PRAISE F

JENNIFER MOORMAN

"*The Magic All Around* is brimming with lyrical Southern beauty, page-turning mystery, and delightful magic. With a house built of enchanted wood, a mother-daughter bond that changes a life, a family saga that brings you home, and a captivating love story, *The Magic All Around* is a work of storytelling-art. For readers of Sara Addison Allen and Lauren K. Denton, this is your next captivating read. If we have eyes to see and ears to hear, Jennifer Moorman is here to remind us that there really is magic all around."

—PATTI CALLAHAN HENRY, *NEW YORK TIMES* BESTSELLING AUTHOR OF *THE SECRET BOOK OF FLORA LEA*

"Brimming with love, and crackling with magic, this story will feel like home on a page—whether it's the home you miss or the home you're hoping to find."

—NATALIE LLOYD, BESTSELLING AUTHOR OF *A SNICKER OF MAGIC*, ON *THE MAGIC ALL AROUND*

"Charming, enchanted, and delightfully Southern, Jennifer Moorman's *The Magic All Around* is a cozy story of family, love, and finding yourself. Perfect for fans of Heather Webber and Sarah Addison Allen!"

—LIZ PARKER, AUTHOR OF *IN THE SHADOW GARDEN*

"Full of Southern charm, second chances, and an opinionated old house that's as (lovingly) meddlesome as a well-meaning aunt, *The Magic All Around* is sure to delight. Jennifer Moorman's latest is equal parts magical and hopeful, revealing the healing power of love."

—SUSAN BISHOP CRISPELL, AUTHOR OF *THE SECRET INGREDIENT OF WISHES*

"Combine four parts love, two parts excitement, a dash of humor, and a pinch of magic and you have Jennifer Moorman's delightful *The Baker's Man*. Moorman's sweet, heartfelt confection will please anyone looking for a charming, witty, utterly delectable read!"

—LAUREN K. DENTON, *USA TODAY* BESTSELLING
AUTHOR OF *THE HIDEAWAY* AND *A PLACE TO LAND*

"Jennifer Moorman's *The Baker's Man* is a teaspoon of love, a dash of magic, and a whole heaping cup of Southern charm. Anna's legacy of unconventional romance and luscious baked goods is a treat from start to finish. Perfect for fans of Amy E. Reichert and Jenny Colgan."

—AIMIE K. RUNYAN, BESTSELLING AUTHOR OF *THE SCHOOL FOR GERMAN BRIDES* AND *THE MEMORY OF LAVENDER AND SAGE*

"*The Baker's Man* is a charming recipe of magic, romance, friendship, and the importance of staying true to yourself.

—HEATHER WEBBER, *USA TODAY* BESTSELLING
AUTHOR OF *MIDNIGHT AT THE BLACKBIRD CAFÉ*

"*The Baker's Man* hits my sweet spot with mouthwatering baked goods and an enchanting romance. Jennifer Moorman's scrumptious tale has all the magical ingredients: best friend banter, small town drama, and the mysterious arrival of the perfect man!"

—AMY E. REICHERT, AUTHOR OF *ONCE UPON A DECEMBER*

The

MAGIC
ALL
AROUND

A NOVEL

JENNIFER MOORMAN

HARPER MUSE

The Magic All Around

Copyright © 2023 Jennifer Moorman

Published by Harper Muse, an imprint of HarperCollins Focus LLC.

This book is a work of fiction. The characters, incidents, and dialogue are drawn from the author's imagination and are not to be construed as real. Any resemblance to actual events or persons, living or dead, is entirely coincidental.

Any internet addresses (websites, blogs, etc.) in this book are offered as a resource. They are not intended in any way to be or imply an endorsement by HarperCollins Focus LLC, nor does HarperCollins Focus LLC vouch for the content of these sites for the life of this book.

Library of Congress Cataloging-in-Publication Data

Names: Moorman, Jennifer, 1978- author.
Title: The magic all around: a novel / Jennifer Moorman.
Description: Nashville, TN: Harper Muse, 2024. | Summary: "Sometimes a family treasure hunt unfurls new paths in life. This enchanting and whimsical tale of mothers and daughters, home, and love will open readers' eyes to the magic all around them"—Provided by publisher.
Identifiers: LCCN 2023028440 (print) | LCCN 2023028441 (ebook) | ISBN 9781400240487 (paperback) | ISBN 9781400240517 (epub) | ISBN 9781400240524
Subjects: LCSH: Mothers and daughters—Fiction. | Women—Fiction. | LCGFT: Magic realist fiction. | Romance fiction. | Novels.
Classification: LCC PS3613.O575 M34 2024 (print) | LCC PS3613.O575 (ebook) | DDC 813/.6—dc23/eng/20230707
LC record available at https://lccn.loc.gov/2023028440
LC ebook record available at https://lccn.loc.gov/2023028441

Printed in the United States of America

23 24 25 26 27 LBC 5 4 3 2 1

*To Natalie, whose perpetual hope and eagerness
to see the magic everywhere ignites my own
passion to look for miracles every day*

Synchronicity is an ever-present reality for those who have eyes to see.

CARL JUNG

Chapter 1

PENELOPE

PEOPLE ASSUMED JULY WOULD BE THE HOTTEST MONTH IN Ivy Ridge, Georgia—probably because it fell slapdab in the middle of the scorching summer months. But they were wrong. August blazed in behind a sweltering July when people were already melting. Pushing through the humidity was second nature to most Southerners, but everyone had their limit. There was only so much sticky heat a kindhearted person could handle before she turned into a cantankerous old woman with a venomous tongue.

Penelope Russell still had a few more degrees of heat she could stand before her compassion and manners evaporated, but the same couldn't be said of a mother who had flames burning in her eyes as she tried to wrangle two crying toddlers into their car seats in the grocery store parking lot. She'd shouted colorful words to the heavens and startled a flock of geese. The frightened birds had changed directions, pointing their V away from town. Then there was the man who had literally stripped down to his checkerboard boxers on the edge of Highwater Creek right before he waded in. Steam had risen off his body like a lobster in a pot of boiling water.

Indoor fan blades spun fast enough to lift houses a few inches off their foundations. The Pixie Dixie Creamery had a line that stretched around the block from nine in the morning until nine at night. Children begged their parents to let them run through lawn sprinklers all day long, and their laughter filled the streets of the town, offering sounds of joy that helped to alleviate the growing agitation over rising temperatures.

Penelope had felt restless all day, and not just because of the August heat wave. Two air-conditioning units had been installed in the historic Russell home in the 1950s when AC first came into fashion. While many townsfolk had been wary of modern advancements, the Russell family didn't see any reason to suffer through Southern summers another day if they didn't have to. Three years ago when the original units started sputtering and groaning like old copper pipes, they replaced them. Now the more energy-efficient units were blasting cold air, and Penelope stood beneath a ceiling vent in her sewing room, letting the coolness wash over her upturned face. She thought of Sophia and Robert, her retired godparents who shared the house with her. They'd taken a jaunt to Savannah for a long weekend, and she wondered if a cooler breeze blew off the Savannah River, offering temporary relief, or if the whole state of Georgia was dissolving into sweaty goo.

A noise downstairs pulled her focus and she listened, hearing music. Penelope followed the sound of it until she stood in the downstairs parlor. The tabletop radio, bought by her great-grandmother in the 1920s, was on and playing "Best of My Love," which was one of her younger sister, Lilith's, favorite songs when they were kids. Penelope smiled thinking of the time Lilith had danced through the backyard, hands reaching toward the sky, singing the lyrics in her mesmerizing bluesy voice. An ache attached itself to the memory, and Penelope rubbed her fingers across her collarbone.

In most houses it might be unusual, spooky even, for a radio to turn on by itself, but not in the Russell house. There was nothing *usual* about the century-old Victorian. Whether it was true or not, Penelope had grown up being told the house was built from enchanted trees grown in the Appalachian Mountains that were felled during a full moon, and this was why the house was never treated as a *thing* but rather as another member of the quirky, slightly eccentric Russell family. The house was very much alive, and when it had something to say, it found interesting ways of letting you know.

Penelope crossed the room and turned off the radio. Enid, her eleven-year-old gray cat, curled on the parlor sofa, blinking shiny amber eyes at her. Penelope scratched between Enid's ears and murmured, "Did you turn on the radio? I thought you were more of a classical music lover." Enid meowed. "No? Oh, I see. Celtic music fan." Enid meowed louder. "That fits you."

A strong wind buffeted the front of the house, then whipped around the sides toward the backyard. Wind whistled through the eaves and the house protested in response. Penelope walked through the foyer and opened the front door. A gust of wind pushed her backward. Enid meowed again behind her.

A cluster of black-eyed Susans in the front flower bed knocked their blooms together as though sending a frenzied message. In another strong gust, a stalk uprooted and dropped itself onto the front porch, scattering dirt and yellow petals all over the boards. The unexpected wind continued for a few minutes while Penelope returned the battered flower to its spot in the front garden. Then, just as quickly as it had arrived, the wind disappeared, leaving behind temperatures that had dropped a few degrees and an unsettling feeling expanding in Penelope's stomach.

At lunch the strangeness continued. When Penelope went to gather ingredients for a salad, she discovered that all the vegetables in the refrigerator had become bruised or shriveled overnight.

An overpowering scent of roses wafted out of the pantry as soon as she opened it, and a bag of holy basil loose-leaf tea dropped from the shelves onto the floor.

Penelope made herself a peanut butter and grape jelly sandwich and brewed a cup of mango and bergamot tea. Enid wandered into the kitchen and weaved around her legs when Penelope sat at the table. "What are you trying to tell me?" she asked the kitchen, but it didn't respond.

Later in her sewing room, while stitching blue lace to the inside of a wedding gown, Penelope pricked her finger with the needle three times before she laid down the project and decided to work on something less frustrating.

She'd thought the tea would help to calm her, but something else was brewing today. Eventually whatever *it* was would reveal itself. Organizing and cleaning usually relaxed her mind, so for the next hour Penelope worked in the sewing room. She had always loved this flamboyantly colorful room with its cramped shelves and cubbyholes that stretched all the way to the ceiling. It was like a hive of treasures stowed away in what might have appeared to be chaos, but Penelope knew where every golden ribbon was spooled, every bolt of silk tucked away, every piece of dreamy lace lying in wait. There were dozens of hues and almost any fabric imaginable, from shiny turquoise satin to delicate ivory chiffon to sturdy black cotton. There were demure floral patterns, one with tiny tulips running along one edge, and outrageously bright florals the young Southern women liked to don in the summer. Soft wools, in oyster and charcoal and tan, whispered of fall and winter when days were short and nights required extra comfort. Spools of thread for any task were organized by colors of the rainbow, and her four sewing machines were parked in each corner of the room where they awaited their next project.

Fabric and thread and sequins—Penelope understood these much more than people. People were complex and frayed when you least expected; they wore holes in themselves from repeated wear and tear, even though they had explicit instructions for how to care for their well-being. Their colors changed and faded over time, and you could start with one version and end up with an entirely different one years later.

Penelope suspected whatever was going on today had to do with her family, but rather than try to sort it out, she straightened bolts of fabrics and rummaged through boxes of pins, ribbons, and fabric tape. She cleaned up stray spools of thread and rewound yarn that Enid liked to bat around the room while she worked.

Then Penelope draped the female dress form mannequin in the indigo-and-black bohemian-style dress she'd sewn to give Mattie, Lilith's daughter—and Penelope's only niece—on their next visit. Mattie's upcoming twenty-fifth birthday was on Halloween, and Lilith and Mattie often visited during the holiday so they could celebrate. It had been two years since Lilith and Mattie visited, missing the past few birthdays and holiday seasons. Penelope had repeatedly invited them, but Lilith had a dozen excuses that all sounded valid while simultaneously sounding empty of truth. Most often she said Mattie didn't have any time off since whatever job Mattie worked seemed to be closed only on Christmas and New Year's Day, which left no time for travel. Because Halloween fell on different days every year, for the past two, Mattie's job had kept her away. Penelope hoped Mattie's birthday this year would be different; maybe she'd see them both soon.

During Mattie's childhood and teenage years, Lilith had dropped off her daughter in Ivy Ridge every summer so Lilith could have some alone time. For those three months in between school years, Penelope and Mattie were an inseparable pair, looking every bit the part of mother and daughter, and Penelope missed those days. She missed the sounds of Mattie's rapid footfalls on the staircases, of her laughter echoing through the kitchen. She missed seeing Mattie outside in the garden with her easel and even missed wiping smudges of paint from the counters and floors when Mattie tracked it inside, oblivious to the trails of colors she left behind. After Mattie's high school graduation, her visits only happened during the holidays since she spent her summers working odd jobs in whatever city she and her mother were living in at the time.

Penelope fiddled with the fabric on the dress. Although playful and curious, Mattie had also been a serious child, often taking on responsibility and soberness like an adult, the opposite of Lilith. Penelope wondered if Mattie hadn't felt forced to be the responsible one since Lilith lived life like a hummingbird, flitting from here to there, never landing anywhere for long.

Penelope hoped that with a few extra silver threads and a string of tiny tiger's-eye stones sewn into the waist, Mattie would try on the dress and dance through the house, laughing the way she used to as a young girl. Penelope turned the mannequin to face the falling sunlight so it could watch ribbons of coral and amber light the sky, as if she were sharing the moment with Mattie too.

In the early evening Penelope repotted a few plants in the greenhouse and then ate an apple for dinner while sitting on the back patio. Enid toyed with fireflies, rising up on her back paws and swatting at them, intentionally not making contact. They seemed to be playing a game of chase. The almost-full moon shone through the tree branches, turning the edges of everything silvery. A warm breeze blew the scent of roses through the backyard, which reminded her of the pink roses her daddy used to bring home to her and Lilith when they were girls.

Pink roses, Penelope thought. *A flower that conveys elegance and refinement, something Lilith and I were slow to practice.* Pink roses also symbolized joy and happiness, two states of being that teased Penelope with their existence but never quite settled into her hands. She stood and called Enid inside.

⚘

A loud banging noise caused Penelope to jerk upright in bed. She'd been tossing and turning all night, kicking off the covers in a sweat and then yanking them back up when she started to shiver from the air-conditioning.

She lifted her cell phone from the nightstand. The face lit up, displaying the time—12:12 a.m.

Had she dreamed the sound? The thumping started again, softer but more persistent. Penelope crept out into the hallway. The noise was coming from the bedroom Mattie always stayed in. *Thump, thump, thump.* The sound reminded Penelope of a loose shutter knocking against the side of a house during a storm.

Penelope flipped on the bedroom light. Enid sat on Mattie's bed and stared at the closet. Was someone in there waiting to jump out and grab her? *Thump, thump, thump.*

She flung open the louvered closet doors and something heavy fell out, covering Penelope's head and draping down her shoulders. Her scream pierced the night, and Penelope shamelessly flailed around, knocking backward into the bed. Enid yowled her displeasure.

She yanked the object from her head and stared down at the wad of fabric in her arms. It was the colorful quilt she'd sewn for Mattie years ago. Every October she put it on Mattie's bed for the fall and winter. Penelope's gaze drifted to the closet. Nothing else was in there. No monster trying to get out. Only a determined quilt.

Penelope folded the quilt and left it on Mattie's bed. She shouted an apology to Enid, who had disappeared to somewhere in the house. No chance she would be able to fall back asleep now, so she shuffled downstairs to make herself a cup of chamomile tea. In the kitchen Penelope filled the kettle and set it on the stove. She walked into the pantry to get the honey, but it had crystallized and formed intricate honey-flavored shapes on the jar. So she grabbed the sugar canister instead and placed it on the counter. When she scooped a small spoonful of sugar into her mug, a clinking noise sounded.

Penelope tilted her mug and inspected the inside. A blue stone the size of a pebble sat among the sugar granules. She plucked it out and rested it in her palm. Lapis lazuli. Penelope's throat tightened. "I see you," she said to the stone. Then she looked around the kitchen. "I don't understand. What truth are you trying to tell me?"

Saying she didn't understand wasn't completely honest because Penelope had a strong sense that *whatever* was unfolding had to do with Lilith and Mattie. She'd like to think they were both on their way to Ivy Ridge for a surprise visit. But the knot in her stomach hinted otherwise.

When the tea was ready, Penelope sat in the window seat in the kitchen nook with her knees pulled up toward her chest, cupping the mug in both hands. She stared out into the dreamy moon-lit backyard, drinking her tea, until she dozed off with her head leaned against the windowpane.

A ringing phone awoke Penelope as the sun rose. She opened her eyes, disoriented and with a crick in her neck. Why was she in the kitchen? The phone rang again, and Penelope's mind snapped to attention. She scrambled out of the window seat and snatched her cell phone from the kitchen island. When she swiped to answer the call, her voice failed her.

"Penelope?"

Words jumbled together for another second before Penelope could use them. "Mattie? Is everything okay?" But Penelope already knew the answer. Mattie responded with a sob. "Oh, baby, tell me what's happened."

"It's . . . Mom."

Penelope's legs buckled, and she sagged down onto the tile floor. She clutched the cell phone like a life preserver as air squeezed from her lungs.

"She's gone," Mattie whispered in a heartbreaking voice. "She died last night in her sleep."

Chapter 2

MATTIE

THREE DAYS AFTER HER MOM DIED, MATTIE RUSSELL stood on the sidewalk on North Wells Street outside of Century Tower in Chicago. They had lived in eleven cities across the United States. Two years was the maximum time her mom wanted to stay anywhere, but they'd lived in Chicago longer than anywhere else. For the past two and a half years, she and Lilith had called this luxury apartment home. When Mattie questioned Lilith about why they weren't packing up and leaving at their usual two-year mark, Lilith flashed her brilliant smile and said, *"Time will uncover all secrets."* Cryptic as ever. Years ago Mattie stopped trying to figure out her mom. Whatever motivated Lilith's life choices was as transparent as oil paint, but living and traveling with her was the only kind of life that Mattie knew.

In the August heat, downtown Chicago smelled sweaty with a funky hint of raw sewage wafting from the river. The winds mingled the scent of lake water—part fog, part fish—with an aroma of warm chocolate coming from the cocoa bean processing at Blommer Chocolate Factory.

Their apartment was only a few blocks from Grant Park, where Mattie and Lilith had taken picnics in the spring, ridden bikes in the summer, strolled arm in arm admiring the jewel tones of the autumn leaves, and ice-skated in the winter. For two nomads living paycheck to paycheck, Mattie often marveled at how they'd resided so close to such wealth.

Lilith had a way with people—an unexplainable quality that drew people to her almost as soon as she arrived in any town. For years Mattie thought it was her mom's striking beauty, the way she glided through the world like a being not *of* this world. Her attractiveness definitely contributed to her magnetism, but as Mattie grew older, she knew there was more to her mother's appeal.

Mattie sometimes wondered if Lilith emitted a frequency that certain people could feel. Someone might be standing on a street corner about to turn right, but she'd pick up on Lilith's energy and take a left instead. Then she'd bump into Mattie and Lilith, and they'd become instant friends. Or someone would order three lunches instead of one and find Mattie and Lilith looking for a place to eat.

Because of Lilith's ability to draw people to her, she and Mattie were never in want of anything. In Asheville, North Carolina, they were researching apartments they could afford, and a woman in the grocery store parking lot heard them and said she had a guesthouse that had just been vacated. And in Austin, Texas, while her mom scrolled through job openings online and chatted with Mattie about her qualifications, the man having coffee next to them on the park bench said he needed an executive assistant since his had just retired. These types of wonders happened in every town, multiple times.

It was no different in Chicago. The week after Lilith decided to leave Portland, she and Mattie bought tickets for a flight bound for O'Hare. The airline had oversold the flight and offered first-class tickets to anyone who wanted to pay a few hundred dollars more. No one was interested, so Lilith made her way to the counter. In less than five minutes, she and the airline worker were laughing. Lilith wrote on a page torn from her notepad and handed the paper to the woman behind the counter. When her mom returned to her seat beside Mattie, she held two first-class tickets in her hand, whispering that she'd been given them at no extra charge.

Mattie had never flown first class. The oversize plush seats wowed her. A flight attendant offered free champagne before takeoff, along with squishy pillows and fuzzy blankets. Lilith struck up a conversation with the man across the aisle from her, who looked vaguely familiar. Turned out he was Orion Aboiye, an actor famous for his roles in sci-fi and adventure movies. He'd just wrapped up shooting a film in the lush Oregon forests.

The next evening in Chicago, Orion took Mattie and Lilith out to Boka, an exquisite seasonal-food restaurant, where Mattie ate grilled Spanish octopus and kampachi for the first time. Her dinner of Tasmanian ocean trout followed by a roasted blueberry sorbet was some of the best food she'd ever eaten. Mattie only joined in the conversation when they directly brought her into it. She'd seen a similar scenario play out dozens of times, but each time it was slightly different. The town, the man, the restaurant, the scenery all changed. The power of Lilith's charm was the only constant, an inescapable force. Even Mattie was often captivated by her.

When Orion hailed Mattie and Lilith a taxi outside the restaurant that night, he asked for their address, which was a downtown hotel until they could find more permanent lodging. Orion offered the apartment he rented near Grant Park. When Lilith protested, Orion assured them it was no trouble. The next morning he would be off again for a promotional tour. He insisted Mattie and Lilith stay at his place rent-free for as long as they needed. As absurd as the whole offer sounded, Mattie had long ago lost her sense of surprise over what people, often strangers, gave her mom.

Orion and Lilith continued to spend time together when he had days off from publicity tours or filming, which wasn't often, but they spoke on the phone a few times every week. Orion never asked them to vacate the apartment. Anytime he was in Chicago, he stayed with his brother, and Lilith would disappear with him for days, leaving Mattie on her own, which suited her just fine at the time.

But now, two and a half years later, Mattie stood alone on the Chicago sidewalk, and she wasn't fine. Not at all. The keys to a rental car warmed her palm. She didn't have any close friends, only acquaintances. After traveling for years, she learned not to accumulate stuff or attach to anything, including people. The few personal belongings she did hang on to were in cardboard boxes she'd gotten from the neighborhood pizza restaurant where she'd been working. All her clothes fit into one suitcase—the same beat-up, hardback teal one she'd had for years.

Mattie didn't know what to do with her mom's stuff other than pack it up and figure it out later. Lilith's vinyl collection and acoustic guitar were safely stowed in the trunk of the rental, and her jewelry and clothes were packed into a fancy rose-gold suitcase that had been a gift from a man in Portland. Two suitcases, eight boxes, Mattie's canvases and paints, and five potted plants crowded the back seat, leaving the passenger seat open for emptiness and sadness to occupy.

A man wearing a red baseball cap, aviator sunglasses, and running clothes whistled a tune as he walked up the sidewalk toward Mattie. Sweat glistened on his face and arms. He played imaginary drums in the air above him, and his grin caught the sunlight.

Mattie watched him for a few seconds, envious of his ability to lose himself in a moment of joy. She moved out of his way and stood by the driver's door. The man stopped a few feet away, lowered his arms, and turned to look at Mattie as she slid behind the wheel and closed the car door. He stared at her for a moment, rubbed the back of his neck, and then continued in the opposite direction.

Mattie buckled her seat belt and turned on the ignition. The radio came on, playing "I Put a Spell on You." A buried memory tried to unearth itself, but her exhaustion halted it. She drove out of Chicago toward the only town she'd ever repeatedly visited: Ivy Ridge, Georgia.

The drive south to Ivy Ridge would take at least fourteen hours, and since Mattie hadn't planned to leave until midmorning, Penelope insisted Mattie stop halfway, book a hotel room, and sleep. But Mattie was restless, and when she stopped for too long, even to pump gas, her mind filled with despair and thoughts of her mom, creeping her closer to the edge of collapse.

She and Lilith had spontaneously traveled to new places dozens of times without a solid plan, and Mattie never worried about the lack of preparation. Lilith's style of planning was hoping for the best and going with the flow, but this unplanned trip to Ivy Ridge felt different in the worst kind of way. Even when she didn't know where they were going, Mattie always trusted her mom. Somehow Lilith had a knowing about what lay ahead of them. Whenever and wherever they arrived, Lilith would have everything arranged like there *had* been a plan.

But Mattie didn't have a plan; she didn't even have a speck of knowing. She felt completely untethered, like someone had cut her kite string during a tornado. Her future had suddenly been swallowed up by the vast nothingness gobbling up every part of her—except her sadness. The nothingness left that, as though despair was something too heavy for even it to take. Her grief expanded while her world shrank.

She'd lost her sole companion, her best friend, and her mom. All at once.

Being an only child raised by a free-spirited single mom had felt like a spectacular gift, until this moment when she was abandoned. Her aunt would argue that Mattie wasn't alone because she had family in Ivy Ridge—the small Russell family unit. Although Lilith didn't talk much about her hometown, she'd shared plenty of stories about their extraordinary family, explaining numerous times that the Russells weren't like other families. You'd never catch them doing ordinary things. Generations of Russells would be more likely to walk barefoot in the moonlight, grow extravagant gardens, and keep prisms near windows. They burned homemade candles while reading fairy tales and novels about ancient civilizations. Russell women opened doors to unexpected guests before anyone even rang the bell, they knew which herbs healed and which ones harmed, and they could see the secret truths in your heart.

Lilith swore the Russell family was enchanted, if a little unusual. Mattie couldn't deny the strangeness she'd seen in their lives. Others believed these whispers about the Russell women, and so in Ivy Ridge they were often met by those pretending indifference though inwardly burning with curiosity. Were the Russells magical or just peculiar? Did they sew courage into clothing or have singing voices that caused men to fall in love with them like the mythological Sirens?

JENNIFER MOORMAN

Ivy Ridge, Georgia, was a place Lilith spent as little time in as possible since she'd escaped on a Greyhound bus when she was eighteen. Lilith rarely talked to Mattie about her life in Ivy Ridge, only once admitting that she had never fit in with the locals. Not with her blue-streaked hair, and certainly not with her uncanny ability to charm other people's boyfriends and husbands. Being different in a small Southern town was worse than wearing white after Labor Day—an unfortunate circumstance that people couldn't help but gossip about. Combined with her bohemian beauty and her candidness, the likelihood of Lilith being widely accepted in Ivy Ridge was about as probable as someone being struck by lightning.

But Ivy Ridge was where Penelope still lived in the family home—a place Lilith had used when the walls around her felt too close and her lungs squeezed tight, when she needed a retreat from parenting. Rather than feeling discarded when Lilith dropped her off, Mattie loved her time there with Penelope every summer. To her, running rampant through the quirky Victorian home was the best sort of fun. She anticipated summers the same way children vibrated with excitement for Christmas morning.

Mattie's summers in Ivy Ridge exploded with possibility. The house, the garden, and even the town felt full of secrets waiting to be discovered. Being in Ivy Ridge was the only time Mattie felt free to truly be a kid because Penelope took care of everything. There was always food in the kitchen, clothes were always washed, and painting supplies were endless. Mattie, of course, had to help out around the house, but Penelope kept life organized and easy, and Mattie never worried about responsibilities being forgotten. Summer was one of Mattie's favorite times of year—along with Halloween, her birthday. As a special gift to Mattie, Lilith always made sure they spent Halloween in Ivy Ridge so they could celebrate together as a family, but the last two years had been different.

Mattie drove the fourteen hours, stopping only for gas and snacks, until she reached the city limits of Ivy Ridge. In the wee hours of the morning, heat pressed inside the car, dampening the cloth seats with humidity, so Mattie cranked the air conditioner higher. She parked on the street in front the Russell family home, which had been built in the early 1900s and was a grand Victorian settled among other impressive historic houses. At nearly four thousand square feet, the house was absurdly large for only three people—Penelope, Robert, and Sophia. Until a few years ago when Robert and Sophia retired, Penelope had lived in the house alone. It was way more space than a small family needed, let alone a single woman. Mattie knew this intimately because she and her mom had lived in apartments smaller than this house's kitchen.

She peeled her cramped hands off the steering wheel and opened and closed her fingers into fists a few times to get the blood flowing. The lights in the house were off except a lamp illuminating a window in the primary bedroom.

Her aunt was awake and expecting her because Penelope *always* waited up. She seemed to know Mattie would ignore the suggestion to break the drive into two days. As Mattie eased the car door closed, the interior staircase light turned on, then the foyer light, followed by the front porch light.

By the time Mattie's foot touched the bottom porch stair, the front door opened. Penelope stood backlit by the house's now-bright interior. She reached her hands out toward Mattie, opening her arms. The last of Mattie's energy went out like a blown match. She stumbled up the stairs, released her suitcase, and fell into Penelope's arms, letting her aunt hold her like she was a little girl.

Penelope rolled Mattie's suitcase into the foyer and led her up the stairs to her bedroom. "I'll come back for your bags."

Mattie's bedroom hadn't changed much through the years. A silvery harlequin pattern overlaid the solid teal background of the wallpaper. The cocoa-brown wooden bed had a carved headboard with two posts and a smaller matching footboard. A hand-carved armoire with crafted panels was pushed against one wall. For additional storage, a closet with sturdy louvered doors had been added when Mattie was in middle school. One double window allowed in late-afternoon sunlight, but Penelope had sewn heavy drapes with blackout liners to block out the light if needed.

"Don't worry about my stuff," Mattie said, sitting on the edge of the bed. She smoothed her hand over the colorful patchwork quilt her aunt had sewn for her years ago. Her fingers tingled against the fabric, and exhaustion spread through her. A framed photo of Penelope and Mattie smiled at her from the bedside table, on which she also spied a brand-new set of paintbrushes and a small fabric bin full of unopened paints. Mattie brushed her fingertips across the unused bristles.

"I thought you might need those," Penelope said softly. "There are empty canvases upstairs."

Through the years, even while she and Lilith traveled, Penelope always kept Mattie's paint supplies stocked. Just when Mattie painted on her last canvas and knew she would need to sell it to afford more supplies, a new pack of canvases would arrive from Ivy Ridge.

"I called Robert and Sophia," Penelope explained. "They're leaving Savannah first thing in the morning." Mattie nodded. "Sure you don't want me to get the rest of your bags?"

Mattie shook her head. "I don't need much, just that one suitcase, and I won't be staying long."

"Oh?" Penelope said.

Mattie fell back onto the bed, lying sideways and dangling her legs off the side. "I'll do the funeral, and then I'm leaving."

Penelope's expression was unreadable. "And where will you be heading? Back to Chicago?"

"No. I'm done there, and . . . I don't know where I'm going," Mattie said. She rolled onto her side and curled into a ball, hugging her knees to her chest as if pulling everything close would help fill up her hollowness. "Nowhere. Anywhere." Tears squeezed out of her closed eyes.

"Try to get some rest, sweet girl," Penelope said. "It's okay to feel this way. It's allowed."

"To feel what way?" Mattie's voice cracked.

"Everything all at once. And nothing. Swinging like a pendulum from one extreme to the next," she said. "I'll at least grab the plants from the car. I wouldn't feel right about leaving them out there all night."

Mattie peered up at her from the bed. "How do you know I have plants?"

Penelope touched her temple. "I can hear them."

Mattie smiled sadly. Penelope had been talking to plants for as long as Mattie remembered. "They'll be fine. No one is going to steal them."

Penelope smiled softly. "Oh, I'm not worried about that. I'm worried about *them*. I don't want them to feel sad and left alone in a new place. I'll put them downstairs, and you can decide what you want to do with them tomorrow."

Mattie pointed to her purse. "Keys are in there."

Penelope turned off the light and left the door partially open. Mattie guessed to keep the cat, Enid, from yawling at the door later. Mattie rolled onto her back, stared up at the ceiling, and felt the swell of tears inside her, but no more would release.

How did Mom do it? she wondered. How did she always know just where they should go next? Mattie had zero ideas about what to do or where to go. Nothing seemed to point her anywhere. No signs from heaven, no nudges from her subconscious. The only thing she'd been certain about recently was that she needed to return to Ivy Ridge, if only for a few days. The rest of her future steps were nonexistent.

Mattie had forgotten how *quiet* Ivy Ridge was. Chicago, although not as noisy as New York City, still swelled with constant commotion—construction, traffic, and emergency sirens blaring toward the sky. The long, straight avenues lined with tall, concrete buildings echoed the sounds of traffic and jackhammers, and the sirens bounced off the buildings and reverberated all around. Voices carried up the streets all day, anything from people hawking wares to laughter to arguments to languages from all over the world. At first Mattie hadn't been able to sleep well through the noisy activity of the city, but eventually it became a steady rhythm that was the soundtrack of her life there.

Ivy Ridge was so incredibly silent that Mattie could hear her own breathing. She also heard the front door open as Penelope went out to the car. A few minutes later, she heard the front door close and lock. Penelope eased back into Mattie's bedroom. She brought in her suitcase, returned the car keys, and whispered good night. Not long after, the bedroom door pushed open wider, and a draft of cooler air swirled through the room. Mattie looked for

Enid but didn't see her. Then the staircase creaked, sounding like someone was either coming up or going down it. Mattie listened for a few more seconds but didn't hear anything else. She got out of bed, walked into the hallway, and stood in the dark house for a few heartbeats. Quiet music drifted up the stairs. Had Penelope decided to make a cup of tea?

The music grew more distinct as Mattie neared the parlor. She poked her head into the room, and the antique radio crackled its music. Mattie made a pass through all the downstairs rooms, thinking she'd find her aunt, but she didn't. She returned to the parlor and stared at the radio across the room. It was playing one of her favorite songs, Kenny Loggins's "Celebrate Me Home," which soothed her. The music coaxed her farther into the room.

Mattie curled onto one side of the crushed-velvet sofa, breathing in the scent of the room. The combination of music and scents of parchment paper and woodsmoke relaxed the tension in her muscles. She rested her cheek against one of the plush pillows and closed her eyes. Her breathing slowed. A window downstairs must have been open because a warm summer breeze swept across her cheeks, bringing the sounds of cricket song with it. It was as if the house—*the whole town*—wanted her to rest. And for the first time in days, she gave in to the desire to put aside the heavy burden of her sorrow and try to quiet her mind.

Just before she fell asleep, she murmured, "I'm not staying in Ivy Ridge."

As if in response, the song shifted to "The Weight," telling Mattie to lay down her heavy load. Was there someone there who'd pick it up and carry it for a while? The radio sounded like someone was turning the dial because the song faded out, followed by static, then distant news, and finally became "Lean on Me."

For a flicker of a second, she wondered whether everything was going to be okay. *Maybe I'll get through this. Maybe I'm not completely, devastatingly alone.*

Chapter 3

MATTIE

MATTIE AWOKE LATER THAT MORNING SPRAWLED OUT ON the velvet sofa in the parlor. In her sleep she'd knocked all the pillows askew. She sat up, blinking in the lemony sunlight, and leaned down to pick up a stray pillow. Voices traveled up the hallway. The scents of baking dough and coffee wafted into the room. Mattie recognized Penelope's voice and the soft Southern accent of Sophia Russell, Penelope and Lilith's godmother and aunt. After the death of their parents, the young sisters had been raised by Sophia and her husband, Robert.

Mattie combed her fingers through her long, tangled hair and realized how much she had missed the cherished birthdays and holidays spent with her family. She could have insisted she and Lilith celebrate in Ivy Ridge the way they'd always done. Lilith hadn't pressed the issue, but why hadn't Mattie? If Lilith was finally exhausted with traveling to Ivy Ridge, why hadn't Mattie gone on her own? Probably because she never argued with her mom or went against her wishes.

Mattie went and stood at the bottom of the staircase and rested her hand on the round finial top. The varnish was worn on one side from years of people touching it as they started up the stairs or reached the bottom. Mattie debated whether she should take a shower or at least brush her teeth before socializing.

Sophia walked out of the kitchen at the far end of the hallway. "Good morning, beautiful darling," she said, her accent making her words flow like music. An ankle-length black skirt that rippled as she walked was paired with a plain white T-shirt. She wore an apron dusted with powdery handprints, and even with the slight mess she looked elegant and refined. Everyday fashion never looked simple on Sophia, and Mattie had never seen her without her signature fire engine–red nail polish and matching lipstick.

Sophia was voluptuous with long, shapely legs like a 1950s pinup girl. She still wore her hair long with soft waves like she had as a young woman, and because she had no interest in going gray, she regularly had a stylist dye her hair the rich auburn shade of her youth. She had chocolate-brown deep-set eyes, high cheekbones, a narrow nose, and full lips on a mouth that was almost too wide for her face, but her smiles were so expansive and vibrant they could change the mood in a room within seconds.

At almost seventy, she looked at least ten years younger. People begged her to tell them how to find the Fountain of Youth she'd obviously been drinking from. They wanted to know about her diet and her skin care routine, whether she preferred yoga or Pilates, and what daily supplements she took. Sophia told them the same secret she'd been sharing for years, which wasn't a secret at all: youth and beauty and magic all came from the same place—the heart. *"You can tell a lot about the state of a person's heart by looking at their face. If they look run down and sickly, chances are their hearts are suffering and their thoughts are reflecting in their eyes. If they are full of life and vitality, if you can feel the joy all around them, you can bet those are the people you want to know, to listen to. Those are the ones to keep close. They are truly alive."*

"Hey, Sophia," Mattie said. She pointed up the stairs. "I was going to brush my teeth." She gazed down at yesterday's wrinkled clothing hanging drearily on her body. "And change."

"Nonsense," Sophia said, pulling Mattie into a hug so tight it felt like she was trying to convey a lifetime of love in one embrace. When Sophia pulled away, Mattie could see a hint of puffiness in her face, left over from a night spent crying. "It's been too long. Come have coffee—or tea—with us. Penelope made cinnamon rolls and buttermilk biscuits." Sophia grabbed Mattie's hand and led her down the hallway.

"I thought you weren't leaving Savannah until this morning."

"We couldn't sleep," she said as they entered the sun-drenched kitchen.

Every surface sparkled in the rays of summer light that warmed the room by degrees. It smelled just like Mattie remembered, a home full of life and ease. The original Victorian kitchen had been dark and much smaller, a space not intended for cooking with a family crowded around. One holiday when the sisters' parents, Elena and Douglas, weren't on tour, Elena had the kitchen remodeled. They knocked down a few walls and created an open, airy space that included more windows, an island, and a breakfast nook with a bay window and cushioned seat. The kitchen transformed from a cramped room into a place where the family gathered easily and often.

The island was now crowded with baskets of fruit and casserole dishes covered in a mix of tinfoil and plastic wrap. Penelope stood in front of the open refrigerator doors. She glanced at Mattie over her shoulder.

At forty-five, Penelope didn't look like other women her age. She looked much younger, and Mattie wondered if that bothered women just as much as others were bothered by Sophia aging in reverse. Penelope and Lilith resembled each other, so it was obvious to anyone who saw them together that they were related. But Lilith was tall and willowy, and her features were sharper and more angular, giving her an edginess that spoke of late nights and wild parties. Penelope was petite, shorter than her younger sister by a few inches, and her body was made of softer lines. She looked like someone you could trust with your car keys. Someone who wouldn't steal your boyfriend.

Penelope's striking green eyes, high cheekbones, and small stature reminded Mattie of a forest pixie who might try to convince you to dance barefoot or create mischief. But Mattie doubted her aunt ever entertained mischief of any sort. Where Lilith had been an untamed spirit, Penelope was responsible and organized, infinitely more serious than Lilith ever had been.

Just like with her mom, people were drawn to Penelope, even though she tried to keep to herself. They often stopped and stared at her before they realized how inappropriate it was of them. Straight black hair hung long down her back, and this morning it was pushed back from her forehead with a stretchy emerald cloth band. Her tank top revealed toned arms, kept in shape by hours of gardening, housework, yoga, and her seamstress work. She wore a flowy blue-green boho skirt covered in purple spirals that swished around her ankles when she moved.

Penelope pointed at a plate heaped with cinnamon rolls. Silky cream cheese melted onto the perfectly shaped rolls and the scent of warm spices wrapped around Mattie like a comfort blanket. Another plate had uniform stacks of buttermilk biscuits. The Russell house was an unusual juxtaposition of the comfort foods found in Southern traditions along with whole food and healthy options. For breakfast Mattie could often find foods like today's offerings, or Penelope would whip up a bowl of homemade granola served with fresh berries and a dollop of Greek yogurt swirled with honey. Or scrambled eggs, a side of grits, and crispy bacon.

"Grab one or half a dozen. There's butter and jam too," Penelope said. "Just leave a cinnamon roll for Robert."

"He's already had one," Sophia said.

"He'll pout if we don't leave him one for later," Penelope said. "Coffee's in the carafe. Or Sophia will make you an espresso."

"Where is Robert?" Mattie asked, pouring a mug full of coffee. She skipped the cream and sugar, now preferring to drink her coffee black.

Sophia pointed at the ceiling with a red manicured nail. "In the music room or the attic."

Mattie made her way over to the plates of food and sipped her coffee. Bitterness lingered on her tongue as the warmth washed down her throat. "What's he doing in the attic?"

"He's looking through—"

"Sophia, hand me that red dish, please," Penelope interrupted. "I've made a spot for it. The rest of those we'll have to pack into the chest freezer in the basement until we can get them to the shelter."

"Looking through what?" Mattie grabbed a cinnamon roll from the stack and put it on a small plate, then licked cream cheese icing from her fingers.

Penelope sighed. "The attic is where we send things we aren't ready to let go of but don't really need."

"That's an interesting way of avoiding a direct answer," Mattie said before she bit into the cinnamon roll and exhaled a satisfied sigh.

"Good, isn't it?" Sophia said. She handed Penelope the casserole dish.

"Better than good," Mattie said. "Once a week I bought cinnamon rolls from my favorite bakery over on Grand Street when we lived in New York City. The owner grew up in Alabama and knew how to make the dough extra fluffy with the most decadent cream cheese icing. She also made a pumpkin pie that tasted like the fall."

Penelope paused with the casserole dish in her hands. "I haven't made one of those in years. Another of my daddy's favorites. Mama used to make those when they were home . . . which wasn't often," she said with sadness enveloping the words.

"The bakery's cinnamon rolls were outstanding." Mattie held up her half-eaten treat. "But yours are next-level."

"Penelope's skill rivals my gran's, God rest her soul." Sophia made the sign of the cross over her chest. "I'd never admit that if she were still alive because she'd curse me, but Penelope bakes better than any of the bakeries in town, probably in the whole county."

Penelope smiled. "You taught me everything I know."

Sophia's smile was soft. "Not everything."

Mattie took another bite and closed her eyes as the warm dough and cream cheese melted on her tongue. Penelope stacked three casserole dishes in her arms and disappeared into the basement.

"What's with all the food?" Mattie asked Sophia.

"Ivy Ridge showing their sympathy," Sophia answered. Her hand crept to the space over her heart. "There is healing power in food."

For a few minutes Mattie had forgotten to think about her mom's absence. Eating pastries and sipping coffee had distracted her. But the reminder that the town knew they needed sympathy and support brought back reality. Lilith wasn't upstairs sleeping in; she wasn't dancing through the downstairs rooms singing along with Fleetwood Mac.

Lilith was gone in the most permanent physical way.

Mattie pointed at the nearest dish and frowned. "There's no chance that broccoli and cheese casserole is going to heal anyone." She glanced out the window toward the back garden. "I'm not sure anything will heal this."

Sophia closed her hand around a ruby stone dangling from the long necklace she wore. "No one prepares you for death. They can't, but still they try. We try to prepare ourselves for the day, don't we? We imagine a future without our spouses or children or best friends, as if *thinking* about how terrible it is will help it be less awful when it happens. But you can't actually prepare yourself for the way loss swoops in and closes around you. Not for the way it paralyzes you, trapping you in a world that keeps moving while you feel immobilized.

"But we must let the emotions come, not fight them, and keep moving through them. We can't stay here in this grief. It will turn everything, including us, to dust." Sophia closed her eyes and exhaled a shuddering breath. "Your mama was so wild and so beautiful . . . since the day she was born." The raw ache in her words spread to Mattie, and her chest constricted.

Mattie put the unfinished cinnamon roll on the plate and stepped into the connected sunporch while she shoved down the urge to cry. By the back door sat a small console with an assortment of items cluttering its top, including an antique Tiffany lamp with a bronze base and red roses on its glass shade. Sunlight filtering through the glass projected distorted red roses on the tile. Beside the lamp was a plastic rotary phone in a shade of 1970s blue that called to mind hideous prom tuxedos and Converse All Stars.

Mattie had never seen anyone use the phone, and it had never once rung. It might not even be plugged in for all she knew, and since it seemed more like a retro knickknack than a usable object, she'd never checked.

Penelope emerged from the basement.

"Can I ask you something?" Mattie asked.

"Of course," Penelope said. "What's on your mind?"

"The night Mom passed," Mattie said and paused, inhaling a slow breath and exhaling before continuing. The knot in her chest didn't loosen. "She was already asleep when I came home from work. She left me a sticky note on the counter. It said to call you. Do you know why?"

Penelope's eyebrows rose, but she shook her head.

She blurted the next question out of her mouth before she could rethink asking. "Do you think she knew?"

Penelope looked past Mattie toward Sophia, who stepped onto the porch with them. Unspoken words passed between the two women.

"Knew what?" Penelope asked, her voice cautious and words measured.

"Nothing," Mattie said. The question sounded insane. How could her mom have *known* something would happen? Her gaze moved to the rotary phone. "Why do you keep that phone? Does it still work?"

"It works," Sophia said. "It's a regular landline, and you can call out on it, but we don't use it anymore, not since cell phones. No one ever calls it."

Mattie lifted the handset from the receiver and listened to the monotonous dial tone. "I don't actually know *anyone* who has a landline, and a rotary phone? No way." She poked her finger into the number 2 circle and spun the dial, removing her finger and watching it rotate back to its starting position. Then she chose the 7 and spun it. The dial tone quieted. A blackbird cawed outside the window, and Mattie hung up the phone. "If you don't use it, why keep it? What's special about this one?"

"Special?" Penelope asked. "Nothing." She wiped her hands on a towel she'd draped over her shoulder. "It's just a phone." Penelope cast a wistful glance at the blue plastic oddity.

"Penelope," Sophia said, "I've never been agreeable to secrets."

Penelope's postured stiffened. "It's just a phone."

"That's like saying you are just a seamstress. You're more than that, aren't you?"

"Is it like the Bat Phone?" Mattie asked.

Penelope snorted a laugh.

Sophia smiled. "It's much better than the Bat Phone. There's a story."

"That no one can prove," Penelope said.

Sophia huffed. "Since when do you need proof to believe?"

"Not *me*." Penelope tilted her head toward Mattie. "I'm not sure this is the right time. And Mattie doesn't plan on sticking around long, so it doesn't seem fit to overshare."

A *crack* followed by a loud groaning sounded from outside and startled all three women. Penelope opened the back door and glanced into the yard. The greenhouse door had fallen open and was dangling from loose hinges.

"Oh my," Sophia said, "an open door."

"A *broken* door," Penelope said.

"Some of these doors have been closed for too long and they're breaking open," Sophia said. "We can't keep what we've hidden tucked away forever. Mattie is part of our family."

"She's *leaving*," Penelope argued.

"Hello? I'm standing right here," Mattie interrupted. "Are we still talking about the phone?"

No one responded.

Mattie pointed into the yard. "Should we fix that before it falls off? Prop it up?"

Penelope waved a dismissive hand. "Later. Sophia, if you don't mind, let's get the rest of the casseroles put away. I can call a handyman afterward."

"Nonsense," Sophia said. "Robert can fix that."

Penelope left them standing alone on the porch. "Where are you running off to next?" Sophia asked.

"I'm not *running* anywhere," Mattie said. "I don't know where I'm going yet. It'll come to me. It always does."

"You mean it always came to Lilith," Sophia said. "She was the captain of your ship, wasn't she?"

For a brief second, Mattie had a vision of a sailing vessel captained by her mom. Mattie sat on the bow, wind blowing her hair back and her face turned toward the sun. She never bothered with choosing the adventure because she didn't *have* to make any decisions. Lilith had always chosen everything, always made life spontaneous with the thrill of uncertainty. But without Lilith steering the vessel, Mattie realized the empty feeling inside her had a name. *Adrift.*

"Let's help Penelope put away the food," Sophia said. "You'll figure out what's best for you. We Russell women always do."

Chapter 4

JONATHAN

JONATHAN CARLISLE HADN'T SLEPT THIS LATE SINCE NEW Year's Day five years ago, and that was because he'd been out watching the sunrise in Grant Park and hadn't gotten home until eight in the morning. He'd argue with anyone that Chicago held one of the best New Year's Eve celebrations in the country. But last night's gig hadn't been nearly as entertaining as an end-of-the-year blowout. The lingering champagne headache definitely wasn't.

The bedroom featured floor-to-ceiling windows with views of the Chicago River and his favored running path near the waterfront. His fifty-seventh-floor apartment had spectacular views of the cityscape. Jonathan rolled out of bed with a groan and lifted his cell phone from the bedside table.

Twenty-seven text messages and seventy-five emails. Jonathan scrolled through the texts and clicked on only the ones that caught his interest. His mom wrote, *Call us this week. I'm making plans for the holidays.* "It's not even Halloween, Mom." But he made a mental note to call his parents. He tried to remember the last time he'd talked to his brothers, David and William. Months, probably. He'd shoot them a text this week too. Do his brotherly duty.

At two in the morning an unknown number had texted, *Hey, it's Stefanie! It was great to meet you last night. Let's get together soon! Call me, okay? Anytime this week is great! Can't wait to see you! XOXO!* Jonathan closed his eyes. That was a lot of exclamation points for this time in the morning, or any time for that matter. He remembered meeting Stefanie—a nice, if tenacious, young woman. She'd asked for his number and, ever the nice guy and perpetual networker, he'd given it to her. But Stefanie was looking for a date, and Jonathan was looking for a client. Not a perfect match for either.

Last night's event was at Fusion Lounge—one of the most hyped clubs in the city and the most difficult to get into, especially after Jonathan had been promoting it for the past month. Last night he'd packed a half dozen runway models and just as many high-profile celebrities into the VIP area, drawing in hundreds of people hoping for admittance. Hiring a band with a current number one hit on the charts added to the mania. Jonathan had been surrounded by people all night. Between the free alcohol, the packed dance floor, and schmoozing into the wee hours of the morning, Jonathan could barely remember his name. He'd do both himself and Stefanie a favor and not text back. Jonathan swiped to delete the message.

There were a dozen messages from clients raving about the success of last night's Fusion Lounge event, including the owner. Every one of them was ready to book their next event with him. All he had to do was open up his planner and start scheduling. Jonathan calculated the revenue he'd generate from these client messages alone. If he booked only this handful of events, he'd earn enough to pay his rent for a year. And there would be more—he was confident of that. There always were when you lived among those who thrived on excess.

During college at St. John's University in Queens, New York, Jonathan knew he'd make a fortune playing professional baseball. As one of the top players in the college league, Jonathan was a naturally athletic shortstop with solid hitting stats. He was as skilled at offense as he was at defense. Jonathan was also charismatic and a team favorite because he had a way of bringing everyone together and raising morale. People believed he knew what he was talking about, even if he didn't.

A teammate knew Jonathan had grown up working at his dad's corporate event planning business and asked Jonathan to help his girlfriend organize a musical concert for a club opening in New York City. Jonathan's skills weren't on par with the professionals in the area, but he took what he'd learned from his dad and found mentors in the business who could guide him. He turned that one-night success into a concert-and-venue-promoter side job with a steady income. He squeezed the part-time work in between his academic and sports schedules by sacrificing his sleep and his freedom.

Jonathan didn't think his side gig would last past college. He'd dreamed of one day playing with his home team, the Atlanta Braves. He would have settled for the New York Yankees, but that was before the compound leg fracture from a collision with another player at second base during his senior year. In the span of a few seconds, Jonathan's entire life changed, and his dreams of pro ball disappeared faster than a one-hit wonder.

After his college graduation and knowing his baseball career was over, his family thought he'd come back to Ivy Ridge, Georgia, and work for the family business. Instead, Jonathan threw himself completely into being a full-time promoter. New York City was competitive and often cutthroat, so when an opportunity in Chicago presented itself, Jonathan pulled up what little roots he had in New York and caught the next plane out of LaGuardia. Living in Chicago, promoting other people's aspirations, wasn't how he'd imagined his life, but he had everything he wanted that money could buy.

Except food in the fridge. Jonathan opened the stainless steel refrigerator that dominated the kitchen space. Premade juices were delivered every four days, and he noticed he'd skipped the last two days' bottles. Had he eaten yesterday? He remembered hors d'oeuvres at the bar—prosciutto-wrapped figs, mini beef wellington, togarashi seared ahi, and lobster crème puffs. He taste-tested everything, but then his focus had been on mingling, introducing powerful influencers to one another, making sure the client was happy. Free drinks were always part of his contracts. Even though he no longer drank himself into forgetfulness as he'd done when he was younger and just starting out, he still drank enough to keep his stomach satisfied, which meant he often forgot to eat real food.

The leftover Chinese takeout stared at him from the middle shelf. It was at least a week old and starting to smell like the soles of his tennis shoes with extra funk. His stomach growled. Jonathan closed his eyes and imagined a homemade breakfast. He thought of his mom's buttermilk waffles with melted butter and syrup. For holidays and special occasions she'd added festive sprinkles to a glob of Reddi-wip she sprayed onto each waffle. He wondered if she still did that. With Halloween approaching in a couple of months, would there be an avalanche of pumpkin and black-cat sprinkles?

Although Jonathan stayed busy all year long, his holiday schedule was extremely booked, sometimes overbooked, so he hadn't been home to Ivy Ridge in a few years. Guilt poked at his chest. His mom never failed to tell him he was always welcome to come home, even for a day if that was all he could manage. And every year he explained how he didn't have even *one hour* to spare.

He grabbed a juice bottle labeled The Night After. The

ingredients of grapefruit, ginger, aloe, burdock root, basil oil, and milk thistle touted they would expel all toxins from his body.

He cranked up Phil Collins on the surround sound, played air drums while he drank toxin-annihilating juice, and let the music pull him away from his thoughts about being the disappointing son who never made the time to come home and see his family. David and William always made time. Maybe that was enough.

An hour later Jonathan stood on the street corner, sweating in the sixty-five-degree weather with the sun shining down on him. Rays of light beamed off the skyscraper windows, and Jonathan looked up at clouds reflected in the silver glass panes. Two cabs raced up the street, honking their horns and making hand motions that seemed to be the secret language of taxi drivers. A bike messenger zoomed in between the street traffic, and a man on the opposite corner sold hot dogs, sausages, and pretzels from his rolling cart. The air smelled like cooked meat, car exhaust, and the neighborhood pizza joint two doors down from where Jonathan stood.

He turned down the music blasting in his Bluetooth earphones and listened to the city noise. Compared to Ivy Ridge, with its summer nights so quiet you could hear crickets chirping from pond reeds and owls hooting from the hollow, Chicago was shockingly loud—so loud he couldn't hear his own thoughts. And that was exactly what he loved about the city. With all the wind blowing, car alarms blaring, people laughing, trucks rumbling up the streets, and dogs barking, Jonathan's inner dialogue couldn't compete.

He ducked into a small market and grabbed a water, an apple, and a bacon, egg, and cheese on a roll. Stepping onto the sidewalk while still unwrapping his food, Jonathan almost walked right into someone. He stopped himself just in time.

"Sorry," he mumbled before taking a huge bite of his roll.

"Jonathan?" the young woman asked.

He made eye contact and forgot to keep chewing. Through a mouthful he said, "Laura? Hi . . ."

"Wow, hi," she said, flashing the unchanged gorgeous smile that had mesmerized him when he met her two years ago. "It's been . . . a while."

Indeed it had. At least six months. Not that he was counting. He'd kept busy with work, which helped him suffer less through the breakup. But that had been the problem, hadn't it? Too much work, too little play *together.*

Jonathan folded the wax paper around his roll and dropped it into the brown sack with his apple and water bottle. He wiped the back of his hand across his mouth. "Good to see you. You look well."

She looked better than well. Laura looked stunning enough to cause a traffic jam on Lake Shore Drive. She was the kind of beauty that cowboys in Western movies would drape their only coat across a mud puddle for. And she knew it. Everything about her was intentionally placed, adorned, and manicured.

"You too," she said with a flip of her styled hair.

"I just finished a run," Jonathan said with a laugh. "I'm sweating and eating a sandwich out of a bag."

Laura laughed, and for a second, the sound of it tempted him like a bad habit he hadn't quite given up. She squeezed his bicep and then wiped her hand on her designer jeans. "You pull off that athletic look, and you know it. You make sweaty look good."

Jonathan stared down at his shoes. Was she flirting with him? Had she hoped to meet him here and rekindle their relationship?

They hadn't exactly been the most compatible couple, but he'd be lying if he said he hadn't missed having someone to spend time with . . . *when* he had spare time. He cleared his throat. "So what're you doing—"

A sharp-dressed man who looked to be in his fifties wrapped an arm around Laura's waist, leaned over, and kissed her temple. He may as well have been a walking advertisement for Ralph Lauren.

"Honey, this is Jonathan Carlisle," Laura said, leaning into the man. "You remember me telling you about him. He's the big promoter who did Fusion Lounge last night. Freddie was talking about it over brunch." She grinned at Jonathan. "Freddie said it was the best event he's been to all month, and that's saying a lot because Freddie goes to *all* the biggest deals. Jonathan, this is Dominique Laurent."

Jonathan squared his shoulders, and Dominique, who was a head shorter than him, mimicked the movement. Dominique held out his hand. "Pleasure to meet you. I've heard a lot about you, about your work."

Laura's new boyfriend was French. How *not* surprising. He probably jetted her off to Paris every other weekend. "Always good to hear," Jonathan said. "I put everything I have into it."

"You can say that again." Laura punctuated her words with a laugh.

Dominique chuckled. "We should get going, *mon chérie*, if we're going to make the train."

"We *can't* miss tea with the Brinkmans," Laura said in a mock-serious tone. "I love hearing all about their travels." She smiled at Jonathan. "Good to see you. Enjoy your bag sandwich."

"Sure, yeah, nice seeing you," he mumbled, but Laura and Dominique were already hurrying off to make a train, probably on its way to Happily Ever After. "Tea with the Brinkmans," he said to no one. "Right after we have scones at Downton Abbey." Both of which sounded exactly like what Laura would want and exactly like what Jonathan never could have offered her.

Jonathan walked home in a mood that continued to sour, and he ate his roll with half the fervor he started with. He stood at the floor-to-ceiling windows in his living room, staring at the river. A group of people practiced tai chi in the park. *Send me some of your zen-ness.*

Seeing Laura with Dominique bothered him more than it should have. She was attractive, well-spoken, and knew how to handle herself at prominent parties. She stayed aware of the fashion trends and knew how to use them to her advantage. How had such a beauty ended up with him? She joked that they were well matched in the looks department, saying that Jonathan had a face for movies.

Other than expensive parties and nice clothes, he and Laura didn't have much in common. She wanted someone to take her out to fine dinners, show her off at galas, and adorn her with jewelry from Tiffany's. The one, and only, time Jonathan suggested they go to a Cubs game together and eat hot dogs while drinking beer, she said that was the grossest idea she'd heard since someone told her crimping irons were coming back into style. He shouldn't have been surprised when she wanted a change, but he'd been side-swiped by her leaving.

After returning to his apartment, he showered and then sank onto the couch. He flicked on the TV to the news and muted it. Then he opened his laptop to scroll through more than one hundred emails. Maybe his apartment and his refrigerator were empty of life, but at least he had his work to occupy his mind, to keep him distracted from the uncomfortable feeling expanding in his gut.

Chapter 5

MATTIE

AFTER HELPING PENELOPE PUT AWAY CASSEROLES, Mattie took the back stairs to the third floor, a floor that housed the primary bedroom, a combination office and music room, and a multipurpose room that Mattie used as an art studio when she was there but Penelope used as a craft room and for yoga when the weather wasn't favorable outdoors. There was also a walk-in attic and a small but cozy library only big enough for a chaise lounge and a single end table with a lamp. Bookshelves covered all the wall space, but it was a perfect room for anyone who wanted to curl up and lose herself in a book.

The combination office and music room had belonged to Douglas Davenport, Mattie's grandfather. The room hadn't been redecorated or repurposed through the years. Penelope wanted to keep it exactly as it had been when her father was alive, as if he might come home one day and need it.

Most of what Mattie knew about her grandfather she'd learned from her mom, and even her mom's knowledge of him had holes big enough to drive a double-decker bus through. Douglas, an accomplished and incredibly successful musician until his death at age forty, had started touring right after he dropped out of college, and he never stopped. Not when he married Elena Russell and not when his two daughters were born. Douglas wanted to take his children with him on the road, to keep the family together, and he had, but only until Penelope was old enough to start kindergarten. Then Elena insisted the girls needed a more "normal" life.

For as long as anyone knew, if a Russell woman married, she kept her maiden name, so there had always been a Russell living in the family home. Sophia, Elena's older sister, had married Robert Adams, and they were the girls' godparents. So it was a natural choice for them to raise Penelope and Lilith in the Russell family home while Douglas and Elena toured all over the world. The family spent a scattering of weeks and weekends together throughout the years, and a couple of months every fall, Douglas and Elena took the girls on family vacations to make up for lost time.

Douglas and Elena were on a private jet to LA when their plane crashed after the engines malfunctioned, killing everyone on board. Penelope was a junior in high school, and Lilith was in eighth grade. Sophia and Robert then raised Penelope and Lilith as their own. Four years later, while Penelope was in college, Lilith left a note on the kitchen counter that read, *I'm leaving Ivy Ridge. Don't worry about me.* She was eighteen.

The next year Penelope graduated from college and came home. Robert accepted a job in Pensacola, and he and Sophia moved away for a short time, leaving Penelope to care for the family home. After being gone from Ivy Ridge for almost two years, Lilith returned on Halloween with a one-year-old daughter in tow. Mattie couldn't even imagine how shocked the family must have been, but maybe when it came to Lilith, they were used to the unexpected.

When Mattie visited Ivy Ridge through the years, Sophia and Robert drove up from Florida to see her. Even though they were technically her great-aunt and great-uncle, Sophia and Robert were like her grandparents, people who gave her gifts for Christmas and birthdays. About two years ago, Robert had retired, and Penelope insisted they move back in with her.

Mattie leaned against the music room's doorjamb. Robert sat in the creaky wooden chair that paired with the writing desk, and his long legs stretched out before him. He strummed a song by the Beatles on a guitar. Cardboard boxes were open, and their brittle packing tape hung from the flaps. Mementos, photographs, and knickknacks were placed around on the floor as though each piece had been studied.

Robert saw her and stopped playing. "I should have known you were coming up. The music always knows." He hummed the last few notes to "Here Comes the Sun" as he placed the guitar snug inside its case.

Mattie stepped into his arms and hugged him. He smelled like patchouli and autumn leaves. "How did I not know you played the guitar? You play well," she said with a smile.

"For an old man," he joked.

"For anyone."

Robert's salt-and-pepper hair fell over his ears, and his shocking blue eyes reminded her of cornflowers. A blue so bright they looked lit from within.

"Music has always been part of the family. I'd ask how you are," he said in his deep, slow voice, "but it's an idiotic question that people always ask you when you lose someone, isn't it? 'How *are* you,' they ask. 'Well, Joyce, I'm lousy. I'm a train wreck. I'm so pissed off I could rip that car in half.' But we don't want to shock the curls off the sweet little ladies, do we? So we nod and say, 'I'm getting by.'"

Mattie glanced around at the scattered memories on the office floor. "How *are* you, Robert?"

They shared a smile. "I'm getting by. It sure is good to see you, little one. How are my girls doing downstairs?"

Mattie nodded. "They've been putting away food from the neighbors. And from the looks of the kitchen, Sophia has plans to cook. As if we need more food." Mattie pointed at the boxes. "What're you looking for?"

His expression drooped. "Just going through some of Lilith's things."

Mattie knelt and lifted a fading photograph. Her mom looked young and hopeful, barely a teenager. Mattie had seen less than a handful of photos of her mom growing up. This felt like a rare treasure, and she wanted to sit and stare at it, to memorize the way Lilith had been caught laughing. Her mom pointed toward something just outside the camera's lens, and Mattie's imagination created possibilities of what—or who—had made her mom's smile stretch wide with unbridled happiness.

"Did your mom ever talk about people she knew when she was young? Other kids from Ivy Ridge? Friends or boyfriends?" he asked.

"Not much. She might have mentioned a few girls, but not in a long time."

"For someone so outgoing, she kept a lot to herself." He reached out his hand to pull Mattie to her feet. "Probably to avoid the town gossip about superstitions and magic." Maggie's eyes widened, but Robert led her toward the door without further explanation. "You know Sophia will whip up more food than the whole street will be able to eat. We don't need it, but the neighbors are good people to drop off their dishes."

Robert walked out of the room. Mattie's curiosity urged her to stay behind, to go through the photos, but he called to her.

"You think we can invite them all back over to eat? Is that inappropriate? Invite them to eat the food they made?"

"Do you really care if it's inappropriate?" Mattie asked.

"Nope," he said with a smirk that matched her own.

As they walked down the back stairs, the doorbell rang. "Potential eaters?" Mattie said.

They found Penelope in the foyer talking to two women whose arms were full of a casserole dish and a potted peace lily. Their eyes drifted to Mattie and Robert, who walked up the hallway, and the sincere compassion Mattie saw on their faces caused her to press her palm against the wall. She stopped moving, but Robert spoke to the women and took the offered casserole with gratitude.

Mattie stood like a statue on the carpet runner, and one of the women moved her hand over her heart and exhaled loudly. "You look just like her."

Hundreds of people had said as much to Mattie through the years. She could see some similarities between herself and Lilith, but the two of them were in no way identical. People saw what they wanted to see, and the people who knew her mom would always see Lilith's features reflected in Mattie's. Regardless, Mattie loved the idea that she had even a portion of her mom's beauty; it made her believe she could carry a part of Lilith with her.

Mattie smiled faintly at the women and then backtracked up the hallway. With Robert and Penelope busy speaking to the visitors, Mattie wanted to return to the music room and have another look at what Robert had pulled out of the boxes. She had one foot on the back staircase when Sophia called to her from the kitchen.

"There will be time for that," Sophia said. "Come here first."

Spinach leaves, fresh tomatoes, potted basil, pears, walnuts, gorgonzola, and other items were spread across the island. A loaf of sourdough had been sliced and arranged on a tray. Water boiled in a pot on the stove. Sophia's thick auburn hair was pulled into a loose bun.

"Time for what?" Mattie asked.

Instead of answering the question, Sophia gazed at her, a knowing in her eyes that caused Mattie to stand taller. "Lilith wore a lapis lazuli necklace." Mattie nodded, picturing the lapis lazuli oval stone wrapped in a thin ribbon of silver. The silver strand coiled around the top of the stone, forming an infinity symbol that hung from a long chain. "It's yours now. It was given to her years ago." Sophia made a motion toward the front of the house. "Bring in your boxes. It's in one of them."

"I'll find it," Mattie said. "I know which one her jewelry is in."

Sophia clicked on another stove-top gas burner. She placed a saucepot on the eye, and orange flames licked the metal bottom. "Bring in *all* your boxes."

"Sophia," Mattie said, feeling her shoulders tense, "I'll be leaving soon, probably right after the funeral."

Sophia turned away from Mattie and grabbed a glass dispenser of olive oil. She swirled the pale-yellow liquid into the saucepot. "Suit yourself. You can bring them in today or bring them in tomorrow."

"I'm *not* staying," Mattie said in frustration.

The lights in the kitchen flickered like a lightning storm, and an unnerving shudder rippled through the downstairs, sounding as though the house quaked on its foundation. Within seconds, the lights returned to normal, but a feeling of unease lingered. Mattie cupped one hand lightly around her throat and stared at Sophia's back.

The back staircase creaked, and Mattie poked her head out of the kitchen to see who was on the stairs, but Robert and Penelope were still in the foyer speaking with the guests.

Mattie shrugged. "I don't remember this house being so creaky."

Sophia dropped two garlic cloves into the saucepot and moved them around with a wooden spoon. "It's reminding you that you wanted to go upstairs." Sophia waved her hand to shoo Mattie out of the kitchen. "Don't forget the necklace."

Mattie slipped up the back stairs. She stopped by her bedroom on the second floor, plugged in her almost-dead cell phone, and grabbed her car keys. She'd find Lilith's necklace once the visitors were gone and she could walk outside without being forced into conversation with strangers.

Once on the third floor, she grabbed the open boxes from the music room and carried them into the walk-in attic for privacy. She hurried back for the loose items and then closed the attic door behind her. The attic was one tick away from being stifling, smelling of sawdust and brittle cardboard. The scent of old plastic and moldy clothes drifted through the rafters. One round window near the roofline let in light, and dust motes floated through the sunbeams.

Mattie flipped the light switch near the door, illuminating the attic in a yellow-orange glow. A dust-coated oscillating fan rattled in the corner as though something knocked into it. Mattie held her breath, waiting for a raccoon or a squirrel to pounce out. When nothing appeared, she glanced around the walls for an electrical outlet and plugged in the fan, turning it on high so it could spin off its dusty blades. Then she positioned it to blow less stifling air over her head and sat on the floor among her mom's forgotten things.

Mattie smiled at the photo of her mom laughing, and again she wondered who had caught her attention in that moment. Anyone who knew Lilith knew that her attention was intense yet temporary. She'd find you dazzling until the next falling star shifted her focus. Lilith had a way of staying detached from a situation—especially from men—while still being able to enjoy the experience.

There were a half dozen more photos of Lilith, and in all but one she looked radiant. Mattie studied the one somber image of her mom. Someone had snapped a photo of Lilith sitting near an outdoor fire. Shadowy trees were silhouetted behind her and a nearby rock formation looked like an oversize garden gnome watching over her. Lilith sat cross-legged on a blanket, staring at the flames beneath a starry sky. Her expression was one Mattie had never seen in person. Lilith looked sad, withdrawn . . . and lost. Obviously someone had taken the picture, but if Mattie hadn't seen there were two glasses nearby that suggested company, she would have assumed her mom was alone. The energy radiating off the image made Mattie's chest ache. She'd never seen Lilith look anything but confident and carefree.

Mattie flipped over the image and saw it was date-stamped, taken the year Mattie was born, but Lilith didn't look pregnant. Did her mom know she was pregnant? Did she know she'd be leaving Ivy Ridge soon?

Along with the loose photos there was a movie stub for *Footloose* from a local drive-in that featured classic films, a dinner receipt from The Pizza Box in Ivy Ridge, and a folded map of the United States. Curious why there would be a US road map in Lilith's collection, Mattie unfolded it. She was careful not to tear the fragile paper. The folded lines were stiff and created rigid peaks across the country. A small tear had already formed across Kansas.

As her eyes scanned the states, she noticed there were hearts drawn around twelve cities across the US. She laid the map on the floor and trailed her fingertip across the hearts, which were all pink except one. Only one city, Ivy Ridge, had a purple heart drawn around it. In the side margin of the map, another purple heart was drawn, and beside it were the words *You are here.* Mattie shivered.

When she realized the significance of the chosen cities, Mattie felt like she'd stumbled off a ledge. She always assumed her mom had chosen their next "home," their next big adventure, on a whim, but looking down at this map with a copyright date before Mattie was born, she could see that Lilith had chosen their path from the beginning.

"Mattie!" Penelope's muffled call slipped beneath the gap at the bottom of the closed attic door.

Mattie scrambled to refold the map and toss the other items into an open box. She switched off the fan and darted out the attic door, closing it behind her just as Penelope came up the back stairs.

"There you are," Penelope said. "What are you doing up here?"

"Nothing," Mattie said, not yet able to articulate what she'd found.

The house shuddered a complaint. Even the floorboards beneath Mattie's feet rattled. The attic door creaked open. Mattie grabbed the knob and slammed it shut.

Penelope tilted her head. "Uh-huh." She motioned with a thumb over her shoulder. "Sophia and I are running to the nursery to grab the arrangements for tomorrow. Why don't you come with us? Get a shower and change. Let's give the house a break." Without waiting for a response, she descended the stairs.

"The house?" Mattie asked, glancing back at the closed attic door. Then she followed Penelope. "What do you mean *the house*?"

"Emotions are high right now," Penelope said. "We all miss Lilith, even the house."

Mattie laughed, surprising herself with the sound. But she stopped when Penelope didn't join in. "Wait, you aren't serious, are you? Houses don't have feelings."

Penelope cringed when the smoke alarm sounded on the first floor. The rest of the alarms went off one by one, filling the downstairs with earsplitting beeping. Mattie cupped her hands over her ears. Penelope touched her hand to the wall. Mattie read her aunt's lips: *I'm sorry. She doesn't understand.*

One by one the smoke alarms stopped beeping, and Mattie stood in the silent hallway with her mouth hanging agape.

Chapter 6

PENELOPE

PENELOPE PARKED AT GREEN CLOVER, AND A MAN WEAR-ing a pecan-brown polo exited the nearest greenhouse. His athletic build was accentuated by bronze skin and a head full of unruly black curls barely tamed beneath a ball cap with an Atlanta Braves logo. He noticed them and lifted his hand in a friendly wave, then kept on his way.

"That's Raoul Moreno, isn't it?" Sophia asked, sliding her sunglasses down the bridge of her narrow nose to watch him walk away. "He was a good-looking kid, as I remember, and grew into a handsome man, didn't he?"

Penelope turned off the car, along with the air conditioner. The interior warmed almost instantly. "I don't see him much around town, but I think that's him."

"How could you see him much around town?" Sophia asked. She opened her car door, letting in the sticky outside air. "That would require you *going* into town often. What would you do without delivery services?" Sophia glanced back at Mattie before getting out. "Raoul is the owner. He went to school with Penelope and Lilith."

Penelope opened her car door. "I go into town, but delivery is easy when I'm working." Ordering groceries and supplies to be dropped off on her doorstep gave her the ability to avoid interacting with too many people—or with anyone at all. For all of Lilith's wayward behaviors, not entangling herself in others' lives was one Penelope understood.

Green Clover was the largest local nursery in Ivy Ridge, situated on three acres of land, and sold pretty much anything you were looking for. They offered a multitude of plants native to the area as well as more exotic varieties. Trees, shrubs, ornamentals, vegetables and herbs, flowers, and indoor plants could all be found at Green Clover. They also had landscape architects available for home or business needs and an in-house florist who created arrangements for any occasion. Penelope trusted their horticulture knowledge and knew they stocked healthy plants. She had never needed them for floral arrangements until now, but they were the first people she thought of to call once she started planning Lilith's funeral.

Penelope wiped the lenses of her sunglasses on her tank top and slipped them back onto her face. The August sun blazed like fire and heated her skin instantly. "Mattie, feel free to roam around."

"This is like a botanical garden," Mattie said.

Penelope's smile reflected in Mattie's mirrored lenses. "Or a wonderland maze."

Mattie looked out at the rows and rows of plants and trees. "Even better. Call me if you're ready to go and you don't see me."

"Don't fall down the rabbit hole," Sophia called after her.

Mattie lifted her hand in a wave to show she heard, and without turning toward them, she replied, "No promises!"

Penelope could see hints of Lilith in the way Mattie walked, graceful and gliding, through the plant rows. Except Mattie moved with a slight hesitation and caution about her, the opposite of Lilith's boldness. Lilith would have taken off at a sprint like a wild mustang let loose from a fenced corral. Mattie eased along, taking in her surroundings before proceeding too quickly. Even in their mother-daughter relationship, Lilith had always blazed the trail, which left Mattie at a huge disadvantage now that she was alone without a leader. Would she discover her own self-assurance and make her way, or would she retreat from the world and flounder? *Don't do what I did, Mattie.*

"She'll find her way," Sophia said as though reading Penelope's mind. "Her sense of purpose is strong, and she has the trademark Russell stubbornness."

Penelope pointed to a nearby greenhouse. "The arrangements will be in there."

As they passed by a potted hydrangea, Sophia reached out and touched a bright green leaf. "I've always thought honesty was the best choice."

Penelope raised her eyebrows and glanced at Sophia, whose eyes were hidden behind her oversize black sunglasses. "I sense there's more."

"I sense you already know," Sophia replied, adjusting her wide-brimmed hat against a gust of wind.

Penelope spotted Melissa MacAllister, who owned the home decor store in the town square. Melissa was friendly but inquisitive. Anything Penelope told her would make its way around town in less than a week. As much as Penelope loved Ivy Ridge, her time here had taught her that most people didn't understand her or why she didn't conform to societal norms. Sure, they came to Penelope for her unmatched seamstress skills, and they were always generous with their praise and kindness. But an element of curiosity surrounded the conversations as though they were all trying to *figure out* Penelope Russell and how to mold her into their groups, rather than just accepting her as she was.

Through the years she'd heard their questions, often whispered miles away but carried on the wind like secret messages. *Why isn't a beautiful woman like Penelope married? And why does a woman her age not have children? Does she ever date? Does she drink tea only when there's a full moon? Can she sew magic into dresses and repair hearts with red ribbons? Why does she spend so much time alone?*

Penelope didn't want to risk the possibility of a conversation today, so she grabbed Sophia's arm and tugged her in the opposite direction, taking the long away around the greenhouse. Sophia didn't argue but followed alongside Penelope.

"There's no advantage to opening up about everything. Mattie is leaving," Penelope said once they were far enough away from others. "Better to keep her free of all this."

"Better to give her a choice rather than making it for her," Sophia said. "Where is she going?"

"She doesn't know."

"Exactly," Sophia said. "She doesn't know anything. Not whether she's leaving. What if she stays?"

Penelope laughed but stopped when her heart seized. Some of her favorite memories were of when Mattie visited Ivy Ridge. For those summer months, birthdays, and holidays, Penelope felt like Mattie was her own daughter. Her fingers fluttered over her stomach. "In Ivy Ridge?"

"What if she wants to live with us?" Sophia said. "Will you tell her all the things she doesn't know about our family? Will you let her in, or will you keep her out like you keep everyone else out?"

Penelope frowned. "I don't keep people out. You're here, aren't you?"

Greg Prince, a local sports trainer and physical therapist,

walked out from a row of azaleas in front of Penelope and Sophia, blocking their way to the back door of the florist's greenhouse. His wife, Trisha, stepped into view carrying two geraniums in her arms. Penelope grabbed Sophia's arm and sidestepped through a row of skinny potted pear trees.

"That's Trisha, isn't it?" Sophia said. "Didn't you alter her daughter's wedding dress last week? Your handiwork gave her the confidence to sing a song dedicated to her groom at the ceremony."

"Yes," Penelope whispered, looking around for the quickest way into the greenhouse. "But I don't feel like talking today."

"Do you ever?" Sophia asked.

Penelope didn't stop walking. She skirted along the side of the florist's greenhouse, darting her eyes around to avoid any unwanted encounters. They'd have to circle back around to the front door. The tension in her shoulders caused her temples to throb. "I don't see anyone now. We can probably get in the front."

"This is exactly what I'm saying," Sophia said.

Penelope stopped and looked at Sophia. "What exactly are you saying?"

Sophia's soft expression almost caused what remained of Penelope's strength to leave her. She felt so close to unraveling, and except for the couple of hours after Mattie's phone call to tell her about Lilith's death, Penelope hadn't been able to openly grieve. She wondered if she'd ever been able to fully grieve her losses.

When her parents died, Penelope took on the role of the responsible sister, the strong one, so Lilith could stay carefree and not have to worry about the details of how they would move forward. Penelope had meted out her grief in increments. Then when Penelope was a young woman, she'd fallen in love and had to let him go. She'd wept only when she could hide away in the greenhouse or a closet, and only when she was certain no one would catch her in a moment of weakness. Now after losing her only sister, Penelope felt like an overstuffed beanbag that might explode with one more squeeze. At the rate Penelope was releasing her heartbreak, in tiny pieces here and there, she'd still be grieving in a hundred years.

Sophia lowered her dark-tinted sunglasses so Penelope could see her teddy bear–brown eyes. "I only want to encourage you to start pulling down the walls you've built around yourself. Mattie needs you. I loved Lilith like my own, but she pulled Mattie along with her because it was what *she* wanted. Lilith could bend anyone to her will, make them believe it was their choice. She didn't do it maliciously, but your sister was self-ish sometimes. She was never going to let Mattie fly free until she left this world. And we both know that Lilith knew her life would be short. She knew Mattie would be free soon enough."

Penelope toyed with the carnelian bracelet on her wrist. The Russell women had heightened abilities, but they didn't all share the same natural talents. Lilith's gifts were obvious as early as six years old, but she never claimed to have the ability to predict the future. However, when she was sixteen, Lilith woke from a dream in a panicked sweat. She swore the dream revealed her future, and while she withheld most of the details, what she did divulge to Penelope was that she knew exactly the month, day, and year when she would die. Lilith never doubted the truth of her dream, but Penelope hadn't believed it until now.

"After she was gone, Lilith expected you to be there for Mattie," Sophia continued. "Like she always did. You've cleaned up her messes or righted her ship whenever she needed it."

"Someone had to," Penelope said, staring at her feet and blinking away tears.

"You wanted to," Sophia said, touching Penelope's arm.

Penelope nodded her head because she didn't trust herself to speak.

"You loved your sister no matter what she did or didn't do, and Mattie needs *that* kind of love," Sophia said. "And she needs the truth."

Penelope swiped a tear from her cheek and straightened her shoulders. "There are many versions of the truth."

"What if you start with yours and the truth about our fascinating family?" Sophia said gently. "If you don't start soon, the house is going to give it all away."

Penelope almost smiled. "The house is a busybody if there ever was one."

Sophia turned her face toward the fiery sun. "Let's give Mattie the opportunity to embrace all of us."

Penelope watched the gusting wind ripple through a row of zinnias arranged in the colors of the rainbow. "I wish I had your faith."

"You do," Sophia said, linking her arm through Penelope's and walking them toward the front entrance to the florist's greenhouse. "It's just buried below a few things we need to move out of the way first."

Chapter 7

MATTIE

MATTIE STOOD ON THE SUNPORCH STARING AT THE flower arrangements for tomorrow's funeral. The sprays were simple, using mostly greenery with white roses and red poppies. There was a single arrangement of pink roses. When Mattie asked about these, Penelope said their dad used to bring home bouquets for them every time he returned from tour.

If asked, Mattie wouldn't have known her mom's favorite flowers. As long as she'd known her mom, Lilith seemed to cherish all aspects of nature, everything from the happy daisy to the prickly pear. They'd never had cut flowers in vases where they lived, and she never expected flowers for birthdays or celebrations. Yet Penelope knew exactly what to order from the nursery's floral designer for Lilith's service, which twisted Mattie's stomach.

Sophia, Robert, and Penelope arranged to have a small service in the backyard and then drive to the cemetery where Lilith would be buried in the Russell family plot. They weren't expecting a lot of people, for which Mattie was thankful. She didn't have the energy for random chitchat laden with condolences. She felt empty and flat, like a used-up paint tube.

Mattie's mind drifted to the photos of Lilith in the attic and to the map that had predetermined their lives across the United States. A squirmy feeling slid through her. Mattie had spent twenty-four years with Lilith, someone she considered her best friend, and had thought she knew everything about her mom. But after finding only a few photographs and the map—and now staring at the flowers—she wasn't so sure. What if all she knew about Lilith was surface level? Maybe her mom had been hiding parts of herself from Mattie her whole life.

The warmth of the sunporch became oppressive. Mattie wiped sweat from the back of her neck.

The stairs creaked as Robert walked down. He entered the kitchen and said, "The upstairs feels like the inside of an oven."

"And you know what that feels like, do you?" Sophia asked.

"Penelope!" Robert called. "What's going on with the AC?" He swirled melting ice cubes around in a half-full glass of sweet tea.

Sophia walked onto the sunporch with Mattie. "Don't forget to get the lapis lazuli necklace out of the box. You'll need it."

A vine of ivy wound through an arrangement. Mattie rubbed one of its leaves between her fingers. "For what?"

"For what's coming." Sophia offered her a peppermint candy.

Mattie enclosed it in her palm. "I don't remember you being so cryptic."

Sophia unwrapped an extra piece of candy and popped it into her mouth. "People remember what they want to. Lunch will be ready soon."

Mattie started up the back stairs. "I'm going upstairs for a minute."

She took the stairs two at a time. Robert was right; the higher up she went in the house, the hotter it felt. She'd left the car keys in the attic earlier, and she needed them if she was going to sift through boxes in the car. By the time she reached the attic door, she felt winded from the oppressive air. Mattie turned the knob on the attic door and pushed. Nothing happened. The door didn't budge. Mattie shoved her shoulder against it, causing the door to groan but nothing more.

She found Penelope on the second floor, staring at the thermostat. "The attic door is stuck."

Penelope tapped her finger against the plastic thermostat casing and then turned the dial back and forth. "That happens in the heat or when . . ." She shook her head. Looking at Mattie, she added, "It'll open again when it's cool."

"The car keys are in there," Mattie said in irritation.

Penelope raised an eyebrow. "Going somewhere?"

"Eventually, yeah," Mattie answered. "I'm not staying here forever."

The pipes hidden in the walls gurgled, then made popping noises. A picture frame on the wall tilted sideways, causing the family portrait to look as though it could slide out of the image.

"*No one* is staying here forever," Penelope said, straightening the picture.

Mattie rolled her eyes. "Sophia thinks I need Mom's lapis lazuli necklace."

"She's persistent," Penelope said, "as is the house. The door will open when it's ready. Let's go out and check the units."

Crouched outside beside the air-conditioning system, Penelope inspected the units and then checked the connected pipes in the back of the system. Mattie opened the weather app on her phone: *Ivy Ridge 97°, humidity 92%*. Everything was sweating. Even the bricks on the house were tacky with moisture. Sweat slow-rolled down Mattie's back, dampening her T-shirt.

"Do you even know what we're looking for?" Mattie asked.

"Hear that?" Penelope asked, standing and brushing off her

hands. "That hissing? I think we're leaking refrigerant, but I don't know why. I just had this serviced." Penelope held out her hands, palms up, and closed her eyes. "At least there's a breeze, even a humid one. Let's open the windows in the house to get the air circulating, and I'll call Eddie at the shop." Penelope rubbed her hand down the side of the house, whispering something Mattie couldn't hear.

"What's with the house?" Mattie asked. As a child she believed the house was magical and full of life. Had she imagined it? Houses weren't *alive*, were they? But even as the thought filled her mind, a swirl of doubt followed behind it.

"These things happen," Penelope said, walking toward the back porch. "Hopefully Eddie can get it fixed fast so we don't have to sweat it out for long."

Mattie followed behind Penelope, hurrying to match her aunt's quick pace. "That's not what I mean—"

"Robert!" Penelope said, rushing over to help him as he tried to lift the broken greenhouse door by himself. "You need to let someone help you with that."

Robert had already removed the pins holding the door to the hinges, and together they lifted and placed the door beside the greenhouse. He tapped a finger against the top hinge. "I'll need to replace this one. It's bent out of shape and not repairable. Once I get a new one, I'll have the door working again."

Penelope smiled at him. "I'll run to the hardware store. You go on in and have lunch. We can fix this afterward."

Mattie stared into the open greenhouse. In her mind she saw the shadows of two people crouched near the potting table, but the sunlight shifted across the panes and the vision faded.

Penelope looked at Mattie. "See if you can help Sophia finish preparing lunch. I'm going to water the greenhouse plants. This heat is getting to them. We're all a little droopy around here."

Robert washed his hands beneath the outdoor spigot, and Mattie went into the house. Sophia bustled around the kitchen. A bowl of fusilli pasta tossed in a pesto sauce was placed alongside a spinach salad adorned with tomatoes, basil, sliced pears, walnuts, and a small handful of gorgonzola.

"Need help?" Mattie asked.

Sophia grabbed glasses from a cabinet. "I'm all set. You want to make a plate?"

Other than the few bites of the cinnamon roll she ate that morning, Mattie hadn't eaten much since the last bag of potato chips on the drive to Ivy Ridge the night before. But the void inside her was swallowing everything, including her appetite.

"If anybody needs me, I'll be upstairs." She avoided Sophia's gaze as she walked out of the kitchen and took the back stairs.

She went to the third floor and tried the attic door again. When it still didn't budge, she wandered into the art studio that doubled as a craft room. The original hardwood floors were a soft caramel color, and long sunbeams of light poured through the oversize windows, accenting scuff marks and tiny riverlike gouges in the soft wood from a lifetime of use.

Floor-to-ceiling bookshelves held books and a variety of plants—succulents, pothos, and Colocasia. Mattie saw the five potted plants she'd brought from Chicago. Penelope must have brought them up here so they could make friends. The thought made Mattie smile. Lilith had taught Mattie all about plants—their Latin names, how to care for them, how to keep them alive—from a very early age. Mattie knew words like *Hydrangea macrophylla* and *Rhododendron simsii* long before she knew her multiplication tables. She assumed Lilith's love of plants had been because the Russell house boasted a glorious garden year-round.

The shelves in the craft room were full of more than just plants. Baskets, bins, and metal jars helped organize arts and crafts supplies and were neatly arranged on the shelves. A rectangular craft table sat near one window, and an easel holding a blank canvas stood nearby. Mattie walked over to inspect the stacks of painted canvases leaning against one wall.

Surprise filled her when she realized the artwork was all hers, pieces she'd painted throughout the years—pieces she thought had been either lost, sold by Lilith, or forgotten in whatever town they'd lived in last. Why did Penelope have these specific paintings, and why had she kept them? They were a random assortment of subject matter.

Mattie flipped through the canvases. They led her down a path of memories that blossomed like wildflowers. There was the three-eyed jack-o'-lantern with the off-center, goofy grin she painted one October when they lived in Austin, and the close-up garden view of orange coneflowers blooming alongside wild lavender she painted after visiting a botanical garden in Atlanta. In New York City she painted a grass-green basil plant in a cherry-red pot that was positioned in front of a blurry uncut pizza in the background. She'd wanted to commemorate her first official New York–style slice.

Mattie looked over the painting of a walking stick with a silver handle designed with swirls and ivy leaves. She'd painted the stick lying on spring grass beside a scattering of cherry blossoms. Mattie remembered painting it while cooped up with chicken pox in Nashville when she was six. The style was more juvenile than her later art, but she was impressed with how detailed it was. Another canvas showcased a blurry image of a dark-skinned woman wearing a cheerful yellow apron seen through a storefront window. The painting captured the play of light on the sidewalk out front and the woman's visage in the shop window. She held a plate of cookies in one hand and the faintest smile touched her lips. Mattie remembered painting that one in Asheville after she and Lilith hiked a wildlife trail near Looking Glass Rock.

Pineapple sage was the focal point of the next canvas. After visiting the town center in Sedona, Mattie had wanted to rush home and paint, and this was what she'd created. She'd perfectly captured the herb's yellow-green leaves and their fuzzy edges. Tubular, scarlet-red flowers rose like hot pokers from the center of the plant. A black hummingbird with translucent wings fluttered near one of the blooms. Mattie touched blue blobs below the sage bush, near where its woodsy stalks disappeared into the earth. She felt the crinkly raised edges of the dried paint. Lapis lazuli stones—she'd forgotten her obsession with them when she was younger. Or had that been Lilith's obsession bleeding onto Mattie?

The final painting was of a campfire burning red and orange with yellow-tipped flames set against a backdrop of a midnight-blue sky covered in shimmery silver dots. The silhouette of a couple was just visible if the light hit the painting at the right angle. She'd been inspired to paint this one in Fort Myers after a day spent at the beach with her mom.

A tangle of love, grief, and confusion erupted inside her, and her legs trembled, so she sat on the floor and went through the paintings, studying the brushstrokes and the colors and remembering her mom's face each time she presented her final work. Adoration and love. Two things she'd never see on Lilith's face again.

Sorrow swelled inside her with a desperate need to fill every cell in her body. She doubled over, pressing her forehead nearly to the floor. She tried to inhale, but her chest constricted, becoming too tight to breathe. With her face scrunched up and her temples throbbing, sobs squeezed out of her and tears dripped onto the hardwood. How was she going to live without her mom? Without her guidance and zest for life? How was she going to live out the rest of her days with this gaping hole in her life?

After a few minutes of crying, Mattie sat up and grabbed a wad of tissues from the box. She blew her nose as quietly as possible because the last thing she wanted to do was heave her sadness on the others. They had their own heartbreak to carry, and they didn't need hers to drag along too. Sitting among the paintings, she slowly let the past return to her and tried to find comfort in the memories of her mother.

Mattie didn't know how much time she spent staring at the paintings, seven in all, but the sound of voices outside pulled her attention. She stacked the art against the wall and headed downstairs for a glass of water and to see what was happening outside. Mattie slipped on her sunglasses to hide the telltale signs of her crying jag and then found Robert and Sophia in the backyard tending to the vegetable garden. The greenhouse door had been rehung on its new hinge. Penelope and a wiry man—presumably Eddie from the shop—stood at the side of the house discussing the air-conditioning units. He squatted at the rear of one unit, resembling a praying mantis with his excessively long, thin legs, and pointed as he talked to Penelope.

When Eddie caught sight of Mattie, he used an oil-stained cloth to wipe the sweat from his brow and stood to his full height, which was at least six feet, four inches. He reminded Mattie of a scarecrow wearing somebody else's faded overalls. Mattie lifted her hand in a wave after he'd been gaping at her without speaking for an uncomfortably long time, and he responded with a nervous laugh. "Begging your pardon," Eddie said with a glance toward Penelope. "I thought I was looking at . . ." He smiled awkwardly at Mattie. "You must be Lilith's daughter. You're the spitting image of your mama in high school. I was crazy about her, must have asked her out a dozen times before she finally said yes."

"I didn't know you dated Lilith," Penelope said. She looked as stunned as Mattie felt. Her mom had dated a guy like Eddie? The kind of men her mom attracted were handsome, wealthy, confident, and charismatic. Eddie didn't fit the stereotype.

Eddie nodded. "Best month of my life," he said sincerely. "Senior year. She let me take her to the homecoming dance, and then, well, she said we were better as good friends. She wasn't rude, ya know, always real nice to me. But I couldn't expect a girl like Lilith to want me forever. I was sad when she left after graduation. She took a part of my heart with her." He rubbed the back of his neck and laughed uncomfortably again. "Listen to me, sounding like a love-struck buffoon. I need to get a tool out of my truck. Be right back."

"He was dating Lilith before she left?" Robert asked, startling Penelope and Mattie, who were watching Eddie high-step off toward the front of the house.

"So it seems," Penelope said. "She never stops surprising me."

"Do you think there's any chance—"

"No," Penelope said, abruptly cutting off Robert's question.

Uneasiness traveled over Mattie and the breeze died. The downstairs windows were open, and Fleetwood Mac's "Little Lies" started playing on the radio inside the sitting room. Penelope's head jerked in the direction of the music.

"Any chance of what?" Mattie asked.

"Nothing," Penelope snapped. "Let's focus on fixing the AC."

Sophia appeared around the corner of the house, gloves dirty from gardening and a trowel hanging loosely in one hand. Her wide-brimmed hat kept her face in shadow. She removed her sunglasses. "Penelope, honey, you can't control everything."

"Yes, I can!" she argued, color rising in her cheeks. "This is my house, too, and I have a say in what goes on here and what we discuss."

The radio's volume rose as though someone inside the house were turning the dial. Mattie shivered, and an idea so unnerving rose up within her that she almost squashed it. But instead, words whispered from her lips. "Is this about my birth father?"

The radio channel switched to a baseball game and lowered in volume. She swayed on her feet in the heat. Everything before her blurred, and colors melted together like a painting left out in the rain.

"But I-I don't have a father," Mattie babbled to herself. "I was left on the doorstep in a pumpkin." She knew the words weren't the truth, but it was the story her mom had told her for years. The story she convinced herself was as close to the truth as she'd ever know. "Why are we even thinking about him? If I cared about who he is, which I don't, he hasn't looked for me in twenty-four years. He obviously hasn't wanted to know where I've been or how I'm doing—"

"Mattie, this is *none* of our business," Penelope said, casting a displeased glance at Robert. "But I don't think he even knew about you."

If Mattie didn't care about knowing who her father might be, then why was her heart racing and her stomach aching so badly?

Fearing she would have a full-on meltdown in front of them, she raced off toward the street.

She passed Eddie, who asked if she was okay, but she kept walking until she reached the sidewalk, where she finally slowed down and stopped beside a maple tree. Why did the mention of her father unsettle her so much? She didn't know anything about him, so there weren't any emotional ties to him, no memories to haunt her. When it came to her father, there was nothing but empty space. Why should she care about empty space?

But maybe that was the answer. *Emptiness.* The emptiness continued to spread, now reminding her of a man Mattie had never known. Not only had her mom left her alone in a world she didn't know how to navigate, but Lilith's absence triggered a collapsing inside Mattie. She thought Lilith was her best friend, that they had shared everything about their lives with each other. If her mom hadn't thought Mattie's father should be a part of their lives, then Mattie trusted her judgment. Or that's what Mattie had done in the past: trust her mom. But should she rethink that now?

More secrets. In less than two days, Mattie had uncovered disquieting things about her mom. How many more would she find? Was her biological father meant to be one of the discoveries? Even Penelope was keeping secrets from Mattie, not wanting to tell her too much about the family or about the house. Regardless of whether Mattie was sticking around—and she wasn't—what could Penelope possibly have to say that would disrupt Mattie's world even more than it was right now?

"Not there, dear," a woman said, "over here by the pink roses."

The neighbors, the Carlisles, were in their front yard positioning a birdbath near the roses lining their front porch. Mattie hadn't seen them in years. Virginia Carlisle wore a pair of khaki shorts and a pin-striped sleeveless blouse. The intense heat hadn't stopped her from rolling her hair and pinning it up in a sophisticated bun at the back of her head. Her gold sunglasses reflected the sunlight, sending bursts of light toward Mattie. Thomas Carlisle grunted as he repositioned the stone birdbath, careful not to separate the top bowl portion from the base. He sweated heavily through his plaid polo shirt, and more sweat dripped down his face. Mattie almost felt sorry enough for him to offer help.

Virginia caught sight of Mattie and raised her hand in greeting. "Hello there, dear." Thomas glanced over his shoulder to see who Virginia was talking to and welcomed the break. He wiped his forehead against his shirtsleeve. A cell phone rang just as Mattie lifted her hand in a return wave. Virginia reached for a phone on the porch and answered. "Jonathan! How are you? I've left you a half dozen messages. Finally found the time to call your mom?"

Jonathan. The name pushed through Mattie's mind, dislodging a memory of a handsome young man sitting in the backyard eating birthday cake with her, followed by a goodbye kiss that held so much promise and hope. Her stomach flip-flopped. She hadn't thought about that boy in a while. She'd never been able to shove him completely out of her mind, not even after his no-show summer. A sense of longing swelled inside her. Why couldn't she keep herself together? Her emotions were as erratic as a wasp trapped in a mason jar.

"Mattie." Penelope stood in the front yard. "Can we talk?" she asked, walking closer.

"Doesn't seem like you want to tell me *anything*."

Penelope sighed. "You're right," she agreed. "And it's not fair to you. If you'll come inside, I'd like to try."

Mattie glanced down the sidewalk. Virginia paced the front

yard talking to Jonathan, her youngest son, and occasionally pointed and spoke to Thomas, who had moved the birdbath twice more.

"Not right now," Mattie said. "I need to clear my head." And she started walking.

"You're coming back, right?" Penelope called after her.

Mattie pointed at the rental car. "Until the house gives me back the keys, I don't have much choice." She set off at a quick pace on the sidewalk, hoping to outrun her thoughts about her mom, her mysterious father, and a young man who had awakened her heart ten years ago, but she was well aware those thoughts followed behind her like a personal entourage.

~

Mattie followed the neighborhood sidewalks lined with majestic oaks that had grown so large they created a thick canopy that shadowed the road. She walked through the historic neighborhoods all the way into downtown Ivy Ridge, which was about two miles from the Russell house. As a kid Mattie thought of Ivy Ridge as an ordinary, uninteresting small town with not much happening. Most of her time had been spent around the Russell house, playing in the backyard or taking day trips with Penelope. As an adult, Mattie could see Ivy Ridge was more than a stereotypical Southern, dirt-roads-only, one-traffic-light kind of place.

It was no bustling metropolis like Chicago, but Ivy Ridge had its charm. If Savannah and the fictional town of Andy Griffith's Mayberry were mixed together, the product would be Ivy Ridge. Its incredibly diverse architecture boasted styles that spanned the eighteenth and nineteenth centuries, from simple Colonials to the gingerbread accents of the Victorian period. Wrought iron gates covered in moss-green ivy were tucked among homes painted in pastels that mixed alongside redbrick structures.

In Ivy Ridge people knew your name and wanted to help, whether you wanted them to or not. They brought casseroles to your house when someone was born or someone passed away. They noticed when you changed your hairstyle or when you needed encouragement. Neighbors brought you flowers from their garden just because. Holidays were celebrated with festivals, bountiful decorations, and impressive community effort. The celebrations called forth an exuberance unmatched even by the big city, and Mattie was reminded of the closeness she'd felt during festivities in Ivy Ridge.

By the time she reached downtown, her emotions had settled enough for the vise grip on her chest to loosen. Mattie and Lilith had lived in all types of climates—places with mild winters and others with winters bitter enough for you to understand why New Yorkers flew away to Florida. Some places never experienced what Mattie knew to be a *real* summer, and then she'd been in towns like Ivy Ridge that had summers so hot the houses nearly melted into their foundations. If Mattie had to choose, she'd pick Southern summers over Northern winters every time.

But she'd almost forgotten how humid and sticky Ivy Ridge was during the summer. After a couple of hours in town, Mattie reluctantly returned to the house. By the time she got back, it was nearing dinnertime. Penelope looked relieved to see Mattie walk through the front door. The house was only a few degrees cooler than the outdoors and smelled humid and earthy like a greenhouse.

"Guess Eddie couldn't fix the AC?" Mattie asked, walking into the kitchen in search of something cool to drink.

Penelope followed her. "He needed a part that won't be here until tomorrow." She pulled a glass from the cabinet and handed it to Mattie. "How was town?" She slid a charcuterie board across the island. "No, I didn't follow you. There are only so many places to wander off to around here. I guessed downtown or through the woods to the Degaré estate."

Mattie filled the glass with ice and found a pitcher of lemonade in the refrigerator. She sat on a barstool at the island. "I haven't thought of that place in ages. Do kids still throw wild parties there?"

Penelope shot her a curious expression. "What would you know about wild parties in Ivy Ridge?"

"Not much." Mattie took a long drink of the cool lemonade and closed her eyes. She remembered the party on the Degaré estate on her fifteenth birthday, mostly because it was the night she met Jonathan Carlisle. "What actually happened there? Since no one has torn down the manor and built a shopping mall on the land, I'm guessing it's still privately owned? The estate must be at least five hundred acres." She reached for the pitcher. "Want some?"

Penelope shook her head. "I don't know much about what happened there, and most of what you'll hear is gossip."

Mattie eyed the charcuterie. She grabbed a seed cracker and smeared goat cheese on it, finishing it off with a fig slice. Then she went for a slice of prosciutto and wrapped it around a pitted date. Penelope continued while Mattie snacked.

"The Degarés were a wealthy family. They were one of the old families in Ivy Ridge, been here since it was founded, I think. The father was a peanut farmer and also had one of the largest pecan orchards at the time. He shipped his goods all over the state and then the country. He built that mansion for his family—a beautiful wife and four children. The kids were young, little stairsteps. I think the oldest was eight at the time it happened."

Mattie listened with rapt attention. She knew something mysterious had happened on the Degaré estate, but she'd never had enough curiosity to ask anyone until now. "When what happened?" She loaded a cracker with cheddar and a paper-thin apple slice.

"The mother, Adrianna, disappeared," Penelope said. "One day she never came home. They searched for her for weeks until someone finally found torn, bloody clothing on the property. They accused the husband of killing her."

Mattie gasped. "Why?"

"After her disappearance it was discovered she was having an affair with a man from the next town over. That man also went missing," Penelope explained, "so the authorities believed that Mr. Degaré killed them both and buried the bodies. They never found the proof, but because Mr. Degaré's fingerprints were on the clothing they found, which turned out to be Adrianna's dress, they put him in prison for murder. The children were shipped off to distant family, and the estate was left to ruin. It's possible one or more of the children are still alive, or maybe one of *their* children owns the estate now. I don't know why they've never sold the property. As you obviously know, local kids use it as a secret party house that isn't so secret."

"Those poor Degaré kids," Mattie said. "Do you think he was guilty?"

Penelope walked to a kitchen window and glanced into the backyard. "No," she admitted. "But that was long before I was alive, so I have no reason to have an opinion at all. I don't feel like it was the truth though. I think there was more to the mother than anyone knew. That poor house, too, left all alone and empty." Penelope ran her hands along the countertop, and the refrigerator started to hum as though responding to her soothing presence in the kitchen.

Sophia breezed into the kitchen carrying a vase of white daisies. "Look at these beauties," she said. "Virginia walked these over. She grows them in her backyard." She looked surprised to see Mattie had returned. "Oh, hey, darling, how was your walk?"

"Town hasn't changed much, which is somehow comforting." She pointed at the flowers. "The Carlisles' backyard?" Mattie asked, curious why her heart responded with a quickening beat.

Sophia nodded and placed the vase of flowers on the round table in the breakfast nook. "They moved in next door the same year you were born, Mattie. Their boys were the rowdiest kids I'd ever seen, but they turned out all right," she said with a laugh. "They're a bit older than you, but their youngest is close in age, I think."

"Jonathan," Mattie said, the name almost a whisper on her lips.

Sophia nodded, opening the refrigerator and pulling out containers of food. "He's the baby, maybe a couple years older than you. The two older brothers, William and David, both live nearby."

Unable to dampen her curiosity, Mattie asked, "But not Jonathan?"

"He moved to New York," Penelope answered, helping Sophia open the food containers to prep for dinner. "He went to college in Queens on a baseball scholarship."

"That's right," Sophia agreed. "He was an incredible baseball player. Everyone thought he'd end up in the major league."

"But he moved to Chicago a few years ago," Penelope interjected. "Lives in the Loop area, if I remember correctly. I'm not very familiar with the different areas of the city, so I could be wrong. He rarely comes home, so we haven't seen him in years."

"He lives in the Loop?" Mattie asked incredulously. "That's where Mom and I lived."

"I think you're right about the area," Sophia said, looking at Penelope. "Virginia says it's a fancy apartment with amazing views, but he works all the time so she doesn't understand why the views matter." She waved her hand through the air. "But it's a big city and unlikely you would have run into him, don't you think?"

"Yeah, big city," Mattie agreed. What would she have done if she'd run into him anyway? Would she have even recognized him? Her speeding pulse seemed to think she would have *known* it was him. She still could picture his smile and the way the moon lit his eyes that night.

Sophia continued, "Virginia said he hasn't been home in five years or so."

Mattie's momentary daydream evaporated. So not returning was typical of Jonathan, something she learned about him ten years ago.

"If you want," Penelope said softly, "I'm still open to talk. We have some time before dinner."

Mattie shrugged. She wanted to bury her feelings half a mile below the surface of the earth and leave them there to ferment like kimchi. Possibly for all time. And as curious as she was about the family and its secrets, she also felt exhausted by the possibility of anything else sideswiping her. "Maybe later."

They prepared a simple dinner of leftover spaghetti noodles

with red sauce, fresh zucchini, basil, and mushrooms, along with a simple salad with summer vegetables from the garden. Since the house felt sticky and heavy from the humidity combined with a feeling of loss, they ate dinner on the back patio to take advantage of the occasional breeze that moved around the muggy air.

Just as Mattie finished the last of her spaghetti, Robert cleared his throat and looked at her. "I understand you're not interested in staying in Ivy Ridge long."

Mattie glanced around the table. Everyone watched her and waited. Apprehension rose from the flagstones like waves of heat. "That's right. I plan to leave right after the funeral tomorrow."

"Tomorrow?" Penelope blurted.

"Yes, tomorrow," Mattie said, pulling her napkin out of her lap and dropping it on the table.

"Where will you go?" Penelope asked. "Do you have a place to live?"

Mattie hesitated. The pasta churned in her stomach. "No . . . but I'll figure it out." Never mind that her mind was screaming, *And how exactly are you going to figure it out?*

"There's a will reading you need to be present for," Robert said.

Mattie's brow furrowed. Why would she need to listen to a standard legal agreement that would likely tell her she was granted ownership of her mom's belongings currently boxed up in the car? "Someone has to read the will to us? Can't they mail it here?"

Robert met Sophia's gaze before continuing. "No," he said. "As Lilith's only heir, you need to meet with the lawyer to discuss what happens next. There are special stipulations."

Enid mewled below the table and eased out onto the patio. Penelope's eyebrows lifted. "What stipulations? I've not heard anything about this."

"That was intentional," Robert said. "But you'll find out everything because you're the one going with Mattie to meet with the lawyer."

"Why does everything have to be so secretive in this family?" Mattie said. "Can't anyone just be straightforward?"

Robert looked apologetic. "Lilith orchestrated this. I'm merely the messenger."

Mattie rubbed her temples. "Obviously I don't have a choice, so I'll go to the will reading, but I'm not staying in Ivy Ridge a second longer than I have to."

Every bulb in the string lights looping through the backyard trees went out instantly, and the house gave a groan before going dark. The electricity had gone out. The four of them sat in the dim light of the setting sun.

"Would you mind," Penelope said, reaching out to touch Mattie's arm, "kindly offering the option that you might stay a little while longer?"

"Why?" Mattie asked. Moving on was what she and Lilith did. Coming to Ivy Ridge was a temporary stay, as it always had been.

"You don't have to mean it," Penelope said, glancing toward the house, "but I would appreciate a little help here. Your staying in town *could* be an option, just as your leaving is another one. Not everyone is thrilled with the idea of you not being home with us."

"This isn't my home," Mattie said.

"But it could be," Sophia offered. "Is there somewhere else you'd like to call home right now?"

Home had never been a permanent place for Mattie. Home was wherever she and Lilith were together, and the word didn't carry the same affectionate meaning it did for others. For Penelope and

Sophia, home meant Ivy Ridge. For Mattie, home meant *nowhere* because her mom—her one constant—was gone.

"Please?" Penelope said.

The gentle tone of her aunt's voice slowed Mattie's racing thoughts. If it made Penelope feel better to think Mattie might stay, then she'd give her aunt that small consolation. "I'll consider staying in town a little longer."

The lights in the house flickered on, and the string lights illuminated.

"Thank you," Penelope said. Exhaustion ringed her words.

Mattie looked up at the string lights. *What is going on here?* In a quiet voice, she asked her aunt, "Happy now?"

"Oh, that wasn't for me," Penelope said, sliding her chair back and standing. She collected the dirty dishes. "You keep saying you're sticking around, and I bet the house will even open the attic door again."

Mattie gawked at the house, and Sophia chuckled.

"What does that mean?" Mattie asked. Goose bumps traveled over her skin, and the light in her second-floor bedroom winked off and on at her.

Chapter 8

PENELOPE

AFTER CLEANING UP FROM DINNER, ROBERT AND SOPHIA retreated to their room for the evening. Penelope stepped out of a scalding shower, which wasn't the best idea given the over-heated state of the house, but she needed to scrub away the day and the sorrow and frustration that encased her skin, making her feel stiff and brittle.

There was nothing more to plan or prepare for tomorrow's funeral, and all she wanted to do was crawl into bed and sleep until her alarm forced her to wake up at six o'clock tomorrow morning. At seven, a local service was delivering two dozen folding chairs and two long tables with tablecloths for the backyard ceremony. She already had the floral arrangements, and the Methodist pastor officiating the service said he'd bring a lectern. There was plenty of food supplied by friends and neighbors.

Penelope dressed in a pair of loose pajama shorts and a tank top, then pulled a brush through her long, wet hair while staring at her reflection in the bathroom mirror. Seeing her sister's eyes mirrored back in her own, she asked, "You left me in a mess, didn't you? Mattie seems lost. How could she not be after losing you?" She lowered her hands to the marble countertop, stared at her splayed fingers, and exhaled. "But I still want to blame you."

Enid pranced into the bedroom doorway and meowed. "You have answers for me?" Penelope asked as she walked out of the bathroom. Enid bounced out of the room, meowing louder as though calling Penelope to follow her, then walked into Mattie's room. Penelope paused outside the half-open door and knocked. "Mattie?" No answer.

Penelope pushed open the door. Enid paced back and forth in front of the bedroom windows, and Penelope looked out into the backyard. Mattie had taken an easel onto the patio, and she stood in front of a blank canvas with a paintbrush in her hand. Enid weaved in between Penelope's legs. Penelope bent down to scratch between her ears. "Thank you."

By the time Penelope joined Mattie outside, the canvas had two globs of blue paint spattered on it. "What are you painting?"

"Can't you tell?" Mattie said sarcastically without looking at her aunt. "My life." Penelope didn't know how to respond, but she didn't have to because Mattie continued. "Messy. Disastrous. Irregular. No purpose."

"Mattie—"

"Don't," Mattie argued. "Don't tell me that everything will be okay and it will all work out." Mattie flung another blob of paint—rich violet—onto the canvas with such force that specks of purple bounced off the canvas and splattered Mattie's shirt.

"What if that's all true?" Penelope asked.

"Why did she do all of this? *Why?* I'm a grown woman, and I should be capable of figuring out my life, but I can't. She did everything. *Everything.* And I let her. I want to yell at her. All these years of dragging me to city after city, promising that life would be fun and happy and exciting. But it's not. This is god-awful, and I feel like she took *me* with her and all that's left is this pathetic nobody. But if she were here, I'd just let her tell me what to do and

I'd go along with it. Sophia is right. I let Mom dictate my entire life. I feel *so angry*." Mattie sagged onto the flagstones, hung her head, and cried.

Penelope's heart ripped open listening to Mattie's devastated sobs. She sat down beside her niece and rubbed Mattie's back. "Even if you don't want to hear it, it's going to be okay. We'll figure this out."

"How?" Mattie asked, wiping her wet cheeks. "I quit my job in Chicago, so I'm jobless with no college degree. I don't have any real friends because who needed them when I had Mom?"

"You have us—me, Sophia, and Robert," Penelope said. "And you don't need a college degree to find a job you love. You've worked all kinds of jobs, and you have more skills than people twice your age. You ran a newspaper route, worked as a hot dog girl at a stadium, sold paintings, delivered flowers, worked as a sous chef on a food truck, led hiking tours, made the best pizzas at that neighborhood spot, and what am I forgetting?"

"That stint as a dogwalker." Mattie's smile was small, but there was still a glimpse of it. She hung her head again. "My life sounds even more absurd out loud. None of those jobs are what I want long term, but I have no idea what I want to do long term."

Penelope nodded. "Because you've never been anywhere long enough to figure it out. But you can stay here for as long as you need."

Mattie grabbed a dirty rag from her supplies and wiped at the paint splatters on the flagstones. "Mom never wanted to come back and live here, so why would I?"

A fire sparked in Penelope's stomach. She clenched her jaw and hands before releasing her held breath along with the tension.

"You used to love it here during the summers, didn't you? We had the most fun together, didn't we?"

Mattie nodded, and that simple motion filled Penelope with relief. She couldn't handle Mattie not loving those memories of her growing up.

"Lilith chose to leave Ivy Ridge because that's what was best *for her* at the time," Penelope said, working to keep her voice steady. "But you are not Lilith. You've never had the same needs or desires. Maybe you thought you did because she was the leader of your pack, but now you have a chance to figure out what *you* want. Maybe that's Ivy Ridge and maybe it's not. Whatever you decide, I'll support you."

New tears sprang into Mattie's eyes. She resembled a lost little girl, and all Penelope wanted to do was hold her. "We could look at a map together," Penelope offered, "and find interesting places that you might like to live."

Mattie's expression sagged. "I have pretty much zero money. I got paid last week, but that won't stretch far."

Penelope squeezed Mattie's hand. "Don't worry about the money. I'll give you anything you need—"

"I won't let you do that," Mattie argued. "It would be no different from depending on Mom for everything."

"Honey, if you'll let me finish," Penelope said softly. "I'll help you until you find the right place for you and get a job. I don't plan for you to be dependent on me indefinitely. I know you don't want that, but until you get settled, let me help you. There's no reason for you to struggle unnecessarily. You also don't have to settle for a job you don't like. Think about what you enjoy or what you'd like to learn more about. You could start painting again. You never had trouble selling your work. People pay a lot of money for great art." Penelope nodded toward the splotchy canvas. "Maybe not this one depicting *your life at the moment.*"

Mattie snorted a short laugh. "You don't think this hot-mess painting will sell for big bucks?"

"I didn't say that," she joked. "To the right buyer this could be exquisitely abstract."

"Or just blobs on a canvas," Mattie said with a small smile. She leaned her head against Penelope's shoulder. After a long pause she said, "Thank you."

Penelope slipped her arm around Mattie's shoulders and hugged her. Then Mattie sat up. "Any idea what the stipulations are in Mom's will? It seems unnecessary for us to sit through a standard will reading . . . unless it's not so standard."

Penelope sighed heavily. "It's like you're reading my mind."

"As far as I know, there's nothing to leave me in a will. I know you both inherited a ton of money when your parents died, but we didn't live like we had money. Do you know what Mom did with hers? She must have given it away, right?"

Penelope's disquiet expanded. "I don't know."

"You never asked?"

"I asked," Penelope said, "but she always brushed it aside or diverted the conversation, and it wasn't my business what she did with it. But, yeah, I was curious." Penelope shifted into a more comfortable position on the hard flagstones.

"Do you think it's possible she *did* leave me an inheritance?" Mattie said, her voice sounding hesitant but lifting with a hint of hope.

Penelope stared off at blinking fireflies grouped near the back fence. "We could guess all night about what Lilith did and still be wrong. We'll find out soon enough tomorrow. Why don't we go inside, and I'll make us a cup of tea."

They gathered Mattie's supplies while Penelope tried, and failed, to control her thoughts about what kind of stipulations Lilith could have left behind for her daughter. She desperately hoped whatever they discovered would help Mattie and not harm her.

Chapter 9

JONATHAN

JONATHAN STOOD AT THE FLOOR-TO-CEILING WINDOWS, staring at the Chicago River aglow with the brilliant oranges of an August sunset falling over the city. His day hadn't been as busy as usual, and without the constant flow of texts, phone calls, and emails to keep his mind busy, he'd gone running, visited the corner market for groceries, gotten a haircut, and bought a new pair of tennis shoes all before early afternoon, which left him feeling aimless late in the day. The last thing on his schedule for the day was a phone call with the owner of a downtown venue. When his phone rang, he answered it on reflex.

"This is Jonathan."

"Who else would it be?" asked a man on the other end.

Jonathan paused, confused by the unexpected call but also recognizing the voice of his oldest brother. "David?"

"You were expecting someone else?" David laughed.

"As a matter of fact, yes," Jonathan said. He sat on the couch and propped his feet on the coffee table. "Work call."

"So that's why you answered," David said. "I figured it would go straight to voice mail. I'm glad I caught you. I'm calling for Mom."

Jonathan sat up instantly as a sinking feeling dropped his stomach. "Is she okay?"

"Yeah, yeah, she's fine," David said. "It's about Dad, and before you freak out, he's okay too. You know he turns sixty next month, and Mom's going all out on a party that he knows nothing about. You can probably guess where I'm going with this—"

"She wants me to be there," Jonathan finished. He rubbed the back of his neck. September wasn't the busiest month of the year for work, but Jonathan made sure his schedule was full. The thought of sitting around his apartment doing nothing nearly made him break out in hives. This afternoon was a perfect example of why he preferred busyness to the stillness of a day without purpose.

"Think about it," David said. "Think *hard* about it. It's only a weekend. You could fly in and fly out—Thursday through Sunday. It's not a big ask. I know you're busy. *Everyone* is busy, so that excuse is overused. It would mean a lot to Mom, to both of them."

"You're getting good at this," Jonathan said, opening his laptop and pulling up his scheduling app.

"Good at what?"

"Guilt-tripping me into coming home."

David laughed. "This isn't guilt-tripping, brother," he said. "This is the truth. We haven't seen you in, what, five years? They miss you. Why? I have no idea because you've always been obnoxious and spoiled—"

"Hey!"

"I'm joking. Mostly," David said good-naturedly. "Baby brothers are always the worst. But we all miss you, so think about it."

Jonathan scrolled through his schedule and then gazed toward the sunset. The sky was already darkening to a shade of melancholy blue. "It's not the easiest for me to shift around dates because I don't schedule the openings or the events. I'm at the mercy of the owners and agents. Let me make a few calls, and I'll let you know this week. But just so everyone is clear, if I *can* make it, it would be only for a weekend. I won't be staying in Ivy Ridge longer than that."

"I'll make sure everyone gets the memo," David said. "Let me know either way. So . . . how're you doing?"

"Good, good," Jonathan said, giving the same answer he always gave when people asked about his work. "Staying busy, making money."

The phone was silent for a few beats before David said, "Money's good, but are you doing all right? Dating anyone?"

Jonathan got off the couch and paced in front of the windows. Why did everyone always ask the same questions, and why did it matter if he was dating anyone? Couldn't he be fine without a steady girlfriend? His high-rise apartment was proof he was doing just fine on his own. "I don't have time for dating."

"You don't have time or you don't make time?"

After Laura, Jonathan hadn't slowed down long enough to ask himself whether he even wanted a serious relationship anymore. "Is there a difference?"

David chuckled. "You know there is. You just haven't found the right girl. You will."

"Easy for you to say," Jonathan replied. "You married the perfect woman."

"The perfect one for *me*," David said. "When you find her, you'll know. You won't be asking how to make time for her because you won't be able to imagine *not* making time for her."

Jonathan scoffed. "Who says I need a serious relationship anyway? Maybe I want to live the bachelor life."

"Do you?"

In the falling night, the interior apartment lights cast Jonathan's reflection against the windows. He stared at the transparent version of himself in the glass. David's question sat unanswered and stirred long-sleeping desires inside Jonathan.

When he didn't answer, David said, "You'll figure it out. You always do. Text me this week to tell me you're coming home so I can tell Mom her baby will be home soon."

"What makes you so sure I'll be there?" Jonathan asked.

"I have a feeling you'll be home before you know it."

David disconnected, and Jonathan stared through his reflection at the lights turning on all over the city. He had no intention of trying to rearrange his schedule so that he could be home for his dad's sixtieth birthday. There were a few reasons Jonathan didn't want to return to Ivy Ridge, and his busy schedule was the easiest excuse to use. David had already touched on one of the real reasons. Jonathan had zero desire to explain, on repeat, why a guy like him was still single and listen to people say he'd better get on that before he was too old to be interesting, as if age disqualified you from being able to find love and partnership. The other reasons for staying away from Ivy Ridge were knotted together with his own shame and disappointment, and those parts of his past he didn't want revealed to anyone.

Chapter 10

MATTIE

By the time Mattie got up and dressed the next morning, the backyard was filled with white folding chairs. Two rectangular tables covered in white cloth and adorned with sprays of flowers were set up on the right and the left of the chairs. One table would hold refreshments, and Penelope and Sophia were decorating the other table with photographs of Lilith and the family. Robert's shadow moved inside the greenhouse.

Eddie had obviously already been by to fix the AC because the house felt less like a marshland and more like a mild Southern morning. It would likely be midday before the house cooled to a comfortable temperature. Mattie grabbed a mug of coffee and watched her family through the kitchen window. The sound of a door creaking open pulled her attention. She caught sight of Enid's gray swish of a tail disappearing up the back stairs. Mattie followed.

By the time Mattie reached the third floor, Enid had disappeared. She called her name, but the cat didn't show herself again. Mattie walked to the attic and tried to open the door again, but it still wouldn't budge. Sipping her coffee, she thought of the night before in the garden when the electricity went out and how quickly it turned back on . . . but only after Mattie said she'd consider staying in Ivy Ridge. Feeling ridiculous while doing it, Mattie tested out an idea.

She rubbed her hand in a circular motion against the attic

door and whispered, "I'm sorry I keep talking about leaving. This doesn't feel like my home, but maybe that's because I've never had a home. It's not you, I promise. It's me, and I'm still trying to figure things out. I would really appreciate you opening this door so that I can get the car keys." Mattie held her breath and turned the doorknob.

This time the door swung open, and Mattie gasped. Hot, sticky air pushed out of the attic and shoved her back a step. "I can't believe that actually worked."

Mattie hurried inside the attic in case the house decided to change its mind, if that was possible. She put her coffee mug on a shelf and checked the box of her mom's things. The photos she'd gone through and the map still rested inside, so she tossed in the car keys. She glanced around for forgotten photographs of Lilith but didn't see any stragglers. Balancing the box in one arm, she grabbed her mug, closed the attic door, and whispered a thank-you.

Her aunt walked out of the music room and caught sight of Mattie. Enid circled around her aunt's feet before slinking down the staircase. Bluish circles marred the skin beneath Penelope's eyes, and her smile was slow to show itself. "Convinced it to open?"

Mattie shrugged with the box in her arms. "Coincidental probably. The house is cooling off, so the door isn't as stuck."

"Uh-huh," Penelope said. "If that's true, why did you thank the house? What's in the box?"

Mattie walked toward Penelope but stopped at the doorway to the art studio. "Some of Mom's things. Hey, why did you keep those paintings?" She tilted her head at the canvases stacked against the wall.

"Lilith asked me to," Penelope said. "She mailed them to me through the years and insisted I keep them for you. She said one day you'd need them."

"Need them for what?"

Penelope's laugh was dry and tired. "As if I know. As if she told me much of anything," she said, walking down the stairs.

"Must be a family trait," Mattie said, following Penelope.

"Ouch, but true. Sometimes I think Lilith was constructing this elaborate game for all of us to play, and she was the only one who knew the rules. But, like most everyone, I did what she asked even though it made no sense to me. Do the paintings mean anything to you?"

Mattie shook her head. "I remember them, but they're random."

Penelope hummed in her throat. "The older I get, the more I realize nothing in life is truly random."

⤛

Mattie had never attended a funeral before. She and Lilith didn't stay anywhere long enough to build close connections who would ask them to attend a gathering so personal.

Mattie wore a simple black dress and watched mourners mingle in the backyard with Sophia, Robert, and Penelope. A few people were crying into wadded tissues. Mattie didn't know how to act. Her heart felt smothered by a mountain of blankets, making her emotions feel muffled and inaccessible.

She stood on the sunporch near the blue rotary phone. She wondered what its story was and why Penelope didn't want Mattie to know about it. Then Mattie's thoughts jumped to another phone. Why had her mom wanted Mattie to call Penelope the day she died? *Had* Lilith known she was going to die that night? The medical examiner said she'd died of a heart attack. How could Lilith have known that ahead of time?

Mattie touched the phone's plastic receiver, which warmed beneath her fingertips. Sophia opened the back door and told Mattie they were getting ready to start. Mattie followed her outside and seated herself between Penelope and Sophia in the first row. All during the service, Mattie's thoughts wandered, never landing anywhere for long. The pastor's words flowed through her mind like a distant radio channel. She thought seeing the casket would cause a surge of sorrow within her, but she felt detached from it and from the whole experience, as though she were watching the funeral from somewhere outside her body, and no matter what logic told her, that Lilith's silent body was in the casket, some part of her didn't believe it. She wasn't denying her mom was gone, but her mind refused to allow her thoughts to consider the casket as anything more than a piece of furniture that everyone stared at.

Mattie was surprised that all of the chairs were filled and additional people stood in the back. She assumed most of them were friends of Penelope and Sophia and possibly didn't know Lilith at all. Their neighbors, the Carlisles, sat a few rows back from the front. Mattie had never officially met them in all her years visiting Ivy Ridge. Jonathan was the only Carlisle she'd seen and held a conversation with. Until yesterday, she hadn't thought much about the Carlisle family in years, aside from her occasional stray musings about Jonathan. As an August breeze blew through the backyard and the rosemary waved its long woody limbs, Mattie's mind drifted back ten years ago to a Halloween when she ate cake with a handsome high school senior who made a deal he didn't keep.

Chapter 11

MATTIE

Ten years earlier, Mattie's fifteenth birthday, Halloween night

MATTIE TAPPED THE FACE OF HER CELL PHONE ON THE bedside table. It lit up the time—11:11 p.m. She had dropped onto the bed, still dressed in her Halloween costume, a couple of hours earlier, but she'd spent most of that time with an overactive mind, slipping in and out of sleep with the sound of the town's fireworks in the distance. So she got out of bed and went downstairs, not bothering to turn on lights. A cloudless sky acted as a blue-black backdrop to a full moon, whose glow smudged the sharp edges of the world and blended all the lines together like a charcoal sketch. Yet even if the yellow moon hadn't been beaming through the windows, Mattie would have found whatever she looked for. Penelope kept everything sensibly organized, but she also swore that if anything was lost, the house would help you find it. Things just *turned up* right when you needed them in the Russell house.

The house was a playground for Mattie's imagination, with its hidden areas, cluttered attic, and three sets of stairs, each one creakier than the others. There were also doors that opened to empty spaces not even big enough for an adult to stand in, and the attic sounded full of whispers, which Penelope said was the wind. Except Mattie could never *feel* the wind or find a crack that allowed in outside air.

The sitting room perpetually smelled like parchment paper and woodsmoke, and its crackly radio from the 1920s turned on by itself when Mattie was around, playing songs that seemed to fit her mood exactly. The ingredients in the pantry rearranged themselves based on what someone wanted to make. Like this morning when she'd opened the pantry in search of sprinkles for their pancakes and noticed nutmeg, cloves, allspice, ginger, and a can of pumpkin puree sitting on the middle shelf. They clinked together when she looked directly at them, as if saying, *You need me!* Mattie had smiled, knowing Penelope was going to make her favorite birthday treat: pumpkin spice cake slathered with cream cheese icing.

Mattie walked alongside the island in the moonlit kitchen, humming and dragging her fingertips down the cool butcher-block countertop. The kitchen smelled like a mix of cinnamon and sugar with a punch of spicy peppers, no matter the season. Tonight Mattie could also smell her birthday cake. She'd already eaten a piece during her earlier celebration, but when faced with the choice between staring at the ceiling for one more second or getting out of bed and eating cake, traipsing downstairs for cake was the obvious course of action. And as it wasn't yet midnight, it was technically still her birthday.

Mattie lifted the glass cake dome and breathed in the distinctive scent of autumn, of birthdays, and of all things cozy. She inhaled deeply, then grabbed a cake knife conveniently sitting nearby on the counter and cut herself two pieces of cake. One would have been enough, but the urge to cut two pieces was so strong that when she questioned why, her mind said, *Why not?* A lone cricket chirped outside the nearest window, a hesitant staccato rhythm, reminiscent of a warning chant. Mattie stood still and listened, then shrugged.

By the back door, she slid on her thick-soled black boots, tied the laces, grabbed her cake, and wandered out into the garden. Mattie exhaled puffs of glittery breath. The scent of wood-burning fireplaces, the distinct smell of the seasons shifting, carried on the wind. The evening was quiet except for a scattering of noises drifting through the night: a dog howl; a startled, clipped yelp followed by laughter; a backfiring truck. Mattie sat beneath a maple tree, leaning against its cool trunk. She balanced the plate on her outstretched legs and stared up at the string lights that twisted through the tree branches. Every tree in the backyard was strung with the same lights, making it look as though a legion of fairies twinkled all around. Quivering candle flames, drowning in melting wax, danced inside carved pumpkins, sending capering shadows across the grass. Pumpkins of various sizes and colors nestled beside gourds, and the potted mums lined the perimeter of the flagstones, marking off the back patio's boundary.

The perfect Halloween setting, Mattie thought. *Now all that's missing is unforeseen mischief.*

Cream cheese icing smeared across the fork tines as she closed her lips around a bite and pulled it into her mouth. Suddenly a group of blackbirds burst noisily from the trees at the far back of the garden. Mattie startled at their exit.

A six-foot fence created a boundary around the spacious backyard, separating the Russell property from the houses on either side. The back fence had a three-foot-wide gate that was never used, and the vintage padlock, now coppery brown with rust, had been secured on the opening mechanism so long ago that no one knew where to find the key to unlock it. Mattie never thought much about the gate and why no one ever needed to use it . . . until now.

The gate rattled as though suffering through a storm. The

corroded padlock slapped against the wood, knocking thirteen times, like an omen. Then the padlock snapped off and dropped into the grass below, and the gate creaked open.

Mattie's breath caught, and she stared at the gate. The buffeting wind stopped. She placed her fork and plate on the patio table, keeping her eye on the open gate as though waiting for someone or *something* to walk through. Nothing corporeal appeared, but voices tumbled across the grass, haunting and traveling toward her like fog. They came from a distance, muffled by the night, by the trees.

A small wrought iron garden stake with a glittery blue gazing ball attached to the top caught her eye, and Mattie tugged it out of the cold earth. She pulled open the gate wide enough to slide through into the empty land behind the houses. Closing her eyes, she concentrated on the noises in the night. An owl hooted. The creek, nearly dry this time of year, offered intermittent sounds of trickling water. Whispering voices and distant music reached out to her. Mattie opened her eyes and set off in a southeasterly direction.

Less than ten minutes later, Mattie stood in the gnarly woods behind the abandoned Degaré mansion that was anything but empty tonight. Even from where she hid in the darkness at least fifty yards away, the volume of the party was incredible. If the teenagers in attendance wanted to keep the party a secret, they were failing. The Bat-Signal would have been less noticeable.

Partygoers spilled out of the run-down estate home, which had been left to succumb to the elements. Without electricity, a few parked cars pointed their headlights at the home. Cell phones with blue-and-white lights illuminated patches of shadow and bounced through the rooms like rectangular ghosts. A choking scent of beer and a haze of cigarette smoke swirled out of the house.

Two teenagers laughed in an exaggerated way, too loud and nasal to be natural. They ran toward where Mattie stood in the woods. Fearing she'd been spotted, Mattie leaped behind the nearest pine tree. They stumbled right past her without stopping until they reasoned they were far enough away from the house. Then they dropped onto the ground in a wrestling move. For a few seconds, Mattie thought the boy was fighting the girl, but she quickly realized something more *adult* was happening.

Stifling a groan, Mattie tiptoed away from them. Although the chance that those two would hear her above their own embellished noises was doubtful. She gazed up at the full moon, questioning why she'd been led on such an uneventful outing when she could be back home eating cake. Drunken teenagers and handsy, lust-filled ones were *so typical*.

And normal, Mattie reminded herself. *This is what regular, everyday teenagers do.*

They went to parties on Halloween, they laughed with their friends, and they snuck off with great expectations of how high the next kiss would take them. But Mattie's teenage years weren't comparable. She'd spent the years traveling with her mom.

Mattie had cheered for the Atlanta Braves during an entire home season from a fancy suite behind home plate, drinking Coca-Colas and eating hot dogs on steamed buns. While living in southwest Florida, Mattie had gone sailing on a yacht bigger than the apartment she and her mom lived in. She'd attended South by Southwest in Austin and watched her mom sing onstage with a real band. In Sedona, a Navajo guide had taken them to a spiritual vortex. Every hair on Mattie's arms had stood on end. Both her heartbeat and time had slowed, imprinting something on her soul. Her mom had stopped talking for three days after that.

Most of these kids had probably never even been outside of Ivy

Ridge. Mattie's teenage years had been so much better and more fun than theirs. Spending every weekend with your friends at a rinky-dink party was dead boring. Wasn't it?

Blue and red flashing lights interrupted her thoughts. Three cop cars drove into the Degaré yard. A uniformed policeman emerged from the first car. A bullhorn magnified his voice as he informed the teenagers that the party was over and told them to come out. Then he added that if they complied now, no one's parents would be called.

Clever tactic, Mattie thought. *Clever but deceitful.*

Murmuring and gasps spread through the party. The music abruptly ended in the middle of "Monster Mash." Lights flicked off. A few heartbeats of silence followed.

Then people exploded out of the house like ants bursting from an anthill on fire. They scattered everywhere at exceptional speeds. Mattie, too stunned to move, stared with her mouth agape.

Fearing she'd be included in the police roundup, she turned and sprinted away too. With her arms pumping and her legs burning, she ran, not knowing the quickest way home. A few kids, reeking of fear and alcohol, rushed past her. Mattie pushed herself harder. She didn't want to get swept up in the partygoers. The cops would never believe that she wasn't part of the group.

Mattie noticed that most of the teenagers were funneling one way, which could be the best escape route. She slowed enough to question her direction. Should she follow them? She didn't want to get lost in the woods.

Tree branches above her creaked. Mattie glanced up. The trees were not only moving; they also appeared to be pointing their branches toward a darker forest path, a path leading away from the rest of the group. She hesitated. It was absurd to think the trees were helping her and even more absurd to follow their path. So of course Mattie ran in the direction pointed out by the swaying branches. *When in doubt, choose the absurd.*

As she ran, Mattie swore the roots pressed closer into the ground to make sure she didn't trip. The wind rushed through the trees, and the mature branches groaned, sounding like encouragement. Mattie thought she heard footsteps slapping the ground behind her, but when she looked over her shoulder, she saw nothing in the shadows.

Wheezing and sweating, Mattie finally arrived at her backyard gate. She slipped inside, closed the gate, dropped the wrought iron garden stake from her cramped hand, and then slid her back down the wooden planks until she sat on the cold grass. A few seconds later, someone banged into the gate, knocking Mattie forward.

"Let me in!" a male voice demanded in a panicked whisper.

Mattie leaped up and grabbed the wrought iron garden stake.

"Let me in! I know you're there. I could hear your heavy breathing a mile away."

Mattie gasped. "Who are you? Why would I let you in?"

The silence dragged on, and Mattie stepped toward the gate. She leaned her ear close to the planks and listened for movement.

"Come on!" he pleaded, sounding as though his face was pressed into the crack between the boards. "You can trust me."

"Says every psycho."

"You're in *my* yard!" he said. "Open the gate or else!"

Shock and confusion had Mattie opening the gate. The young man on the other side shoved his way into the yard and slammed the gate behind him.

"Or else what?" she asked.

He stomped a few paces away from her and then stopped. "This isn't my yard."

"Well, aren't you a genius," Mattie said. She opened the gate again and pointed into the night. "Now, get out."

He walked toward her with a newfound swagger. Mattie stiffened, wondering if she should run for the house. Would he catch her before she could disappear inside? She tightened her grip on the iron stake, trying to recall every fighting movie she'd ever seen, which were a sad few. When he stepped within a slant of moonlight, she recognized him. He was her neighbor, one of the Carlisles. Jonathan maybe, the youngest son, who was a few years older than her.

"Why would I leave?" he asked. "You just let me in." He was dressed like Danny from *Grease*, wearing a black leather jacket, white shirt, jeans, and shiny black shoes. His hair had been slicked back on the sides with a bouffant in the front that had probably fared better earlier in the evening. Now his windswept hairstyle had a maple leaf stuck in the gel and hair spray.

She loosened her grip on the stake. "You sounded desperate."

His embarrassed laugh was almost charming. "I've never been desperate a day in my life."

"Is that so?" Mattie said. "*Your* heavy breathing and the begging are a solid argument to prove otherwise. And there's a leaf," she said, pointing toward the side of her head and then to his, "stuck right there."

He plucked off the leaf and looked around, taking in the surroundings. Flickering candlelight mixed with moonlight on his face. He was nearly a head taller than her and built like a quarterback. His jeans were so tight she saw the outline of car keys in his front pocket.

He creased his brow. "This is the Russell house."

"You were hoping this was *your* yard," Mattie said. She pointed toward the Carlisles' house. "You missed."

"Slight miscalculation. I was in a hurry," he said. "I'm Jonathan, by the way. Are you planning on knocking me out with that or casting a spell on me?" He pointed toward the stake in her hand. Then he flinched when his cell phone rang. He cursed and struggled to get the phone out of a pocket in his too-tight pants.

"Interesting ringtone," Mattie said with a smile, humming along with a few bars. "Halloween inspired?"

"Huh?" he asked, silencing the phone.

"That's 'I Put a Spell on You,'" she said, walking past him to return the stake to its spot near the tree.

"That's not my ringtone," he argued. "I have no idea why it's playing that song." He shoved the phone back into his pocket. "So are you gonna introduce yourself, or are you going for mysterious?"

"I'm Penelope's niece, Mattie," she said.

The look of recognition on his face surprised her. "Oh yeah, I've seen you here every summer." He moved closer. She caught a whiff of alcohol and sweat.

He had? Mattie was shocked that he would have noticed her. She mostly kept to herself during summers and holidays in Ivy Ridge, but she'd noticed the Carlisles coming and going, sometimes at all hours of the night. Jonathan had two older brothers, David and William, and none of them, parents included, were strangers to parties and late-night sneaking around.

She backed away from him and grabbed hold of the gate. "Now

that we've made proper introductions, good night, Jonathan. I think you know the way home."

He clasped his hands together behind his neck and looked up at the fairy lights in the trees. "Normally, people take the shortest route. You know, the quickest way between two points. If point A was the party and the fastest escape route was toward point B"—he lowered his hands and looked at her—"why did you take point A to point C?"

"Are you drunk?" Mattie asked.

Jonathan's laugh startled her, but the sound of it also pleased her. His smile was wide and genuine. "The opportunity was taken from me, so no, but I was on my way. What I mean to say is that even though you took the longer escape route, I followed you home."

Mattie's skin prickled. "You realize that sounds totally creepy, right?"

He laughed again and rubbed his hands down his face. Mattie noted that he had hands like a quarterback too, large enough to wrap around a football with ease. "Cut me some slack. My thoughts are jumbled. I barely escaped being caught, and I ran a couple of miles following a trail of fireflies."

Mattie snorted out a laugh and opened the gate wider. "You definitely need to go home. I think delirium has set in."

"It was you," Jonathan said, his voice having gone quieter, almost questioning. "*You* were the fireflies."

He stepped closer to her and touched the fabric of her skirt. She almost slapped his hand away but didn't.

"One minute we were all running toward town because it's a fact that three cops can't catch all of us. Survival of the fastest. Then I tripped over a tree root that came outa nowhere—"

"Right. 'Cause they do that."

"This one did because I might be a lot of things, but clumsy ain't one of them," he said. "I nearly face-planted into a tree, but that's when I caught sight of the fireflies. There were dozens, and they were all clustered together like I've never seen before. And they were darting through the trees in the opposite direction of everyone else. So I followed them."

"Why would you follow a group of bugs?"

"Have you ever seen something so weird that you just *have* to find out what it means?" Jonathan asked.

Mattie stilled. *Like the gate tonight? The trees making a way for me?*

"It must have been your skirt, reflecting the light," he said, twisting the fabric between his fingers and then letting it drop back against her leg.

"This fabric doesn't do that," she said, but Penelope had sewn this skirt for Mattie's birthday, and it was no secret that Penelope's creations were infused with her own special magic.

Jonathan shrugged. "I know what I saw." His grin returned. "Sounds crazy, but I followed you when everyone else was going the other way, and here we are. Safe and sound. Why *did* you go the long way? Did you know which way the police were going to go?"

"I . . ." Mattie heard the faint echoes of creaking trees. If she told him that she'd been led home by the trees, she would sound crazier than him saying he followed the fireflies. "Lucky guess . . . I guess."

"Hmm," he said, sounding unconvinced. He tossed a thumb over his shoulder toward the house. "I'll go out the front gate, if that's okay. The downstairs window I left unlocked is closer to the front."

Before Mattie could argue, Jonathan strode across the yard

toward the back patio. Mattie closed the gate and hooked the latch even though she couldn't lock it. She picked up the broken padlock and closed her fingers around it. The rusted metal felt warm in her palm.

"Is that cake? I'm starved," he said as he picked up Mattie's plate.

"Hey!" she said. "That's mine."

The gleam in his pale eyes caused her stomach to flip-flop. "Both pieces?"

"Are you food-shaming me right now? It's my birthday, so I'm entitled to as much cake as I want." Was this why she'd cut two pieces earlier?

Jonathan plopped down into a patio chair and grabbed the chair beside him. He slid the empty chair across the flagstones so that it was right next to his. Mattie cringed at the scraping of metal against stone. She glanced at the house, but no lights turned on.

He patted the seat of the empty chair. "It's your birthday, on Halloween? Aren't you a spooky one. Let's share, birthday girl. You can't possibly eat both of these by yourself, and it would be rude not to share now that I'm here."

Mattie hesitated before she placed the broken padlock onto the table and sat beside him. "Weren't you leaving?"

He didn't answer but instead picked up the fork and handed it to Mattie. "I'll eat this one because you've obviously already started on that one."

"Are you going to eat with your fingers—"

He picked up the whole piece and bit into it. Crumbs tumbled back onto the plate. "Man, that's good," he said through a mouthful. He moved the plate closer to her. "Eat."

"This is weird," Mattie said. "We don't even know each other and it's almost midnight and—".

"Are you about to tell me that you turn back into a pumpkin at midnight?" he asked and took another huge bite of cake.

Mattie laughed. "Cinderella turned back into a neglected maid-servant, not a pumpkin."

Mattie cut off a piece of her slice. She opened her mouth and closed her lips around the fork. Icing melted on her tongue, and she closed her eyes, humming in pleasure. When Mattie opened her eyes, Jonathan was shamelessly staring at her. Insecurity clamped her stomach. The gap between their ages seemed to widen exponentially. She felt like a child, and he was, what? Seventeen? Eighteen? Did she have icing blobbed on her face?

She wiped her mouth with her fingers and cleared her throat, which shook him out of his intense staring mode.

"When you're not here in the summer, where do you live?" he asked.

"What year?" Mattie asked. "I've lived in Anaheim, Boston, Nashville, Atlanta, Fort Myers, Austin, and Sedona. A different city every couple of years."

Jonathan's eyes widened. "Is your dad in the military?"

Mattie inhaled, flaring her nostrils. "No."

He could have asked her a year's worth of questions about her dad, and the answers always would have been no or I don't know. *Do you and your dad get along? No. Do you and your dad look alike? I don't know. Do you and your dad watch movies or go to baseball games or take hikes? No.* Mattie didn't know anything about her dad.

Lilith used to tell Mattie that she was left on the doorstep Halloween night in a pumpkin that was carved into a baby's cradle. But Mattie knew that story was meant to make her feel special. And she had . . . for a while. She had a biological father somewhere, but she had no viable proof of that since her mom refused to elaborate on the subject. Mattie assumed he hadn't wanted her. Although no one had actually said that, based on his complete lack of presence in her life, it had to be the truth. Dads who loved their children were there for them.

Her gaze met Jonathan's, and it was clear he was waiting for her to elaborate. "My mom likes to travel." In truth, staying in one place too long made Lilith restless and irritable. After she'd squeezed all the life out of a city, had enough men captivated by her beauty and eccentricity, Lilith would pack their few belongings, and they'd head off on a new adventure to a city they knew nothing about.

Normally, on the way home from a job she had resigned from that very day, Lilith would swing by the local bookstore and buy a guide to a new city. She'd come home and toss the book on Mattie's bed with a wild look in her eyes, saying, "Time to hit the road, baby."

"That's cool," Jonathan said, "living in all those places." He shoved the last of his cake slice into his mouth.

"It's not boring, that's for sure," Mattie said. Leaving had gotten easier after the first couple of cities, once she learned not to become too attached to anything or anyone.

Jonathan leaned back in his chair and stared up at the string lights. "I'm going to New York City after I graduate this year. Summer trip before college." He turned his face toward her and they locked eyes.

An autumn wind gusted through the yard, and Mattie's long hair blew back from her shoulders.

He said, "Maybe you could share your secrets with me."

Her skin tingled under the intensity of his gaze. "My secrets?"

His smile was slow and easy. "You know, insider tips about city sights. You've traveled a lot. I bet you have ideas about what to look for, where to eat, sights to see, that sort of stuff. But if there's anything *else* you want to share with me, you can."

Mattie tilted her head. *Is he flirting with me?* She didn't have much experience to compare their conversation with, but Jonathan's voice had deepened and taken on silky tones that rippled over her skin in the cool night air. His gaze hadn't moved from her face, and he looked like he could wait all night for her to respond.

His cell phone started ringing again, and they both jumped. "I Only Have Eyes for You" by the Flamingos blasted from his phone. Mattie's heart pounded like a kick drum solo. Jonathan stretched out his legs and nearly performed a backbend out of the chair so he could tug his phone out of his jeans. Mattie laughed.

"What the hell is going on with this thing tonight?" he growled. Once he held the phone in his hand, the music stopped. "The damn thing's on vibrate."

Angry, panicked voices raced over the back fence and across the backyard, causing the pumpkin candles to flicker wildly. Someone banged into the fence and cussed.

"Hey! Let us in!" a male voice called from the other side of the fence.

Mattie leaped to her feet. "They followed me!" she blurted, thinking they'd seen the unusual fireflies too.

"You?" Jonathan asked in confusion. He shook his head. "No, they're here for me."

"Jump over it!" someone said from the other side of the fence.

Tension rippled across the grass.

"No one can jump over this fence. It's your fault the cops caught up with us. If you hadn't run through the Dawsons' backyard yelling, then she wouldn't have freaked out and started screaming. We would have gotten away."

"Shut up. We lost the cops a block over. Give me a boost. Jonathan said to meet him at his yard. Jonathan, let us in!"

"I forgot I said that." Jonathan paced the patio.

Police lights swirled into the backyard, reflecting off the maple leaves.

"What's going on?" Mattie whispered beside him.

"Jonathan!" Someone kicked the fence.

"You wanna tell me who's over there," Mattie warned, "or should I hand you over to them before the whole neighborhood wakes up? I refuse to be involved."

"Short version?" he asked. "We—the band and I—"

"You're in a band?"

"It's not that hard to believe."

"You seem like a jock."

"And you seem like an emo kid," he said. She opened her down-turned mouth to speak, but he stopped her with a hand signal. "I'm a drummer. We played a few sets at the festival tonight. Then everybody wanted to get some drinks and party in the old Degaré house . . ."

She knew where they'd been, but curiosity had her saying, "It's an abandoned house. Why there?"

"Lots of people go there to . . . mess around. Much less chance of being caught—but, hey, you already know that because . . . wait, were you there tonight? At the party?"

"Not really. I was . . . out for a walk."

"In the woods on Halloween? Who's buying that story? 'Cause I sure ain't."

"Just finish what you were saying!"

"You obviously know this part, but the cops showed up, and we scattered 'cause we're all underage. I told the guys to meet me at the house, but we got separated 'cause I followed you, and—"

"You ended up in the wrong yard," Mattie finished and pointed toward the fence. "And they want you to let them in. Why is everyone at the wrong place tonight?"

"I should have gone home and let them in," Jonathan said, "but I forgot they were coming."

Mattie shook her head. "How could you *forget*?"

"I got distracted with you and the cake. I *can't* get arrested. I could lose my baseball scholarship if that's on my record."

One of the guys slammed into the back fence. Then it sounded like he was scrambling up the wood. A hand, followed by an arm, hooked over the top of the fence. A shadow heaved itself up and teetered on the top of the fence boards, groaning, just before he fell over the fence into the backyard. He dropped like a stone into the pile of raked maple leaves, which exploded into the air like a scene from a cartoon. More grunting and groaning came from the dispersed pile. Another body appeared at the top of the fence.

"No way I'm getting caught up in this with you and your drunk friends," Mattie whispered. "They'll never believe I wasn't there, not with us together, and I'm not going to jail for a bunch of idiot strangers."

Jonathan looked pleadingly at Mattie. "Please help me."

Mattie almost said no, almost pointed at the fence and demanded Jonathan grab his hooligan friends and get out. This was one reason she avoided making friends: they dragged you into their problems. They got you caught up in their dramas and landed you in detention with them for something you didn't even do. Or worse, they became your best friends, and then you had to leave them.

And *how* exactly was Mattie supposed to help him?

Jonathan whispered the word *please* again, and Mattie felt a shift in her heart. Some soft part of her swelled when she looked in his eyes, when she saw the vulnerable version of him staring back at her. She grabbed Jonathan's hand and, avoiding the glow of the fairy lights, pulled him through the semidarkness, skirting the edge of the side yard toward the greenhouse. She eased open the glass door.

The boy in the pile of leaves pushed himself up into a sitting position just as a second boy dropped into the yard.

When Jonathan didn't move to enter the greenhouse, Mattie nudged him forward, and he crept inside, barely making a sound. She pulled the door closed behind them. The earthy scents of composted soil and wet terra-cotta surrounded them. As they passed a grouping of potted plants, the herbaceous smells of rosemary and basil followed them like shadows.

"This is made of glass," Jonathan whispered. "They'll see us."

With her hand on his shoulder, she pushed him into a crouch so that they were positioned behind a potting table. The bright moon bathed the greenhouse in a shimmery glow. The moonlight made them look like phantoms haunting the space. Plantings and minimal furniture created pockets of shadow, and Mattie hoped this would be enough to conceal them.

"People only see what they're looking for." Mattie peered out the windowpanes beneath the table. "They aren't expecting people to be in here, so the chance that they'll see us is slim to none."

They watched as another shape dropped over the side of the fence, followed by another. In total four young men stumbled around in the backyard.

"Jonathan!" one yelled. He was gangly and tall and moved like

Jack Skellington from *The Nightmare Before Christmas*, which made his choice of a skeleton costume near perfect. He lifted a liquor bottle in his hand and drank. "No thanks for letting us in. Good thing we figured it out."

"This doesn't . . . this doesn't look like his yard," another said. This bandmate was dressed like an '80s rocker with his ratty blond wig askew, pushed too far back on his wide forehead, and tangled with leaves. He swung his gaze around, taking in the backyard layout. "This isn't Jonathan's yard." He stared in Jonathan and Mattie's direction. "They don't have a greenhouse."

Jonathan flinched, knocking into the table leg. A hand shovel rocked back and forth and then fell from the potting table. It dropped onto a terra-cotta pot beside Mattie. All four boys went still. The pungent scent of tomatoes filled the greenhouse.

"Who–who's there?" the rocker called.

The skeleton pointed at the greenhouse. "Somebody's in there. I see them. Jonathan, is that you?" He strode quickly toward the greenhouse door with the other three hurrying behind him.

He snatched open the door, but a cell phone blasted out "Somebody's Watching Me" by Rockwell. The earsplitting volume of the song sounded extraordinarily loud for such a small device.

The door handle slipped from the skeleton's hand. "Turn that off," he demanded.

Another cell phone rang, this time playing Stevie Wonder's "Superstition." One of the boys cursed and pulled his phone from his pocket. Another phone went off, playing "Breaking the Law" by Judas Priest.

"What the hell is going on?" the skeleton barked.

Mattie could see the other two boys more clearly now, a *Top Gun* pilot and Batman with his mask pushed on top of his head. Mattie pulled Jonathan into a lower crouch, and her stomach clenched. She squeezed Jonathan's fingers, and he winced before rubbing his hand on her arm, causing her to release her grip. The red and blue swirling lights flashed a few more times and then turned off. The sound of a car driving away hummed through the backyard.

"Let's get out of here," Batman said.

"What about Jonathan?" the pilot asked. "Are you sure the cops are gone? My dad will *kill* me if we're caught. I'll never see daylight again. You think Jonathan ratted us out?"

"Hell no," the rocker said. "He's probably hiding out until he's sure he can get away."

"Come on," the skeleton said. He dropped the liquor bottle and tried to kick it out of sight.

The four boys ran across the backyard and slipped out the front gate. Mattie stood and eased open the greenhouse door. Jonathan followed her out into the yard. Voices echoed from the street, and then the night was quiet again.

"I can't believe I forgot," Jonathan whispered. "I should have gone home and let them in."

"You should have," Mattie agreed. "But it sounds like they made a mess of things on their way to your house anyway. The cops might have caught all of you." She awkwardly patted his arm a couple of times to try to ease the tension on his face. "And you would have missed out on the most delicious birthday cake."

He gripped the back of his neck. "And missed out on meeting you."

"Total disaster that would have been," she said.

He shifted closer to her, and Mattie's breathing paused.

"For a minute there, I thought you were going to desert me," he said.

"For a minute there, I was," she admitted.

"What changed your mind?" He stepped closer still.

"Your total desperation," she said with a small smile. Then she smoothed her hands down her skirt. "You'd better get out of here."

"You kicking me out?" he teased.

"Most definitely." She glanced at the house, staring up at the second-floor windows with the distinct feeling that they were being watched.

Jonathan's grin was mischievous and tempting in a way that made Mattie's stomach flutter. Wind whirled through the backyard, causing leaves to dance in circles and extinguishing half the candle flames. Just as he started to reach out for her, to possibly touch his hand to her cheek, his cell phone rang again. "Goodnight Sweetheart, Goodnight" by the Overtones blasted from his back pocket.

Mattie covered her mouth and snickered. Jonathan cursed. He snatched the phone from his pocket and silenced it. Then he swiped through a few screens and turned the phone over in his hands, as if examining it for defects, before finally switching it off.

"You really should have that looked at," Mattie said. "If your friends don't get you busted," she added, pointing at his phone, "then that's going to."

"This thing's possessed."

"It *is* Halloween." He gazed at her in the same way she'd seen some men looking at her mom, as though mesmerized. "Good night, Jonathan."

He nodded, seemingly reluctant to leave. Mattie swung open the front gate and waited for him to walk through. He hesitated. "Hey, thanks. This was . . . unexpected."

"Most of the best things are."

He looked like he wanted to say more, but he shook his head at the ground and strode through the gate. He snuck around to a downstairs window a few feet away. As she moved to close the gate, Jonathan paused and looked at her. Within seconds he ran over to her, placed his hand on her cheek, and leaned down and kissed her. His lips were warm, and the kiss was quick and chaste at first, but she felt herself sway. Jonathan pulled her closer and deepened the kiss, and the world around her melted away until there was only her and Jonathan, locked in a perfect birthday kiss. Jonathan ended the kiss by pecking her lips quickly one more time, then he grinned at her like no one else ever had.

"Wow," he whispered. "Good night indeed." He rushed off, slid open the window, and climbed into his house.

Mattie closed the garden gate like someone in a trance. Jonathan Carlisle had just kissed her. On purpose. She'd never been kissed but had often wondered what it would be like. She thought she'd be nervous or the first kiss would be awkward, but Jonathan's unexpected kiss hadn't given her the chance to *think* about anything.

She peered up at his house, wondering if he'd be able to sleep after everything that had happened or if he'd lie awake, like she thought she would, replaying the night's events that ended with her first kiss. She locked the back door and removed her boots. Then she tiptoed up the hallway, hoping to sneak up the stairs and back into her room unnoticed.

She eased her bedroom door shut and paused when she heard muted music. She moved slowly toward the window. Someone was humming "Chances Are." The curtain rings glided against the wooden rod as the velvety fabric pushed aside. Mattie unlocked the window and slid up the sash an inch.

"Hey!" a voice called.

Mattie startled and spun around to see who'd entered her bedroom. But no one was there. The voice called again. From *outside*.

Jonathan was leaning out his bedroom window, which was directly across from hers. She lifted the sash higher, knelt down on the floor, and leaned her arms on the windowsill.

"What are you doing?" Mattie asked, feeling pleased and surprised to see him.

"I was just about to throw something at your window," he said with a crooked smile.

"Nothing that would break it, I hope."

"Nah," he said, "I was gonna start small." He held a blue racquetball in his hand.

"That doesn't answer my question about what you're doing."

"Stargazing," he said and laughed. "I've been waiting for you. I wanted to thank you for helping me tonight." He leaned farther out his window. He'd changed into a T-shirt emblazoned with the local high school's mascot. Now that his hair wasn't styled and slicked back, it lay flat and long against his head.

"You already thanked me. It's not a big deal," Mattie said.

"It's a big deal to me. I wasn't joking about potentially losing my scholarship. It took a helluva lot to get chosen, and they're picky, so I wouldn't be surprised if the university tossed me out because of breaking a stupid underage-drinking law."

"Now you're in the clear."

"Thanks to you," he said.

"Don't forget the fireflies."

Jonathan's laugh stretched between their windows and skittered across her skin. "I'll be going to New York City for a summer trip after I graduate, but I'll be home for the summer. My parents wanted me to enroll in the university's summer classes, but I want to wait until the fall so I can have one more summer of freedom."

"You're going to college, not prison," Mattie said.

He laughed again, and the sound of it had her leaning forward, dangling her arms out the window and catching moonlight in her hands.

"Yeah, yeah, I know, but it'll be different. Between the classes and baseball practices and games, free time will be nonexistent. I think I've convinced them to let me stay here one more summer. Will you be back?"

His question startled her. A shiver shimmied through her stomach. "Probably," Mattie said.

"Don't you always come back here?"

"So far."

"Are you always so vague?" he teased.

Mattie smiled. "It's just that with my mom, I never really *know* where we're going to be. But it's highly probable I'll be back next summer because I've been spending my summers here for as long as I can remember."

"Let's hang out. Next summer, I mean, when you're back."

Mattie leaned back into the window. "Seriously?"

Moonlight shone off his face and highlighted his smile, and Mattie took a mental snapshot that she wanted to tuck beneath her pillow and remember forever.

"Of course," Jonathan said in his slow Southern drawl. "I have a feeling we're going to have a lot of fun together."

"The legal kind?" Mattie asked.

"No guarantees," he said.

A floorboard creaked in the hallway, and Mattie glanced over her shoulder.

"Hey," Jonathan called softly. When she looked at him, he said, "Happy birthday, Mattie. See you next summer?"

"See you next summer," she confirmed, even though it sounded a million years away. Mattie closed the window, waving good night to Jonathan, who lifted his hand in response. She pulled the curtain closed.

Mattie changed out of her costume and hung it in the closet. One of her graphite pencils lay next to her shoes. Kneeling down to pick it up, a ridiculously girly idea popped into her head. On the lower inside wall of the closet, she wrote her name and Jonathan's and placed a heart between them.

Then she crawled into bed and smiled into her pillow, allowing herself a few minutes to daydream about what a summer spent with Jonathan might look like. She thought of them eating ice cream and walking through the park, heading out to the drive-in theater to watch a summer blockbuster, and watching Fourth of July fireworks fill the sky with glorious light. She drifted off to sleep, pulled into the most vibrant dreams of a boy whose smile shone in the moonlight.

But Jonathan didn't come home the next summer. When his mother, Virginia, stopped by the house that June to pick up a dress for a summer picnic, she mentioned that Jonathan had enrolled in summer classes, wanting to get a head start on completing his core requirements. He didn't come home the following summer or the one after that, either, and eventually Mattie stopped looking for him. And then she stopped hoping for him.

Chapter 12

MATTIE

Present day

AFTER THE FUNERAL SERVICE MATTIE ATTEMPTED TO BE social, but most people understood her lack of interaction. The friends and neighbors were kind and sympathetic, and Sophia and Penelope seemed to find solace in their comfort and conversations. Mattie hovered around the table of photographs, staring at different versions of her mom through the years. Rather than experiencing a deeper sense of connection to her mom, with each new photo or piece of information, Mattie felt increasingly detached from the multilayered woman Lilith Russell had been. Mattie had known her as Mom; these people and these photographs revealed her as someone else, someone more. Someone Mattie possibly never knew.

Was that how all relationships were? Did people shove everyone they knew into specific boxes and not allow them to ever become anything or anyone else? If someone was your mom, she couldn't also be someone else's best friend or a lover or a person with dreams. The hollow channel running through her deepened.

～❧～

A short procession of cars followed behind the hearse to the Russell family plot in the cemetery. Mattie sat in the back seat of

Robert's black SUV, staring out the window in silence, watching as other drivers pulled off the road and turned on their lights. She'd never seen anything like it before—strangers who stopped what they were doing, paused their busy lives, and honored her family in a display of reverence.

At the gravesite, the pastor spoke words meant to comfort and prayers of hope. Mattie stood with her family and stared at the spray of pink roses atop the casket. The breeze fluttered the green leaves, making the arrangement look as though it was waving at her. The others in attendance stood a respectful distance away from the family and clustered together in a group bound by somberness.

When the pastor dismissed everyone, Mattie stood where she was near the grave while Penelope, Sophia, and Robert spoke with the pastor and their friends. She thought of the conversation she'd had with her mom the night of her fifteenth birthday before she met Jonathan.

Mattie had stood outside her bedroom in the Russell house. Moonlight streamed out of Lilith's room and cut a diagonal line across her mom's body in the hallway.

"Some people need a place to call home," Lilith said, "a place that feels kind and soft, a place for dreams. And it's okay to want that."

"Ohh-kay," Mattie said.

Lilith toyed with her dangling earring. "What I mean is that it's okay for you to want that."

"Want what?" Mattie asked. An ache pinched her chest and moved to her stomach. Was her mom about to release a serious piece of information, a piece too heavy for Mattie to carry around?

"A home, Mattie. We're always moving, and maybe . . ." Lilith stared off into her empty bedroom. Moonlight glinted off the lapis lazuli pendant hanging around her neck. The vulnerability on

her face made her look like a young girl, almost a mirror image of Mattie. "Maybe that's not what's best for you."

As though mother and daughter switched roles, Mattie crossed the hallway and reached for Lilith's hand. "I like our life."

Lilith looked at her and brushed Mattie's hair from her face. "Oh, baby, it's the only life you've ever known. You have nothing to compare it to. And you're adaptable." Mattie frowned. "I mean that as a compliment. You can be happy anywhere with your paints and brushes." Lilith sighed. "My point is that one day it's okay if you decide to live your life a different way. If you stop agreeing with everyone around you and choose something for yourself. You might have the kind of heart that needs a home."

"Staying in one place sounds boring," Mattie said.

Lilith pulled her into a hug. "Perception," she said, "is all about how you choose to see the world around you. Staying in one place has its advantages."

"Like what?" Mattie asked.

"Stability, dependability, predictability."

"Boring, boring, and more boring," Mattie teased.

"You feel that way now, but you won't always be this same person. You'll keep growing and changing."

"Are you implying that I'm going to grow into a dead-boring adult?"

Lilith laughed. "Mattie, you will never be dead boring." Then her expression turned grave in the moonlight.

"Hey, Mom," Mattie said softly, "I like our life. I don't want it to change or be anything else. I have you, and that's all I need. And food. You, me, and food? I'm happy."

"I won't always be here," Lilith said.

"What are you talking about?" Mattie said, feeling heat in her cheeks. *Thinking about a world without her mom in it felt like being suffocated.* "We're always going to have each other, traveling the country together, maybe even the world when I'm old enough. Two wandering travelers carried by the winds of change. Then one day you're going to grow old and wrinkly, and you and Penelope are going to be two old crones, sitting here in the backyard cackling, and I'm going to be with you, only less wrinkly."

"Why are Penelope and I turning into old witches?" Lilith asked.

Mattie shrugged. "How is that different from what you are now? I'm kidding!"

Lilith pulled her into another, uncharacteristically tight, hug. "Just know that this will always be a home for you. Here, in Ivy Ridge. If anything were to happen to me—"

"Mom—"

Lilith released her. "Just remember what I've said."

Nearly ten years later, Mattie wondered: Was hers the type of heart that needed a home? She'd never once imagined a life without her mom, a life not moving, moving, moving. How did one rebuild a life? How did anyone decide what to do next? The same question that had risen to the surface dozens of times since she'd left Chicago rose up again. *What do I do now?*

At some point someone led Mattie back to the car. As they drove home, Sophia and Penelope chatted quietly about the service and how they appreciated so-and-so, but Mattie couldn't tune in to anything they said. Her senses had dulled like someone who was waiting for anesthesia to wear off.

Once home, she changed out of her dress and into a pair of shorts and a tie-dye T-shirt in shades of purple and blue. She grabbed the rental car keys and went out the front door. Mattie hesitated, wondering if she should unpack the car, but she assured herself she would be leaving right after the will reading. Whatever the stipulations were, it was unlikely they would keep her in town.

Mattie shifted around the boxes until she found the one containing Lilith's jewelry. Tucked in between layers of clothes, Mattie found the zip-top bag with the necklaces. She removed the lapis lazuli necklace and dangled the chain from her pinched fingers. She tapped the stone and watched it spin in the sunlight, then hooked the clasp around her neck. A green hummingbird flew out of the Carlisles' azaleas and zoomed right toward Mattie's face. It hovered in front of her before rushing off toward the flowers lining the front porch. Mattie watched it, mesmerized by its nearly imperceptible wings and quick movements.

Inside she followed the sound of voices to the kitchen. Penelope stood on the sunporch and held open the door. Sophia and Robert were out back. Robert was stacking the funeral chairs and breaking down the tables while Sophia gathered up the photos and personal belongings.

Sophia stepped onto the porch and said, "I just saw a hummingbird. It hovered right in front of my face."

"I did too," Mattie blurted.

Penelope and Sophia looked at her with surprise. "A green one?" Sophia asked.

"Yes."

"That was Lilith's favorite bird," Sophia said and unloaded the items onto the kitchen island. She smiled at Penelope. "Remember how much you both loved spotting them in the garden? I can still hear Lilith's squeal. It's a sign, that bird, from her to you."

"You believe in signs?" Mattie said, feeling silly but wanting to believe she could somehow still hear from her mom.

"Doesn't everyone?" Sophia said.

"No," Mattie and Penelope said simultaneously, which made Sophia smile.

"They should," Sophia said. "Especially you." She crossed the kitchen and touched the lapis lazuli stone in Mattie's necklace. "You found it. Keep it on and keep looking for those signs. Once you start noticing them, you'll see them everywhere."

"Signs for what?" Mattie asked.

"For exactly what you need exactly when you need it."

"That's helpful," Mattie said sarcastically.

Sophia patted her cheek. "You'll see."

Mattie helped Robert finish stacking chairs in the backyard. The rental service arrived not long after they finished, and Sophia started preparing lunch. Mattie grabbed an apple from a basket on the counter and slipped up the back staircase.

In her room Mattie sat on her bed with the box she'd taken from the attic and ate the apple. Even though she never fully believed all Lilith's talk of how the spiritual and the physical worlds overlapped, Mattie would give anything for wisps of her mom to materialize out of the box, to be surrounded with the essence of her mom's spirit.

Mattie removed the old map and opened it on her bed, smoothing out the creases. Where was she going next? She placed her finger on Ivy Ridge with its purple heart and slid her fingertip across the country, stopping for a moment on every place she'd lived with Lilith. Then her finger wandered over state after state, not pausing anywhere for long, not feeling drawn to any specific place. Could there possibly be nowhere she wanted to live?

She pulled more items out of the box, and a button pin the size of a baseball fell out of her hand and rolled across the floor into the open closet. Mattie hopped off the bed and followed it.

The button slowed and wobbled in a small circle before landing facedown next to her flip-flops. She knelt in the closet and reached for the button, but something on the closet wall caught her eye—her name and Jonathan's with a heart drawn between them. She reached out and rubbed her finger across the penciled words, which normally would have smeared the letters, but nothing happened. She licked her finger and then rubbed the letters again. Still the words looked as bold and pristine as the day she wrote them.

Mattie grabbed an unopened white tube of paint and a brush from the end table. Returning to the closet, she squirted a blob of paint onto the brush and painted over the names and the heart. Satisfied with her work, Mattie picked up the button pin and flipped it over. The button was designed with a logo of a baseball team, the Richmond Braves, a team she hadn't thought of since she was a kid. When she was a little girl, she and her mom attended a few minor-league games in Nashville, Tennessee, and she remembered that at one game, the team opposing the Sounds was the Braves. Why had Lilith kept this button and brought it to Ivy Ridge?

Penelope knocked on the open door. "Mind if I come in?"

Mattie looked up from the button and shook her head.

"Are you unpacking?" Penelope asked.

There was so much hope in her aunt's voice that Mattie wasn't sure whether she wanted to feel grateful or irritated. Why did everyone want her to stay in Ivy Ridge? Didn't they know she was a free bird, that she could do whatever she wanted and go anywhere without attachments? Never mind her frustration that even though she could go anywhere, she had no idea *where* she wanted to go.

"No," Mattie said. "These are Mom's things I found in the attic.

Did you know . . ." She lifted the map. "Did you know that at least thirty years ago Mom mapped out every single place we would live?"

Penelope took the offered map. "I've never seen this before. I never knew where y'all would end up next. Once she got to a new place, she'd call and send a postcard or a letter with your new address." Her gaze fell to the map.

"I always thought where we ended up was a spontaneous decision," Mattie said. "Why would it matter for me to know it wasn't? Why would Mom care if I knew she had a plan?"

"That's a good question." Penelope glanced toward the closet. "Are you painting something?"

Mattie's cheeks warmed. She threaded her fingers together in her lap. "Sorta. I wrote my name in there years ago and forgot, so I just fixed it. It's not really my style to write on walls."

Penelope placed the map on the bed, then walked over to inspect the closet wall. "I'd forgotten about this too. You know, I've tried to wash this a few times over the years, but it doesn't work."

"What do you mean, it doesn't work?" Mattie joined Penelope and peered down at the wall. The names and the heart showed through the white paint as though she'd barely tried to cover them. In fact, it looked as though the letters were pushing their way up through the paint and intensifying as she stared at them. "I literally just painted over that."

Penelope laughed. "Looks like the house isn't going to let you."

Mattie dropped onto the edge of her bed with goose bumps shivering over her skin. She whispered, "You talk about the house as though it's alive."

"Everything is alive," Penelope whispered back. "And whispering won't stop it from hearing you."

Mattie shook her head. "Everything is *not* alive," she argued and immediately wished she hadn't chosen those exact words because an image of Lilith rushed into her mind, followed by a vision of a casket being lowered into the ground. A shadow moved across Mattie's face, and she closed her eyes for a moment.

Penelope walked over to the bedroom window and looked down at the garden. "We can agree to disagree. People talk to plants, don't they? Not because they're cuckoo but because plants are alive and respond to words just like people do."

"We're talking about a *house*, not plants. I know plants are alive."

"What are houses made of? Plants, trees, sand, rocks. All living things," Penelope said, turning her attention back to Mattie. "I was told this house was built from magical trees that grew high in the Appalachian Mountains. To keep the magic inside the wood, the trees could only be cut during a full moon, so that's why this house is so special."

Mattie snorted a laugh. "You believe that whopper of a tale?"

"People believe in stranger things, and I've experienced too many phenomena in my life not to have some belief in the mystical."

"Let's pretend for a minute that I believe the house is alive and has *feelings*. Tell me, what's with the phone downstairs? Sophia said there's a story."

Penelope sighed dramatically. "There's always a story. That phone was special to your mom. It was her . . . dream phone."

"As in she always wanted a hideous blue rotary phone the way other girls want diamond rings?" Mattie asked.

A dry, deep laugh rose up Penelope's throat. "She believed that when that phone rang, we would know our dreams were coming true."

Mattie's face fell slack. "You can't be serious."

126

"She wholeheartedly believed that ever since we were kids, and none of us had the heart to toss it out. I guess we were all hopeful it would ring one day."

"You don't even know the number anymore. How would anyone call it? Although you could just use it to call your cell and caller ID would show the number."

Penelope rotated the tiger's-eye bracelet on her wrist. "You think we haven't tried that? It shows up as an unknown number. When you try to call back, nothing happens."

Mattie leaned back on her elbows, sinking into the mattress. "That's bizarre."

"Sophia says houses have energy. They respond to us," Penelope said. "She says houses hold memories and emotions and maybe even a little bit of magic. They keep a record of all we do and hold on to those things we say we don't want. That phone has been in the family for so long now, all tangled up with our hopes and dreams. It's a *part* of the house, a part of us."

Mattie sat up and picked up the Braves button before dropping it back into the box. "Do you think it will ever ring?"

Penelope shrugged. "Lilith did."

Mattie's eyes drifted toward the names in the closet. Were they part of the house's memories, now ingrained in the history forever?

A series of loud bangs erupted from the third floor, sounding like a cascade of books falling from shelves. Penelope rushed out of the room. Mattie glanced back at the closet wall and gasped. The pencil heart between her and Jonathan's names now had an arrow going through it—something she had not drawn herself. Penelope's footsteps echoed up the stairs, and Mattie suspended her disbelief long enough to ask, "Okay, house, I know you're up to something, but what?"

Chapter 13

PENELOPE

PENELOPE FLUNG OPEN THE ATTIC DOOR AND IMMEDIATELY saw the cause of the banging. A cardboard box and a stack of books had fallen from one of the top shelves installed along one wall of the attic. The box had busted open, the brittle, discolored tape tearing away from the top flaps. A cascade of pastel clothing had tumbled out and stretched a river of fabric across the floor.

Penelope dropped to her knees and gathered up the clothing, her mind slow to comprehend that she scooped up baby clothes. She had hand-stitched the clothing more than twenty years ago when she was first learning to sew. She held up a smocked peach dress with tiny pink flowers bordering the hem. Another dress was hyacinth blue with a white collar and matching bloomers. There were onesies, bonnets, booties, and dresses tiny enough for a preemie.

Penelope held up a pink-and-white gingham dress stitched with watermelons that was meant for a baby around six months of age, and she felt as though her chest split open at the sight of it. She pressed the dress against her heart like a bandage meant to cover the wound.

"Everything okay?" Mattie asked from the doorway.

Penelope's eyes popped open. She hadn't heard anyone coming up the hallway. Her response came out hoarse. "A box fell. And books." Penelope hurried to shove the clothes back into the box.

Mattie grabbed a pair of daffodil-yellow bloomers before Penelope could return them to the box. "Whose baby clothes are these? They smell like they've been boxed up for centuries, but they look new." Mattie's eyebrows rose on her forehead. "Did you make these?"

Penelope grabbed the bloomers from Mattie's hand and tossed them into the box. "A long time ago." She folded the box flaps together and returned it to the shelf. Then she gathered the fallen books, all children's stories she purchased years ago. Handing the books to Mattie, she said, "Let's take these downstairs. They're not doing anybody any good up here. We can donate them."

Mattie nodded toward the box. "Did you make those for me?"

Penelope shook her head and half smiled. "They're a bit too frilly for Lilith's taste. She preferred to dress you in rough-and-tumble clothes. I'm not sure you ever wore dresses unless you were here with me."

Mattie shuffled through the books in her arms. "Mom liked that boho style. I don't even know if I have a style. Does random count?"

"There's still time for you yet," Penelope said.

"What about the baby clothes?" Mattie asked innocently. "Should we donate those too? They're beautiful. It seems a shame to keep them in a box."

Penelope glanced at the box and felt an ache so strong that her whole body shuddered. She placed her hand on her stomach.

Mattie touched her arm. "Hey, you okay? You look pale."

The intensity of the emotions attached to the memories of those baby clothes shocked her. She thought she'd wrung out all the possible grief. How could there be any left? Penelope exhaled her held breath. "I think I'll lie down for a few minutes."

"Good idea," Mattie said. "I'll take these downstairs."

Mattie walked out of the attic, and Penelope braced one hand on the wall. "A little break here, please?" she said out loud. "There's only so much family heartache I can handle in one day." The box on the shelf trembled before the whole room fell into silence.

※

The next morning after a restless night with little sleep, Penelope stood at the kitchen window, drinking a second cup of mint tea and staring into the backyard, lost in thought.

Mattie sipped an espresso at the kitchen island. She picked at a piece of a biscuit slathered in butter. "After the will reading, I'll come back and get my stuff together so I can leave."

Penelope's hand shook slightly. She lifted the mug to her lips only to realize it was already empty. The air conditioner switched on and caused the basil and small ZZ plants on the windowsill to wave. "Figured out where you want to go?"

"Not exactly," Mattie said. "South, I think. I haven't lived near the ocean in years. It might be easier to find temporary work in a beach town."

Penelope washed out her mug and looked at her niece. The thought of Mattie leaving so soon intensified the grief mushrooming within her. "You're welcome to stay here as long as you need, but I'll support whatever you decide. My doors are always open, should you need a place to stop over and rest."

Mattie slouched forward over her coffee. "I wish I *knew* what I needed."

Penelope glanced at the clock. "For now, we need to get going. Let's start with that."

The August morning offered a mild breeze that stirred the dampness in the air. The sun was arcing across a pale blue sky with thin white strands of clouds. Creedence Clearwater Revival sang about Willy and the Poor Boys, and Penelope tapped her fingertips on the steering wheel to the beat as she drove Mattie across town to the law offices of Allen & Patterson, two local lawyers who'd been practicing in Ivy Ridge for more than thirty years. When Penelope parked in front of their brick building, Mattie switched off the radio and turned toward her.

"We'll learn what this is all about soon," Mattie said, "but I have this eerie feeling in my gut. Like something is *off* or . . . not wrong exactly, but—"

"Me too," Penelope admitted. She had felt uneasy about this unexpected will reading ever since Robert mentioned it. Why hadn't Lilith said anything to *her*? Why had her sister gone to Robert instead? Lilith trusted her only daughter with Penelope but not her last will and testament? "Could be that our emotions are heightened because of everything and there's actually nothing to worry about."

Mattie nodded. "As far as I know, there's nothing to leave me in the will."

Penelope turned off the car and grabbed her purse. "Let's get this over with, shall we?"

Inside the law office was cool, a welcome relief from the rising morning temperatures. Penelope assumed their appointment was with the family lawyer, Daniel Allen. His administrative assistant, Marla, greeted Penelope and Mattie before leading them into Mr. Allen's office. They sat in two cushy leather armchairs across from his oversize mahogany desk.

"Mr. Allen, unfortunately, had to have an emergency root canal this morning," Marla said, "but we're borrowing his office because of renovations. His colleague is assisting you today."

"Should we reschedule?" Penelope asked. "If Mr. Allen is the executor, isn't it mandatory that he be here to probate the will?"

Marla smiled in a professional, detached way. "I'll let his colleague discuss the legal aspects with you. He'll be with you shortly."

"Mr. Patterson must be going to help us," Penelope said to Mattie.

"Good morning," a man called from the doorway as he entered. "Sorry to keep you waiting. My office is being repainted, and it was supposed to be done by today, but they're doing touch-ups. Mr. Allen has graciously allowed us to borrow his office while he's out."

Penelope's entire body tensed, her back stiffening as though her chair produced an electric shock. Mattie looked at her with a curious expression. The familiarity of the voice resonated through Penelope's chest, causing a sudden squeezing sensation in her lungs.

A well-dressed man wearing navy-blue slacks and a matching blazer over a crisp white shirt breezed around the desk, staring intently at the files in his hands. He pulled back the rolling chair so he could sit. It was only then that he lifted his gaze to meet Penelope's.

"Good morning," he said again, this time looking at Mattie. "I'm Stephen Sloan. I'm the executor of Lilith Russell's will. I'm deeply sorry for your loss. Thank you for taking the time to come in today."

Penelope's hearing dulled and her brain shifted to static mode. Then her vision tunneled, narrowing in on Stephen Sloan's handsome face.

He smiled slowly, cautiously, at her. "It's good to see you, Penelope."

The dark edges on the periphery of her vision closed in, and Penelope's body temperature spiked. She leaped out of the chair and ran out of the room like someone fleeing a ghost.

Chapter 14

MATTIE

ONE SECOND MATTIE WAS LISTENING TO THE LAWYER talking; the next she was watching Penelope run out the room.

"Whoa, what's happening?" Mattie said in a rush of panicked breath.

Within another second, Stephen was out of his chair and running after Penelope. "Penelope, wait!" He caught up with her just outside the door but only because he latched onto her arm.

Penelope whirled around with the wildest look in her eyes that Mattie had ever seen. "I can't do this," she said, her voice barely above a whisper.

"Please," Stephen said, "come back and sit down."

Mattie stood from her chair. "What's going on?"

Penelope's dry, short laugh raised goose bumps on Mattie's arms. "There isn't enough time in this day to explain *what's going on*. But let's start with the obvious. What are you doing here?"

Stephen motioned toward her vacated chair. "Please, sit."

Penelope returned to the chair and sat, rigid and unhappy. Mattie sat and leaned over, clutching the lapis lazuli pendant in her hand, worrying her fingers over the smooth stone. "You okay? We can come back another time. We don't have to do this today."

"No, I'm fine," Penelope said. Then she clenched her jaw before asking, "You're the executor of Lilith's will?"

Stephen nodded. "I know this must be a shock—"

"A shock? That doesn't adequately describe this development. My sister, Lilith, chose *you* as her executor? On purpose?"

"It would appear so," Stephen said.

There was history between these two. Mattie did a quick study of Stephen. He looked to be around her aunt's age, midforties. His rich brown hair looked recently cut. His blue eyes followed Penelope, and Mattie noticed a look of concern in them. He was physically fit but not overly muscular, and his skin was browned by the sun. He was a handsome man, and Mattie would wager he was Penelope's type: intelligent, put together, and health conscious. "You two know each other, I assume?" Mattie said.

"Simply put, yes," Stephen said.

"There's *nothing* simple about this," Penelope said.

"Ohh-kay," Mattie said, feeling something akin to anger radiating off Penelope's skin. She focused on Stephen. "Mr. Sloan—"

He shifted his blue-eyed gaze toward Mattie. "Stephen."

"Stephen, I'm Mattie, Lilith's daughter," she said. "Is it common for strangers to be executors of wills?"

"It's common for lawyers to be appointed as executors," he answered. "And for the record, I'm not a stranger. To you I am, but not to your family."

Penelope huffed beside Mattie. "There's probably a time limit on when you go from *knowing* a family to reverting into a stranger. I'd say twenty years is plenty long enough to qualify, and we're past that."

Stephen looked at Penelope. Was that hurt in his eyes? "Maybe so, but why don't we agree to put aside the past for today?"

Mattie reached over and touched Penelope's arm. "We don't have to do this right now," she said. "Can we get someone else to be the executor?"

Penelope glanced at Stephen, then back to Mattie. "Not without a lot of trouble and extra time involved. You'd have to stay in town longer, which I wouldn't mind, but I know you have other ideas. We'd have to file a petition with the probate court to have Stephen removed for wrongdoing, which he hasn't done in relation to Lilith's will."

"In relation to the will—nice clarification," Stephen said with a hint of dry wit.

"I thought we were agreeing to put aside the past?" Penelope responded. "Or are we discussing other wrongdoings?"

"If we can't oust him," Mattie said, trying to distract Penelope from her verbal sparring with Stephen, "then let's get this over with."

Penelope and Stephen locked gazes for so long without speaking that Mattie shifted uncomfortably in her chair. They weren't sharing a lover's gaze, but it was passionate and complicated, and whatever passed between them ran deep like the roots of an oak. The room crackled with tension. "Penelope?"

Her jaw clenched and unclenched. "Yes, let's get this over with."

Stephen cleared his throat and sorted through the file folder and the papers within it. "About six months ago, Lilith reached out to me when I was living in Atlanta. She asked me to be the executor of her will and also the trustee. I moved back to Ivy Ridge shortly after."

Mattie frowned. "You moved here from Atlanta to execute a will?"

Stephen shook his head. "Not exactly."

"There's a trust?" Penelope asked, sounding surprised.

"What does that mean?" Mattie asked.

Stephen nodded. "There's a testamentary trust created by the will." He lifted a stack of papers, tapped them together on the desk to align the pages, and moved everything out of the way so only the stack sat in the middle of the desk. "This is Lilith's will. Most of it is standard legalese, but the part that most concerns you, Mattie, is that your mom left in trust $750,000 for you contingent on you satisfying specific requirements within a time frame."

Mattie's mouth fell open in shock, and she gripped the armrests. "I'm sorry, what?"

Stephen folded his hands together on the desk. "It sounds more complicated than it actually is. The simple version is that you stand to inherit $750,000 when you satisfy the requirements your mom set forth. There's a time limit for you to fulfill them, which is standard, and she gave Penelope the power to decide whether or not you've completed them in a satisfactory way."

Mattie's mind raced off without her. Her mom had been hoarding money for years, squirreling it away for Mattie to inherit? Mattie couldn't even imagine $750,000. Her mind could picture only colorful Monopoly money or the bonus faux-gold tokens used to play Skee-Ball. "We have money—I mean, *Mom* had money? This whole time? We lived like bohemian travelers, paycheck to paycheck. I sold my paintings, for Pete's sake, so I could buy more art supplies. And she had a secret stash?"

Penelope closed her eyes and pinched the bridge of her nose. "For when she was gone. She knew you'd need—or you'd *want*—a more stable lifestyle."

A stable lifestyle? As if Mattie knew what that was like. The only firm thing on her calendar right now was the date she had to return the car. She focused on Stephen. "What are the requirements?"

Stephen shuffled through the papers. "There are seven tasks you'll need to complete."

Was he serious? "Tasks? Are we talking Hercules? Or something more elementary, like selling wrapping paper at Christmas?"

"Somewhere in between, although you won't be required to slay the Hydra this time," Stephen said with a small smile.

"Can I see the list?" Mattie asked. "What's the time frame?"

"Four months." Stephen passed her a typed sheet of paper.

"Four months?" Mattie said, glancing at the numbered list and holding it so Penelope could see it too. "Will it actually take that long to . . ." Her words died in her throat.

1. Plant these twelve plants in the Russell family garden. Each plant must be labeled with its coordinating symbol/number: black-eyed Susan, 5; bleeding heart, 6; columbine, 2; coneflower, 7; geranium, 6; hibiscus, 3; hydrangea, 1; lantana, 8; peony, 9; petunia, 2; poppy, left side of a halved heart; white daisy, right side of a halved heart.
2. Take a local pizza cooking class.
3. Take a local baking class.
4. Paint a picture for someone that changes their life in a positive way.
5. Participate in a beautification project in Ivy Ridge.
6. Go on a picnic date and share s'mores and secrets.
7. Throw a Halloween bash with Penelope at the Russell family home.

Mattie's scowl deepened. "Are you serious about these?"

Stephen held open his hands and shrugged. "Your mom was. I don't question my clients' requirements. I'm only here to make sure their requests are met."

"'Take a local pizza cooking class . . . Share s'mores'"—Mattie read out loud as she skimmed the tasks—"plant flowers in the garden." Disbelief mingled with frustration. "'Participate in a beautification project'? What am I trying to do, become an Eagle Scout? I actually have to do these things *before* I can inherit the money?" Mattie laid the paper in her lap, her hands shaking with an emotion that bordered on outrage. She clenched her fists. "Penelope gets to say whether I've completed them?"

Stephen rolled a ballpoint pen between his hands. "That's correct."

Mattie looked at Penelope for alliance. "I'm not staying in Ivy Ridge for four months, so you'll just say I've done them, and I can get my money and leave."

"She *could* do that," Stephen agreed, "but she'd be breaking the law, and as the trustee, I won't condone that. I'll need proof of completion for each one."

"Oh, give it a rest, Stephen," Penelope snapped. "Do you honestly have to be such a rule follower about this? Just give Mattie the inheritance. Who knows why Lilith came up with this nonsense, but there's no reason to prolong Mattie's suffering."

"I must uphold my client's wishes and the requirements of the trust," Stephen said, "regardless of what others want to do. Mattie must complete the tasks or the money will stay in the trust indefinitely. This is a lot of money to reject, so I encourage you to go home, think about it, and decide if you can stick it out for four months, or less, and complete these tasks."

"Home?" Mattie punctuated the word with a sarcastic laugh. "I don't even *have* a home. Let's go," she said to Penelope. The paper crumpled in her grip.

Stephen stood behind the desk. "I'll store the original will here, and you can keep that copy of the tasks. I'll be here if you have any questions, and let me know what you decide. If I don't hear from you and four months pass, I'll assume you aren't interested in claiming the inheritance."

Without waiting for Penelope, Mattie stormed out of the office. When Penelope caught up to her, Mattie faced her aunt on the sidewalk outside the building. "I can't *believe* this," she said, waving the paper through the air as tears gathered in her eyes. She didn't want to cry, but a volcano of anger bubbled inside her in a way that might be unstoppable. "Why would Mom *do* this to me? Spend our whole lives living like we might not make it through the week, hoard all this money here, and then make me *work* to get it? Did you read this list? Beautify Ivy Ridge? What for? She didn't even want to *be* here. These are asinine! Mom didn't force me to make my bed, but she's now forcing me to take a class and learn how to toss pizza dough into the air? My last job in the city was at a pizza joint. I don't need a class." She sucked in a few deep breaths and swiped at her eyes. When she could speak again, she asked, "What's with that Stephen guy?"

Penelope dug the car keys out of her purse and clicked the car unlocked. "Let's finish this conversation at the house."

Mattie got into the car and stared at the wrinkled list in her lap, fighting an internal battle. Now that her initial response of anger had ebbed, she focused on the logical next steps. She knew she should put aside her frustration and complete the tasks. They weren't overly difficult, but they would require planning and time. She would have to stay in town for at least another two months, which wasn't what she wanted, but if she was honest with herself and everyone else, staying in town a while longer wasn't a bad idea. It would give her time to come up with a solid plan for her future, and now she'd have the money to do whatever she wanted. But what *did* she want to do?

Penelope didn't speak the entire ride back to the house. The rigidity of her clenched jaw revealed her own frustration. Was she angry about Lilith's mindless "tasks" for Mattie, or did her anger have more to do with the lawyer, Stephen Sloan?

Penelope parked on the narrow strip of driveway alongside the house. Without saying anything, she got out of the car and slammed the door. Mattie barely caught up with her aunt as Penelope marched into the house like a woman on a mission. She shouted for Sophia, who didn't answer, so she continued through the house until she flung open the back porch door and found Sophia deadheading roses in the garden.

Sophia wore an emerald-green sundress that cinched at her waist and brushed against her ankles. Her auburn hair was pinned into a bun at the base of her neck, and she stood barefoot in the grass. She stopped her clipping and peered up at Penelope, who flew down the stairs fast enough to set fire to the boards.

"Did you know about this?" Penelope demanded.

Mattie joined them in the backyard, standing on the flagstones in the shade of a maple tree. She folded the task list and shoved it into her pocket.

"Know about what, darling?" Sophia asked. Her wide-brimmed sun hat shaded her face.

"The testamentary trust."

Sophia placed the bucket of dead flowers and clippers on the grass. "That's vague, Penelope. I need more context."

"Lilith left an inheritance amounting to hundreds of thousands of dollars for Mattie," Penelope said, stomping across the grass like an angry child. "But only if Mattie completes a series of tasks, *and* Lilith appointed Stephen as the executor of her will."

Sophia removed her sunglasses. "Stephen Sloan?"

"Did you know about this?"

Sophia placed one hand over her heart. "Oh, honey, of course I didn't know."

"Why would she *do* this?" Penelope asked, her voice breaking in a way that brought tears to Mattie's eyes. "Didn't Lilith do *enough* through the years? She always got to do whatever she wanted, *live* however she wanted, never caring about the rest of us or how she hurt us or left us or burdened us. I always had to carry her weight and make sure everything got done. She never did *anything*! She left *her own daughter* with us for months while she flitted off to wherever and *whoever* she wanted to—"

"That's enough, Penelope," Sophia said, nodding toward Mattie.

But more words tumbled out of Penelope's mouth. "I'm so sick of her games and her lack of concern and responsibility. I loved her and I always stuck up for her and defended her, but I'm done pretending she was this perfect, wonderful creature. And Stephen? How could she *do* this to me?"

"Stop it!" Mattie yelled. "Stop talking about my mom like that!" Hot tears rolled down her cheeks. "You've been acting like a sad, heartbroken sister, but you're nothing but a hypocrite. How can you say those things about her?"

Penelope swiped at her own tear-streaked cheeks. "You have no idea what you're talking about."

"I know what I'm hearing!" Mattie argued.

Penelope's shoulders slumped forward, and for a few moments, she covered her face with her hands. Then she looked up at Mattie. "You only know one small piece of your mom, of who she was to

141

you. I loved Lilith. I worried about her. Worried that you both would end up lost or dead or stranded somewhere—"

"We were *fine*," Mattie said.

"Were you? You described your lifestyle as bohemian travelers living paycheck to paycheck. Mattie, you were a child who thought she needed to sell her paintings for money. How is that okay? In general, yeah, sure, you were fine. Lilith was *always* fine," Penelope said bitterly. "That didn't stop me from worrying. And I loved having you here for the summers, don't misunderstand that. But Lilith did whatever she wanted no matter who it hurt or inconvenienced, which is something you'll never understand because your blind devotion to her keeps you from seeing *all* of her."

"I'm not blindly devoted," Mattie said. Heartbreak closed up her throat as more tears filled her eyes. "She was an amazing person and the best mom. And if you weren't so self-absorbed and judgmental about what you think she should have been doing with her life, you'd see that. She *never* wanted the kind of life you have. Who would? This dead-boring existence where you never go anywhere and you stay closed up in this house with no friends?"

Sophia gasped, and Penelope's stunned expression instantly ignited Mattie's guilt. Shouts sounded from next door, rushing over the top of the fence and surrounding the Russells. A woman screamed for help.

"That's Virginia!" Sophia said, and she was off and running through the front garden gate toward the Carlisles' house.

Chapter 15

MATTIE

MATTIE AND PENELOPE HURRIED AFTER SOPHIA. THE backyard gate to the Carlisles' was open, and they found Virginia leaning over Thomas's prone body in the soft backyard fescue.

Virginia looked up at them when they entered the backyard. "Oh thank God," she said. "We were standing out here talking about the garden, and then Thomas stumbled sideways, like his legs were giving out, and his speech slurred. I tried to get him to sit down, thinking he'd gotten too hot, and then he dropped like a mayfly. I thought he'd . . . but he has a pulse. I think he's only passed out," she said and started crying.

Sophia knelt beside her and rubbed Virginia's back. "It's okay. We're here."

Penelope dropped down beside Thomas and pressed her fingers to his neck. She touched her wrist against his forehead. "Was he complaining of numbness or chest pain?"

"No," Virginia said. "No pain, although he did mention that his face felt strange this morning during breakfast."

"Strange how?" Sophia asked.

"Numb maybe," Virginia said. "I forget. He said it felt odd to eat, like his face was slow to respond, but I thought he was being silly, rambling like he does sometimes. I wasn't paying attention. I was too busy fretting over the coffee I spilled on my new rug." She pressed her hands to her chest and made a sobbing noise. "I should have taken him seriously."

"Don't blame yourself," Penelope said. "Sounds like it might be a stroke. Mattie, call 911."

Mattie hadn't moved since she entered the garden and saw Virginia leaning over Thomas's unmoving body. Except she wasn't seeing Thomas; she was seeing her mom lying peacefully in the bed, her face so calm and pale in the growing sunlight that she looked like Sleeping Beauty waiting for her prince to come. But there had been a stillness in the bedroom that morning, and instantly alarms had gone off in Mattie's brain even as her mind resisted the truth. The bedsheets weren't moving with a steady rise and fall of Lilith's breaths, and her lips were a fading shade of pink that reminded Mattie of rose petals littering the ground. She could still hear the echo of her voice as she called her mom's name—first as a question and then with a rising sense of panic.

"Mattie!" Penelope repeated, louder this time. "Call 911!"

Mattie's memory shattered with the urgency of her aunt's voice. She pulled the phone out of her pocket and dialed immediately. Thomas made a soft groaning noise, and his eyes opened. Everyone exhaled in relief, and Virginia's crying momentarily stopped. She called his name a few times and touched his face.

A dispatcher answered, saying, "911, what's your emergency?"

"I think my neighbor had a stroke," Mattie said. "But he's conscious now."

Mattie gave the dispatcher all the necessary information, and he assured her that emergency personnel were already on their way. Mattie relayed this information to the others.

Now that Thomas was awake, Sophia and Penelope shifted him to his side, and they elevated his head using an outdoor chair pillow to promote blood flow. He tried to speak, but he struggled to form words and his speech was muddled. Virginia spoke soothingly to him, and he seemed to understand, but his responses were slow and confused.

Mattie stood nearby but wanted to keep some distance between them. Even though the situation was different, she knew Virginia's anxiety and fear, the feeling of being completely helpless while staring at someone you love.

"Is there anyone else you want us to call while we wait?" Penelope asked.

"Would you call my son David?" Virginia asked. "He lives the closest."

Penelope glanced over her shoulder at Mattie. "Do you mind?"

"Me?" Mattie asked in surprise. She wanted to argue that she didn't know these people and wouldn't it be better for David Carlisle to hear about his dad from a trusted friend or at least a name he recognized?

"Thank you so much," Virginia said, looking at Mattie with an expression of such gratitude that Mattie couldn't say no. Virginia called out David's number, and Mattie dialed.

A man answered. "Hello?"

Mattie walked away from the others and paced along the roses. "Hey, David? This is Mattie Russell. You don't know me, but I'm Penelope Russell's niece—"

"I know who you are," David said.

"You do? Oh . . . so I know this is odd, but I'm at your parents' house, and your dad has possibly had a stroke. He's awake and responsive though. We've called the ambulance, and they're already on their way. Your mom asked me to call you."

There was a pause before David responded. "He's okay?"

"I think so," Mattie said. "I'm no expert, but he's awake, and he seems to understand something has happened, but he's confused and . . . and I'm probably not the right person to give you all the details since I don't want to say anything wrong or tell you something inaccurate. Maybe it would be best for you to come over as soon as you can or meet them at the hospital."

"Tell Mom I'll be there in less than ten minutes," David said. "And, Mattie, thank you."

Virginia's courage was bolstered knowing that David was on his way. Mattie wouldn't wish for anyone to have to do this alone. She would have given anything to have had even a stranger be with her when she called the ambulance the morning she found Lilith unresponsive, someone to be with her while she tried to make sense of what was happening.

The ambulance and David arrived at the same time. He appeared in the backyard like a godsend for Virginia. The oldest Carlisle son exuded an air of confidence and comfort. Mattie assumed he was the son they depended on to keep everything and everyone floating with their heads above water. David looked like an older, slightly stockier version of the seventeen-year-old Jonathan from Mattie's memory.

Once Thomas was loaded into the back of the ambulance, Virginia went inside to grab her purse so she and David could follow the EMTs to the hospital. Before he left, David thanked the Russells. He touched Mattie's arm briefly. "Thanks again for the call. It means a lot to all of us that your family was here today and even more so that you were in the backyard so you could hear her call for help."

Mattie nodded, but his words reminded her *why* the Russells had been in the backyard and how ugly the conversation had been. Sophia walked with David toward his car, and Penelope and Mattie followed them out of the yard.

"Please keep us updated," Sophia said. "If you need *anything*, don't hesitate to ask."

"I appreciate that," David said. He glanced behind him and caught Mattie's gaze before looking away. "Your family has a lot going on right now. I know Mom wouldn't want to burden you more."

"Never a burden," Sophia said. "We've been neighbors since you were eating crayons."

David laughed unexpectedly. "You knew about that?"

Sophia patted his arm. "Not much escapes me. You call us or we'll come over and ask what you need."

"Yes, ma'am."

Chapter 16

JONATHAN

"HOW'S THAT BLACK FORBIDDEN RICE?" JONATHAN ASKED, placing his hand on Leo DiFederico's shoulder. Leo was one half of the million-follower foodie influencer power couple known as Eat It Slow. Having this couple attend and review the soft opening of a new eatery in Wicker Park had massive potential to generate buzz and turn the restaurant into a local gem. "Have you ever seen tiger shrimp that size? And that's only an appetizer portion. Wait until your entrée arrives."

Leo flipped through images on his iPhone, displaying a dozen different angles of his appetizer *before* he'd started devouring it.

"You got some great shots," Jonathan complimented.

"He's the main photographer of our duo. I'm the main eater." His partner, Flora, forked oozing monterey and pepper jack cheeses dotted with diced poblanos onto a folded warm tortilla. "Speaking of eating, I'd give away a pair of my Manolos for this queso fundido. It's legit plus some."

"Can I get you to quote that to your followers?" Jonathan asked with a wink. "Don't forget we have a table set up near the side windows that offers the best natural light this time of day. And don't be shy about taking your dishes over there for optimal shots. A house assistant can get you any props you might need to enhance the photos."

"Flora shy?" Leo joked. "A word that will never be used to describe her."

Jonathan smirked at Flora. "What's that they say? Fortune favors the bold?"

"Exactly!" Flora agreed. "Leo wouldn't do well with a shy girl. He needed someone brassy."

"And evidently someone bossy," Leo added, but he reached across the table and gave her hand a squeeze. Flora beamed at him in return.

"Don't skip dessert," Jonathan said. Looking at Leo, he added, "Photo-worthy for sure. Thank you both for coming."

"Wouldn't have missed it," Leo said. "It's hard to pass up free food created by one of the best chefs in the city."

Jonathan leaned closer to the table and whispered, "In the *world*. And you can quote me on that."

Jonathan passed between the crowded lunch tables full of foodies, food bloggers, food influencers, and local media. He spoke to them, checked to make sure they were satisfied, and soothed any complaints, although there weren't many. The chef and owner, waitstaff, bartenders, and hosts had buttoned up their processes and executed everything smoothly. As with any soft launch, there were a few issues that would need to be addressed, but fortunately today they were minimal and not upsetting to the invited guests.

Jonathan's work for the day was almost complete. He'd invited specific members of the press and media and targeted food influencers, and he'd pulled all the strings to ensure most of them were in attendance for today's lunch opening. They agreed to share their experience with millions of followers in exchange for a free meal. Jonathan also reminded them to tag the restaurant and chef in their photos and in their shout-outs on all the social channels. The people sitting at these tables had the potential to skyrocket the restaurant's success, and from his view, Jonathan felt confident today's trial run cemented the eatery's guaranteed triumph. In a few weeks, reservations would be booked months in advance and seating at these white tablecloth–covered tables featuring the new American cuisine would be in high demand.

Jonathan's cell vibrated in his pocket. He glanced at the notification illuminating his screen. His brother David was calling. He assumed David wanted to ask him *again* about their dad's upcoming birthday party next month—the party Jonathan wasn't going to attend. His schedule didn't allow for him to take enough days off to make the short weekend trip. He'd text David a few days before the party to send his regrets.

A voice mail notification popped up on the phone screen followed by a text message notification from David. Jonathan frowned. It was out of character for David to phone stalk him. Jonathan swiped to open his texts.

It's Dad. Call me ASAP.

Jonathan's stomach clenched, but he pasted on a smile as he moved through the front room toward the door. He slipped out quickly, stood on the noisy Chicago sidewalk, and called David. As soon as his brother answered, Jonathan said, "What's going on with Dad?"

"He's stable," David said, "but he had a stroke. He's in the ER now. They're running tests to find the cause and assess the severity. He's responsive but confused and upset. He has some paralysis and memory loss, but there's a possibility it could be temporary."

Jonathan sagged against the building and gripped the back of his neck. "Paralysis? What happened?"

David relayed the events as told to him by their mom and finished with, "The neighbors were outside and called 911."

"How bad is it?"

"Hard to know for sure at this stage," David said. "Lots of stroke victims have a barrage of complications at first and then they lessen or heal completely once the body balances again. At his age, there's no way to know what's long term and what might get better in the next few days. I know you're probably working and busy, but Mom wanted me to call everyone," David said. "I'll keep you updated as we learn more."

Jonathan imagined his mom's stricken face and his dad lying in a hospital bed, connected to tubes and unable to move his body like he'd been able to. "How's Mom?"

"She'd like to think she's keeping it together, but she's a mess. A classy mess. You know, wearing her pearls with her nails done, but one look at her face and you can see she's not okay."

David's calm honesty pulled a small smile from Jonathan. "Sounds like Mom. I'd ask what I can do to help, but . . ."

"From there? Nothing much you can do. Call her later and check in," David said. "William and I have been talking. We have to make plans for Dad's business."

"What about it?" Jonathan asked.

Thomas Carlisle had started a corporate event planning business in Ivy Ridge more than thirty years ago. His company devised meetings, conferences, trade shows, seminars, retreats, and other events for businesses. He planned corporate events using a small internal staff, and he also hired out vendors for clients or for any interested professionals within a specific industry. Through the years the success of the business gave him the opportunity to expand and open two additional branches in large neighboring cities. Now his dad's company was a financial powerhouse, and they planned events for businesses all over the country.

"Dad's not going to be able to get back into his work routine for at least the next couple of weeks," David said. "And depending on his recovery, it might be longer. William and I aren't equipped to step in and help."

"How could you be? You've never worked that kind of business and you have jobs," Jonathan said. "Doesn't he have a VP in Ivy Ridge, someone who can take over while he's out?"

"He did," David said, "but she's just gone out on maternity leave. The other employees don't have the experience to head the operation. They're efficient in their areas but not to organize the whole."

"How fast can he hire a replacement?"

The phone went silent for a few beats, then David said, "Would you consider coming home and helping out? Temporarily?"

The question stunned Jonathan into momentary silence. A car horn honked and a cyclist sped by, stirring a crumpled paper bag along the curb. "Are you kidding me? I *have* a job. A job that keeps me busy every day all year long."

"Aren't there people who could step in for a few weeks and cover for you? Surely you have colleagues or peers you could call. I wouldn't ask you if I had other options. You are the *only* person I know who could handle this kind of work."

"No way," Jonathan said, unwilling to relent and accept such an outrageous ask—and it was a *gargantuan* ask. "I can't up and leave town for weeks. It's taken me years to build this kind of clientele."

"Same here, brother," David said. "Dad has spent his whole life building this company. Think about it. You don't have to decide right now, but call Mom later." David ended the call.

People hurried by on the sidewalk, oblivious to Jonathan's mounting sense of shock. When had his dad gotten old enough to be a stroke survivor? Thinking about his dad paralyzed in a hospital bed didn't align with the vision of the strong, capable, energetic man he knew, and going home to take over the family business in Ivy Ridge? Not possible. He had a life in Chicago—a good, successful life.

The front door to the restaurant opened, and the chef and owner, Rosa Martinez, stepped out. Her thick, wavy, dark auburn hair was pinned up on the top of her head, and her cherry-red lips popped against her brown skin. She made eye contact with Jonathan. He pushed himself off the building, slid his phone back into his pocket, and shoved his personal life aside so he could put on his business persona.

"Rosa," he said with a smile, "I hope you're as pleased as I am. Everything is going far better than we imagined."

Although Rosa was petite and barely five feet tall, her vivacious and passionate personality was anything but diminutive. She quirked an eyebrow at him. "What's going on with you?"

Jonathan hesitated. Had he forgotten a vital to-do? His mind quickly scrolled through the tasks he'd arranged to ensure today was a success. He mentally checked all the boxes. "I'm not following."

"Out here," Rosa said. "I'm not talking about the opening. Because of you and my staff, this event is *in the bag* as they say. But I saw you through the windows talking on the phone. *Qué pasó?* I know that look on your face."

Jonathan exhaled. He touched the white sleeve of her chef's coat. "Nothing for you to worry about. Focus on your restaurant."

"Don't tell me what to worry about, Jonathan Carlisle," she said, stepping closer to him and poking her index finger into his chest. *"Dime ahora."*

"It's my dad," he admitted. "He had a stroke, and he's in the ER. My brother said he's stable, but we don't know much else yet."

"Oh, Jonathan, *lo siento*," Rosa said. "You're off the clock. You've done what you need to do here. *Vete a casa*. Go home. Be with your family."

Jonathan laughed unexpectedly. "Home? Not an option. I have work, and *home* is almost a thousand miles south."

Rosa blinked at him without speaking. Jonathan cleared his throat.

"There's nothing I can do right now."

"Not from here, no," she said.

"I have events every day this week and the next week and the next."

"You'll never run out of work," Rosa said. "There will always be something to do—a party to throw, a bar to open, a restaurant to promote. You're one of the most in-demand promoters, Jonathan. If you want work, you'll find it. And if you go home to be with your family, you'll still have work when you come back. This town is full of people who would step up and help you with your upcoming events should you need to go home."

Irritation chiseled away at Jonathan's calm. "Would you let someone else run your kitchen?"

"*Sí*," Rosa admitted. "Would they run it exactly like I would? No, but I'd trust that whoever I gave the task to would take care of my restaurant while I stepped away for a few days." She touched his arm. "Is your family intolerable?"

"No."

"Do they make you miserable in a way that causes you to stay away? Are they toxic?"

"No. But they want me to take over my dad's company in Ivy

Ridge temporarily while he recovers. My brothers aren't in the business, so it's not really an option for them to step in."

"It sounds like they need you," Rosa said gently, "and you once mentioned to me that you haven't been home in a while. How long?"

Jonathan counted the time in his mind. "Five years, maybe?"

"Go home, Jonathan," she said. "The rest of life—your job, your clients—it'll sort itself out. From one workaholic to another, for once do the opposite of what you would normally do and take a break from your work here."

"Just so I can go home and work there?"

Rosa smiled. "At least you won't have to completely give up your workaholic ways. Maybe you'll find what you're looking for there."

Jonathan frowned. "I'm not looking for anything."

Rosa smirked. "We're *all* looking for something."

An hour later, after Rosa reassured Jonathan his work with her was done for the day, he started heading back to his apartment. His thoughts were all over the place, leaping from one possible scenario to the next. Could he run his business in the city from Ivy Ridge? Did he have to call in reinforcements? Did he have to hand off his clients? Would his clients still work with him when he returned? Would years of hard work and long hours disintegrate within a few weeks of being "out of touch" with the city?

He stopped at the market on his block and bought two bags of Jolly Ranchers. He hadn't eaten the candy in years, but today felt like a green apple–blue raspberry–cherry kind of day. Once inside his apartment he paced the living room, sucking on the hard candies and mentally pushing against the idea that he had to leave town for an unknown number of weeks and give up his upcoming events. He didn't relish the idea of calling his clients to tell them he wouldn't be able to promote their events person-ally. But how could he *not* go home and help his family? How could he tell his dad no and force his brothers to find another way to keep the flagship Ivy Ridge branch open and running?

Jonathan opened his laptop and pulled up his work schedule. On a notepad he wrote down every event professional he knew within his network of business associates and neighboring peers. He worked with only high-level vendors who were capable of handling their portion of an event, but most of them still appreci-ated direction from a main promoter.

He then made a list of which events he could keep while asking the partnering vendors to step up their responsibility, the ones who could take the lead without issues. The next list was for the events he would *have* to hand off to another promoter to coor-dinate. These were too high-profile to run smoothly without a designated leader.

Jonathan shoved his hands through his hair and tossed out a few desperate prayers that he could not only find peers to help him out but also return to the city in a few weeks and pick up where he left off without problems. Then he unwrapped a blue raspberry candy before picking up his phone and making calls.

Chapter 17

MATTIE

WHEN THEY RETURNED TO THE BACKYARD LATER THAT day, Sophia picked up her gardening tools and resumed deadheading the roses. Penelope hadn't said anything to them and went into the house. Mattie wandered into the garden and lingered on the flagstones, feeling uncertain about what to do next. Guilt tore through her. The anger she'd felt after hearing Penelope bad-mouth Lilith was gone. Seeing Virginia's heartache and Thomas's motionless body had placed life back into perspective.

But how could Penelope say such hurtful things about Lilith *and* about Mattie? Mattie hadn't been blindly devoted to her mom. She simply hadn't questioned Lilith's plans. What did it matter that Mattie hadn't offered many opinions? It wasn't as though Lilith never asked. Mattie's own words from a few nights prior returned to her. She herself had acknowledged that Lilith left her without the experience to know what to do with her life. Now who was the hypocrite?

"Penny for your thoughts?" Sophia called from the roses. "From the looks of it, they might cost me a lot more than a penny." She pointed to an extra sun hat resting beside the greenhouse.

Mattie crossed the yard, grabbed the sun hat, and placed it on her head. Sophia handed her an extra pair of clippers.

"We have to cut away the dead ones," Sophia said, "so new growth can start. It's a waste of energy for the plant to keep sending life to these dead ends."

"Wish you could cut away the dead ends for people too," Mattie mumbled.

Sophia's smile comforted Mattie. "You can." They trimmed the roses in silence for a few minutes, then Sophia spoke. "Want to talk about the will reading?"

Mattie dropped cuttings into the bucket at Sophia's feet. "Who is Stephen Sloan, other than a lawyer? He's *someone* to Penelope."

"How about you tell me about the tasks first."

Mattie pulled out the folded list of tasks and handed the paper to Sophia while she explained what Stephen had conveyed about the will. Sophia read through the list, and her eyebrows rose higher and higher on her forehead. When she finished reading, she looked at Mattie.

"Four months?" she asked.

"Basically by December," Mattie said. "I don't think the tasks have to be done in order, but I'm not sure I can pull those off any quicker. Take a look at the seventh task. Host a Halloween bash with Penelope at the Russell house. That's *very* specific, and I don't mean location. I mean *time*. Halloween." Mattie's stomach tightened. A thought had been niggling in the back of her mind. "Hypothetically, if Mom had passed on the first of the year, I would have had to wait ten months before I could complete the tasks, but the time frame she gave for completing them and inheriting the money is four months, meaning she must have *known* the time of year. Sure, we could host a Halloween bash in the summer, but did she really think that was when this would happen? The note she left me the night she died said to call Penelope.

"And a couple of weeks before she died," Mattie continued, the pent-up thoughts tumbling out, "Mom made all these plans for us. We went to theater shows, ate at restaurants we'd never been to before, took a pottery class, went on tours of the city. Anytime we weren't working, we were doing something new and she was marking it off her list. Sometimes she got those kinds of whims to live life to the fullest, so I didn't think it was odd. But now . . . is it crazy to think that Mom *knew* something was going to happen to her?"

Sophia returned the list to Mattie. "She knew."

Mattie's mouth dropped open. A strong gust of wind snatched the paper from her hand. She chased it across the yard but didn't catch it until it wedged itself into the rosemary. Mattie folded the list and shoved it into her pocket while she walked back to Sophia. "She knew? How?"

Sophia sighed. "There are many things about this family I wish someone had told you years ago. People often think they're protecting you by withholding information. Sometimes this is true. Sometimes it's not. In this case, I think it's not been for your benefit. Did Lilith ever tell you about the family's talents?"

"Like how I can paint and Mom could play guitar and sing?"

Sophia motioned for Mattie to follow her to the patio table draped in shade. She sat and removed her hat and sunglasses. "You are a wonderful painter, but those aren't the talents I'm talking about."

"Mom used to say the Russells were enchanted," Mattie said awkwardly. "But I thought those were stories she told me for fun when I was a kid."

Sophia nodded. "Yes, enchanted is a good description. We have special gifts. You love music, don't you?"

"Yes."

"Has anything unusual ever happened with you and music?"

Mattie frowned. "Not that I know of."

"Not that you've *noticed*," Sophia said. "And your art—through the years did you ever notice how whatever you painted, there was always someone who showed up and needed exactly that piece of art?"

Mattie's breath caught. No matter what paintings she displayed for the day, people bought every one. She never took home an unsold painting, and many people had shared comments similar to Sophia's words. *"This is just what I've been looking for,"* or *"It's like you crawled into my dreams and painted what I've been seeing."* A few people even thanked her for the paintings so profusely and with such intensity that Mattie felt embarrassed by her own talent.

Sophia tapped the side of her temple. "I see something is turning in there. Start noticing and remembering moments you thought were coincidental or lucky. I would also bet you noticed things about your mom, *special* things." Mattie nodded. "About your mom's passing, she had a dream when she was younger, and she said it revealed to her all the places she would live and when she would die, even the day."

Mattie gasped in disbelief. "Why wouldn't she have told me?"

"Would you have believed her?" Sophia said. "Would you have done anything differently? Loved her more or less? Traveled more or less? Some things are better left to the unknown so that you are free to make your own choices and not be bound by a forever-changing future."

"Make my own choices," Mattie echoed dully.

"You chose to follow Lilith," Sophia said, "because you wanted to and you loved her. She didn't force that on you. But now, honey, you are free to make different, new choices. Penelope didn't believe in Lilith's dream, but now that we see what has happened, we can all admit it was a premonition."

"Was that one of her talents?" Mattie asked. "The gift of premonition?"

Sophia shook her head. "Lilith's talents were more persuasive and bold. As far as I know, that was the only premonition she ever had. You should talk to Penelope about this too."

Mattie leaned back in the chair, dropped her head back, and stared at patches of blue sky peeking through the leaves arching above her. "I said some harsh things this afternoon."

"You did," Sophia agreed. "How do you feel about it?"

"Not good." She placed a hand on her stomach. "Kinda nauseous."

"She'll forgive you," Sophia said.

Mattie sat up and glanced toward the house. "Who's Stephen?"

"That's Penelope's story to share, if she wants to," Sophia said.

"But you know who he is to her," Mattie said. "And obviously so did Mom. Penelope was really bent out of shape about Mom picking him as the executor. They don't seem like *enemies*, but if there's some kind of animosity between Penelope and Stephen, why would Mom make him the executor knowing Penelope would be involved?"

A blue jay landed on the birdbath and drank, eyeing Sophia and Mattie.

"I want to believe there is a good reason," Sophia responded.

Mattie rubbed her hand across her stomach. "Do you think it's because Mom was selfish and didn't care about how people felt? Would she have hurt Penelope on purpose?"

"Lilith was selfish sometimes," Sophia agreed. "But she wouldn't have hurt Penelope so intentionally without believing there was another way to view the situation. From one angle it's a hurtful decision, but from another angle . . ."

"Putting her in contact with Stephen might not be a bad thing for Penelope?"

Sophia lifted her hands in response. "That's Penelope's choice."

Mattie sighed. "I should apologize, shouldn't I?"

Sophia donned her sun hat and slid on her sunglasses. "I have a few more dead ends to cut, and so do you. Penelope's in her sewing room. She's too stubborn and too hurt to start the conversation, so it's up to you to be the braver one."

Mattie went into the kitchen and filled a glass with ice water before going to find Penelope. While she stood at the window watching Sophia in the garden, music started playing in the parlor. Mattie followed the sound of it, recognizing the tune "We Are Family." She thought she'd find Penelope at the radio, but the room was empty. Goose bumps spread across Mattie's skin. She heard Sophia's voice in her head asking, *"Has anything unusual ever happened with you and music?"*

Something was happening now. The radio crackled and the song changed almost as soon as Mattie's thoughts did. "Magic" by Pilot started playing. Mattie backed out of the room, nearly tripping over the carpet runner in the hallway as she rushed up the stairs to the third floor. She found Penelope in her sewing room standing beside a female dress form. The mannequin wore an indigo-and-black bohemian-style dress. Mattie paused in the doorway, trying to catch her breath and slow her heartbeat.

Penelope glanced at her. Worry ghosted across her face. "You okay?"

Less than an hour before, Mattie had been ungracious and insensitive toward Penelope, and yet her aunt was able to rise above the petty argument. "The radio," Mattie babbled. "The songs change."

Penelope tilted her head. "Is that a question or a statement?"

Mattie stepped into the room. "No, I mean, they *change* because of *me*. Is that possible?"

Penelope's eyes widened, and she turned her gaze back toward the mannequin. "You've been talking to Sophia."

"That's not the main reason I came up here, but yes, she mentioned our family gifts, and the radio just—" Mattie inhaled a slow, deep breath. "We can save that conversation for later. I wanted to say I'm sorry for earlier. I shouldn't have said what I did."

Penelope's features softened. "You weren't wrong. Tactless, but not way off from the truth." She touched the lace neckline of the dress. "I think *dead boring* was a bit dramatic, but mildly boring is probably accurate."

"I was angry, and angry arguments are ugly and unfair, and I always regret what I say."

"I'm sorry too," Penelope admitted. "I'm hurting and I'm frustrated, but I love Lilith, and I shouldn't have let my temper get the best of me. Forgive me?"

Mattie touched the dress form. "Of course. This is beautiful. Who did you make it for?"

Penelope smiled. "You for your birthday this year. I wasn't expecting you so early, so it's not quite finished."

Mattie mirrored her smile. "I haven't worn a dress in a while, but I can see myself wearing this. I'll act surprised when you give it to me on my birthday." Penelope's sewing skills were incredible. She had a way of creating pieces of clothing that were different from anything you'd find in a store, which brought Mattie back to the question of the Russell family and their unusual skills. "Care to share what you know about the music and me?"

Penelope pulled a fuchsia scarf through her hands like a magician. "You'd know more than me," she said. When Mattie frowned, she continued, "I'm not the keeper of all our family's wisdom or secrets. You'll know more about yourself than anyone else."

"You must know *something*. Even Robert acted like the town thinks the Russells have powers."

"Powers?" Penelope said with a short laugh. "This town thinks all kinds of things."

Enid crept into the room and weaved around Mattie, pushing her weight into Mattie's legs. "Like what?" Mattie leaned down and scratched her fingers down Enid's arching back.

"It's been said that Lilith cast spells to make men fall in love with her. Laugh it up, but it was confirmed as the gospel truth. Mom supposedly could control animals and sent a scurry of squirrels to eat through the electrical wiring at the Baptist church, causing a power outage just before their Christmas production, because the Methodist church didn't appreciate them planning an event on the same night as theirs."

Mattie laughed. "And you? What do they say about you?"

"That whatever I sew gives the wearer special abilities."

Mattie stopped laughing. "What kind of abilities?"

"Bravery, kindness, comfort," she said with a slow smile. "Helps them find love or lost things."

Mattie's skin tingled. "Now *that* I believe. The squirrels and the love spells, not so much. And me?"

Penelope wound a pink ribbon around her fingers. "Music comes alive when you're around. It has ever since you were little. The songs on the radio, what people were humming. You've always loved music, but that's all I know. Not every gift we have is extravagant. Some are more unassuming, quieter, but that doesn't mean they're less important. To me, your more obvious gift is painting, and I think you've seen evidence of that."

Mattie nodded and, feeling brave, asked, "Is some of your frustration with Mom because of Stephen?"

Penelope visibly stiffened. "That's an old story that doesn't bear repeating, but yes. I hoped to never see him again. It would have been easier."

"What would have been easier?"

"Living." Not waiting for Mattie to ask another question, Penelope said, "Have you given the tasks any more thought? I'm not sure we'll be able to bypass completing them, not legally, and I'd hate for you to forfeit your rightful inheritance."

Sunlight shone through the window and stretched across the hardwood floors. A small basket on the craft table was full of silver and gold sequins, and they sparkled in the light. The skirt of Mattie's birthday dress fluttered beneath the air-conditioning vent. Although the idea of staying any longer than necessary in Ivy Ridge hadn't appealed to her initially, she'd spent more than four months in the cities where she and Lilith lived. And staying for a little while in Ivy Ridge wouldn't be much different from all the times she'd spent summers here.

"The logical choice is to complete the tasks," Mattie said.

Penelope's face revealed her relief, and she agreed. "There are worse places than Ivy Ridge to spend a few weeks."

Being on the road alone, floating aimlessly without an end point, would be much worse. In Ivy Ridge Mattie had people—a family—who loved her. Everywhere else she lived Mattie had learned to keep a safe distance from people, her childhood friend, Julia, being her first painful lesson in why attachments were an unfavorable option.

A faded memory, held together with heartache and regret, materialized, and the sting of sadness still attached to it surprised her. Julia had been Mattie's best friend in kindergarten. The last day Mattie saw Julia she told her friend she was moving. The two best friends held hands and promised to be friends forever, and Mattie believed it. Julia's mom drove her away from the playground with Julia's hands pressed against the station wagon's window, tears causing her eyes and nose to run. Mattie never saw Julia again, and she realized at six years old that being friends forever wasn't possible and becoming too attached to people was a one-way trip to heartbreak.

It wasn't as though Mattie hadn't interacted with people since then. Some of them even called Mattie a friend, but she'd been careful not to get too close, not to be too involved in their lives.

It was undeniable that the inheritance money would significantly change her life. If Mattie stayed long enough to complete the tasks, she could also learn more about the Russell family gifts and about why Lilith chose Stephen Sloan out of hundreds of lawyers to probate the will. There were secrets still to unearth in Ivy Ridge, and Mattie's curiosity had taken hold of her and wasn't letting go.

Chapter 18

JONATHAN

JONATHAN STOOD AT THE WINDOW IN HIS CHILDHOOD bedroom. Sipping a mug of steaming coffee with a splash of heavy cream, he glanced at the alarm clock on the bedside table. Barely six in the morning and the rising sun lit the sky in shades of pink. He'd been up working for more than an hour already, answering emails and sending texts to clients and partners. After being in Ivy Ridge for a whole day, he could describe it in two words. *Quiet* and *slow*. More precisely, it was unnervingly quiet and painfully slow.

A single car motored up the street in front of his house, disrupting the stillness of the morning. When was the last time he'd heard birds singing? Two cardinals chirped at each other from the front yard. Last night while trying to fall asleep, he'd heard an owl hooting. Turning on a white noise app was the only way he could block out the lack of noise and finally sleep.

How did anyone live in this kind of quiet? How did they distract themselves from the inner dialogue that ran on a loop?

His childhood room hadn't changed much since he'd left for college. His mom had repainted the walls and replaced the bedding with a pattern she deemed "more suitable for a grown man." Weren't MLB bedsheets timeless? She'd changed out the kids' books on his bookshelf for contemporary fiction and travel books—nothing he'd read.

But she left a few mementos from his high school days, like the state championship trophy, a picture of his senior year baseball team, and a ticket stub from his spring break trip to watch the Braves' training. The boy in those pictures *knew* what his life was going to be like. He *knew* he'd be playing professional baseball, and his hometown would cheer his name while watching him on TV. If Jonathan could talk to that boy now, would he tell him that life was going to go sideways and baseball wouldn't be an option? Or would he let that boy keep dreaming?

Jonathan needed to get out of the house, to get his body moving and relieve the restlessness. At this time in the morning, it was doubtful he'd run into anyone. He left the room and grabbed his shoes, quietly closing the front door behind him. With his running playlist cued up, he started down the sidewalk at a steady pace. He could run through the neighborhood, down to the local park, past the baseball fields, and then circle back around the house. If his memory was correct, that path would be around seven miles.

As he neared the local park, he noticed a few dog walkers out for a misty morning stroll. One man raised his hand in a familiar wave and started talking as Jonathan neared. Should he slow down? Was the man even talking to him? Jonathan paused the music and slowed to a walk, and that's when he recognized his former high school baseball coach, Ricky Hunter.

"Jonathan?" Coach Hunter said. "I thought that was you. You've stayed in shape. Good for you."

"Coach," Jonathan said, pausing to pet the golden retriever that begged for his attention. "How're you? Still coaching?"

"I retired last year," he said. "But I already miss it. I still think about our glory days when you were playing. Never had a more talented player. You got us to the state championship."

Jonathan felt the ghost of an ache in his right leg. "The whole team got us to the championship."

Coach's dog stretched out his leash and sniffed a cluster of dandelions. "You were their leader though. You could rally them together like nobody else. We all knew you were going to be big. Remember that party we threw you right before college? Your mama made you a Braves jersey with your name on it, didn't she? As a stand-in until you got the real thing. They were so proud of you. We all were. Dadgum shame what happened. I bet you miss it. Last I heard you were in New York City planning parties."

"Promoting events," Jonathan corrected. *This* was exactly what he'd been avoiding for years. The pitying look on Coach's face. On *everyone's* faces. "I'm helping Dad for a few weeks while he's in recovery, then I'm back to Chicago where I run a successful business."

"Good for you," Coach said, reaching out and slapping Jonathan's arm. "I didn't picture you as a businessman, but if you run it like you played baseball, then you're gonna succeed. You were the only kid I ever coached who I knew could go pro."

Jonathan's gut twisted as he remembered how close he came to that dream and how easily it evaporated. "Good to see you, Coach, but I'd better get back to it. Got a full day of work ahead." Before Coach could say anything more, Jonathan cued up his music and jogged off, trying to shake off his irritation at the conversation.

Back at the house Jonathan showered, changed into a T-shirt and shorts, and gathered up his laptop and cell phone. Virginia was in the kitchen steeping a tea bag in a ceramic mug decorated with a turquoise star and the words *Super Mom*.

"I'm going to Deja Brew to work for a while," Jonathan said. "It's too quiet here. I need more activity."

"It's a bit toned down here from Chicago," Virginia said.

"Total understatement," he agreed. "Call if you need anything."

"Activity is good," she said. "But sometimes staying busy is just a means to distract ourselves from what we really need to focus on."

Jonathan zipped his laptop bag and slipped it over his shoulder. "Is that some kind of passive-aggressive statement meant to make me look inward? It's not working," he said with a grin. "Can I borrow the car?"

"Keys are in my purse in the hall," Virginia said, smiling over the rim of her mug. "Deja Brew is a good choice. You remember your high school friend Jamie? He and his wife own it now. They'll be happy to see you and catch up. I bet you haven't talked to him since you played ball together."

Jonathan hesitated. Another conversation about baseball or his career or how great Ivy Ridge had expected him to be? "Maybe I'll skip the coffee shop and work in the backyard. There's shade back there."

"Is this a good time to add in another passive-aggressive statement about avoidance?" Virginia's chuckle followed him out of the kitchen.

Chapter 19

MATTIE

MATTIE SPENT THE NEXT WEEK UNPACKING HER BOXES, moving into her bedroom, and releasing as much built-up frustration and confusion as she could. Focusing on the little details, like hanging her clothes in the closet and filling the dresser, kept her mind off the sadness too. Mattie fell into a new rhythm, which was a skill she'd honed over the years. Moving from town to town, she adapted to her surroundings like a shape-shifter among the people. She could figure out quickly where she fell into the order of things and fit herself into the flow of life in each city. Because she'd been to Ivy Ridge dozens of times, sorting out her place within the Russell house and the town was even easier.

Mattie lined the few pairs of shoes she had along the closet floor. She set up an easel near the windows in case she wanted to paint in her bedroom instead of in the art studio upstairs. A blank canvas watched her movements from near the sun-washed windowpanes.

She'd decide what to do with her mom's things later, but for now, she put Lilith's boxes in the closet. She purposefully stacked the boxes to hide the names painted on the wall—the names the house wouldn't let anyone erase.

Mattie had returned the rental car and had also been helping Penelope and Sophia with final arrangements and paperwork that needed to be completed for Lilith's death. There were so many steps that Mattie had never thought about, like ordering a headstone, requesting multiple copies of the death certificate, contacting the Social Security Administration, canceling Lilith's driver's license, and finding a local accountant who could help them file taxes for Lilith and her estate.

Because they held the funeral service so quickly and invited only close friends, there hadn't been time to run an official obituary in the local paper before the funeral. Sophia and Robert took care of writing it, and the newspaper had printed it a few days ago. A copy of the paper was folded and tucked inside one of her mom's boxes. More food and flowers arrived at the Russell house. The parlor resembled a florist's shop, and the intense perfume of the blooms was enough to knock Mattie backward as soon as she stepped into the space.

When Penelope wasn't finalizing Lilith's business, she spent hours in her sewing room, catching up on projects she'd put aside for a few days while they sorted through the bulk of funerary responsibilities. New projects kept her sewing late into the night too. As odd as it was, it seemed Lilith's death had created more seamstress work for Penelope. Mattie wondered if losing a sister positioned Penelope to the town in a way they'd never thought of her before—as a normal human capable of loss and grief.

After waking up this morning, Mattie decided that today was the day to start the seven tasks. The only way to get her life going again and move toward her future would be to play by the rules Lilith left behind. Although she didn't have to complete them in the order they were written, the first task seemed to be the easiest to tackle.

This task required Mattie to find the twelve flowers on the list and plant them in the Russell garden. Mattie recognized that the flowers were significant to each city they'd called home. Was this Lilith's way of helping Mattie fondly recall memories of where they'd been? Right now reminiscing felt like being dragged over thorns. Sadness lurked around every corner, hid under furniture, ready to spring out at her, and every happy memory was accompanied by an ache. Mattie wanted to focus on the first task and approach it in a clinical way, keeping her heart as detached from the process as possible . . . but could she?

The flowers held varying degrees of significance. Some of them were flowers that had grown in the nearby park or along the sidewalk where they lived. A few flowers she remembered from hikes with her mom or bouquets sold at the flower shop she passed every day on her way to school.

Accompanying the task of collecting specific flowers was the additional strange requirement of including a random number or symbol staked with each plant marker. Mattie's mind whirled with possible reasons for the numbers. Were they a code? A wayward Sudoku puzzle? The number of times Mattie would feel frustrated with these tasks?

Robert offered Mattie his truck for her nursery scavenger hunt. She found him and Sophia in the kitchen sharing a breakfast of coffee and jasmine green tea served with an eater's choice of buttermilk pancakes, sliced banana bread, or avocado toast. Mattie's appetite was slowly returning, so she ate a pancake and a fat slice of banana bread before leaving them sitting in the breakfast nook.

With the flower list tucked into her pocket, she drove to Green Clover. On this midweek morning, the nursery was nearly abandoned. Her tennis shoes crunched along the plant rows, and Mattie saw only a couple of people, who appeared to be employees. The air smelled like freshly tilled earth and damp soil. When the wind blew from the east, she caught a whiff of magnolia blooms and roses. She stopped beside a wooden table covered in potted succulents like aloe, gasteria, and gorgeous pink-tinged aeonium.

"Good morning!" a young woman said as she stepped between a row of white and pale purple blooms on clematis plants. Their skinny green limbs twisted up miniature lattice pieces.

The young woman looked about Mattie's age with shoulder-length brown hair. A green headband held back her glossy waves. She was a few inches shorter than Mattie and enviously curvier than Mattie's straight figure. Over the left breast pocket of her work polo, neat stitching displayed the nursery logo—a four-leaf clover—and the name *Lucy*.

Her chocolate-brown eyes were large and round, framed by long, thick lashes. Combined with her button nose, high cheek-bones, and full pink lips, she resembled a comic book heroine who was in her regular-person daytime disguise. Mattie had just started imagining what Lucy's superhero costume would be—a shiny green design—when the girl interrupted her thoughts. "Can I help you find anything?"

Mattie glanced down at her list. She didn't want help because that would involve mindless chitchat. Rather than being completely rude, though, she answered, "I'm looking for flowers."

The young woman gave Mattie a thumbs-up. "Good news! You're in the right place. I'm Lucy, short for Lucia. Most people call me Lucy, though, or Lou-Lou. My mama calls me Bugaboo-Lou, but that's more than I intended to share." She laughed at herself and continued, "I'm the head florist here, but it's a slow morning, and when that happens, I come outside to help wherever I'm needed. Any specific flowers you're looking for?"

Having Lucy's help would expedite the process. The sooner

she completed the task, the sooner she could start the next one, and the sooner she could get on her way. Mattie handed Lucy the handwritten list of twelve flowers.

"Wow," Lucy said, "this is an interesting assortment."

Mattie agreed. "There are wildflowers, traditional Southern flowers, summer bloomers, fall bloomers, some that thrive out West, and others that are better for warmer climates."

Lucy slid her finger down the paper. "Are these for something special or flowers you've always wanted to plant in your yard? Or did you flip through a gardening magazine, close your eyes, and point?"

Mattie chuckled despite her attempt to remain slightly disengaged. Lucy's peppy personality was hard to ignore and also welcome after so much gloom. Her honeyed Southern accent was disarming, making Mattie feel like Lucy was someone she could trust with her secrets. Not that Mattie planned on sharing *any* of her secrets, but if she wanted to . . . "There are reasons for the choices. Do you have all of them?"

"We do," Lucy said with a megawatt smile. "We advertise that we have anything you're looking for, and it's true. If we don't have it here on the property, we can order it and get it here lickety-split. Follow me." Lucy motioned over her shoulder for Mattie to follow as she walked off. Mattie hustled to catch up. "Wanna share the reason for the choices, or is it top secret? I love a good mystery."

Mattie laughed, surprising herself. Unexpectedly she felt compelled to share the truth with Lucy, which was the opposite of what she would usually do. Access to her private life had always been off limits. "My mom left a will with requirements."

Lucy stopped walking abruptly. "You lost your mom? I'm so sorry."

Her genuine sympathy caused warmth to spread through Mattie's chest. "Thank you. A couple of weeks ago. My name is Mattie, by the way."

Lucy's expression shifted to recognition. "Are you Lilith Russell's daughter?" Mattie nodded. "I made the floral arrangements for the funeral."

"You did?" Mattie said. "They were beautiful."

Lucy's smile returned, and Mattie felt a kinship forming between them. "Thank you. What do these flowers have to do with her will, if you don't mind me asking?"

"It's a weird story," Mattie admitted.

"I *love* weird," Lucy said. "Besides, I bet it's more interesting than it is weird. The peonies are over there. What color? Talk while we walk. We have everything on the list, but they're scattered all over the place. Plenty of time for you to tell your story . . . if you want to."

Mattie realized that she *did* want to share the story with Lucy. While they grabbed a flat nursery cart and pulled it all over the grounds, Mattie explained the unexpected testamentary trust and the seven tasks she had to complete by the end of December. It felt good to be honest with someone outside of her family about how ridiculous and sad and unusual the requirements were.

With a cart full of flowers, Mattie followed Lucy to a checkout station. After promising Penelope she would pay her back once she received the inheritance, Mattie had agreed to use her aunt's credit card for any expenses accrued because of the tasks. At the counter she noticed a stack of flyers advertising an upcoming Green Planet Initiative event in mid-September. She picked up a flyer and read it.

"You should come!" Lucy said while she rang up the flowers and returned them to the cart. "The nursery hosts a few events in the spring and fall. For this next one we'll be planting a butterfly garden and local trees—hey, wasn't that one of your tasks? To create a beautiful environment?"

Sophia's advice to keep her eyes open for signs came to mind. "What are the chances?"

"Coincidental?" Lucy asked. Then, lowering her voice to a conspiratorial whisper, she added, "Or destiny?"

"Do you believe in destiny?" Mattie asked, half teasing.

"You bet I do!" Lucy said without hesitation. "The initiative is my brother and dad's brainchild. They've been doing this for the past couple of years. Luca, my brother, studied to be a plant geneticist. He's working on his master's while assisting at the university. His current project conducts research, and he's also a TA. As if that isn't awesome enough, he also works in the nonprofit sector researching ways to benefit people who live in areas where it's difficult to grow plants and crops. He talked my dad into hosting this initiative to better the lives of others, starting at home in Ivy Ridge."

"What does your dad do?" Mattie asked, rolling up the flyer and sliding it in between the plants on the cart.

"This is his place, Green Clover," Lucy answered. "Owner and head landscape architect."

"And you're the head florist," Mattie said. "That's cool that you all work together and in the same field."

Lucy scanned the barcode on the last plant. "I'm not in the same league as they are. A geneticist and an architect? I just arrange flowers in vases."

Mattie stared at her for a few beats without replying. Lucy told her the purchase total, and Mattie slid the credit card through the machine. "It's not comparable," she said. "Your job and theirs. It's like comparing oranges to apples. Sure, they're both fruit, but each has its own stand-out unique qualities. I'd argue that you do more than arrange flowers in vases. You bring joy and happiness to people. You help them show love and sympathy. I saw the arrangements you made for Mom, and they spoke to people in a way nothing else can."

Lucy's eyes filled with tears, and Mattie felt a wash of embarrassment. She wasn't usually so open to emotional chat. "Wow, that's really sweet, Mattie. I'm glad we met today."

"Me too," Mattie said honestly. Lucy helped load the flowers into the back of Robert's truck and waved goodbye as Mattie pulled out of the parking lot and headed back to the house.

Mattie parked Robert's truck against the curb. She lowered the tailgate and gathered a couple of smaller pots in her arms, then started toward the side gate to take them to the backyard. When she reached the edge of the curb, her tennis shoe slipped and she pitched forward. Though she managed not to fall, the potted bleeding heart tumbled from her arms and bounced against the sidewalk, spilling half its dirt on the concrete. She steadied herself and bent down to clean up the mess. The slap of tennis shoes against the pavement pulled Mattie's attention away from scooping palmfuls of dirt back into the bleeding heart's pot.

A man wearing a red ball cap and sunglasses jogged up the sidewalk. He slowed his pace as he approached Mattie. Pulling out his wireless headphones, he asked, "Need a hand?"

"I'm good," Mattie said, motioning for him to go around the mess.

He glanced at the truck bed full of pots and up at the Russell house, then back at her. He removed his sunglasses and hooked them into the collar of his sweaty T-shirt. Every hair on Mattie's head stood on end, and her heart beat a wild rhythm in her chest.

She rose to her full height, cradling the potted bleeding heart in her arms.

"Mattie?" the man asked.

She knew that voice, that smile, that dimple in his cheek. "Jonathan." It wasn't a question.

Chapter 20

JONATHAN

JONATHAN'S SMILE WIDENED. HE COULDN'T BELIEVE WHO was standing on the sidewalk in Ivy Ridge. He hadn't seen Mattie Russell since he was in high school. She'd been a teenager, and even then, Jonathan had been taken by her beauty. He felt stunned by how attractive she was now.

Unlike the girls he knew in the city who went to the gym wearing full makeup and styled hair, Mattie looked fresh and natural with pink in her cheeks caused by the heat. She wore a plain white tank top, black nylon shorts, and white tennis shoes. Her long hair was braided in a single thick plait down her back, and sunglasses hid what he remembered would be pale blue-green eyes. She was a knockout despite the frown that pulled down her lips and the deep crease between her brows.

He stepped closer to her. "I haven't seen you in, what, ten years? Since I went to college?"

Mattie leaned down to pick up a potted daisy from the sidewalk. "Something like that." She adjusted the pots in her arms like she was creating a barrier between them.

Jonathan looked at the Russell house, and she made a move toward the side yard like someone fleeing a conversation she didn't want to have. He felt compelled to keep her talking. "Are you living here now?"

"No," she said. "I'm only here for a little while."

The disappointment that sprang up inside him caught him off guard. "Yeah, me too."

Mattie glanced toward the side yard again and shifted her feet. Obvious signs of someone who had no interest in a catch-up session. Why did that intensify his displeasure? It had been years since he'd seen her and they'd spent less than an hour together one night. But how many times had he thought of that kiss?

"I came home to be with my family," Jonathan said, taking a wild gamble by playing the sympathy card.

Mattie's body visibly relaxed, and her expression softened. "How's your dad?" As if to explain how she knew about his personal life, she added, "My family and I were the ones who helped your mom that day."

Her discomfort with him made him cautious but also curious. He remembered her being forthright and bold, not a timid woman who scurried away from conversation. "He's home now," Jonathan said. "Resting mostly. The doctors are projecting a slow recovery, but my mom is hopeful it'll be faster than they predict. Dad is a tough one and focused on getting well. This hit him hard, but together, he and my mom are a tenacious team."

Mattie's smile was slow, and the way the movement of her lips lifted her cheeks captivated him. "That's good to hear."

How could he prolong that smile? What would keep her attention on him? He walked to the tailgate and pointed at the plants. "Sure you don't need help?"

"I'm sure," she said firmly. "Go finish your run. I'm all good here."

Her obstinance about not wanting help amused him and reminded him of the first time they met. She hadn't wanted to help him that Halloween night either. "My run is finished. Why make so many trips back and forth when you could cut the work in half?" Without waiting for her to object, he leaned into the truck bed and slid two pots toward him. He picked them up and motioned with his head toward the backyard. "Consider it a thank-you for helping my parents. Lead the way."

She stared at him without speaking, then huffed and stomped through the grass. Progress! She slowed long enough to lift the latch on the gate and pull it open.

"I guess you're helping out with gardening while you're home," Jonathan said, trying to make easy conversation with her even though she was giving off *leave me alone* vibes. "Family bonding?"

"In a way."

Jonathan followed Mattie into the Russells' backyard, which brought back a rush of memories from the night they met. The decorations had been different then. The pumpkins and gourds were gone now, and the pile of maple leaves that his friends had fallen into had crumbled back into the earth. There were still string lights in the trees, and the table where they'd sat eating cake had been upgraded but was still positioned on the flagstones where he remembered.

The greenhouse plants looked like blurry green paint splotches through the milky glass. He could still recall the smell of potting soil and herbs from when they hid in the dark. Colorful flowers grew wild in the backyard flower beds, yet there was order to the chaos. Everything, including the grass, was well manicured.

Mattie stopped walking and gazed around the garden in silence.

Jonathan stood beside her, subtly taking in her figure. She'd grown a few more inches since high school, but so had he. Now the top of her head reached his chin. "Where are you planting these?"

She lifted her shoulders and swiped her free hand across her sweaty brow. "No idea. The garden is full."

He stepped away from her and noticed spots here and there where a plant could be squeezed in between others, but why had she bought so many plants if the garden was already full? "There's always room for one more," he said. "Or a dozen. I've learned that in my line of work. It might *look* like there isn't space, but we find a space we didn't know we had. Where do you want these for now?"

Mattie pointed at the flagstones. "Let's put them on the patio in the shade. I'll grab the rest. Thanks for your help, but seriously, you can go home and . . . take a shower."

Jonathan placed his pots in the shade. He looked down at his sweaty clothes. His T-shirt was damp and sticking to his chest and abdomen. He pinched the fabric between his fingers and pulled it away from his skin, then he flapped it, sending ripples of air up his shirt. "Are you implying I stink?"

"Do you?"

His confidence was boosted when she focused a smile on him. "How long are you staying in Ivy Ridge?"

Mattie put down her pots beside his and headed back toward the truck. "Until December, but I might leave sooner."

Jonathan matched her stride. She was quick, and he wondered if she'd make a good running partner. "That's specific and yet not specific at all."

She side-eyed him. "How long are *you* staying?"

"Until mid-September, but I might leave sooner."

"That's specific and yet not specific at all," she echoed.

They shared a smile, and Jonathan said, "I see what you did there." Standing beside her at the tailgate, he slid more plants their way.

Mattie pulled the pots toward her. "You don't have to keep helping."

"You don't have to keep telling me that," Jonathan said. "If I didn't want to help, I wouldn't." They grabbed another armful of plants and returned to the backyard. With each minute he spent talking to her, more pieces of that night with her came back to him. "This place looks pretty much like I remember. Only things missing are a full moon and the birthday cake."

Mattie turned her gaze to him with an expression of shock that parted her lips.

"What?" he asked, not understanding her surprise.

Mattie placed her pots with the growing group. She headed for the remaining flowers in the truck. "That was a long time ago."

Jonathan called out to her, and she slowed her pace. "I never forgot about that night."

"You never came back home," she said and then looked embarrassed by her candidness.

Memories rushed through his head like a montage. What had they said to each other? The kiss had outshone everything else, and he recalled that moment well. But the rest of the night had faded into a dreamlike remembrance. He'd unexpectedly had to attend college summer classes after high school graduation, which wasn't how he wanted to spend his summer. But to keep his scholarship and train with the team, there hadn't been a choice. Had Mattie looked for him that summer? "I—" From its hidden spot inside his running shorts, his cell phone started playing the song "Everywhere" by Fleetwood Mac. He pulled out the phone and unlocked the screen. A YouTube video was playing, but how?

"Lively ringtone," Mattie said as she grabbed the potted hydrangea and peony.

"It's not my ringtone," he admitted. "I have no idea how that happened."

Mattie's smile vanished and she stared at his phone like it might explode in his hand. He slipped it back into his pocket and grabbed the remaining plants. He followed Mattie around the house into the backyard.

Penelope opened the back porch door and came down the steps. She resembled Mattie, but Penelope's facial features were less edgy. Mattie was leggier than Penelope, who was petite and toned like a woman in her forties who took care of her body, a fair representation of what Mattie could look like in twenty years—still setting fires in the hearts of men without trying. They shared the same long, almost-black hair and light eyes that were borderline spooky. Pale blue-green irises ringed in smoky gray that watched the world with an intensity that made Jonathan squirm.

"Hey, Jonathan," Penelope said. "Your mom said you were home. It's good to see you. How's your dad doing?"

Jonathan updated Penelope and then felt her appearance was probably his cue to go. She intimidated him with her steady gaze. It gave him the feeling she was reading his thoughts, and he needed to get out of there before she uncovered his thoughts about Mattie. He said goodbye, but when he reached the side gate, he glanced back to see Mattie was watching him leave. "It's great to see you again, Mattie."

Uncertainty shone in her expression. "It was unexpected."

He plucked his sunglasses off his collar and slid them back onto his face. "Someone once told me that most of the best things are."

Once inside his house, Jonathan found his mom in the kitchen preparing lunch. The space smelled spicy like diced jalapeños and chili powder. The fixings for tacos were laid out on the countertop. "What's for lunch? Burritos? There aren't any taco shells."

Virginia pointed at a plastic clamshell container packed full of butter lettuce. "Lettuce wraps. I'm working on changing your dad's diet."

Jonathan picked up a package of uncooked tofu and chuckled. "Is this fake meat?"

"Shh," Virginia said, taking the package from Jonathan. "Don't tell your dad. What he doesn't know . . ."

Jonathan grabbed a glass from the cabinet. Using the dispenser on the fridge, he filled it with ice and water. "Mattie Russell is back home."

Virginia placed a skillet on the cooktop and turned on the burner. She sliced open the imposter meat package and dropped the mystery meatless rectangle into the pan. "Oh, I don't believe this is her home, honey. She only came here for the funeral."

The world around him slowed like someone had switched life to half speed. Jonathan lowered the glass from his lips. "Who died?"

Virginia grabbed a wooden spoon from the canister beside the stove. She started breaking up the block of nonmeat as it sizzled on the heat. "Her mom."

"Seriously?" Jonathan's stomach sank. He remembered the feeling he'd had when David called him about his dad's stroke. Mattie's mom was gone, permanently. She wasn't home recovering like his dad. "When?"

Virginia turned on the exhaust fan above the stove and it whirred to life, filling the kitchen with a steady hum of white noise. "A couple weeks ago."

Jonathan put his empty glass in the sink. He'd been trying to flirt with her, and she'd just lost her mom. Her coolness toward him made more sense now. She was grieving. "No wonder she's so . . ."

His mom pushed the food around in the pan, and then she left it to cook. She arranged curved cups of lettuce on a platter. "So quiet?"

Jonathan leaned against the counter and crossed his arms. "That's one way of describing it."

"Get the sweet tea out of the fridge, please," Virginia said. "She keeps to herself. That whole family does, always has. They're good people, though, and they've always helped us when we needed it. We couldn't have asked for better neighbors." His mother gave him a knowing look. "Mattie is a beautiful girl."

Jonathan returned her look and pulled two cookies out of the jar. Yes, she most definitely was beautiful, but he wasn't going to let his mom think he wanted a matchmaker.

She returned her attention to the pan. "Don't spoil your dinner."

"Mom, I'm not a kid anymore."

She pointed her wooden spoon at him. "You'll always be *my* kid. Put one of those back and go see your dad."

Jonathan grunted his displeasure but dropped one cookie back into the jar like an obedient son, left the kitchen, and walked up the stairs. From the window at the second-floor landing, Jonathan caught movement in the Russells' backyard. Mattie hugged a potted vivid-orange geranium in her arms. Penelope was talking and pointing toward a corner in the garden, and Mattie nodded. Penelope said something that made Mattie laugh, and Jonathan moved closer to the window. All the beautiful girls he'd met in Chicago *knew* they were beautiful and most of them used it as a method of manipulation to get whatever they wanted, but Mattie seemed oblivious to the way she could stop traffic or make Jonathan's mind go blank. Then, as though she could sense his presence, she glanced up at the window and they locked eyes.

Jonathan quickly backed away from the window. "Great, now she'll think you're a creep," he muttered.

"Who's a creep?" his dad, Thomas, asked with a slight slur from behind Jonathan in the hallway. His dad's hair had become grayer and thinner since the last time Jonathan had seen him. The lines around his eyes had spread and deepened, and the dimple in his cheek had become permanently etched into his skin. Thomas's posture leaned slightly to the left, which revealed the area of his body where the stroke had caused paralysis, only temporarily they hoped. His left arm hung loosely at his side, and his left cheek drooped, causing half of his mouth to sag downward, but his eyes were bright and alert.

"Are you supposed to be out of bed?"

"I'm not an invalid," Thomas said in a huff. "They told me I should keep my body moving throughout the day. A body that isn't used starts to fall apart, like an old house. Is that cookie for me?"

Jonathan sighed and handed his dad the cookie.

"Don't tell your mom." He bit into the cookie and closed his eyes, enjoying the chocolatey goodness of a favorite family recipe.

Jonathan chuckled. "And risk her wrath? No thanks. But if she finds out, you didn't get that cookie from me."

Thomas finished the forbidden treat in another bite. "I'm supposed to be eating only green stuff. Vegan diet, they suggested."

Jonathan grimaced. "Sounds like torture."

"That's what I said." Thomas walked to the banister and peered down into the foyer. "What's for lunch? It smells good."

Jonathan took a quick glance at the window. Penelope and Mattie were now out of view. "Don't ask. Just eat it."

Thomas walked toward his office door. "Come sit with me. Let's talk about the business. Mine and yours."

Jonathan followed his dad into the office. He pointed at the corner of the desk. "Where is your candy jar?" His dad gave him an exasperated look. "She didn't throw them away, did she? What if we *need* them?"

Thomas slowly lowered himself into his desk chair, bracing his right hand on the armrest. He glanced toward the door, making sure Virginia wouldn't pop around the corner, before he opened a desk drawer and pulled out a small glass jar full of Jolly Ranchers. He opened the lid and removed two wrapped pieces of candy. "Watermelon or green apple?"

"Green apple, and I'll take a blue raspberry if you have one." Jonathan reached over and took the offered candy. "I need extra thinking power today." He unwrapped the green hard candy first and popped it into his mouth.

This ritual was one that Thomas had been doing since he was a kid. Jolly Ranchers were a special occasion treat growing up and given to Thomas when he needed to focus on something, mostly his homework. To his surprise, and to the pleasure of his sweet tooth, the brittle, translucent candies always helped him succeed. Believing they held a kind of lucky charm magic, Thomas continued eating them as an adult for good luck, focus, and victory, and he passed the belief on to his kids.

Thomas unwrapped the watermelon candy. He handed the paper to Jonathan. "To hide the evidence. Your mom will sniff it out on me." After putting the candy into his mouth and savoring the sweet flavor, he said, "I know you can't stay here and help out forever, but I sure wouldn't say no if you wanted to."

"Dad," Jonathan said, pocketing the candy wrappers, "my life is in Chicago."

"Is it?" Thomas asked. "Or is your *work life* there?"

Jonathan bit back a groan and dropped into one of the leather armchairs. "What's the difference?"

"Huge difference. A work life with no life outside of work isn't much of a life, is it?"

"Depends on who you ask," Jonathan grumbled. "I'm doing well financially. *Really* well. I have enough money to get anything I want."

Thomas hummed in his throat. "You know what the Beatles say."

"Here comes the sun?"

Thomas chuckled. "Money can't buy love."

"When did you get so sentimental?" Jonathan joked.

"When did you get so apathetic to love? Regardless, I can't control your mom trying to set you up with local girls while you're here. Anything to make you stick around."

Jonathan puffed out his cheeks and released the air. "She's already started. She mentioned Mattie Russell, Penelope's niece."

Thomas's lips lifted on one side. "Pretty girl, but she's never stayed longer than a few months. But that might work for you since you don't plan to be here long either. Summer crush."

Jonathan laughed. "Seriously, Dad? A summer crush? What am I, seventeen?"

"Son, take it from an old man—you are *never* too old to entertain a crush. In fact, I encourage you to pursue it. Now, let's get down to the real business." He opened his laptop and clicked the keyboard before turning it around so Jonathan could see the screen. "I know you gave up a lot of business and put your life on hold to be here, and I appreciate it. Your mom and your brothers do too. Here's a rundown of the next few weeks. Do you think you can handle these and run my team at the office?"

Jonathan scrolled through the schedule and the list of tasks needed for each booking. The events were straightforward and considerably more moderate than the wild, over-the-top shindigs he pulled off in the city. "Easy as pie," he said with a nod.

"As easy as pursuing a summer crush."

Jonathan leaned back in the chair. "I'm not saying I want to, but I don't think there's anything easy about pursuing Mattie Russell."

"A challenge then," Thomas said with a wink. Virginia called up the stairs that lunch was ready, and Jonathan offered his dad a hand out of the chair. At the second-floor landing Thomas paused and gazed out the window. Mattie and Penelope, trowels in hand, were planting the new flowers in the backyard. "Maybe it's because you were the youngest and needed to prove yourself, but you never turned down any challenge your brothers gave you. Not even when you knew you couldn't possibly win."

"I'm leaving in a few weeks," Jonathan said.

Thomas grabbed the staircase handrail and started down the steps with his other hand on Jonathan's arm for support. "I don't even know what I'm having for lunch today. How can you possibly know what will happen in a few weeks?"

Chapter 21

MATTIE

MATTIE DROVE THE FINAL SKINNY WOODEN STAKE INTO the ground beside the coneflower. Then she knelt on the grass and, using a black marker, wrote the number 5 on a laminated notecard. With Penelope's staple gun, she attached the card to the stake. A humid breeze blew through the garden and knocked the coneflower blooms against the lavender, its closest neighbor. Mattie's body relaxed as the scent of the herb filled the space around her.

She stood and surveyed the yard, letting her gaze find all twelve of the new flowers. Penelope had helped her locate spots where they could squeeze in the additions since the Russell garden was already thriving and full of established plants. Enid basked in the sunshine near a patch of Shasta daisies and lazily batted at a butterfly. Mattie knelt and scratched the cat's stomach, causing Enid to purr.

"All done."

Sophia sat at the patio table drinking fresh lemonade and flipping through a magazine. Her straw sun hat cast a wide circle of shadow over her shoulders. "Any revelations about the numbers?"

Mattie shook her head. "Penelope and I are going with our latest guess, lottery numbers."

Sophia's cheeks lifted, pushing her red-rimmed sunglasses higher on her face. "Have we ruled out latitude and longitude coordinates to a buried treasure? Oh, speaking of unexpected treasure, when I went into town today, I saw The Pizza Box is hosting a cooking class next week. Isn't that on your task list? You have to sign up in person, though, or I would have signed you up myself."

Mattie sat in the chair across from Sophia and wiped her sweaty face on her shirtsleeve. Then she sagged against the chair back. "That's peculiar, isn't it?"

"That you have to sign up in person? No. They don't want someone signing up anyone without their permission."

"That's not what I mean," Mattie said. "The will requires me to attend *specifically* a pizza cooking class, and the local place coincidentally offers one next week?"

Sophia lifted the drinking glass to her lips and smiled against the rim. "Not coincidental. Synchronistic."

Mattie rolled her eyes, but the timing of these events was eerie. She thought of the flyer from the nursery upstairs in her room. She *just happened* to buy flowers from Green Clover today to fulfill a task on the list, and Green Clover *just happened* to be offering a weekend activity that would satisfy another task requirement.

Penelope came outside carrying a tray with two glasses of ice and a pitcher of lemonade. She placed the tray on the table and refilled Sophia's glass before filling the other two. Mattie drank half her glass in one gulp.

"I saw that Jonathan Carlisle is home," Sophia said. "And we were just talking about how he hadn't been home in years. I suppose he's come home to check on his dad."

"He's helping out with the family business too. And helping Mattie carry plants," Penelope said with a hint of a smile. She twisted her hair into a loose bun on top of her head and used a hair tie to keep it in place.

The acidity of the lemonade burned Mattie's throat and she coughed. "I told you I didn't ask him to."

"How polite of him," Sophia said. Her red lips lifted in an amused smile. "I wonder how long he's staying."

"Mid-September," Mattie answered. When Penelope and Sophia turned surprised expressions on her, Mattie added, "He mentioned that while he was *politely* carrying plants."

"Perhaps we'll see more of him then," Sophia said. "You should invite him over for Penelope's lemonade. This is the best I've ever had and a welcome relief from this heat."

"Thank you," Penelope said. "It's the honey I use as the sweetener. I bet the house would like to see him."

"The house?" Mattie said with a laugh.

Penelope lifted one shoulder. "I was thinking about your bedroom closet and the house's insistence that we not paint over the names. Seems it has a fondness for our neighbor."

"What names?" Sophia asked.

Mattie quickly stood, not wanting to fill Sophia in on a silly, impulsive thing she'd done as a kid or discuss why the house might want to have Jonathan over for reminiscing. "I'm going to shower and go into town to register for that class. Might as well keep moving forward with getting these tasks done. Who knows? The way these events are lining up, I might be done before December."

Sophia agreed. "It does appear that a lot is aligning, even Jonathan being home."

Mattie's stomach somersaulted. Why did it feel like she'd reverted back to a nervous, giddy teenager? "That's not connected at all."

Penelope snorted into her glass of lemonade, and Sophia's smile caused Mattie to scowl. "Oh, darling, everything is connected. Once you stop resisting it, you'll see he's home for a reason."

"He's here for his dad," Mattie argued.

"That's true, but I'd hazard a guess that the reason is multi-layered," Sophia said, lifting her glass in a toast. Penelope clinked their glasses together.

Mattie hurried off. She wasn't going to entertain thoughts about Jonathan's return being somehow connected to *her* return. Just thinking about him again made her insides jumpy. The attractive young boy from her memory had grown into an even handsomer man, the kind of handsome she always avoided. Mattie had no desire to have her heart broken, not again.

She put her glass in the kitchen sink and noticed a stack of mail on the island. A glossy cover poked out from the bottom of the pile, and she slid it out. A home design and decor magazine showcased an upscale, sophisticated front porch decorated with a tasteful Halloween display. What caught her eye on the magazine's shiny front cover were the carved pumpkins. Mattie thought about the story of her being dropped off on the Russells' front porch, tucked into a pumpkin cradle. She knew the story was make-believe and she had a mother and a father. Being in Ivy Ridge this time triggered a growing desire to learn more.

Music drifted down the staircase and pulled Mattie toward the sound. She followed it to the third floor. Mattie found Robert strumming his guitar in the music room. A portable satellite radio player broadcast a baseball game at low volume. His laptop was open on the desk, and a screensaver with the word *hello* in rainbow letters stretched across the screen. As a retired financial adviser, Robert didn't work much, but he'd never been able to quit completely. He took consulting jobs to keep his mind busy, but now he had the freedom to work from anywhere he wanted and take breaks to play guitar. She listened to him strum through a few bars of music before interrupting his alone time. "Two questions: Is that the Braves game, and do you think I should find my father?"

Robert startled and then laughed at his own alarm. He lowered the guitar and balanced it on his lap. "Skip right to the good parts, I see. No hellos or how-are-yous? Yes, the Braves are playing today. It's 1–0, Braves."

"They're having a good year. Think they'll make it back to the Series?"

Robert nodded. "I'd love to get my hands on those tickets if they do. As for your father, that's up to you. Sure, we've all been curious now and then, but we know it's your decision."

Mattie stepped farther into the room and lifted a wooden clock from a bookshelf. A dust-free outline remained behind, marking its place. The hands had stopped moving, freezing time at eleven forty-five for years. Flipping it over, she saw there was a place for batteries, so she popped open the back. It was empty. "Why haven't we ever replaced the batteries so this works?"

"Have you seen this room?" Robert asked. "It's a time warp back to thirty-some years ago. When Douglas and Elena died, many things stopped moving forward, and not just that clock. We've gotten stuck in old ways for too long. It's time for things to start moving again. Like you moving toward a chance to know your father."

Mattie returned the clock to the shelf. "What makes you think I want to know him?"

Robert placed the guitar into its case and looked at her with his piercing periwinkle-blue eyes. "You're up here asking about him, aren't you? That means you're curious, which means you're opening up to the idea. It doesn't matter to me which way you choose, but what if you had the option of learning more about him?"

"Mom didn't think it mattered," Mattie said, "or she would have told me. Unless . . . unless you don't think she knew who the father was." A sinking feeling cramped her stomach. She hadn't considered that Lilith might have had multiple flings during high school and therefore might have been unable to pinpoint Mattie's actual father.

Robert shook his head. "Lilith wasn't a *loose woman* as the old folks say." He smiled when Mattie chuckled. "I didn't make up that description, but you understand the meaning. Lilith was flirtatious, but she didn't hang around with lots of boys. In fact, that's why it's so difficult to know the truth. She was secretive and sneaky, like she never intended for anyone to know she was dating at all." Robert shrugged. "Or maybe the boy didn't want people to know about *her*. Wouldn't be the first person to keep their relationship with a Russell woman a secret."

"Why? What's wrong with Russell women?" Mattie asked defensively.

"Not a dang thing," Robert said. He stretched out his long legs and folded his arms behind his head. "But they aren't for the weak. Most men can't handle them or can't keep up."

"But you can," Mattie teased.

"I'm still here, aren't I?" A long pause stretched between them. "So what do you say? Are you interested in finding out who your father is?"

A stab of fear entered Mattie's heart. "What if he doesn't want to know me? What if he's a total jerk who tells me to take a long walk off a short bridge?"

"Then he's a moron, and we'll have Sophia put a hex on him."

Mattie gasped. "Can she *do* that?"

Robert's laugh boomed through the room and out into the hallway. "Lord, no, but the thought of it would scare him in all the right ways."

"Where do we start?"

Robert leaned his elbows on his thighs. Then he plucked a few of the guitar strings and hummed. "I think Lilith left clues—or *signs* as Sophia likes to say. Maybe in those boxes from the attic, the ones you took to your room. Or in the stuff you brought from Chicago. Penelope might have more ideas. You know she doesn't like to push, but she'll burn the midnight oil helping you with anything if she knows you're interested. Could be you'll find answers with those tasks."

"The tasks?" Mattie asked. "How would those random jobs be connected to my father?"

Robert's smile was slow and easy. "Lilith never did anything randomly. She was clever. Very clever. I'd be willing to bet a gallon of homemade peach ice cream that those *tasks* in the will are more like bread crumbs leading you somewhere."

"Leading me where?"

"I don't know for certain, but I know it's somewhere worth going."

"Why do you think that?"

"Because Lilith never did anything that wasn't guaranteed to be fun and worthwhile."

After showering, Mattie returned to her bedroom and noticed her mom's boxes had rearranged themselves in the closet. They no longer pressed against the wall to hide her and Jonathan's names. On closer inspection she saw that not only did the letters in their names look more vibrant, but the heart in between had enlarged and was now neon pink. She pointed at the closet. "What are you doing, house? *Nothing* is going to happen with me and him, so you might as well relent and let me erase those names."

The floorboards in the closet groaned, and a box tipped over. The folded flaps popped open, and two vinyl records slid out. Mattie picked up the record on top, a Kenny Loggins album. Her mom had played his record so often that all the cover's corners were frayed and the original color worn off. The second album, the *Top Gun* soundtrack, was another one of their favorites. Mattie remembered when she and Lilith rented bikes in Fort Myers in preparation for the newspaper route she was going to start. They biked all over town singing "Danger Zone" while pedaling as fast as they could and racing seagulls.

Mattie returned the albums to the box and closed the flaps. Then she moved the boxes back in front of the painted names to block them from view. "Danger zone is right," she said to the house. "Jonathan Carlisle is off limits, okay? I don't need any more complications right now."

As a last-minute grab on her way out the door to The Pizza Box, she packed a blank canvas and a bag of paints and brushes and tossed them into the back seat of Penelope's car. On the way into town, Mattie stopped by the gas station so she could fill up the tank. She pulled her wallet out of her purse and noticed how little cash she had left. Her bank account was dropping its way toward empty, meaning her debit card wouldn't stretch much further either. Without a job to provide continuous income, she would probably run out of money in less than two weeks.

Pressing her forehead to the steering wheel, she sighed. If she could complete the tasks in four months, she'd get her inheritance and her worries over money would disappear.

But during the time it would take to meet the will's requirements, Mattie didn't want to keep depending on Penelope to support her. She needed a job. Who would hire someone short term? During the holidays businesses were always looking for temporary help, but in late summer, who would offer a job to someone who wasn't sticking around? Maybe the local farms needed summer help. She'd been apple picking once, if that counted as "farming" experience.

She could start painting again and sell her work like she'd been doing since she was a kid. When she turned sixteen, she'd taken on her first part-time job in New York City working at Yankee Stadium. She circulated among guests within the assigned sections and called out items for sale. She worked many nights and weekends. It wasn't the easiest job, but she got to watch the Yankees play for free. In each town they lived in after New York, Mattie and Lilith always found work, and when Mattie took on new jobs, she didn't paint as often, but she had never stopped selling a few pieces every couple of months.

While Mattie gassed up, images of paintings she could create swirled in her mind. An image of a half-butterfly, half-flower creation formed, and she took a mental snapshot of it. She paid for the gas with her card and drove into town, eventually parking in The Pizza Box's adjoining lot.

The lunch rush was over, and only a few diners were tucked into booths eating late-afternoon pies. The walls were stained paneling adorned with black-and-white photographs framed with white mats and thin black frames. Tables covered in red-and-white gingham cloths were topped with rectangles of disposable white paper. White ceramic plates and silverware rolled up in white napkins offered simple place settings for the next customers. Oversize red vinyl booths lined two of the walls, and the expansive windows filled the room with light, which kept the heavy wooden tables and chairs and the walnut walls from looking like the interior of a British smoking room. The restaurant smelled like fresh tomatoes, baking bread, and melted cheese. Hints of oregano, rosemary, and garlic hung in the air. An antique jukebox kicked on and started playing "Witchy Woman" just as someone walked out of the swinging door attached to the kitchen area.

The woman looked to be in her early fifties with shoulder-length blonde hair and sun-kissed skin. She wore a black blouse tucked into fitted jeans and black ankle boots. Her gold hoop earrings matched the simple gold necklace with a round pendant she wore. She looked more suited for a fine-dining restaurant than a casual pizza place. "Table for one or pickup?" she asked.

"Neither," Mattie said. "I'm here to sign up for the cooking class."

The woman's surprised expression was quickly replaced with a genuine smile. "Fantastic!" she exclaimed. "Let me grab the clipboard. We're keeping this old-fashioned for now, but I can email you all the details a couple of days before class." She produced a clipboard with a legal pad from beneath the hostess desk while she rattled off the class details, including day and time. A list of names, numbers, and emails filled up half the page. "How did you hear about us? Just write your info there," she said, tapping the next open line on the page.

"My great-aunt. She's my mom's—*was* my mom's—aunt, Sophia Russell."

The woman nodded. "Sophia is one of my favorite people in

town. I'm Linda Spataro. My husband and I took over this place twelve years ago when we moved from New York. Those winters are brutal, and we like the heat."

"I used to live in New York City," Mattie said. "Those winters *are* cold, but Chicago isn't much better, and I just moved from there." Technically she hadn't *moved* anywhere. Saying she *left* Chicago would be more accurate.

Linda's expression changed. She reached out and touched Mattie's hand on the clipboard. "Pardon my slowness. I just realized who you are. You must be Lilith's daughter. I'm so sorry for your loss."

"Oh . . ." Mattie said, scribbling down her email address as a distraction. "Thank you." She lifted her gaze and handed Linda the sign-up sheet. "It smells great in here."

"Best pizza in the state," she said. Then, leaning closer to Mattie, she whispered, "Because it's *real* New York–style pizza. Know what I'm saying?"

Mattie smiled. "I do. I worked at a neighborhood pizza place before I left Chicago, but it's not like New York pizza."

"Nothing is. You'll have to give our pizza the test," Linda said. "Let us know how we measure up."

"Linda!" a man called from the kitchen. Then the kitchen door swung open, and he appeared wearing an apron stained with flour and red sauce. The man was tall and athletic, probably a few years older than Linda, with a shaved head and bright eyes. "Beet pesto, right? Doesn't want the regular pesto?"

"That's right," Linda said. "With kale and goat cheese. We go over this every time. They *never* want to try the regular on this pie. Don't forget the large supreme. They'll be here in five to pick up, so get moving."

"All right, all right," he said and disappeared through the swinging door.

Goose bumps rippled across Mattie's skin. "Beet pesto with kale and goat cheese?" she asked.

"Most of our customers want the usual pies, but we have a few odd ones," she answered with a laugh. "Terry, the head cook and my husband, doesn't like to change the menu, but he makes allowances for our regulars."

That specific pizza combination was Mattie's favorite and had been for as long as she'd been eating pizza. Someone in Ivy Ridge ate the same unusual combo?

"Thanks for signing up, Mattie," Linda said, looking over the sign-up sheet. "We'll see you next week. Are you staying in Ivy Ridge?"

Mattie decided honesty was the best option. "Temporarily, yes. There are some family things I have to finalize before I can decide where I'm going next. I lived with Mom in Chicago, but without her, I'm not interested in going back."

Linda nodded. "Make sure you come back for lunch or dinner. If you close your eyes and eat a slice, you can almost hear the noise and feel the rush of the city." Linda leaned her hip against the counter. "I miss that sometimes, all the chaos and life, but I like the quiet more."

"I'm still getting used to the quiet," Mattie said. "It's uncomfortable being able to hear yourself breathe while trying to fall asleep."

Linda laughed. "Terry insisted we leave the bathroom fan on at night when we first moved here. He said it gave him the willies to hear *nothing*. But once you start listening to the nothing, you find there's a lot of life in that too. Things you *never* hear in the city. Crickets, owls, the wind blowing through the oaks." She shook her head slightly. "Here I am chatting away. I'd better get to work or Terry will be yelling for me. Come back and see us even after the class if you're around."

"I'll be here until December," Mattie said. "So I'll make sure I do." She missed New York pizza, and since The Pizza Box already served her favorite kind of pizza, she'd be able to request it without upsetting Terry. She was tempted to stick around to see who picked up the order.

The restaurant door opened and a man walked in laughing into his cell phone. "Yeah, I'll be there in ten."

Mattie recognized Jonathan immediately. He'd showered and changed from their earlier encounter, and Mattie inwardly groaned about how he could be so good-looking in a faded college T-shirt and shorts.

"Pickup for two pizzas?" Linda said. Before Jonathan could answer, Linda shouted over her shoulder, "Terry, pickup!"

"Mattie," Jonathan said as soon as he noticed her. "What are you doing here?"

"I was heading out," she said, trying not to stare at his smile. "Nice meeting you, Linda. I'll see you next week."

"You too, Mattie," Linda said. She stepped behind the counter and started ringing up Jonathan's pickup order on the register.

Terry pushed open the kitchen door and came out carrying two pizza boxes. Jonathan stepped up to the hostess counter and paid the tab. Just then it clicked with Mattie that *he* had ordered her favorite pizza combo. "These are your pizzas?"

"I'm heading to a friend's place," he said. "You hungry? Want to share?"

"No!" she said so hastily that Jonathan laughed. "No, I was

curious, that's all. I heard the order, and it has . . . unusual pizza toppings."

"The goat cheese one?" he said and curled his lip. "That's for my friend. I prefer meat lover's."

"Of course you do," Mattie said, mentally berating herself for thinking that their shared love of a strange pizza combination might mean she and Jonathan shared a destiny. After standing in awkward silence for a few seconds, Mattie took her opportunity to leave. "Well . . . see you around."

"I hope so," Jonathan said.

Mattie scurried out the door as quickly as possible. She jumped into the car like he might pursue her, though he didn't. As she cranked the engine and drove out of the lot, her heart was pounding like she'd been sprinting from Chicago to Ivy Ridge. In the rearview mirror, she saw Jonathan standing in the parking lot, watching her drive away.

Her jittery insides didn't make sense. She'd been around men before and been on a few dates, so why did being close to Jonathan make her feel like she'd been turned into a silver metal ball and dropped into a pinball machine? Mattie didn't want to go home in this state, so she drove to the downtown city park. She grabbed her bag of painting supplies and the blank canvas out of the back seat and found a shady spot beneath a massive oak tree.

Once she got in the painting zone, everything around her faded to a dull hum. She didn't always know what she would paint when she started and usually preferred to let inspiration come to her, but this time the earlier image she had of a butterfly and flowers returned.

She began to create a monarch butterfly, painting the left wing with the yellow-orange of an early morning sunrise that blended with a brighter, preschool orange. The bottom of the wing became the deeper shades of apricot and bronze. Then she added the recognizable black wing edges and white spots that were unique to each butterfly. The butterfly's body was a simple mix of gold and black with thin antennae. The right wing became an organized arrangement of pink peonies, orange ranunculus, yellow sunflowers, and white daisies.

While painting, Mattie wasn't aware of the creation as a whole. She focused on each stroke, each color, one at a time. Blending and adding dimension. A couple hours later when her artwork was complete, she held it at arm's length and studied it. The depiction of the butterfly transforming into flowers—or were the flowers morphing into a butterfly?—yielded a beautiful result. Mattie had sold paintings of this size for a few hundred dollars in the city. If she could get 75 percent of that in a small town like Ivy Ridge, she'd be satisfied. It would be a start to her earning her keep rather than depending on Penelope to support her for weeks.

Mattie tossed her bag and the canvas in the back seat. Painting had calmed her and settled her back into feeling more like herself than she had in weeks. She'd forgotten how much she loved creating. She cranked up the radio and laughed when Kenny Loggins came on. She sang along with "Danger Zone" at the top of her lungs as she drove back to the Russell house. It was almost enough distraction to make her forget about Jonathan and the way he made her feel like she was coming undone.

Chapter 22

PENELOPE

PENELOPE FELT LIKE THE LAST FEW WEEKS HAD BLURRED into an amorphous span of time. With the abundance of food and flowers, the house felt like a combination café plus florist. She gave most of the food away to local shelters and the churches that regularly fed people. The combined smells of the flowers indoors overpowered her senses, and she could tell the house disapproved because it complained more than usual—opening drawers, rattling shelves, and creaking—until she decided to offer the arrangements to local businesses whose owners she knew and to the assisted living residence.

After putting her alteration and sewing projects on hold in the immediate aftermath of Lilith's death, Penelope made it a priority to get caught up before her customers started complaining. She spent hours in her sewing room until her hands ached. Mattie periodically brought in hot tea, water, and snacks to make sure Penelope was eating. New clients started calling days after Lilith's funeral, which surprised Penelope because her steady client list of repeat customers hadn't changed much in years. But now there were half a dozen new projects coming in every other day. Penelope rarely turned down work, so it didn't take long before she needed to keep sewing long after sunset. Those nights Mattie brought up dinner and stayed to chat while they ate.

On this afternoon Penelope finished hemming a pair of dress pants and needed a stretch break. As she walked through the house, she found it empty and quiet. Enid was curled up on the window seat in the breakfast nook, and she purred her pleasure when Penelope scratched her between her ears. Penelope grabbed her cell phone and water bottle and walked out into the garden. Mattie's flowers were nestled among the established plants, and she wondered again at the numbering system Lilith had assigned. This thought made her realize that one of the seven tasks was finished, and *she* was the one who had the power to say if it was completed satisfactorily.

Which meant she would need to inform Stephen. Resentment flickered to life inside her, and she clenched her jaw. After all this time, how was she still susceptible to this past heartbreak? She thought she'd let it go years ago, but her emotions revealed otherwise.

Penelope wished for the millionth time that Lilith was here *right now* so she could ask her why on God's green earth she made Stephen the executor. She inhaled a steadying breath, took a long drink of water, and dialed the number for the law office. Marla, the executive assistant, answered and transferred Penelope to Stephen's office line. Melancholy saxophone hold music offended her ear.

The music stopped abruptly. "Penelope?" Stephen asked in lieu of a proper greeting.

He sounded surprised and pleased at the possibility that she had called him. Her pulse quickened. "Hey, Stephen," she said. "You might reconsider your hold music. It's—"

"Torturous?" he said with humor in his voice.

"I didn't even know saxophone music could sound so depressing and annoying at the same time," she said. When he laughed, Penelope felt the hard shell around her heart soften. She was reminded of lazy summer afternoons lying on a quilt and staring up at Stephen's face haloed in sunlight. Butterflies fluttered over wild thistle, and time stretched long and wondrous.

"It's good to hear from you today. What's on your mind?" he asked.

A thousand and one things were on her mind, but she focused on her reason for calling. "Mattie finished a task to satisfy one of the requirements."

"She did?" he said, sounding relieved. "I'm happy to hear that. Based on our last conversation I wasn't sure she would willingly agree. Most people would do anything for that kind of money."

"Mattie isn't like most people."

"I don't doubt that," he agreed. "She's a Russell, and before you defend your family, I mean that as a compliment."

Penelope lowered her shoulders, which had risen toward her ears with building tension. Stephen had always been able to calm her. "And *willingly* isn't exactly how I'd describe her attitude. Resigned, maybe?"

"She's going to follow through then and stay in town long enough to complete them?"

Even as a kid, Mattie was logical and responsible, so although Lilith's requirements seemed unfair, her daughter wasn't going to give up the inheritance. "It appears that way. She planted the flowers and has them properly labeled. I approve of the work, so how do I confirm with you? Can I take photos and email them to you?"

"That'll work," Stephen said. "Or I could come by and confirm in person."

Penelope's breath caught. "Come by my house?" Stephen hadn't set foot in the Russell home in more than twenty years.

Would the house even let him inside? Would he be stuck on the front porch indefinitely—like he was stuck in her heart?

"I can," Stephen offered in a hopeful voice. "If it's easier for you."

That option definitely wasn't easier. Penelope felt her heart barricading itself behind new protective walls. Two adults could be friends and nothing more, and they could conduct business without being awkward, but could she and Stephen? "No," she said. "That isn't necessary. No reason to disrupt your workday. I'll email you photos."

There was a pause before Stephen gave her his work email. "Feel free to check in with me as Mattie completes the tasks. I bet it's nice for you to have her around."

She could feel him trying to pry open their past and dig out the memories they shared, hoping to find a common ground between them again. Her first impulse was to shut him down. Instead she said, "It is nice to have her home. I'll take her for as long as I can. She brings a different energy to the house, a good change."

"From the little bit of time I spent with her, I bet she does. She's fiery . . . like you."

Penelope felt Stephen could keep talking, but conversing with him was dangerous territory. "I'll take the photos and get those to you today." They said goodbye and Penelope walked through the garden, taking pictures of Mattie's flowers, thinking about Stephen and how more than twenty years had passed, but while standing barefoot in the grass, she felt like that twenty-year-old lovestruck young woman dreaming of a future she had no idea would unravel before it could begin.

She went back inside, but rather than return to her sewing, she stood in the third-floor hallway and stared at the attic door. Her heart thumped harder in her chest as she neared it. When she reached for the knob, the attic door eased open before she touched it. The attic was expecting her and welcomed her inside.

Penelope pulled down two boxes from a top shelf. One of the boxes had been opened recently when it fell from the shelf and scattered its contents—hand-stitched baby clothes. She opened this box again and pulled out baby dresses and bloomers. She brushed her fingers over the soft fabrics and traced the stitching.

The second box hadn't been opened since college, since Penelope had packed away everything in the hope it would help her forget. She ripped the tape off the box and opened the flaps. A sweet rush of air swirled out. It smelled like ripe strawberries and textbooks, like tennis shoes and wet ink on paper. Inside the box were photographs and ticket stubs from concerts and football games. There was a journal and a poetry book by Mary Oliver with a photo used as a bookmark.

The photo was of her and Stephen sitting on the tailgate of a pickup truck. His arm was looped around her shoulders, and she was leaning into him, smiling at the camera. Dozens of people loitered around on the edges of the picture, wearing bright red and black. She remembered the day. They were tailgating before a university football game. Lilith had already left Ivy Ridge with no warning and no information about where she was headed. Penelope found her happiness in her relationship with Stephen, and she would have been lost without him during that time. She had no idea how much her life was already changing the moment that picture was taken.

Penelope reached into the box and pulled out a white envelope. The front was blank, giving no indication of its contents.

She opened it and pulled out three small black-and-white photos. For a moment all she could do was stare at them. Her eyes filled with tears, blurring the images, but she could still make out the tiny outline of the baby shown during the ultrasound. A little girl. *Her* little girl. Penelope pressed the photos to her chest and felt the whole house shudder with the ripple of grief that flowed out of her. She thought she'd released all the heartache attached to that part of her past, but obviously these roots ran so deep there was still more left to pull out. The house creaked around her in a steady rhythm as though it were soothing her, a gentle tempo like a front porch rocker.

Chapter 23

MATTIE

DURING THE NEXT WEEK MATTIE PAINTED IN HER FREE time, which was most of the day, and by Saturday she had created a half dozen paintings. She brainstormed the most efficient and easiest ways to sell them. Creating a website didn't make sense, not unless she intended to become a full-time artist. She could open an Etsy shop, but could she compete with artists who had dozens and dozens of listings? Ivy Ridge didn't have a local art gallery, but a few downtown shops sold artwork, so she could ask if there was any interest.

While she was researching places to sell her artwork, an internet search took her to a real estate agency in San Francisco. She almost clicked off the web page, but she saw that a space previously used as an art gallery was for sale. After a bit more research into the area, Mattie learned that San Francisco had a thriving art scene, and the art gallery location was in the heart of a creative district. An idea sprouted. With the inheritance money, could she open a gallery? She could sell not only her art but also the artwork of others. She knew almost nothing about owning and running a business. *But I could learn. Or hire someone with experience.* She clicked through a few images of the city, and with a flicker of excitement, she imagined herself living there. She bookmarked the page for later reference.

Focusing back on Ivy Ridge, Mattie searched the city's schedule of events and saw there were upcoming fall festivals where she could rent a merchant's booth. At the pace she was painting, she might have twenty to thirty pieces by October, which could earn her a couple thousand dollars if she sold the lot.

Would Penelope want to split the cost of a booth with her and sell her own creations? Lately Penelope had been working on clients' pieces only, but Penelope sometimes stoked her own creative fires. She had a stash of dresses, skirts, and miscellaneous pieces stitched and ready to sell if she wanted to. Penelope said she made them just for fun, but a festival booth rental would be a great way to push Penelope to try something new.

The cooking class at The Pizza Box was scheduled for midmorning, so Mattie cleaned up her paint supplies, tidied up the craft room, and poked her head into Penelope's sewing room to let her know she was heading out with the promise of bringing home pizza for dinner.

Mattie parked in The Pizza Box's parking lot and "Have a Little Faith in Me" by John Hiatt came on the radio. She climbed out of the car with the lyrics running through her mind and a nervous twitch in her stomach. She heard a *kerchunk* and then a pause and then another *kerchunk*. A young woman stepped back from a wooden power pole posted through the sidewalk. A staple gun swung from her hand, and an open messenger bag slung over her shoulder revealed a stack of green flyers.

Mattie approached her and a smile of recognition spread across Lucy's face. "Mattie!" Lucy wore a fitted, ruby-red T-shirt that had an outline of a white Monstera leaf in the center. The words *Life Is Short Buy the Plant* curved along the top and bottom of the leaf. Her cut-off denim shorts showcased her caramel-colored skin. She pointed at the power pole. "Trying to drum up volunteers for our Green Planet Initiative weekend. You're still coming, right?"

Mattie nodded. "Got to mark that task off the list."

Lucy fisted a hand against her hip. "I hope it's not only for business," she teased. "You could lie to me and say it's because you're pumped to hang out with me. I had fun hunting down all the flowers for you. Hey, how did planting go? Everything still healthy and blooming?"

"So far, so good," Mattie said. The varieties her mom had chosen would grow well in the Georgia weather with its mild winters and insanely hot, sticky summers. But everything thrived in the Russells' backyard, even people.

Lucy's thick wavy hair was pulled into a ponytail, and tortoiseshell sunglasses kept her eyes hidden. Her faded white tennis shoes were stained with dried soil. She fiddled with a ruby stud in her earlobe. "Picking up a pizza?"

Mattie studied the flyer, which was identical to the one she picked up from the nursery. She'd left it on her bedroom dresser as a reminder. "Does this work better than online ads or emails?"

Lucy reached out and patted the stapled flyer like a beloved pet. "There's something timeless about dozens of flyers all stapled on top of each other with the addition of a tear-away ad for piano lessons or a roommate. I like to think people still stop and read these, even if it's just out of curiosity. Look at this pole! It's a rainbow of past events and upcoming possibility. I like that Ivy Ridge clings to some of its old-fashioned traditions. But," she said, looking at Mattie and pushing her sunglasses on top of her head, "we do both—online marketing and these. So . . . pizza?"

"I'm taking a pizza cooking class," Mattie said, "to satisfy one of the tasks."

"Another task! You're not messing around with getting them done," Lucy said. "Sounds like fun. Linda and Terry are supercool people. Not to mention their pizzas can't be beat. I wish I'd known they were hosting a class. I'd have joined. I took one a few months ago to learn how to make garlic bread and pesto. What's today's class?"

"Pizza dough first and then a classic pizza margherita."

"This is my Saturday off work." Lucy shoved the stapler into her messenger bag. "Do you think they have space for more?"

"I don't know if—"

Lucy walked up the sidewalk a few paces and shouted to someone across the street. "Hey! The Pizza Box is hosting a cooking class. Want me to see if they have space for us? We can hang the rest of the flyers afterward."

Mattie followed Lucy's line of sight and noticed two men across the street. A tall guy had a stack of flyers pressed against his chest. He wore a red baseball cap, aviator glasses, shorts, and a white T-shirt displaying a Foo Fighters band image. The other guy lifted a stapler into the air as a sign of acknowledgment. He was slightly shorter, broad shouldered, wearing a blue University of Florida T-shirt. A mop of brown curls covered his head and hooked around his ears. He was built like a college athlete who'd gone a bit softer since then. His high cheekbones and angular jaw were accentuated by summer-tan skin. With his rounded nose and full lips, he reminded Mattie of someone.

"Is that—" Mattie started to ask.

"That's my brother, Luca. We're twins. Did I mention that? And that's one of his best friends, Jonathan Carlisle. They played baseball for the same college. Luca obviously played after Jonathan graduated, but Jonathan used to promote and organize a lot of the team's fundraising events. They realized they had a lot in common—baseball, Ivy Ridge, an obsession with Phil Collins." Lucy laughed as though recalling a funny memory.

Mattie recalled Jonathan's fear over the possibility of losing his baseball scholarship the night they met. Without her help, how different would his life be now? Would he have been caught with his friends by the local police? Would the college have reneged his scholarship? Would he have actually been home that following summer to see her again?

Luca and Jonathan crossed the street and joined Lucy and Mattie.

"I never turn down pizza," Luca said. Lucy introduced Mattie to her brother and to Jonathan.

Jonathan removed his sunglasses and hooked them on his T-shirt collar. "We know each other," he confirmed.

"You do?" Lucy asked with surprise, looking back and forth between them. "How?"

"We're neighbors," Mattie said. "Temporarily. His parents live next door to my family."

Jonathan shoved his hands into his front pockets. "And we celebrated her birthday together one year."

Mattie snapped her head in his direction. "That's totally inaccurate."

Jonathan's laugh surrounded her on the sidewalk.

Lucy and Luca exchanged glances, then Lucy said, "Well, this is an interesting development. I'm going to check for open spots." She hurried off toward The Pizza Box and disappeared into the building. To avoid being left alone with Luca and Jonathan, Mattie followed. Jonathan matched her stride, and Luca fell into step behind them.

"Hey," Jonathan said as they walked, "you here by yourself or are you meeting a date?"

Mattie looked at him curiously. There was an edge to his question, a strained tone that revealed a discomfort with the idea that she might be meeting someone. "I was by myself until—"

"Until Lucy invited herself to the party," Luca joked. "She's good at that, but parties are better with her around."

Lucy bounded out the front door, her smile wide enough to compete with an Oscar winner's exuberance. "There's space for us!"

"Hooray," Mattie mumbled under her breath.

Jonathan pushed his arm against hers and chuckled. "Come on," he said. "You have to admit it's going to be more fun with a group."

Mattie wasn't about to admit anything. Not that she felt a combination of excitement and dread with him so close to her. Not that her brain felt full of summer wind, churning her words and thoughts into nervous energy. "Ask me at the end of class."

Jonathan removed his cap, smoothed his hand over his hair, and popped the cap back onto his head. "This isn't the kind of thing you do alone."

Mattie rolled her eyes behind her sunglasses. "I'm perfectly fine doing lots of things alone."

Lucy held open the door and they stepped into the dim restaurant interior. The air smelled thick with garlic, roasted tomatoes, and Italian spices.

"I get that," he said. "I like my independence, doing my own thing, but it's nice to have someone to hang out with sometimes."

Mattie removed her sunglasses. "Do a lot of hanging out with someones in Chicago?"

"Of course he does," Luca answered. "It's his job to hang out and schmooze with half the city, but only the elite crowd. Am I right?"

Jonathan started to object. "Well, not—"

"What kind of job is that? Professional schmoozer?" Mattie asked.

Before he could answer, Lucy chimed in, "Professional *charmer*. Be careful you don't fall for his perfectly curated lines. He woos people for a living." She nudged Jonathan with her elbow in a playful way.

Jonathan attempted to defend himself again, but Linda ushered them through the swinging door that led to the kitchen. The kitchen area was much larger than Mattie imagined. She'd pictured it looking like the pizza place in her city neighborhood, with its tiny galley kitchen that had only enough room to pass behind someone smaller than the Italian owner, whose rotund belly required him to move out of the kitchen if someone needed to grab something on the opposite side of where he stood.

The Pizza Box's kitchen was four times the size of the one where she'd worked. Different stations were set up for class, and a half dozen people stood at stainless steel countertops full of ingredients portioned in bowls and liquid measuring cups.

Lucy and Mattie partnered up. Mattie hoped that Linda would reshuffle the class and place Jonathan somewhere on the other side of the kitchen, but he and Luca ended up sharing a countertop area with her and Lucy. Fortunately the class directions and prep limited conversations. Lucy and Mattie worked well together preparing their pizza dough, and Lucy prattled on about seeds she planted, flowers she ordered, and a big order she was pulling together for a local event hosted next week.

Once everyone had dough balls rising in bowls, Linda and

Terry brought out previously risen dough for the attendees to use for the next step. Then Terry placed potted basil plants on a community counter. Mattie grabbed the cherry-red pot of basil and placed it at their station. Lucy pressed the dough into a flat circle, and Mattie crushed whole, canned Roma tomatoes in a bowl. She added oregano and salt and stirred the tomatoes while Lucy went to wash her hands. When Lucy returned Mattie was spooning the red sauce onto the flat dough.

"I ran into Lenora Jackson at the hand-washing station," Lucy said as she sliced fresh Roma tomatoes and strategically placed them on the red sauce in a circular pattern. "She owns Butterfingers, the bakery, and we were chatting about how much we love classes and how she hopes that her own baking class will be as enjoyable. She's hosting her first one soon."

Mattie ripped chunks from the mozzarella ball and scattered them around on the pizza.

"Isn't that one of your tasks?" Lucy asked when Mattie didn't respond.

Mattie had been only half focused on Lucy. When she started a project, whether painting or cooking, her ability to pay attention to surrounding distractions was limited. "Oh, sorry. I wasn't making the connection. Yeah, it's one of the tasks."

"We could take it together!" Lucy offered.

Lucy seemed confident Mattie would agree, and Mattie didn't have an immediate reason not to. Telling Lucy she preferred not to get attached to people and interact much with them on a personal level would be offensive given how happy Lucy looked.

"Tasks?" Jonathan asked, joining the conversation without an invitation. "What does that mean?"

"It's nothing," Mattie said, and Lucy looked apologetic for sharing what might have been a secret. "Focus on your pizza, and tell Luca the basil goes on *after* it's baked."

Jonathan caught Luca ripping basil and dropping it onto the top of the pizza. The two of them picked off the shreds, leaving a few slivers behind, which would turn into charred bits in the oven. Linda and Terry came around and helped each group slide their pizzas into the ovens for a quick bake. Lucy chatted with Lenora across the room while Mattie cleaned up their station.

Jonathan leaned against the countertop, blocking part of her space. "Are they part of your bucket list?"

Mattie paused in swiping a clean rag across the stainless steel countertop and looked at him questioningly.

"The tasks," he said.

"No," Mattie answered and resumed wiping a small pile of flour into her palm.

His cheek dimpled. "I get the feeling you don't want to elaborate."

She dropped the flour into the nearest trash bin and brushed off her hands. "I get the feeling you don't give up easily."

At some point during the cooking class, he'd turned his ball cap around backward to keep the brim out of his way. His hair poked out from underneath the edges. "Who would give up getting to know you?"

Mattie's body stilled. The noise in the kitchen around them dimmed, and Jonathan's eyes met hers. She wanted to press her finger into his chest and demand he stop whatever it was he was doing. Maybe Lucy's warning was one Mattie should take seriously. Jonathan Carlisle was a top-notch charmer, and he was using his skills on her. Her skin tingled with the intensity sparking between them.

Lucy bounded back over and ended the connection between Mattie and Jonathan. She was saying they *had* to take the baking class. Mostly because she'd verbally already signed them up. But also because they would be baking oatmeal crème pies, which happened to be one of her favorite childhood treats. Lucy asked for Mattie's phone number so she could add her to her contacts. Instead, Mattie handed Lucy her phone and told Lucy to add herself to Mattie's contacts. This tactic often worked because it gave Mattie the option of texting or not.

The rest of the class passed quickly with everyone eating slices of their fresh-from-the-oven margherita pizzas and oohing and aahing over their new skills. Mattie sent the rest of their pizza slices home with Lucy and ordered a veggie pizza to go since she promised Penelope she'd bring home dinner. Jonathan hung around in the lobby with her while Lucy and Luca went outside to finish hanging flyers.

"Are you ordering something to go?" Mattie asked him.

"You told me to ask you after class if it was more fun with a group. Was it?"

Mattie rolled her eyes. "Do you always have to be right?"

"Not always, but I told you it would be better with us. I know it was more fun for me having you here."

Mattie locked her gaze with his. He was flirting with her, possibly trying to charm her, but for what purpose? Neither one of them was sticking around long. Guys like Jonathan were often only after the thrill of the chase. Well, he could keep chasing her all he wanted because she was determined not to let him catch her.

"Don't you have flyers to hang? Or people to schmooze?"

Jonathan laughed. "So subtle. See you around, Mattie." He pushed open the door and walked out into the sunlight.

"Not if I can help it," she whispered.

❧

Back at the house, Mattie grabbed a couple of plates and stacked them on the pizza box. Then she filled two glasses with lemonade and carried all of it to the third floor where she knew she'd find Penelope in her sewing room. Penelope was hunched over a complicated beadwork dress but glanced up when Mattie entered the room.

"Whatever that is smells delicious," Penelope said. She lifted the dress gently from her lap and draped it over her sewing table. "What day is it?"

Mattie laughed. "Still Saturday. Veggie pizza and lemonade. A dinner fit for college kids . . . although I don't really know what college kids eat since I never went." She sat down on the rug and arranged an indoor picnic for them.

Penelope stretched her arms over her head and cycled through a few yoga poses before she sat down with Mattie. "I can't speak for all of them, but I ate a lot of fast food from the student union food court and more french fries than is decent to admit."

It was hard to believe Penelope had eaten anything processed or greasy, at least not based on the kind of foods Mattie had seen her aunt eat regularly. She doubted there was a boxed food item, with the exception of emergency pasta, in the house—except when Mattie visited. Then the pantry additions included breakfast cereals, potato chips, and crackers. As an adult, Mattie preferred homemade meals, too, but she still had a soft spot for her childhood favorites.

"I pegged you for a tree hugger who only ate granola," Mattie said.

Penelope's laughter rolled out of her like a melody. "Oh, the things you'd be surprised to learn about me. How was class?"

Mattie flipped open the pizza box lid. "It was . . . fun?"

"Are you asking me or telling me?" Penelope pulled a slice from the box and slid it onto her plate.

Mattie's slice was lukewarm, but the cheese was still slightly gooey. "I was paired up with a local girl. I actually met her at the nursery. Lucy. She talks a lot, but she's nice."

"Lucy Moreno?" Penelope asked. "The florist at Green Clover? I don't know her family that well, but they seem like nice people. Her dad used to live here, but he was younger than me by a few years. Your mom's age, I think. His family moved away when I was in college."

Mattie nodded. "Have you given any more thought to working a festival with me? With all the customers you get without advertising and how happy they are with your work, I *know* you could sell your own stuff."

Penelope sipped her lemonade. "I've been thinking about it."

Mattie grinned. "You should go ahead and say yes. Think how much happier people would be with your enchanted clothes."

Penelope's loud laughter pleased Mattie. "Enchanted?"

"Are you saying you don't stitch bravery, kindness, and comfort into your work?" she asked with a slow smile. "Your exceptional skills don't help people find love or lost things?"

Penelope's mischievous grin lifted her cheeks. "I didn't say that, did I?"

"Have you ever made anything for yourself?" Mattie asked.

"Does it work that way? Can you boost your own life with your talents?"

"That's a great question," Penelope said, humming in her throat. "I've never tried."

"You should," Mattie said. She took a bite of her slice and chewed. "With another task done, what do we do now? Call the lawyer and tell him? Does he need proof?" And realizing she didn't have proof, she added, "I didn't take any pictures. I guess he could call the owners."

A somber expression turned Penelope's lips downward. "I'll call him."

When she didn't elaborate, Mattie braved a topic she'd been curious about for days. "What's with you and Stephen?"

Penelope's body tensed, and the plate wobbled in her hands. "There's nothing with us."

Who would believe that? What wasn't her aunt saying? "But there was."

Penelope inhaled a slow breath and released it, but the tension didn't quite leave her body. "Yes."

Something heavy and intense brewed in the air around them. The room lights flickered and Mattie saw something in Penelope's eyes that she'd never seen in her mom's. Lilith had spent time with lots of men, probably the most time with Orion. But Lilith's eyes never carried a look of suppressed longing, never revealed that glimmer of long-held desire. "You were in love with him?"

Penelope stared down at the half-eaten slice on her plate. "I was, wholeheartedly. But that was a long time ago."

Understanding and truth blended together inside Mattie. She reached up and rubbed the lapis lazuli stone in her necklace.

"You still do . . ." she said quietly. Penelope met her gaze. "You're still in love with Stephen."

Penelope didn't answer. A skein of red yarn fell out of its organized cubbyhole and unrolled itself across the floor, wobbling straight toward the two women. It traveled a meandering path as though the floor was uneven and tilted, stopping only when it rolled into the pizza box. Both women stared at the curling trail the red yarn had made on its journey toward them. It was asymmetrical and reminiscent of a child's handiwork, but it was most definitely the shape of a bright red heart.

Chapter 24

MATTIE

September rolled in, offering mild relief from the brutal Southern heat with temperatures in the mid-80s. After learning of the personal connection between Penelope and Stephen, Mattie hadn't mentioned Stephen again, nor had she pressed her aunt for additional details. She'd seen the raw emotion in Penelope's eyes, and she understood a lot more about why Penelope had reacted so strongly to Stephen being the executor of Lilith's will. Why *would* her mom have made that choice? Was there a significant reason Lilith willfully brought Penelope and Stephen together again?

The tasks set forth in the will didn't feel significant, more akin to senseless. Maybe Mattie was trying to find logic where there wasn't any. Sophia didn't believe that, though, and neither did Robert, who thought Lilith might have left clues behind in the tasks. Mattie had yet to see any connections between her father and her mother's past.

A local arts and crafts festival was taking place in Ivy Ridge's downtown park starting tomorrow, and Penelope agreed to renting a booth together. Mattie gathered her recent paintings and began leaning them against the wall in the downstairs hallway in preparation for loading them into the car before tomorrow's early morning setup. While she was gathering the last two paintings from the art studio, the doorbell rang.

Penelope hollered from her sewing room. "Can you get that?"

Mattie carried the paintings downstairs, leaned them against the wall, and opened the front door. Jonathan stood on the front porch. She blurted, "What are you doing here?"

A sheen of sweat covered his face, neck, and arms. He wore a lightweight blue polo made of wicking material and a pair of khaki shorts. His feet were bare except for thin black flip-flops. "Not much for hellos, are you?" he joked.

A green hummingbird did a flyby behind Jonathan's head before returning to the foxgloves. "It's a valid question, but not how I was taught to greet people. You caught me off guard. Hello, how are you, what are you doing here?" she said in one breath.

He tapped the toe of his flip-flop on the porch boards and shoved one hand through his brown hair. Stray pieces stuck straight up before he patted them down, and Mattie grinned. "Wow, that was so much better. I feel all warm and fuzzy inside."

Lucy was 100 percent right. Jonathan was über-charming. A twinkle of sunlight reflected off his toothpaste commercial–grade smile, and Mattie felt a thin connection forming between them, pulling her closer to him. Her memories offered her a brief flash of the kiss they shared ten years ago, and she felt a glimmer of excitement. To which she almost responded with a groan. It wasn't like she hadn't kissed another man since then. Why on earth did her memory want to make *that one kiss* so special?

Jonathan's cell phone dinged in his back pocket. He pulled it out and did a quick check before sliding it out of view again. The radio in the parlor kicked on and started playing "I'm So Excited" by the Pointer Sisters at max volume.

Jonathan leaned forward as though trying to see around Mattie into the house. "Are you having a party?"

"Hardly," she grumbled. "Be right back." She walked away from the front door and into the parlor. "Knock it off, will you?" The volume lowered but the radio didn't turn off, so Mattie manually switched it off. When she turned around, Jonathan stood in the foyer and the front door was closed. He bent down to look at her paintings. "I don't recall inviting you in."

He glanced up at her from his crouched position. "I assumed that was next on your hospitality list. Did you paint these?"

"Yes," she said. Did he like her painting style? Why did she care?

"These are good," he said. He gently flipped through the canvases. "*Really* good. What are you doing with them? Do you have an art exhibit some—" He picked up a painting of Central Park in the fall, which she'd painted from the perspective of someone on the water looking at the stone bridge arching over it. The cityscape rose in the background toward a pale blue sky. A smudged outline of a person leaned on the bridge. The lone figure stared down at the blurs of red, orange, gold, and blue reflected in the water.

Mattie shifted on her feet in the silence. Why was he gaping at the painting like she'd stolen it from the Louvre? "That's Central Park. My mom and I lived up the street from there."

His expression of disbelief intensified as his mouth dropped open. He stood holding the painting in both hands and glancing from the art to Mattie's face. "You lived in the city? When?"

"When I was about sixteen. We were there for a couple of years."

He returned the painting to the stack against the wall. "I would have been in college then. I used to go into the city all the time. We could have passed each other on the sidewalk."

"Doubtful," she said, not wanting him to know that she had thought the same thing.

"But possible." Jonathan pointed at the canvas. "This image, what inspired it?"

Mattie shrugged. "Just something I saw in my head." The look of wonderment in Jonathan's gaze ratcheted up Mattie's nervous energy. The radio switched on and started playing "Crazy Love" by Van Morrison at a low, seductive volume. To distract Jonathan's attention from the radio, Mattie asked, "Was there a reason you stopped by? Sugar, eggs, milk?"

"Lucy," he said. "You haven't texted her about the baking class."

A rush of guilt flooded Mattie's stomach. She'd been busy, and that's why she hadn't called or texted Lucy. At least that's the excuse she'd been telling herself for days. Truth was, she'd been purposefully avoiding Lucy. "Who are you, the phone police? How do you even know I haven't texted her?"

"She texted me a few minutes ago," Jonathan said. "She's worried you lost her number, so she asked if I'd come over and check. Judging from that look on your face, you haven't lost her number, so why haven't you texted her?"

"I . . ." Mattie hesitated. She debated honesty versus lame excuses. "I prefer to keep to myself. It's simpler."

"Simpler than what?" he asked.

"Simpler than getting attached and involved in people's lives," she admitted. "I'll be leaving soon anyway."

She could tell Jonathan hadn't been expecting her to answer so bluntly.

After a beat, he said, "Unless you're a hermit, and maybe you are when you're not in Ivy Ridge, it's impossible to stay completely disengaged from people's lives. They'll find ways to meddle and squeeze in. As for leaving soon, you can have friends anywhere. You've heard of the internet, right? It allows you to connect with people all over the world, which means you can make friends and *keep* friends even if you're leaving soon."

The staircase groaned, and Mattie looked to see whether Penelope was coming downstairs, but it was only the house, probably warning her to stop talking. "What makes you think I *want* friends?"

He chuckled. "Lucy won't give up. She likes you for some reason, and she's an optimist. She thinks the only reason you haven't texted is because you've lost her number. But—"

"But instead I'm being a jerk to the nicest person I've met in town," Mattie finished. She hadn't tried to be a real friend to anyone, not since Julia, but Lucy made her *want* to rethink the possibility of friendship. "I'll text her."

The chandelier in the foyer creaked, and Jonathan glanced up. It swayed slightly as though agreeing that Mattie needed to text Lucy. She rolled her eyes in response.

"You didn't say what you're doing with these paintings," Jonathan said.

Footsteps sounded on the steps. Someone was definitely coming downstairs this time. "Penelope and I have a booth at the festival this weekend."

He picked up the Central Park painting again. "How much for this one?"

Mattie smirked. "For everyone else, two hundred dollars. For you, five hundred."

Jonathan reached for his phone. "Sounds like a fair deal. Upcharge for the high-maintenance clients. I do the same. PayPal, Venmo, or Cash App? Or is cash better?"

His unflinching acceptance of the price startled her. "I was kidding."

"I never joke about money," he said. "How about I pay five hundred and toss in having lunch with me as part of the deal?"

Penelope appeared on the staircase with a box in her arms, sparing Mattie from having to respond to the lunch request. Was he asking her out on a date?

"Hey, Jonathan," Penelope said. "How's your dad?"

"A little better every day," he answered. "Thanks for asking."

Penelope put down her box in the hallway next to Mattie's paintings. "Your mom said you're helping out with the business while you're in town?"

"Yes, ma'am," he said. "Until he's ready to take the helm again. It's not much different from my work in Chicago, so that makes it easier for all of us. In fact, I've been working remotely today on both jobs while sitting in the backyard. Organizing events here for Dad and checking in on the status of my clients in the city. I like to stay busy. The fast-paced life works for me."

"I'm glad you know what makes you happy. I bet your folks appreciate you helping out for a while," Penelope said. She picked up one of Mattie's paintings. "Is this the Degaré house?"

Jonathan moved to stand beside Penelope as though she'd been asking him instead of Mattie. "No," he said. "That can't be. The Degaré house is falling apart."

"It wasn't always," Penelope said. She looked at Mattie for confirmation.

Jonathan leaned in closer to the painting, which Mattie had finished days ago. It captured the mansion and its surrounding estate, with its majestic magnolia and oak trees and verdant landscaping, at the height of summer. The front porch was adorned with grand terra-cotta pots bursting with blooming lantana, pink petunias, and draping potato vines. The gleaming-white

Greek Revival–style mansion boasted a columned exterior, wide porches, sweeping galleries, and the belvedere that crowned the structure.

Jonathan asked, "This is what it used to look like? Did you recreate this using old photos?"

Mattie shook her head. "That's how I saw it in my mind." When he looked questioningly at her, she shrugged self-consciously. "What?" Did he think that was a crazy comment? Surely he knew lots of painters "saw" things in their heads and recreated them using different mediums.

"I'm impressed, that's all," Jonathan said. "I used to wonder what it looked like before it was abandoned."

"It's a guess," Mattie said. "It might not be an accurate representation."

Penelope placed the painting with the others. "I have a feeling it might be more accurate than any of us know. You see life in a way we don't."

"My thinking too," Jonathan said. "Good to see you both, but I'd better get back to work. I'll see you at the festival this weekend."

"Do you have a booth?" Mattie asked. Jonathan didn't strike her as a crafter.

He opened the door and stepped onto the front porch. His expression was serious when he said, "Yes, and I hope to sell out of my macramé plant holders." His expression broke and he grinned. "I'm kidding, Mattie. No, I just meant I'd stop by and see you."

"On purpose?" she asked. Why couldn't she control her words around him?

Jonathan's laugh joined Penelope's and echoed through the foyer. "That's what friends do. They see each other *on purpose*.

And I need to stop by so I can buy that painting and we can decide where we want to go for lunch."

Before she could argue with him and tell him that they were not friends and she hadn't agreed to have lunch with him, Jonathan closed the front door. Mattie exhaled loudly. She needed to find her phone upstairs so she could text Lucy. When she saw the delight on her aunt's face, she said, "Whatever you're thinking, stop. No, no, and more no." Penelope's laugh reverberated through the foyer.

⚬⚬

By midmorning the Ivy Ridge arts and crafts festival was jammed with people meandering among the rows of tented booths that bordered the downtown park's walkways. The day was filled with sounds of talking and laughter. Music drifted out from a small stage set up at the far end of the park where a rotation of singer-songwriters were scheduled to perform all day. The sun rose high in the sky like a sparkling citrine, and temperatures were steadily rising too. Mattie bet the snow cone vendor would sell out today. The Pixie Dixie Creamery's ice cream truck was somewhere because she spotted people with waffle cones filled with oversize scoops of chocolate and vanilla, some covered in rainbow sprinkles and others with walnuts. If the truck had any left at the end of the day, Mattie wanted a scoop of dark chocolate caramel ripple with brownie bits.

Mattie and Penelope's booth was an explosion of color. Mattie's art hung alongside her aunt's stunning creations. Boho dresses with simple ruffles and layers mingled with swing-style skirts, and vibrant scarves with intricate patterns looped through hooks hanging from the tent poles on the inside structure. Embroidered blouses and comfy pajama pants hung beside paintings of Pike Place Market in Seattle and an emerald-green hummingbird darting among peach and golden daylilies.

So far, Mattie had met dozens of Ivy Ridge residents, although she'd already forgotten half their names. Even though she wasn't usually talkative, she knew how to work a crowd to make a profit on her art, a skill she'd been perfecting for years. Penelope had surprised her by being more than just friendly to the visitors; she'd been downright sociable. Mattie heard her promise to attend a book club meeting next month, which shocked everyone within earshot. Jonathan hadn't shown up yet, and that was fine with Mattie. She half hoped he wouldn't so she could stay relaxed and not overthink every word that came out of her mouth.

"You've been particularly chatty today," Mattie said to Penelope after a customer paid for a brilliant blue scarf and skipped away with her new treasure.

"Have I?" she asked innocently. With a half shrug she said, "Sophia's been hounding me for years about *opening up* and letting people in. And then after you reminded me what a dead-boring person I am, I wondered if I should make a few changes."

Mattie groaned. "I didn't mean it."

"Oh, but you did, and we both know it's true. I also made this skirt just for the festival, and I might have stitched it with golden threads of courage and confidence."

Mattie's eyebrows lifted. "So your talents *do* work on you."

"So it seems. But this is new for me, being more outgoing. I'm testing the waters, as they say, easing into it. I'm hoping the town will be receptive rather than creeped out."

Mattie snorted out a laugh. "You are the least creepy person I know. Eccentric maybe, but never creepy." Mattie straightened the painting of Central Park. Would Jonathan actually buy it?

That would require him coming by, and she'd already decided she didn't want that. Hadn't she?

"Mattie!" Lucy bounded into the tent wearing a fluorescent green shirt with the words *Loyal to the Soil* written in white script surrounded by graphic prints of miniature gardening tools. Her white tennis skort showed off her curvy, muscular legs. "You weren't kidding when you said you'd been busy painting. Hello, Ms. Russell."

"Call me Penelope."

Lucy's energy was contagious and welcome. She bounced around the tent like a ball of happiness. "Wow, wow, wow, Mattie. You should be selling these for real."

"I *am*," Mattie said.

"I mean like an Etsy shop or in a gallery or on the streets of Paris," Lucy continued. "And if you *do* sell them in Paris, please invite me over to stay with you indefinitely. I'd love to see the Eiffel Tower one day while eating a croissant and a macaron."

"At the same time?" Mattie teased.

Lucy laughed and scanned the crowd outside the tent. When she spotted what she was looking for, she lifted her whole arm and waved like a kid. "My parents and my brother are here."

Mattie followed Lucy's gaze toward a tall black-haired man and a shorter, voluptuous woman who looked like a more mature version of Lucy. They were strolling through a booth that sold old baseball cards and antique sports paraphernalia. Luca stood off to the side with someone.

"And Jonathan," Mattie said. Just saying his name caused her palms to sweat. She pulled her fingers through her hair in a make-shift comb.

"He's only here for a minute," Lucy said. "He's organizing a company retreat today. For his job, or his dad's job, or both maybe.

He's a workaholic, but now that I say that, he's been taking more downtime lately. This is the most Luca's been able to see him *and* talk to him in years. Oh, I officially signed us up for baking class." She tossed a thumb over her shoulder. "Lenora has a booth set up a ways down, and she had the sign-up list with her."

"Baking class?" Penelope interjected. "At Butterfingers? That sounds fun. What're y'all making?"

"A total classic, oatmeal crème pies."

An older woman walked into the tent. She wore a silky navy-blue blouse with gray slacks. Her white hair was thick and parted in the middle, stopping at her shoulders in a stylish cut. She walked using a wooden cane with a distinct silver handle. Unlike most shoppers, she didn't browse through the offerings. Instead, she went straight toward the Degaré painting and stood in front of it, looking like she'd seen a ghost. The eeriness of her demeanor quieted the other women, and Mattie held her breath, waiting for something to happen.

The older woman turned away from the painting and looked at Penelope with pale gray eyes. "Where did you get this?"

Penelope glanced at Mattie. "My niece painted it."

"How?" the woman asked. Her voice warbled, sounding like a radio losing its station.

Jonathan chose that moment to wander into the tent. Lucy stepped over to him and gripped his arm.

"With oils," Mattie said. "Sometimes I paint with acrylics, but for a job like this, I needed oils for the proper blending. I wanted to catch the interplay of light and shadows more accurately. It's an old estate in town."

"I know what it is," the woman said, returning to the painting. "I grew up there."

A wild wind blew through the tents and the hanging scarves fluttered like tangled birds. She reached out her hand toward the canvas but stopped short of touching it.

"How could you have known exactly what it looked like?" The woman was crying now, quiet tears leaving wet tracks on her wrinkled cheeks.

Mattie stood beside her. Should she try to comfort the woman or pretend she didn't notice her sadness? "I don't know. I painted what I saw in my head. You said you grew up there? Are you a Degaré?"

The woman nodded. "Mona Degaré. How strange this all is. I just left the lawyer's office. There was an official reading of a statement about my family. You're so young, you don't likely know anything about my family, but we've been marred by a tragedy for more than seventy years. My father was accused of murdering my mother and her supposed lover, and when my father went to prison, the state split my siblings and me up among family, and we never truly recovered from that broken home. I'm the only remaining member of my family now."

Mattie's curiosity overstepped propriety. "What was the official reading for? Did you sell the property?"

Mona shook her head. "My mother wasn't murdered," she said, still sounding dazed by the news. "Neither was her lover. They framed my father so they could run away together. Through the years, my mother and her lover had other children, and on his deathbed last week, their oldest child revealed the truth. He hadn't known about my mother's previous life until just before she died. He felt conflicted about it for years and didn't feel compelled to share it until now. Until he was dying.

"All these years . . ." Mona pulled a handkerchief out of her pocket and dabbed at her cheeks. "My mother abandoned us, and my father was an innocent man. I haven't wanted to be anywhere near the estate. I preferred to let it fall into ruin, just as my family disintegrated throughout the years. But now, seeing this picture . . . *this* is exactly how I remember it from my childhood when we were happy and free." She pulled the painting from its stand and held it in her arms. "This makes me wonder if I should restore the old estate, maybe donate it and its gardens to the city. The gardens were glorious, and if they could be revived, then maybe, despite the fact that everyone is gone, the gesture could offer my family redemption and peace. It could bring goodness back to a name that has been tainted for so long." She looked at Mattie. "How much?"

Mattie felt too stunned to speak immediately. Penelope nudged her arm. "Take it," Mattie blurted. "I mean, it's yours for free. I couldn't possibly charge you for it. Not after everything you've been through."

Mona lifted the painting in her hands. "Thank you. Seeing this brings back so many sweet memories that I forgot for too long."

"Let me wrap it up for you," Mattie said, and Mona thanked her again.

When Mona moved toward the table where Mattie wrapped the painting in craft paper, Mattie and Penelope saw that Stephen Sloan was also in the tent.

He looked starkly different from how she'd seen him at the law office. Stephen had exchanged his suit and tie for a button-down cotton shirt tucked into khaki shorts. His white-and-tan tennis shoes were trendy and transformed lawyer Stephen into casual, surprisingly good-looking Stephen. He waved shyly. "Hey, Penelope." Then he acted as though he was interested in the swing skirts. Mattie's aunt had the look of someone who wanted to bolt out of the booth. Mona, the last Degaré heir, walked out of their tent with the wrapped painting and a lightness she had not entered with.

Stephen spoke up. "Correct me if I'm wrong, but you just completed another task." He moved closer to the group huddled inside the tent.

"Can you believe that?" Lucy asked. "For years I've thought of that place as the murder estate, and the rumor was all wrong."

Jonathan's mouth pulled down. "What tasks?"

"What are you doing here, Stephen?" Penelope asked.

Mattie snapped out of her daze. She'd been watching Mona disappear into the crowd and was momentarily amazed by her own ability to create art that was so meaningful to someone else.

"Browsing," Stephen said.

"For skirts?" Penelope questioned. Her tone made it clear she wanted him to stop browsing their booth.

"He's right though," Mattie said. "One of the requirements was to paint a picture that affects someone in a positive way."

"Definitely positive results there," Lucy chimed in. "I'd even say life-changing. Did you see her face? Mattie, you are incredible. You might have single-handedly convinced her to donate the house and land to Ivy Ridge to preserve her family's name in a *positive* way for all time. That's huge!"

"What requirements?" Jonathan asked.

Ignoring Jonathan, Mattie addressed Stephen, hoping to give Penelope some relief from his presence. "Since you were here for this one, we won't follow up with formal proof. But that's three of the seven, and Lucy and I will complete the fourth one, taking a baking class, next weekend. I'm almost halfway through. So if there's nothing you want to purchase today, we'll reach out to you as needed."

Stephen glanced between Mattie and Penelope, who was avoiding his gaze. He looked crestfallen at her obvious rejection, but he nodded and walked out of the tent. Penelope lifted her eyes and watched him go. Mattie saw a fleeting glimpse of regret in her aunt's expression, but Penelope made herself busy shifting around the paintings to fill the hole where Mona's painting had been.

"Are you in some kind of legal trouble?" Jonathan asked.

Lucy groaned. "For Pete's sake, just tell the man what's going on before he makes both of us crazy."

Mattie didn't want Jonathan any deeper into her life than he already was. But it seemed no matter how many steps backward she took, he took double the amount toward her.

"If it means you'll stop poking into my personal life," Mattie said in a huff. "My mom left a testamentary trust for me, and in order to receive my inheritance, there are certain requirements I have to meet."

Jonathan's eyes widened. "A baking class is one of them?"

"Sounds ridiculous, doesn't it? That's because it is," Mattie agreed. "There are seven tasks, and yes, attending a baking class is one of them. So after next weekend, I'll be over halfway through them."

"That's why you're staying in town until December, but you might leave sooner. What are the other tasks?"

"I'm starving," Lucy interrupted. "The Salsa Shack's truck is here. Anybody wanna grab food?"

"You two go," Mattie said, motioning to Lucy and Jonathan. "I should stay here and work the booth."

"Sounds good!" Lucy said. "I'll talk to you soon."

"Why don't you go with them?" Penelope said to Mattie. "I'll be fine here by myself." When Mattie tried to disagree, Penelope gave her a look that said, *Go and see what happens.*

Outside the tent, Lucy linked arms with Mattie and leaned in close. "Sorry about that. I didn't mean to pressure you into coming with us. For all I know, you might have been trying to avoid me," Lucy joked. "You're not, are you?"

"Of course not," Mattie said. "Not *you.*" Lucy's eyebrows lifted and Mattie tossed a quick glance at Jonathan. "I'm trying not to complicate life."

Lucy nodded her understanding. "He's taken an interest in you. Anybody can see that. We'll eat quickly and then you can ditch us."

Mattie glanced over at Jonathan. Was she feeling excitement or anxiety? When Jonathan caught her looking at him and smiled in response, her heartbeat quickened. "Just a Kiss" by Lady A started playing in a nearby booth.

Halfway to the taco truck, Jonathan got a phone call and had to bail on them, which he didn't look happy about. He told Mattie he'd stop by her tent later, which had Lucy wide-eyed and Mattie unable to respond before he rushed away. Lucy had the decorum not to ask Mattie questions about why she didn't want Jonathan around and instead filled the time talking about an upcoming certification she was hoping to obtain from the Institute of Floral Designers. They shared a bag of tortilla chips and salsa, and Mattie ate two street-size tacos al pastor, happy to listen to Lucy talk about flowers and her future.

After eating, Mattie finished the afternoon with Penelope in the booth. The run-in with Stephen and Mona left both of them quieter than they had been that morning. At the close of the day, Penelope had sold more than half her inventory, and the only painting remaining was the one of Central Park. Jonathan never returned to the booth. Why had she believed he sincerely wanted the painting? Her hope in his return frustrated her. If she was steadily pushing him away, why would she care if he was *staying away*? She needed to focus on the tasks. Four more to go and she could buy a car and maybe open that gallery in San Francisco.

Chapter 25

JONATHAN

JONATHAN PACED HIS DAD'S UPSTAIRS OFFICE WHILE taking a phone call. A vendor in Chicago was partnering with him on the reopening of the Electric Eel. After an extensive remodel, the once-aging bar had been transformed into a hip lounge with nightly music. The investors and owners wanted to draw in a large enough crowd to entice A-list musicians into performing there. Jonathan hadn't worked with the owners before. They'd been referred to him by a current client. Most days Jonathan could handle high-maintenance demands or whining from spoiled clients, but today his patience was more worn down than the soles of his high school sneakers.

A few of today's demands were ensuring the temperature in the lounge would stay at seventy-three degrees all night, as if Jonathan were some kind of thermostat god. The newest ultimatum, the one that nearly sent him over the edge, was a request for Maine lobster, but not the smelly or aggressive kind of shellfish. What did that even *mean*? Was he meant to call his seafood guy and request only the polite and well-behaved lobsters? The client rushed off the phone, leaving Jonathan to sort out their needs. He rapped his forehead against the doorjamb.

He could toss on his athletic gear and go for a run to empty his mind, but he'd already been for a seven-mile run this morning. Jonathan thought his daily runs energized him and kept his mind active and ready to problem solve. But since returning to Ivy Ridge he realized the running was a stress reliever from the tension he carried in his body *because* of his job.

The much easier requests and polite thank-yous he'd been getting from his dad's clients for the past few weeks made dealing with the imperious demands more challenging. His dad's clients' biggest concerns were about having enough food for everyone and making sure the air-conditioning worked efficiently in whatever venue they booked. They didn't want their attendees passing out from low blood sugar or overheating. The level of professionalism was just as high as with businesses in the city, but his dad's clients were more appreciative and flexible. In Chicago, clients were hyperfocused on appearances, on who among the elite would make an appearance and how much media publicity they were receiving. That was part of the business, and when the client made money, so did he. But Jonathan hadn't missed the intensity and the constant need to be "on" as much as he thought he would. When he first arrived, the slower pace in Ivy Ridge made him antsy, but now there were aspects of it that he was starting to prefer.

The biggest downside to quieter workdays and nights without the city noise was that he was left alone with his thoughts. With no evening distractions other than hanging out with Luca, Jonathan kept thinking and rethinking about his past and his future. Questions without answers rose like air bubbles from the depths of the ocean. Had he made the right decision staying in New York after college and working full-time as a promoter? Should he have returned to Ivy Ridge and worked with his dad? What if his baseball career hadn't ended? Could he imagine himself living in Ivy Ridge again? What was Mattie Russell doing right now? How far along was she with her tasks?

Thinking of her drew him to the second-floor window at the staircase landing. To his surprise, Mattie was in the Russells' backyard. She'd set up an easel and canvas on the flagstones and held a paintbrush in her hand. He instantly remembered he'd never gone back to her festival booth to buy the Central Park painting, the one that had stunned him with its accuracy. The one that looked identical to a photograph someone had taken of him a few years ago. With all the work calls on the day of the festival and organizing the business event that same night, he'd forgotten. Did she think he was a jerk for saying he'd come back and never returning? Was she the forgiving kind?

His stomach growled, so he closed his laptop and took the stairs two at a time. He yelled to his parents that he'd be back after lunch and was out the door before they could question him further. Jonathan decided to come through the garden gate like friendly neighbors were apt to do, at least on TV sitcoms. Once he was in the Russells' backyard, he heard noise coming from a portable radio on the patio table. Mattie painted an open book with blackbirds flying out of it as though they'd been released from the pages. She still hadn't noticed him, so he cleared his throat. Still nothing.

"Howdy, neighbor," he said in an exaggerated accent that made him sound like a Texas cowboy.

Mattie flinched and then relaxed. She lowered the paintbrush from the canvas. There was a smudge of green paint on her cheek. Her white T-shirt looked to be the designated painting shirt because it was covered in bright-colored splatters and smears that would make any '80s kid envious, extra points if it was puffy paint. Her long hair was pinned up on top of her head in a style that made her look like a mad scientist at work—a beautiful scientist, no doubt. "Hey, how are you, and what are you doing here?"

He heard the humor in her voice. "Still needs some work, but I'll give you a half point. I didn't make it back to you during the festival. Any chance you still have the Central Park painting?"

"I thought you'd forgotten. It's the only one that didn't sell." She put her paintbrush and palette on the table. "Still interested?"

"Definitely." He pulled out his cell phone. "Can I send you money or do you want cash? Five hundred dollars, right? Lunch included?"

"Tempting to take the money and run," Mattie joked, "but two hundred is fair for the size and work involved. No need to add lunch. Let me grab it from upstairs."

Her words conveyed she wasn't interested, but the way it *felt* when they were near each other revealed otherwise. He knew he wasn't wrong about their connection, but Mattie kept her distance. Why was it simpler for her to keep out of people's lives? What had happened to make her choose loneliness over friendship? Was it the loss of her mom or something more? "What if I want to take you to lunch?"

Mattie glanced toward the house and then at her canvas. "I'm ... busy."

"You do eat, don't you? I need a mental break from work and to get out of the house. I eat lunch with my parents almost every day." His attention shifted to the radio as the volume increased. "Are you listening to the Braves game?"

Her eyes lit up. "Yeah, they're ahead by two. Robert and I think they have a shot this year at the Series."

That was unexpected. "You're a Braves fan?"

"Don't sound so surprised," she said. "Girls like baseball too."

"I'm not a Luddite. I know girls like baseball. I've seen *A League of Their Own*. We have something else in common. I'm a *huge* Braves fan. It was my dream to play for them."

"You played in college, didn't you? Why did you stop?"

Jonathan tried to sound nonchalant about what happened, but a vein in his temple started throbbing. "Same story most players have. I got injured my senior year and that was that." The compound fracture had broken more than his body; it had broken his spirit for a long time. Before he tumbled down into a black hole of lost dreams, he switched the attention back to her. "So how about we grab sandwiches from Toasties? It'll be easy and quick, and then you can get back to being busy. They have the best grilled cheese this side of the Mason-Dixon Line."

"You're good at this," Mattie said. "Lucy was right. Is professional charmer on your résumé?"

"You think I'm charming?" Was she complimenting him?

She didn't answer as she gathered her supplies and told him to meet her around front. Then she disappeared into the house. When Mattie came out the front door, Jonathan was in his dad's pickup truck, idling next to the curb and playing air drums to Phil Collins's "In the Air Tonight." She'd changed into a pair of shorts and a Braves T-shirt. The green paint was washed from her face, and her hair was down, falling around her shoulders. He tried not to stare. She made casual look sexy.

Mattie opened the door and held the painting. "Is there room for this? You want it to ride in the middle between us?"

He turned down the radio. "Like a barrier we can't cross? You stay on your side, I stay on mine?"

"Works for me," she said and hopped in, positioning the

painting in between them on the middle of the bench seat like a third passenger. "Do you mind if we turn on the game? It's the bottom of the ninth."

Jonathan chose his programmed channel 2 on the satellite radio, which broadcast MLB Network Radio. He pulled away from the curb and glanced over at her. Mattie Russell intrigued him. Maybe it was better he hadn't been home the summer after his high school graduation, because he was an idiot back then, and he would have screwed up with her. But now maybe he had a better than average chance of convincing her to spend more time with him. He'd already swayed her to have a lunch date, so things were looking up. They were both only temporarily in Ivy Ridge, so what was the harm in hanging out until they left?

They parked and headed for the restaurant, noise spilling outside. Toasties was packed with a chatty lunch crowd. Jonathan scanned the two-top tables and booths and saw no open spots. "Plan B?" he asked Mattie.

"Which is?"

"We could picnic in the state park," he offered, guiding her toward the order line. This would also help him avoid being recognized by any locals eager to ask questions, specifically about baseball. The word *picnic* seemed to arouse suspicion on her face. He held up both hands in a sign of peace. "Fast, friendly, get us out of this crowd."

"Since the temperature is no longer at melt-your-face-off highs, I guess eating outside isn't a bad idea," she conceded.

"Jonathan Carlisle?" a woman's voice asked from behind them.

Mattie and Jonathan both turned to look at the woman. Myra Murphy, a cheerleader he'd taken on a couple of dates during high school, smiled at him with glossy pink lips. She looked much the same as she did back then, minus the more intense tan and dramatically teased hair.

Myra toyed with a string of pearls hanging around her neck. "I'd recognize you anywhere. You haven't changed a bit. I haven't seen you in Ivy Ridge in years. What are you doing home?"

"Good to see you, Myra," Jonathan said, using what he called his professional voice. "This is my friend Mattie Russell. We're having a . . . working lunch." He caught sight of Mattie's smirk and refocused. "Dad had a stroke, and I'm home assisting him with the business for a few weeks."

Myra's expression softened. She squeezed Jonathan's bicep. "Oh, bless your heart. You're a good son. I hope he's doing okay now. I bet they love having you home. They were always so proud of you, so sure you were going to rocket off to being a famous baseball player. We *all* knew you were going to get out of this small town." She leaned in and whispered, "You're one of the lucky ones, getting out of here. Some of us are *stuck*." Her lip curled for a second, and then she straightened. "I felt so bad about how it worked out for you. It was such a shock—"

"Myra!" a burly man shouted from the front door of the restaurant.

Myra rolled her eyes. "Duty calls," she said. "So good to see you again. *Really* good. If you're in town long, look me up." She spun on her bejeweled sandal and sashayed across the restaurant.

"I have a new superpower," Mattie said.

"Huh?" Jonathan said, watching Myra and the burly man leave.

Mattie's mischievous smile caused her eyes to crinkle at the corners. "My new superpower. I'm invisible. Myra didn't even *see* me."

Jonathan chuckled and rolled his eyes. "Believe me, she saw you. You're hard to miss. Let's order and get out of here."

With their orders bagged, they headed the few miles to the closest state park entry. By the time they arrived, the Braves had won, and Mattie tapped her hands on the dashboard in a victory rhythm.

Jonathan parked in the lot that led to Blackberry Bluff and where he knew there were open grassy areas. He'd come up here a few times during high school with friends and also on dates when taking a date back to her house with her parents nearby wasn't appealing. He grabbed an old drop cloth out of the back of his dad's truck and carried it to a shady spot. Mattie followed behind with the food bags but stopped when they entered the clearing.

He unfolded the cloth, rippling it through the air before letting it drop to the grass. Mattie walked to the rock ring surrounding a fire pit and then gazed out at the forest . . . or was she staring at the rocks?

"You okay?" he asked.

She pointed at one of the rocks that had been chiseled away by time and now looked like a chubby man wearing a pointy hat. "I've seen that before."

"You've been here?" He felt a twinge of jealousy. Had a date brought Mattie to Blackberry Bluff?

She sat down on the drop cloth. The wrinkled, stiff cloth crunched and crinkled beneath her movements as she placed the food bags in the center. "No, but I saw that same rock in a picture of my mom. I thought it looked like a gnome." She pointed at the firepit. "And that was in it too. I found the picture recently in a box of her things in the attic."

Jonathan sat down near her. "That's an uncanny coincidence, me bringing you to the same place."

"Sophia would say it's a sign."

Jonathan reached for a brown bag and unrolled the paper to open it. "A sign of what? That you and I should be here having lunch together?"

Mattie stared at the gnome rock and shrugged. He handed her a wrapped sandwich, a bag of chips, a bottled water, and a wad of napkins.

He opened his water bottle. "Hey, I haven't had a chance yet to say I'm sorry about your mom."

Mattie nodded but didn't respond.

Jonathan drank from his bottle and desperately wanted to lighten the mood. "So why are you so into baseball? Is your dad a fan?"

Mattie stopped unwrapping her sandwich. Wrong question? So much for lightening the mood. Mattie had never once mentioned a dad. Was he deceased or a deadbeat or the last person on the planet she wanted to talk about?

"I never knew him," she finally answered. She paused so long that he thought the conversation was over, but she started up again like someone who needed to get the words out of her body before she exploded. "And I never cared to. Mom said I was dropped off on the doorstep at Halloween in a pumpkin—of course I knew that wasn't true, but it was *my* story of where I came from, and that's all I needed to know. I was fine with it being just me and Mom, and I didn't need a dad, didn't think about him or wonder where he was. I thought if he wanted to be in my life, he would have been. But Penelope thinks maybe he never knew about me, and ever since I've been in Ivy Ridge, I don't know what I want."

He couldn't read her expression. "Do you want to find him?"

Her shoulders drooped forward. "I don't know. Yes? No? Maybe? But what if he's a total loser?" She looked abashed at her openness. "I have no idea why I'm info-dumping all of this on you. I'm sorry. You wanted a nice, quiet lunch and you got *The Mattie Show* instead."

Jonathan chuckled. "I happen to like *The Mattie Show*. It's the most interesting thing I've watched all day." When she smiled at him, he felt victorious. "Seriously, though, if he's a total loser, then you don't have to do anything. You don't have to spend time with him, and you'll know why your mom never wanted him in your life."

Mattie picked at the melted cheese stuck to the thick crusty bread. "What if Penelope is right? What if he never knew about me?"

"He never had the option to be in your life."

"That's a possibility."

Jonathan opened his chip bag and popped a few chips in his mouth. "I'm guessing no one else in the family has had luck finding him."

Mattie shook her head. "All I've found are random mementos like that photo taken here, buttons from baseball games, movie tickets, that sort of thing. And all she left for me more recently was a will requiring random tasks that lead me nowhere."

"All of it led you back to Ivy Ridge." *Back to me*, he thought but wasn't about to vocalize.

"Temporarily."

"Right. Temporarily."

Mattie finally bit into her sandwich. "You were right. This is an excellent grilled cheese—still gooey inside with a good toasty crunch on the bread. And to answer your question, I'm into baseball because Mom was. We went to a lot of games, no matter what city we lived in. I remember going to minor-league games in Nashville when we lived there. When we lived in Atlanta we went to a lot of Braves home games. Mom always managed to get tickets for the best seats. She had a special talent for that. And I worked for the New York Yankees selling snacks for a season."

Jonathan bit into his grilled cheese with bacon and nodded. He displayed his sandwich bite toward her. "The bacon makes this next-level. I know you told me you moved around a lot, but remind me again where you've lived?"

"We moved about every two to two and a half years. We lived in Anaheim and Boston, but I don't remember either place because I was so young. Then Nashville, Atlanta, Fort Myers, Austin, Sedona, New York City, Asheville, Portland, and Chicago."

Jonathan swallowed before he answered. "Did you like moving so much?"

Mattie opened her chip bag and looked toward the gnome rock. "I guess I liked the adventure of it all. No chance of getting bored anywhere. Just when we were starting to put down roots, it was time to dig up everything again. It didn't feel unusual at the time, but now it's unsettling."

"What's unsettling?" he asked.

"The idea that I don't belong anywhere. Mom was comfortable being a free bird, but now that she's gone . . . I'm not sure I want that life anymore."

She turned her pale green eyes on Jonathan and gazed at him

in a way that made him squirm. "What?" he asked, wiping a hand across his mouth. Did he have crumbs on his face?

"I've never admitted that out loud before," she said. "I'm not sure I realized it until this moment."

He thought about his own sense of belonging. For years he described himself as a New Yorker, a transplant for sure, and although he'd never called himself a Chicagoan, he never said he was a Southerner either. He left Ivy Ridge after high school and hadn't wanted to come back, especially not after his injury. "Do you want to belong somewhere?"

"Possibly. At first I knew I'd be leaving here after the tasks were done, but—"

"But you don't know where you want to belong?"

She half smiled at him. "Something like that, but I have an idea forming."

He tried to picture Mattie somewhere other than right here with him, but he couldn't. "Want to share?"

"Not yet," she said. "What about you? Is Chicago going to be your forever home?"

"You make me sound like a rescue animal," he joked. "Maybe I am, in a way. I love Chicago. There's an energy there, and you never feel alone, unless you want to be, not with humanity everywhere every day. You feel like the city is one big family. You can find anyone to help you with anything. For example, I needed people to help me continue my business there, and I found someone for every event, and they didn't act like it was a hardship. They were happy to help me."

"The museums were a favorite of my mom's. She loved sitting on the steps and people-watching. We did a lot of that in Grant Park too."

Jonathan finished his sandwich. "Christmas was a fun time to be in the city, wasn't it? People go all out for the holidays. I'm mostly working all the time, but I catch glimpses of it." Catching glimpses of the season was a slight exaggeration. Jonathan's work schedule was packed from sunrise to long after sunset every day starting in mid-October and didn't let up until after New Year's. He hadn't properly celebrated any holiday in years. Having a lunchtime picnic? No chance of that.

Mattie leaned back on her hands. "You didn't answer the question. Do you think Chicago is where you'll stay? Or would you rather end up in a place like Ivy Ridge?"

She'd opened up to him, and Jonathan felt emboldened by her honesty. "Being in the city and working all the time distracts me from myself." She cast a questioning gaze his way. "I haven't been home in a few years. On purpose. Everyone always asks me about baseball, just like Myra today. They were all so *sure* I'd be a famous ball player on TV." He shrugged and looked toward the bluff. "I thought that too, but after my injury I couldn't face their questions—or worse, their pity. And I felt . . . well, like a huge disappointment to everyone. Like I'd destroyed their dreams *for* me."

"That's a bit dramatic, don't you think?" she said, although her tone was gentle.

"Probably," he admitted with a sheepish smile. "But moving back to Ivy Ridge and working at my dad's company felt like a massive failure. And I'm unmarried with no children. Totally failing at life."

"Wow," she said sarcastically, "you really are the absolute worst kid anyone could have. A college graduate with a successful job who supports himself *and* comes home to help keep his father's company running. You have all your teeth, you appear to be healthy, and you aren't a deadbeat from what I can tell. I can see why you consider yourself a disappointment."

Jonathan chuckled. "Saying it out loud does make me sound a little over-the-top."

"Drama queen," she teased. Then Mattie's expression sobered. "I get it though. Life didn't work out how you imagined, so you felt embarrassed because everyone had such high hopes for you and you thought you'd let them down. But it seems like you're doing okay for yourself. From my perspective, you look like the opposite of disappointing."

Jonathan grinned. "Isn't handsome the opposite of disappointing? So you're calling me handsome?" Mattie rolled her eyes and laughed. "What about you—can you see yourself living in Ivy Ridge?"

"It's growing on me," Mattie admitted. "And I like being around my family, strange quirks and all."

"Quirks like how you can paint things you've never seen?" he asked, feeling unsure of how she'd respond. "That painting of Central Park. Do you want to know why I'm so interested in it?" He opened a social media app on his phone. He scrolled through his pictures and stopped to enlarge one. Then he handed the phone to Mattie.

Her eyebrows rose on her forehead as her mouth dropped open. "Is that you?" she asked.

"Uncanny, isn't it?" The photograph looked exactly like Mattie's painting with him standing on the Central Park bridge. "It's like you painted my memory. Like how you did with Mona Degaré."

Mattie stared at the gnome rock in silence for a minute. "That surprised me as much as anybody. I don't know *how* it works, but it does. Or how the tasks Mom left for me are happening so easily, like she knew everything would come together this way, but how could she have?"

Goose bumps rose on Jonathan's skin. Even the timing of his dad's stroke was eerily coinciding with Mattie's return and their reconnection. "Maybe she was special just like you are."

They locked eyes, and he thought he saw a blush in Mattie's cheeks, but she broke eye contact and started gathering their trash. Was the conversation over? Had he pushed it too far? Said too much? She stayed quiet the whole ride back to the house, but when she climbed out of the truck, she said, "Thanks for today. It was . . . nice."

"You sound surprised," he said.

"I am," she agreed. "But in a good way." Then she closed the door, and Jonathan sat in the truck, grinning at the steering wheel like a lovestruck teenager.

Chapter 26

MATTIE

A WEEK LATER MATTIE HEADED INTO TOWN TO MEET Lucy at Butterfingers for the baking class. Despite her best efforts, Jonathan's voice in her head kept saying, *"You can make friends and keep friends even if you're leaving soon."* What if keeping everyone at arm's length, never letting anyone in, wasn't the best idea—and never had been? Penelope had siloed herself in a way too, and it hadn't brought her abundant happiness.

Mattie parked up the street from Butterfingers. While walking up the sidewalk she glanced through the front window of an empty shop. She couldn't tell what had been there. Retail maybe? The long narrow room had redbrick walls and planked flooring covered in a layer of dust. The next shop was Butterfingers, and Mattie found Lucy was already waiting for her inside. The bakery popped with color. Bold yellow accents were everywhere, from the front counter design to the shelving to the smiling sunshine clock hanging on one wall. The black café tables and chairs were pushed to one side of the front room and rolling stainless steel tables were arranged in a U shape with Lenora's setup in the center, including her bright yellow mixer. Mattie donned the coordinating yellow apron Lucy handed her. Then they read through the oatmeal crème pie recipe and looked over the preproportioned ingredients while they talked about their shared love of Little Debbie cakes.

A young strawberry blonde–haired woman came out of the

kitchen. She carried extra ingredients to a couple across from Mattie and Lucy. The woman's short hair was pinned back on the sides with barrettes. Her chestnut-brown eyes were set into a full face with rosy cheeks. She looked every bit the friendly girl next door. Lucy waved and caught her attention.

"That's Elisa. She helps Lenora bake," Lucy said.

When Elisa weaved her way over to them, the apples of her cheeks were lifted in a jovial smile. "Hey, bakers. Got any questions so far?"

"Any insider secrets to how we can make sure our oatmeal crème pies turn out?" Lucy said.

Elisa adjusted her apron. "This is top secret and foolproof." She leaned toward Mattie and Lucy and whispered, "Follow the recipe." All three girls laughed. Lenora called for Elisa, and she wished them luck before she hurried off.

Lucy picked up the recipe again, then lowered it. "I'm glad we're doing this but also weirdly sad."

"Sad?" Mattie picked up a rubber spatula and bounced it in the palm of her hand. "Sorry you chose me as a baking partner because I'm seriously lacking in experience?"

Lucy's smile flashed before her expression turned serious again. "The more tasks we finish, the closer you are to leaving. You *are* leaving, aren't you? You haven't said for sure, but I assume you're going back to Chicago. Jonathan mentioned that's where you were living."

Mattie squeezed the spatula in her hand before putting it back on the counter. What would Lucy think about the plan growing wings in her mind? "I'm not going back to Chicago. I quit my job, and the apartment belongs to someone else. He'll probably rent it or leave it open for when he's in town. I was thinking . . . San Francisco maybe."

"Whoa," Lucy said. "That's really cool! And really far away. What's there? Friends? A boyfriend?"

Mattie's face scrunched. "Boyfriend? Hardly." That was one label she'd never bestowed on anyone. "Just an idea I'm kicking around."

Lucy's smile stretched across her face. "And . . . ? I know there's more to this *idea*."

What was it about Lucy that caused Mattie to *enjoy* sharing her secrets with her? "There's a gallery for sale."

Lucy bounced up and down. "And you're going to buy it?"

"Shh!" Mattie grabbed Lucy's arm to stop her from drawing so much attention their way. "I'm *thinking* about it. Once I have the inheritance money, I could buy it and open a gallery. I've emailed the sellers and asked for more information."

"Wow, Mattie," Lucy said, looking childlike and sincere, "you are so brave."

Was she? Or was she grasping for anything to make her life feel stable and normal? "I haven't told anyone else yet, so keep it between us, okay?"

Lucy nodded her agreement.

Lenora started the oatmeal crème pie lesson, and Mattie was able to give most of her attention to making the fairly straightforward cookie recipe. But her mind wandered to San Francisco, to opening a gallery, and to the possibilities of what that life could be like. Would she enjoy being on her own without a companion? Could she learn to make friends? So far she wasn't doing too terribly with Lucy.

While the cookies were baking, Lenora walked around the room talking with each student. When she made it around to Mattie, Lucy had wandered off to talk with the couple across the room.

"Mattie, right?" Lenora said. Her shoulder-length, springy hair was held back by a decorative elastic headband, and her corkscrew curls framed both sides of her face in a cloud of spirals. She wore black-framed glasses that complemented her wide eyes lined in swooping eyeliner. Plum-purple lips flattered her friendly smile. She touched Mattie's arm briefly. "I was sorry to hear about your mama. Lilith was a fun lady. I met her a few Christmases ago after I first opened. She came in one afternoon when I was flustered and wondering if opening this bakery was a bad idea. But she was so kind and offered me great business advice."

"*My* mom did?" Mattie asked. Mattie was sure the only business knowledge her mom had to give was how to start a new job and then how to leave one. What kind of business insight could she have possibly offered?

"Mm-hmm," Lenora said, pushing her hands into her apron pocket. "She encouraged me to keep going and to keep focused on my dreams. Never give up. Just take the next step even if I couldn't see the end point and how it might work out."

"Not exactly business advice," Mattie said mostly to herself.

Lenora nodded, and her curls danced around her head. "*Life advice* is a better description. I wish I could thank her in person for encouraging me that day not to give up on my dream. I'm happy you're here, Mattie, and I hope you're enjoying the class. Let me keep moving and checking on everyone before our cookies are done."

Lucy bounded back over to their station. The timers started going off on the ovens, and there was a flurry of activity and excitement about seeing how the cookies turned out. At the end of class, Mattie and Lucy munched on their near-perfect oatmeal crème pies. A few were flat and wonky, but they tasted even better than the boxed brand. Lucy pulled out her phone to check a text and frowned at the illuminated phone face. Then her shoulders hunched.

"What's wrong?" Mattie asked, almost overcome by the urge to hug Lucy.

"They didn't accept me."

"Who?"

"The Institute of Floral Designers. They said I don't have enough real work experience, that working at a nursery isn't enough." Even though it didn't seem possible, her shoulders slumped more. "I wanted that certification to show that I'm legit, that I'm a real florist with talent."

"I'm sorry," Mattie said as she packed their cookies into small to-go boxes. "But you don't need a certification to be a real florist with talent. You already are that."

Lucy nodded but stayed unusually quiet while they packed up their things. They thanked Lenora for the class and said goodbye. Outside on the sidewalk, Lucy lingered with a lost expression.

Should she get involved? Wasn't it her style to drift along the outskirts without seeming too withdrawn or antisocial? Mattie had spent years perfecting the art of not committing. But seeing Lucy's downcast face tugged at her compassion. "Hey, what's so important about a certification? You probably have more talent than half the people in that group."

Lucy sighed. "Everyone in my family is certified or degreed or part of some accredited association that proves they're important and worthy. But not me. I have a college degree, but it's in mass comm, which I don't even use, unless you account for my exceptional talking skills. I just wanted to show that I'm qualified and good enough too."

Mattie noticed the edge of a canvas sticking up in the back seat of her car. "Walk with me." She unlocked the car and grabbed the painting she'd created in the park a few weeks ago—the monarch butterfly with one traditional wing and another wing created by a cluster of blooms. She handed the canvas to Lucy. "Why do you need certifications to prove yourself? If you stopped striving so hard, you'd see how great you already are. Your life might not look like everyone else's—like this unconventional butterfly—but it doesn't mean you aren't perfect just the way you are."

Lucy held the painting in both hands. "You cut right to the heart of the matter, don't you? But you're right. I *am* trying to prove I'm good enough, and for what? Nobody in my family has ever made me feel like I'm not. It's me being hard on myself. This painting is beautiful, Mattie. It speaks to me."

"Gentler than I do, I hope," Mattie joked. "It's yours. I painted it weeks ago with the intent to sell it, but I forgot about it."

"It was meant for me," Lucy said. She unexpectedly pulled Mattie into a side hug and squeezed hard, causing the air to whoosh from Mattie's lungs in an *oomph*. "Oops, overzealous! I know you're only planning to be here until your tasks are finished, but I'm glad you're here now." She smiled at the canvas. "Thanks for this, and let's get together soon."

On the way home Mattie thought about the will requirements and about Lucy's gratefulness that Mattie was in town for a while longer. The number of people who wanted her to be in Ivy Ridge was growing fast enough to make her consider staying—even after the requirements were fulfilled.

Chapter 27

JONATHAN

"DID YOU KNOW THIS WAS FAKE MEAT?" LUCA ASKED. HE poked his finger into the portion of the hamburger where a huge bite was missing. Red juice squished out onto his finger. "But it bleeds."

"Beet juice," Jonathan said. "Anything to get my dad to eat healthy while believing he isn't."

"Your mom is sneaky," Luca said. "I like that. This fooled me." He glanced at the three-tiered birthday cake with a sparkly gold 60 pressed into the white icing on the top tier. "Is the cake real?"

"As opposed to imaginary?" Jonathan joked.

Luca took a bite of his hamburger and chewed. "As opposed to vegan or sugar-free or some other poisonous fake-cake monstrosity."

Jonathan laughed. "You'll have to try it and find out."

He and his brothers had spent all morning hanging up string lights with retro light bulbs in the backyard. They stretched blue-and-white bunting between tree trunks, along with a large white-and-gold Happy Birthday sign that draped across the cake table. Tables and chairs were placed around the backyard, and Lucy had arranged daisies and mums in blue mason jars on the linen tablecloths. There were lemonade and sweet tea glass dispensers on a drink table, and another long table was covered in platters of deviled eggs, pigs in a blanket, sausage balls, and chips and salsa. There were ceramic bowls of spinach dip, cheese dip, and buffalo chicken dip, along with fresh fruit, an assortment of crackers, and blocks of cheese. His brother William was manning the grill, and beside him a hamburger bar had been set up with all the standard burger fixings.

This food spread was nothing like what he would have arranged in Chicago for his clients. They would have laughed him out of the room if he'd suggested pigs in a blanket or store-bought chips and salsa. But these birthday food choices were not only some of his dad's favorites but also Jonathan's. It was the kind of food he instantly associated with Ivy Ridge.

Looking around the backyard, Jonathan shook his head at the thought that he could have missed all this.

It wasn't just the food that felt like *home*. It was also the people crowding his childhood backyard. There were clusters of his dad's friends talking about laying concrete in their driveways and about the outrageous cost of a new set of tires. There were well-dressed huddles of his mom's friends wearing pearls, sipping wine, and looking like they all shopped at the same boutique for Southern women. His brothers, David and William, were both there with their wives. David's two sons and William's son and daughter, all under six years old, raced around the yard with balloons taken from the decorations. They laughed wildly while playing some invented game with rules that changed every few minutes.

Virginia had invited all their closest neighbors, including the Russells, and Jonathan's eyes constantly searched for and found Mattie, who was presently snickering with Lucy and eating from a plate heaped with party food. Unexpectedly so, Jonathan felt an overwhelming sense of belonging and comfort. For the first time in a long time, he realized he didn't wish he was in the city instead.

"Your mom says you've been a real gem," Mrs. McGuire said,

interrupting Jonathan's thoughts. She held the narrow flute of a plastic wineglass in her fingers and sipped. "Coming home like you did and helping with the company." She took another sip and leaned in so close that Jonathan could smell her floral perfume. "Bet you miss Chicago though. I know I would. Ivy Ridge must pale in comparison. It's so small here, and Chicago is"—she sighed dramatically—"so much more exciting. When are you going back?"

Her words broke apart the calm feeling he'd just been enjoying. "I'm not sure. When Dad is well enough, I guess."

Mrs. McGuire's eyes found Thomas in the crowded backyard. "He's looking great. It probably won't be long before he's ready to get back to it. Bet you're counting down the days." She patted his arm. "Good to see you, Jonathan. I need a refill." And she flitted off toward the drink table.

When he first arrived in Ivy Ridge, he had been, in a way, counting down the days until he could return to Chicago. He had a great life there, an apartment he loved, and a job that kept him busy and paid well. But he didn't have *this* in Chicago. He didn't have backyard cookouts or family birthday celebrations. He didn't have his nephews and niece running barefoot through the grass. He didn't have his parents smiling at each other with an expression of gratefulness.

Virginia picked up a small bell and rang it, bringing the attention to where she stood at the cake table. She called everyone over to sing "Happy Birthday to You." While Jonathan made his way toward the table, his phone rang. One of his wealthiest clients in Chicago was calling, probably to offer a job. This was the type of call he would never let go to voice mail. Could he slip away to the back of the crowd unseen, answer the call, and be back before anyone missed him? One less voice singing wouldn't be a big deal.

Virginia called his name, and Jonathan looked away from his flashing phone. She motioned him to the front to stand with his brothers. Jonathan silenced the call and joined his family around the cake.

They sang loudly and slightly off-key, but it was a joyful rendition of the birthday song. Then David's wife started cutting the cake and handing out slices. His gaze found Mattie's, and she smiled at him. He grabbed two slices of cake and walked to her.

"We're making a habit of this," he said. "Me and you sharing birthday cake together."

She took the offered plate and laughed. "I'm not sure you can call anything a habit that only happens once every ten years."

Jonathan realized there was something else he didn't have in Chicago. He didn't have the sound of Mattie's laughter stirring something deep and forgotten inside him.

Chapter 28

PENELOPE

THE NEXT SATURDAY MORNING BROUGHT IN THE END OF September and also an end to the stubborn heat. Wisps of pale white fog circled around tree trunks and created sparkling dewdrops on the grass as a pale pink sunrise colored the sky. Leaves had started to change, deepening into crimson and gold. Yellow sycamore leaves tumbled down the sidewalks like children skipping off on adventures.

The crispness in the air made Penelope want to drink warm apple cider and stroll through an orchard, something she hadn't done since she was in college. Not since she and Stephen had driven to Ellijay for a long weekend during fall break.

She hadn't thought about Stephen this much in years. But for the past few weeks it seemed that every time she found herself without something to focus on, her thoughts drifted to him. Memories of their time together waited everywhere for her to find. Ordinary objects with little-to-no previous meaning now caused her to think of him. A chipped silver-rimmed teacup in a store window reminded her of the set he bought her from an antique store in Savannah. The grocery store tulips were the same color as the ones he gave her on their first date. The local drive-in was hosting a flashback series and was currently playing the last movie they watched together. Now with Mattie and the will tasks, Penelope couldn't get away from him. She wondered for the millionth time why Lilith would have made such an arrangement.

Thankfully today Mattie's next task would keep Penelope's mind busy. They were participating in the Green Planet Initiative hosted by Green Clover. She saw Robert and Sophia off early that morning as they headed to Jacksonville to spend the day with former clients turned friends. The house was quieter without them, but Mattie's presence had a way of filling up the rooms with good energy. At almost eight o'clock that morning, Mattie bounded downstairs, drank a cup of espresso, and the two were off to help plant a fall butterfly garden.

Two hours into the event, Penelope, Mattie, and Lucy—one of the many teams designated with specific jobs—had established a rhythm that comprised Lucy coordinating plant placement, Mattie digging holes, and Penelope chatting up the plants while she put them into their new homes.

"There you go, lovely little aster," she cooed while scooping dirt over the exposed roots. "You're going to love your new home here."

Mattie leaned against the shovel and wiped sweat from her brow. Her blue cotton T-shirt was speckled with dirt, and her ponytail had slid off-center. "How do you know it's going to love it here?"

"Wouldn't you?" Lucy asked. Looking down at her color-coordinated plant map, she said, "Ironweed is next."

Mattie rammed the shovel into the earth to keep it upright. "Water break is next," she said.

Plastic Igloo coolers filled with ice water were set up on a card table along with recyclable cups. Penelope hadn't seen this type of spigot water dispenser in years. Someone had probably dug these out of their garage, a relic unseen since T-ball games in the 1990s. While she filled up her cup with water, Penelope glanced around at the other teams. Some were planting small trees, while others were setting up butterfly feeders. A voice floated to her, and Penelope snapped her head in its direction. Stephen was placing a pineapple sage bush into a newly dug hole. Wearing a red T-shirt and khaki shorts, he looked just like the young man she fell in love with. The sight of the victorious grin on his handsome face caused her heart to stutter. He looked in her direction, and she quickly turned away. Did he think she was staring at him?

Luca and Jonathan approached the water table with a dozen pizza boxes. The smell of hot cheese, meats, and vegetables overpowered everything else. After putting the food on the card table next to the coolers, Jonathan pulled a stack of paper plates out of a shopping bag. Luca yelled to everyone that lunch had arrived. He slid the top pizza box from the stack and placed it behind the coolers.

"I'm sticking with Chipper Jones," Luca said to Jonathan.

"Hey, ladies," Jonathan said. "How's the planting going?"

Mattie's expression noticeably brightened. This was a new development. Hadn't Mattie been actively trying *not* to pay attention to him? What changed?

Lucy responded for all of them, going off on a tangent about the importance of having food for overwintering butterflies right up until the cold weather sent everything into hibernation. In the middle of her discussion about how monarchs needed their strength for their long journey south, Mattie chimed in. "Were you talking baseball?" she asked Luca.

Luca grabbed a cup and pressed the button on a cooler spigot to fill it. His deep brown curls spilled out from the edges of his ball cap. "The Braves' all-time best player. I say Chipper."

"But Austin Riley is crushing it," Jonathan argued.

"Hmm," Mattie said. "What about Andruw Jones?"

"You're into baseball?" Luca said dramatically, placing one hand on his chest. "She's a keeper."

Jonathan gave him a playful shove. Someone was humming an upbeat song behind Mattie, and she turned to see Raoul Moreno, Lucy and Luca's dad. His friendly smile made him instantly likable, and Mattie returned his smile. Up close Penelope could see how much the twins favored him. His tall, athletic build matched Luca's, and he shared the same large, round, chocolate-brown eyes and full lips as Lucy. Raoul asked how everyone was doing.

Without responding to Raoul's question, Mattie asked, "Were you humming 'Footloose'?"

"Please don't ask him to dance," Lucy joked, "because he will most definitely reenact that scene from the movie. He has a love affair with Kenny Loggins music."

"My mom loved Kenny Loggins," Mattie said. "By default, so do I. 'Footloose' is a classic."

Raoul's wide, boyish smile made him look even more like Luca. "Finally someone with taste." Looking at his son, he said, "Thanks for picking up lunch. Did Terry agree to make mine?"

"Doesn't he always?" Luca said. He pointed to the pizza box behind the water coolers.

Raoul flipped open the box, and Mattie stepped forward slowly. "What kind of pizza is that?"

Raoul dropped a slice onto his plate and displayed the pizza to Mattie. "Beet pesto with kale and goat cheese. It sounds weird, but it's delicious. Try a slice."

Mattie visibly stiffened and then locked eyes with Penelope. Penelope had never known anyone other than Mattie who wanted that combination, one Mattie had been eating since she was a little girl.

"We need a tiebreaker," Jonathan said, looking at Raoul. "Best Braves player of all time."

Raoul looked at his son. "You said Chipper, and I bet Jonathan said someone younger. Riley? Acuña?"

Mattie stepped closer to Raoul. "What about Andruw Jones?" Raoul's dark brown eyebrows rose on his wide forehead. "I went to a lot of baseball games growing up, but my mom had a deep love for the Braves."

"Dad played for the Braves," Lucy said.

"Minor league, the Richmond Braves," Raoul said quickly. "Eons ago."

"Really?" Mattie said, squeezing the paper cup in her hands and denting the sides. "I saw them play when we lived in Nashville."

Why were Mattie's hands shaking? Low blood sugar? Penelope suggested they take a lunch break. Mattie went for Raoul's special pizza, and he waited to hear her thoughts. She casually agreed it was a good flavor combination. Why didn't Mattie mention it was also her favorite? Or how bizarre it was that Raoul had the same preference?

They stood around eating pizza off paper plates and making conversation that ranged from herbology to genetics to baseball to rock bands. Jonathan barely took his eyes off Mattie. Did Mattie see how smitten he was with her? While Mattie and Lucy finished eating, Penelope returned to their planting area, which left her alone with the unplanted sedum and salvia.

"Looks good over here," Stephen commented behind her. "Y'all are faster than my team. Looks like you have twice as much planted."

Penelope whirled around in surprise. Dirt smudged his cheek, and a line of sweat followed along his hairline. He removed his sunglasses and hung them on his T-shirt collar. He still had the kindest eyes she had ever seen.

"Another task done. How many does Mattie have left?"

Penelope's hand tingled. She wanted to reach out and wipe his cheek, but that would startle them both. And the very idea that she wanted to touch him infuriated her. "You aren't counting?" she asked with more bitterness than she intended.

Stephen touched his fingertip to a purple salvia bloom. "I'm making polite conversation, Penelope."

The half smile on his face stirred the dust on long-neglected parts of herself. Her whole body suddenly became restless. How did he have the power to resurrect the emotions she'd entombed years ago? "Why?" She sounded like a petulant child, which amplified her frustration even more. Was that hurt she saw in his eyes?

His lips thinned. A response she knew meant he was thinking carefully about his next words. "Why not?"

"Because . . ." Because of a dozen reasons, not one of which she wanted to say out loud.

Stephen's response was unexpected. He laughed. "Should I go with 'because why'? Or directly address the issue?"

"Which is what?" Penelope asked.

"Why are you hell-bent on ignoring me and acting like we're sworn enemies? We were friends once . . . *more* than friends. Yeah, it was years ago, but I was madly in love with you, and you broke *my* heart, and now here I am trying to start over with you, and you can barely be polite to me. What did I do?" He shoved his hands into his pockets. "What did I do to make you hate me so much?"

Penelope gaped at him. He'd been madly in love with her? She'd broken *his* heart? No, that was all wrong. He'd been unable to stop the forward motion of his life. He'd sped away from her at top speed, leaving her in a wake so high it had drowned her. Stephen had *no idea* how much his refusal to fight to keep her had shattered her. He'd just . . . let her go like a kid releasing a balloon into the sky, with no care for where it might end up or what might happen to it. She'd been left to deal with the loss—no, the *losses*—alone.

"I don't hate you," she finally admitted. What she felt for Stephen was, in fact, the opposite. "I never hated you." She inhaled a slow, calming breath before continuing, or else she would unravel in front of everyone. "We broke up because it was what you wanted. Don't you remember your first year of law school? It was the most difficult year you'd ever had—the coursework, the projects, the competition. You had no time for anything else. Making it to the top of your class was crucial to you, and there wasn't room for us in your life anymore. You were coming apart beneath the burden of school, and I was like deadweight you were dragging around. I didn't want to ruin your chances at a successful life."

But that wasn't the whole truth. Having a girlfriend wouldn't have ruined his chances, but what she'd hidden away in the attic would have. It would have derailed him, and she loved him too much to ask him to sacrifice his plans. When she suggested they break up, Stephen agreed. He didn't come after her. He just let her go. That truth still felt like broken glass in her stomach. Penelope tried to smile at Stephen, but it wobbled on her face. "And look at you now. You're successful and happy and living a good life."

Stephen frowned and stayed silent so long that Penelope started fidgeting with the shovel. She glanced over to see Mattie watching her.

"That's not how I remember it," Stephen finally said. "And you're wrong about a few things. My first year of law school wasn't the most difficult. The first year without you was. I remember arguing about how you thought I'd be better off without you complicating my life, but you were never a complication. You were one of the best things *in* my life. I thought that was just your excuse for wanting to break up, and I didn't want to make you miserable. Now I'm successful, sure, but am I happy? Not really. I've not been truly happy since you left."

Stephen stunned her again by walking away without allowing her to say more, and it took every bit of her strength not to crumble into the garden soil as the old fractures in her heart rebroke. She had never truly buried Stephen. She could see that now, how hard she'd been fighting to hang on to those broken shards of who they'd been no matter how much they cut into her.

Chapter 29

MATTIE

FOR THE REST OF THE AFTERNOON, PENELOPE WAS QUIET and withdrawn, even when Mattie tried to engage with her. The conversation with Stephen had obviously rattled her. Plants seemed to lean into her, brushing against her legs when she walked near, as though offering comfort. Stephen's gaze lingered on Penelope with such intensity it was a wonder Penelope didn't have holes piercing through her body from his stares.

Once the plantings were done in their area, Mattie, Lucy, and Penelope helped other groups—except Stephen's—finish up. While positioning a maple sapling into the oversize hole, Mattie's lapis lazuli necklace caught on one of the reedy branches. She tried to stand upright and gasped, realizing she was unable to free the necklace without snapping the chain.

"Hang on, let me help you," Raoul said, appearing at her side. He gently untangled the silver chain from the thin branches without damaging its delicate leaves. "There you go."

Raoul continued to hold the lapis lazuli stone in his hand while Mattie straightened. They were so close to each other she could smell the mix of sweat and topsoil on his clothes and skin. The creases around his eyes deepened with the concentration he placed on the deep blue precious stone. Then he cleared his throat and let go. The stone bounced against Mattie's chest.

"Thank you," Mattie said, pinching the stone between her

fingers. His favorite pizza was *her* favorite pizza. Was there a chance he was more than just Lucy and Luca's dad? She pressed on. "It was my mom's." Raoul nodded without speaking. A warm shiver moved over her like she'd slipped into a hot bath. "Did you know her?"

"A long time ago and not for long," Raoul said.

Mattie exhaled. Maybe she was wrong. "I'm starting to think no one knew her at all. Not even me." Mattie hadn't intended to sound so forlorn. The kindness in Raoul's eyes was so parental and so full of compassion, reminding her of how Robert often looked at her.

"I doubt we ever really know anyone," he said. "Most people are lucky if they know themselves. What I remember about your mom was her excitement for life. She was fun and fearless but not stupid. And she was one of the prettiest girls I'd ever seen. She had a way of making you feel special." He glanced down at his dirty work boots.

"Thank you for sharing that," she said. After the frustration she'd felt about her mom, the tasks, and the will, it was a relief to hear Lilith had left behind goodness too. "I'm learning she was . . . complicated. Complex too."

"Aren't we all?" Raoul said, and they shared a smile.

Later that afternoon Penelope promptly closed herself up in her sewing room, not even emerging for dinner. That evening Mattie stood in the kitchen eating a snickerdoodle from the cookie jar. She yawned just as her phone dinged twice in a row. The first message was from Lucy.

Thank you so much for helping out today! Dad was singing
your praises, off-key of course. Let's grab lunch this week.

The other text was from a number she didn't recognize, but
she could read the first line. *Hey, this is Jonathan.* Mattie hesitated
before tapping to read the whole message. How did he get her number? The floorboards began vibrating beneath her feet, causing her
whole body to tremble.

"Knock it off," she said, but she was smiling. When had she
gone from avoiding Jonathan to feeling this—whatever *this* was?
Excitement? Eagerness? Gut-clenching nervousness? She opened
the message.

Hey, this is Jonathan. Don't be mad at Lucy, because
I bribed her. What are the chances you'd like to get
together? Lunch at Blackberry Bluff?

Her cheeks lifted, and an unexpected noise rose up her throat.
Was that a giggle? She texted back.

Should I even ask what you bribed Lucy with? It better have
been good. Chances of having lunch at Blackberry Bluff
are high. Tomorrow is open.

Jonathan texted back that he'd come over and get her for lunch
tomorrow. Mattie slid her phone into her pocket with a grin on
her face that wouldn't dim. The staircase creaked and diverted her
attention. Penelope still hadn't come out of her sewing room, and
Mattie couldn't let go of the idea that she *needed* to check on her.

Mattie knocked on the closed sewing room door. When no one responded, she turned the knob and pushed open the door. The room was lit only by a table lamp, and the rest of the space was thrown into dark grays and black shadows. Penelope stood at the window with her back to the door. She'd changed out of her gardening clothes and now wore a soft lavender cotton dress. Her damp hair shone like onyx against her back. Pastel-colored baby clothes were arranged on the floor as though the outfits were being photographed for social media or to sell on consignment.

An eerie prickle skittered over her like something was terribly wrong. Penelope didn't acknowledge her presence. Mattie recognized the clothes. "Hey, you okay? What's with the baby clothes?"

Penelope's response was raspy and strained. Without turning she said, "She would be almost twenty-five."

The hair on Mattie's head stood on end. "Who?"

"I never settled on a name," she said. When she faced Mattie, her eyes were swollen and bloodshot, her gaze wild and haunted. Penelope walked to the baby clothes and knelt. She lifted a white jumper in her hands. The cuffs were lacy with a smocked rainbow-striped band across the waist. "I thought maybe Violet or Ruby. I don't know why I kept leaning toward colors. Maybe I thought she would be bright and full of life. She *should* have been." She covered her face with the tiny outfit and her body trembled with grief.

Mattie knelt beside her aunt and gently touched her. A sudden awareness filled Mattie, but she had to ask anyway. "Who are you talking about?"

Penelope sniffed and lowered her hands. She placed the jumper with the spread of clothes. Her shaky smile looked like the face of someone cracking apart while trying to feign strength. "I got pregnant in college. I didn't tell *anyone*, not even your mom. Not that she was around when it happened. She'd already run off, but we didn't know it was to have you. Can you believe that, both of us pregnant at the same time? I was in a relationship, but I didn't want him to know about the baby because it would have changed everything for him. So I came home and decided to do it on my own. I made all these beautiful clothes and dreamed of how my baby girl and I would make it work. But I . . . I lost the baby at five months."

Mattie's hands were over her mouth, and the hot tears on her cheeks surprised her. "I'm so sorry. And you never told anyone, not even after it happened?" Penelope shook her head. "Why? Why did you go through all that alone, on purpose?" Mattie's stomach twisted. "And then Mom came home with me, a healthy baby girl. That must have been gut-wrenching."

Penelope hung her head. "It was bittersweet." She looked up at Mattie. "You were such a beautiful, sweet baby. It twinged a little at first, but I wasn't jealous of Lilith. I was happy for her and grateful for the time I got to share with you. When you were with me during the summer, it felt like you *were* mine."

Mattie had never thought of their lives from Penelope's perspective, never imagined that her aunt had loved her and cared for her like she would have her own daughter. The summers with Penelope had been some of her favorite memories, and Mattie was now realizing they'd been saturated with the feelings of being safe, loved, and *home*. Penelope had been acting like a second mother all these years, making sure Mattie had art supplies, a warm, fun place to stay during summer vacation, and a happy holiday home where there was always laughter, food, and security. For a moment she envisioned how different her time here would have been if she'd had a cousin, someone her age to play with in Ivy Ridge. Would Penelope have married the father? Would they be a tight, picture-perfect family unit so dissimilar from Mattie's own childhood experience?

"Wait . . ." Mattie locked eyes with her aunt. "Is this connected to Stephen?" Penelope's bottom lip trembled, so she pressed them together in a tight line. "You never told him?"

Penelope wiped her cheeks. "I couldn't. He was in law school. He didn't have time to even breathe, let alone start a family. We were kids, Mattie, and he would have left law school to take care of me. I didn't want that for him, and when I lost her, how could I tell him then?"

"Why can't you tell him now?" Mattie asked. Penelope looked stricken and unstable like someone stepping off the Tilt-A-Whirl. "You're just like Mom, then. Neither of you gave those men the opportunity to decide how they might handle it. You both took away their choices. Maybe it was for the best, but . . . maybe not."

Penelope sagged forward and reached for a pink sundress. "I don't even know *how* to tell him. I've been so mean to him since he's been back in Ivy Ridge."

Mattie shrugged. "He'll forgive you. He'll be shocked, for sure, but I see the way he looks at you."

She cast a questioning glance at Mattie. "What do you mean?"

Mattie rolled her eyes. "Like you hung the moon and the stars and the sun and the—"

"You mean the way Jonathan looks at you?"

Mattie's face felt like someone struck a match too close to her cheeks. The lamplight flickered. "He's taking me to lunch tomorrow."

Penelope smiled for the first time in hours. Her whole face lifted with a lightness. Enid sashayed out of a shadowed corner and purred, then circled around Penelope and leaned into her.

"Call Stephen," Mattie said. "Give him the chance to know the truth and the choice to respond."

Penelope nodded and reached out for Mattie's hand. "We're going to be okay," she said like a whispered promise.

Mattie squeezed her hand in response. "Mom used to tell me about a cake you and Sophia made called the Heart Mender."

Penelope looked lost in thought for a moment. "I'd forgotten about that cake. Sophia swore it healed hearts. What made you think of that?"

"Seems like the perfect remedy for us to try soon."

⚶

Mattie startled awake as though jarred from a falling dream. She lay in bed, heart thumping a rapid rhythm, and tried to recall what she'd been dreaming. But *had* she been dreaming or had it been something else—

She sat upright in bed at the sound of someone whispering, and not just anyone. Her mom. Mattie gripped the sheets like a terrified child. Her bedroom door was open. She stared into the dim hallway with wide, wild eyes, listening hard enough to cause a vein in her forehead to throb. The quiet murmurings started again, sounding like her mom's animated voice from behind a closed door. Mattie flung her legs off the bed and crept toward the doorway and out into the hall.

Penelope's bedroom door was closed, and when Mattie pressed her ear to the wood, she heard nothing but the steady hum of the ceiling fan. The staircase leading to the third floor creaked. Enid sat on the bottom step watching Mattie. With one hand on the railing and her face tilted up, listening, barely breathing, Mattie placed her bare foot gingerly on the first stair. Halfway up the staircase, the whispers started again, forming words Mattie could almost understand, followed by muffled laughter. Then something dropped against the floor, followed by a knocking sound, and Mattie almost screamed.

She scrambled up the remaining stairs, thinking every crazed thought in quick succession. *Is it an intruder? A trapped animal? Or worse, a ghost?* The whispers stopped when Mattie stood in the doorway to the art studio. She flipped on the light. The window was open and a tickling wind rustled the curtains and danced across the room. The plants shivered on the shelves, creating a soft *shoosh*ing noise in the room. Mattie's canvases had been moved and one had fallen on its face.

Behind where the canvases had been propped was an imperfection in the wall—the rectangular outline of a gnome-size door with a hole where a doorknob should be. Mattie had never noticed it before, but behind it was the source of the knocking. Forcing herself not to imagine anything with teeth waiting on the other side, Mattie slid her finger into the hole and tugged. She braced herself, but nothing leaped out. The open door revealed a compact storage space barely big enough for Mattie to wedge herself into, and it was completely empty except for a vintage red cardboard pencil box. The box was decorated with a map of the United States on the top.

Mattie flipped open its lid. A pressed four-leaf clover sealed in a mini plastic bag sat on top of a faded, blue-toned polaroid. In the photo her mom stood with a young man who looked vaguely familiar. They looked to be about seventeen or eighteen. Lilith's hands were wrapped around his bicep, and she leaned into him with a look of stunning joy on her face. The young man had one hand on the back of his neck. His expression said, *This girl is into me?* The words *you and me* were scribbled on the bottom of the polaroid in her mom's handwriting.

Underneath the photo was a folded letter. In a different script were the words:

> L,
>
> These past few weeks feel like a dream. I get up in the morning, and I don't know what is real or what isn't anymore. All I know is that I don't want this to end. I have to go back to college, but you and me, we've got something good, don't we? We've made something special. Write to me. I'll come home as much as I can. After you graduate, we can figure out how to be together more.
>
> Love, R

Mattie reread the letter. She picked up the polaroid, and that's when it struck her who the young man looked like. Luca. But the man in the photograph wasn't Luca. It was his dad, Raoul. The photo dropped from her fingers and floated to the floor like a feather. Her mom had been with Raoul before she left Ivy Ridge, exactly around the time she'd gotten pregnant. The probability that Raoul Moreno was Mattie's dad had just become astronomical.

Mattie unintentionally slept in the next morning. By the time she padded downstairs, still wearing her faded gray nightshirt with a pumpkin on the front and her cotton pajama shorts, she found the quiet house empty. Penelope had left a handwritten note on the island. *Gone to see Stephen this morning. Yogurt and sliced fruit in the fridge, granola in the pantry.*

Mattie felt intense admiration for her aunt, warming her from the inside like hot tea. After more than twenty years of holding in a heartbreaking secret from the man she was still in love with, she was about to bravely release it. What would it feel like to finally set free the broken, life-altering thing she'd been harboring all these years? Would Penelope walk lighter, laugh louder?

Mattie had her own secret spreading across her skin like goose bumps. She wanted to tell Penelope about what she'd found in the box, about the possible answer to the long-held mystery of her father's identity. But Penelope was working through her own struggles today. Calling Lucy popped into her mind, but that wasn't the right option either. Mattie imagined the conversation going something like this: *Hey, I think your dad is my dad.* Followed by Lucy saying, *Have you lost your mind?*

Who was left to talk to? Did she know an unbiased listener who could offer advice without emotional attachment? Mattie swiped to unlock her phone and looked at the last text from Jonathan. Was she really considering him as her go-to person for this kind of access into her personal life? While she debated, Mattie opened the pantry to grab the granola. The top shelf wobbled and a bag of jumbo marshmallows dropped to the floor. As she bent down to pick them up, a package of chocolate bars dropped onto her head.

"Hey, knock it off!" she said to the house and looked up just in time to see a box of graham crackers teetering off the edge of a vibrating shelf. Mattie grabbed the box before it beaned her in the head. She cradled the marshmallows and chocolate in her arms. "Oh, I see . . . not a bad idea. Thanks!"

She dropped the ingredients on the island and texted Jonathan.

> Change of plans. How about we move lunch to dinner
> instead and have s'mores on Blackberry Bluff? It's one of
> my tasks from the will.

Jonathan texted back before she could dollop yogurt into her bowl.

> You're using me as a pawn to complete your tasks? Clever.
> And yes. I'll bring dinner. You bring s'mores stuff.

The pantry door squeaked open, sounding like a high-pitched laugh. She pointed her spoon at the partially open door. "It's *not* a date. It's dinner and dessert . . . at a place mostly known as being a teenage make-out spot." Mattie rolled her eyes and mixed granola and sliced pears into her yogurt. Her stomach somersaulted, and it had nothing to do with hunger.

Chapter 30

PENELOPE

PENELOPE PARKED IN THE DRIVEWAY OF STEPHEN'S craftsman bungalow. When she called to ask if he could meet her somewhere, he suggested Deja Brew. No way Penelope was having *this* conversation in a crowded room smelling of coffee and blueberry muffins. She thought his office would be a good option, but he insisted she come to his house.

Why were her palms sweating? She gulped down half her water bottle, grabbed her purse, and squared her shoulders as she walked up the stones leading to the front porch. Why hadn't she sewn a dress stitched full of strength and courage? She should have made an entire wardrobe and worn every piece.

Stephen opened the door before she could knock. Had he been watching for her? The cool inside air rushed out and circled around her. "Come in," he said, motioning her inside.

The hardwoods gleamed in the sunlight, and the entire front of the house was illuminated in soft sunbeams. He led her into the well-organized living room that boasted a stained coffered ceiling, built-ins, and an emerald-tiled fireplace.

"The woodwork is beautiful," Penelope said. "Lots of people these days paint over the original hardwood to lighten it, but there's plenty of sunlight to keep it from feeling heavy." Unlike the conversation they were on the verge of.

"Why change what's already perfect?" He pointed to the tan couch. "Want to sit? Can I get you anything? Water? Tea? Scones?"

Penelope shot a gaze his way. "You made scones?"

Stephen laughed, and her shoulders lowered. "No. I have Ruffles and french onion dip though."

Penelope chuckled. Did he disarm everyone so easily? "Sounds awful, but thank you. I'm fine." She sat on the edge of a couch cushion and placed her purse beside her on the floor. Stephen sat on the couch, leaving distance between them.

"Is Mattie okay? Is this about the tasks?"

Penelope shook her head. "It's about us." Stephen's light expression shifted, and his back straightened. "I'm just going to come out with it. I haven't been honest with you about everything, and I don't even know where to start, but I want to apologize first. I thought I was doing what was best for all of us. And looking at us now and where we've ended up, I still believe it was for the best, but maybe it's time you know the truth."

Penelope didn't realize her hands were shaking until Stephen placed his hand over hers and squeezed. "It's okay, Penelope," he said in that soothing voice that still quieted her heart. "Whatever it is, I can handle it."

Penelope squeezed her eyes closed. Then she reached into her purse and pulled out the white envelope with the sonogram pictures. She handed the envelope to Stephen.

He pulled out the photos and tilted his head, studying them, his brow wrinkling before his eyes widened. "You're pregnant? I didn't know you were dating anyone."

Penelope's laugh came out as a sob. "No." She pressed her hands against her heart. "Was. I *was* pregnant. Years ago. That's why I broke it off with you."

Stephen's expression caused every hair on her body to stand. His eyes moved back toward the images in his hands. "My baby?"

Tears leaked from Penelope's eyes. "Of course *your* baby," she said. "I was crazy in love with you, and when I found out, I didn't want to mess up your life. You know what you would have done?"

"I would have married you!" His voice came out as a shout. "I would have spent every day loving the hell out of you and our baby. I would have done *anything* to make this work."

Penelope covered her mouth and cried. "I know. *I know.* You would have given up everything, and that's not what I wanted for you."

Stephen stood and paced toward the windows. When he turned to look at her, anger flared in his eyes for a second. "What about what I wanted? My God, Penelope . . . I nearly crumbled without you, all because you wanted me to become a lawyer?"

Hadn't it been what he wanted to do with his life? "It was your dream," she argued.

He crossed the room in quick strides and sat beside her on the couch. Grabbing her hands, he said, "*You* were my dream. I could have been a cloud collector, a flower picker, a chimney sweep." He placed the photos gently back into the envelope. "But what happened? Adoption?"

Penelope swiped at her tears. "I lost her after five months. Her little heart stopped."

Stephen wrapped his arms around Penelope and squeezed her so close she could hardly pull in a breath. He smoothed his hand down her hair, and years of pent-up tears rushed out of her. Penelope wept, and Stephen held her against him until she pulled away. His face was wet with tears.

Penelope cupped his cheek in her hand. All the love she'd tried to smother exploded within her, a force so strong it stole her breath. "I am *so* sorry. Can you forgive me?"

He nodded and placed kisses across her knuckles. "I'm sorry you went through that without me. But never again, okay? From here on out, I'd like to be here for you."

Was there a possibility for a second chance? Did she want that? Did *he*? Yes, yes, yes. "Would you— Do you want to give us another try? We could start slow, as friends."

Stephen grinned. "Seriously, Penelope? I've been waiting to give us another try for twenty years. We could go slow and start as friends. Or . . ." He leaned over and placed a kiss on each cheek and then one on her lips, and she folded into him.

Chapter 31

MATTIE

MATTIE SPENT MOST OF THE DAY WORKING OFF HER excess excited energy by painting in the art studio. She wanted to try a drybrushing technique, and by late afternoon she'd created a midnight forest with a path stretching through it like a charcoal ribbon. At the end of the path, a gathering of fireflies illuminated the shadows of two people. Friends? Lovers? Strangers? It was open to interpretation.

Sophia called out for Mattie from downstairs. Mattie shouted a greeting and then put away her art supplies.

In the kitchen Sophia stood by the whistling kettle. She poured steaming water over a tea infuser inside a dainty porcelain cup. "No one should save their fine china for a special occasion. Every day is a reason to celebrate. This was a wedding gift to your grandmother. Beautiful, isn't it?"

Mattie filled a water glass and sat with Sophia in the breakfast nook. Late-afternoon light cast a long beam over half the table, highlighting its worn edges and scratches caused by years of love and conversations.

"How was Jacksonville?" Mattie asked.

"Hot," Sophia said and lifted her cup. "A lot like this tea."

Mattie picked up her water glass. "Is Penelope home?"

Sophia shook her head.

"She left hours ago." Maybe her chat with Stephen had gone

well. But what if it had gone terribly, and she was sitting in her car somewhere bawling her eyes out? "Should I text her?"

Sophia lifted out the tea infuser, letting the amber liquid strain into the cup, before placing it on a plate. "I talked to her an hour or so ago. She was making a few stops before coming home. I'm curious. What did you say to her?"

Mattie tensed. "What do you mean?" She hadn't spoken to Penelope since last night. A quick loop of their conversation spooled through her mind.

Sophia stirred a spoonful of honey into her tea. The spoon swirled the liquid into a miniature whirlpool. Then she sipped and smiled against the rim of the cup. "She sounded fired up about the house. She called me, asking about interior decorators, new furniture ideas, and paint colors." The cup clinked against the saucer.

Mattie leaned back in the chair. "We didn't talk about redecorating."

Sophia tapped her manicured nail gently against the cup like Morse code. "Penelope sounded like she used to, many years ago." Her soft brown eyes met Mattie's. "Hopeful and, dare I say, happy."

So the conversation with Stephen had gone well. Had they reconciled? "Maybe she's excited about making a few changes."

Sophia's laugh startled Mattie. It was a deep belly laugh that resonated through the kitchen. The grandfather clock in the hallway struck the hour. "Penelope hasn't been willing to make *any* changes to this house except necessary upgrades. She wanted to preserve everything like a fossil in amber. Penelope has *never* been excited about change. Until now. Until *you.*"

"Me?"

Sophia lifted her teacup. "I don't know what you said to her, but I'm fairly certain she giggled on the phone with me, and I haven't heard that girl *giggle* since she was a girl." Sophia gazed out the windows into the garden. "I'm going to finish my tea and then grab some tomatoes and herbs from the garden. I'm in the mood for caprese. Don't let me keep you from getting ready for your date."

"Penelope told you?"

"Virginia saw me when I went out for the mail," Sophia said.

Mattie's heart stuttered. "His mom knows? She said we're going on a *date*?"

Sophia's melodic laugh circled them. "She said you were having dinner on Blackberry Bluff, and I just assumed . . ." Sophia nearly snorted into her teacup. "Mattie, honey, don't look so panicked. Believe it or not, I was young once, and Robert and I went to the bluff many times."

Mattie shoved back from the table and urgently stopped her brain from imagining Sophia and Robert making out on the bluff. She couldn't picture them as young people, only seventy-year-olds rolling around on a patchwork quilt. "You're right, I should get ready." Sophia's laugh chased Mattie all the way up the staircase.

As the sun set over Blackberry Bluff, the logs Jonathan had propped into a loose pyramid crackled and popped. Four hot dogs were shoved onto two makeshift coat hanger skewers, and he roasted them over yellow-orange flames. Mattie fidgeted on the flannel blanket. To keep busy, she toasted the hot dog buns and arranged the condiments in a neat line inside the cooler. She positioned the thermoses of hot chocolate alongside water bottles, and she neatened the pile of s'mores essentials for the third time. Her hands felt trembly. Was it because of the way Jonathan kept smiling at her? Or was it because the secret of her parentage wanted to gallop out of her like a wild mustang?

As soon as she climbed into his truck tonight, the radio had been on the fritz, playing every sappy, angsty love song no matter the channel. Jonathan scanned through nearly all of them. Even a talk radio channel was discussing a love affair between athletes. Mattie pretended she was just as confused as he was, but the undercurrent of nerves vibrated her bones.

Mattie reached for the family-size barbecue potato chip bag and pinched her fingers together at the top. She struggled to pull the bag apart along the sealed, crimped edge. "Why are these so hard to—" The bag burst open, creating a rip down the center. Chips jumped out and scattered all over Mattie and the blanket.

Jonathan barked a laugh. He pulled the skewers from the fire, carefully removed the hot dogs, and dropped them on a plate.

Mattie gathered chips and put them back into the torn bag, which was not salvageable. "Five-second rule?"

"I've eaten food from dirtier places," he joked. He touched her hand while she reached for a chip. Mattie's whole body stilled with the contact. "What's with you tonight?"

She stared at him, unblinking, for a few seconds before glancing away. "What do you mean?"

"You seem . . . nervous or distracted," he said seriously. Then added, "Is it my good looks?"

The truth rose up in her so quickly she felt as though she had indigestion. She pulled out of his grasp. "No."

A blackbird cawed from the nearby forest. "No, I'm not good-looking or no, you're not distracted?"

Mattie exhaled. She *had* asked Jonathan to dinner specifically to share her discovery with someone who could help her figure out what to do next. "Let's fix our hot dogs, and then I'll tell you."

They filled their plates with food. A few other couples were taking advantage of the great location and the sunset but were far enough away to muffle their conversation. In the fading light, Mattie could just see the silhouette of the gnome rock. Her mom and Raoul had probably sat right here. Had he taken the photos she found in the attic?

"The suspense is killing me, Mattie," Jonathan said after finishing off his first hot dog. "I'd be dense to assume the only reason you asked me out here is to complete a task. What's on your mind?"

Setting her plate to the side, she reached for her bag. Along with the s'mores ingredients, Mattie had packed the pictures and the letter from Raoul. She handed them over to Jonathan, and he looked quizzically at her.

"Look while I talk," Mattie said. "I found some of those photos packed in the attic with my mom's things. Last night I found another box with that one"—she pointed at the photo of Raoul and Lilith—"and that letter and a four-leaf clover."

Jonathan unfolded the letter and then glanced between it and the photo. "This looks like—"

"Luca? Yeah, I'm pretty sure that's his dad. Obviously that's my mom. I'm guessing the love letter is from him, too, which means they were *together* before my mom left Ivy Ridge to have me. She didn't come back until I was one, and the Moreno family had already moved by then. You see where I'm going with this?"

Jonathan passed the mementos back to Mattie. She could almost see the thoughts forming and connecting in his mind. "You think

Mr. Moreno is your dad?" She nodded and he leaned back and stared up at the silver dots of light poking through streaks of violet and midnight-blue sky.

Once she released the first truth, the rest of them flew up her throat like a flock of startled birds bursting from the treetops. "Everything, *everything*, I've been doing has been leading me to this conclusion, but not only *this* one. The will tasks—it's like she knew exactly where to send me, what to make me do. At first the requirements seemed pointless, a ridiculous wild-goose chase to send me on, but why? I couldn't figure out *why* she would arrange all of this, but now it's starting to make sense." Mattie's heartbeat raced, dizzying her mind, but she couldn't stop the words, like she had to speak all of them out loud to make them real. "Task one sent me to buy flowers, which led me to Green Clover, which is how I met Lucy, who joined me for task two, the pizza class, where she talked to Lenora about a baking class, task three, which led me to Butterfingers. And Lenora mentioned that my mom encouraged her to follow her dreams, which could be why Lenora kept Butterfingers thriving.

"I had *no* idea how I would complete task four, which stated I had to paint a picture that changed someone's life. I wanted to kill time while here, so I painted a lot. I convinced Penelope to rent a booth with me at the festival, and I felt compelled to paint that picture of the Degaré estate, and Mona Degaré *just happened* to be there and came to *my* booth, and you saw what happened. The Green Planet Initiative, task five, happens to be run by the Morenos. Am I supposed to believe it's a coincidence that Raoul played minor league for the Braves—a team my mom loved—and he loves Kenny Loggins—also one of my mom's favorites—*and* his favorite pizza combination is also mine?"

Jonathan held up his hand to stop her. "Wait, you *actually* eat the beet pesto with kale and goat cheese?"

Mattie narrowed her eyes. "*That's* your takeaway from everything I said? I'm serious, Jonathan. Even with Stephen being the executor. Mom knew Penelope would need to sort that out." Her hands clenched in her lap. "I was so angry. It felt like she tossed me out into the ocean without a life preserver, but now I see they were all around me. She didn't abandon me. She left all these ways for me to find myself, to *save* myself. But how? How did she know everything would come together?" The hot tears that sprang up surprised her, and she tried, but failed, to contain them. Her body trembled like an autumn leaf caught in a gust of air.

Jonathan looked uncomfortable. What was he thinking? That she'd totally lost her mind? But then he crawled over to her and put his arm around her shoulders. Mattie sagged against him before thinking it might not be the best choice. He held her against him and made a soft shushing noise, the way someone might comfort a scared animal. He smelled like woodsmoke and laundry detergent with a hint of pine. "It's okay. This is a helluva lot to go through and learn in a few weeks' time. I'm still trying to follow along."

Mattie sniffed against him, relaxing into the warmth of his body.

"Could be she didn't know how it would all work out," Jonathan said when Mattie stopped crying. "But she knew that if she gave you some of the pieces, you'd figure out the rest. She must have believed the right people would come into your life to help."

Mattie sat up, and Jonathan's arm fell behind her. She immediately missed the heat of him and shivered. "I know it sounds crazy, but I think she knew when she was going to die, and because of that, she set all of this in motion for me."

Jonathan reached out for her hand, and she let him twine their fingers together. "Do you know why?"

"I think she knew I'd eventually want to belong somewhere, that maybe I'd want to put down roots, maybe stay in Ivy Ridge. Or have the courage to choose where *I* want to end up." Maybe even as a gallery owner in San Francisco. But California didn't have *this*. This moment with her fingers wrapped around Jonathan's and the comfort of him.

Jonathan nodded. "Bringing all these people into your life, like Lucy, and leading you to your dad, who is possibly Mr. Moreno, could be the start of that. You haven't mentioned me."

Firelight flickered off his grin, and Mattie felt a flare go off in her heart. "Should I have?"

"Damn straight," he said with a laugh. "I helped you with the plants. I was at the pizza class. You painted a picture for me, actually *of* me. And here we are, completing task six. Does that mean your mom wanted you to share s'mores with a handsome man?"

"Should we look for him?" Mattie joked. "He's going to miss out on dessert." She laughed as he tugged her toward him, and Mattie leaned against his body, feeling the rumble of laughter in his chest.

Jonathan smoothed his hand down her hair and caused her to shiver in a different way. "On a serious note, are you planning on talking to Mr. Moreno?"

Mattie inhaled a slow breath and nodded against him.

"I can go with you if you want," he offered.

Mattie turned her face up toward his. The tip of her nose grazed his lips. Looking into his eyes made her forget to breathe, forget that anyone else existed in the universe. Was this how it felt to have a romantic date and let someone get close?

"Thank you," she said, and because she felt his desire like a heat wave, she tucked her head again. If they started kissing, they'd skip right over the s'mores. "We still have a task to complete."

Jonathan chuckled. "Fair enough. This is not a rejection but the intense focus to get a job done first."

Mattie *wanted* to kiss him. She'd been fighting the attraction since the day he showed up on the sidewalk. Part of her wanted to pull the emergency brake, full stop, because he would be returning to Chicago soon and she might be on her way to California. She thought of her mom, how Lilith lived with arms wide open, how she never turned down any opportunity for pleasure. Her mom would say that kissing Jonathan would be worth it, even if he left next week. Because even when the man was gone, the memory would live on. "Definitely not a rejection. You're a party planner, right?"

His lips thinned. "A *party planner*? I'm a promoter who manages high-end clients with marketing, publicity, VIP customers, booking of entertainment—"

"Whoa, whoa, settle down," Mattie said lightly. "I didn't mean to ruffle your fancy feathers. I'm asking because my last task is to throw a Halloween bash at the house, and I wondered if you'd like to help me since you're *not* a party planner."

"On your birthday? Could we have cake at midnight again?"

Mattie crawled across the blanket to grab the skewers. "Not *on* my birthday but before. Maybe next weekend? Does that give us enough time?"

"I can pull a party together in days," Jonathan said, oozing confidence. "Can we dress up?"

Mattie shrugged. "We can make that optional."

"No, I meant *us*. Can we be a pair, like Jack and Jill or Cleopatra and Antony or—"

"You're not serious."

He reached for the marshmallows. "Oh, I'm serious. Bacon and eggs? Woody and Buzz? Han Solo and Chewbacca?"

Mattie opened the bag of chocolate and unwrapped one bar. "How about we go as me and you?"

Jonathan shoved a marshmallow on each skewer. "Are you implying we're a pair?"

Mattie groaned. "Do you *ever* give up?"

"On you? Never." Then he leaned over and did what she'd been wanting him to do again since the very first time ten years ago. He kissed her.

His lips were warm, and he tasted like hot chocolate. Mattie's arms fell slack and the chocolate bar tilted out of her hands. His kiss was chaste at first, but she wrapped her hands around his neck and pulled him closer. Jonathan deepened the kiss and leaned them back onto the blanket. Her mind was wiped clean of anything, *everything*, and she realized she hadn't romanticized their first kiss. She and Jonathan created a magnetic energy together that was unlike any stolen kiss below the bleachers or slobbery smooch at a school dance. A few more minutes of kissing Jonathan, and Mattie would lose herself completely. But Jonathan ended the kiss by pecking her lips quickly and lifting up on his arms so he could look down at her. His goofy grin unwound the last bit of tangled insecurity inside her.

"I could do this all night," he said, "but we have a job to do, and I won't be the reason you have an incomplete task." He grabbed Mattie's hand and lifted her into a sitting position. "I'd like to pick this up later, after s'mores." Jonathan touched her cheek and then grabbed the skewers. "Let's celebrate."

Mattie opened the box of graham crackers and pulled out an unopened sleeve. "What are we celebrating?"

"I've been waiting ten years to kiss you again," he said, cutting his eyes over at her while he held his marshmallow over the flames. "Well worth the wait."

Mattie tapped her marshmallow against his in the fire, a kind of toast. "Here's to not waiting another ten."

"Minutes, right?" he teased. "I'll try to hold off for ten minutes. How fast can we eat these?"

Mattie's laugh caused the flames to lift higher, sending sparks of light into the evening sky.

Chapter 32

MATTIE

WITH JONATHAN'S EXPERTISE, THE HALLOWEEN BASH
was in full planning mode and already nearly finalized. Digital
invitations had been sent, two local eateries were catering—
Toasties and Butterfingers—a DJ was hired, floral arrangements
were chosen (a gift from Lucy), and the Russell women had
already started decorating inside and outside the house.

Mattie's attraction to Jonathan increased every day, and
watching him in his element, the way he took charge of the
party with such finesse, nearly made her swoon. And Mattie
never swooned. When he was around the house, which was at
some point every day, he and Mattie sneaked off into corners
and empty rooms where they could be alone and act like groping
teenagers, which was something Mattie never did when she was
a teenager. But with Jonathan she was someone new, someone
she hadn't had the chance to be growing up.

Midweek in the Russell home found Mattie, Jonathan, Lucy,
and Luca sitting around the kitchen island, which was covered in
old newspapers. They carved pumpkins and talked about their
favorite Halloween movies. There were votes for *Hocus Pocus*,
Practical Magic, *A Nightmare on Elm Street*, and *Halloween*.
Penelope and Sophia made pizzas shaped like pumpkins and
sugar cookies decorated with orange-and-black royal icing, while
Robert entertained them with spooky songs on the guitar.

Mattie and Penelope hadn't discussed what happened during Penelope's talk with Stephen, but old heartbreaks were obviously on the mend because Stephen was currently outside putting up the next phase of outdoor decorations.

Mattie leaned over to look at Lucy's design, but Lucy squealed and faced the squatty round pumpkin away from Mattie's prying eyes. "No peeking!"

Luca's haughty laugh caused Lucy to narrow her eyes. "Lucy *never* wants to show you until she's done, like it's a big deal what she's carving."

Lucy pursed her lips. "I don't want you to feel bad about how stellar my skills are compared to yours."

"How do you know my skills aren't stellar?" Luca argued.

Lucy's laugh sounded almost identical to Luca's, just an octave higher. "I've *seen* your creative skills, and they're something all right."

Jonathan leaned over toward Mattie. "*Psst*, want to see mine?" Mattie responded with a smile, and Jonathan turned his pumpkin toward her. His deep orange, oblong pumpkin sported a goofy one-tooth grin with oversize googly eyes and a lopsided mouth.

Luca walked over to take a look and punched Jonathan lightly in the shoulder. "That's what you look like when you're talking about Mattie."

Mattie's phone dinged on the counter behind her. She slid off the stool, grabbed it, and swiped open the email notification. The gallery sellers in San Francisco were incredibly interested in her offer. So interested they wanted to set up a phone call ASAP. Mattie assumed there would be dozens of bids challenging hers. But she was their first pick? After the past few days in Ivy Ridge, did she still want to consider leaving all this for California? Mattie had never seen Ivy Ridge as a home because Lilith hadn't. The small-town life hadn't appealed to her mom, and what Mattie knew best was packing up and moving on. Jonathan's laugh cut through her tangled thoughts. He was returning to Chicago soon. What then?

"All done!" Lucy announced. "Drumroll, please!" She performed her own drumroll, which Jonathan followed up with air drums. Lucy rocked her pumpkin around to face the others.

The three-eyed jack-o'-lantern with its off-center, silly smile joggled a memory inside Mattie. She felt woozy for a second and her knees buckled. Jonathan caught her and steadied her. She shooed away his look of concern. "I'm okay," she said, trying to laugh it off, but she couldn't stop staring at Lucy's pumpkin. "Looks really good . . . and familiar."

"Really?" Lucy said. "I've never done this face before." She turned the pumpkin back toward her and smoothed jagged spots around the face.

Mattie excused herself from the kitchen, saying she'd be right back, and then hustled up the back staircase to the third floor. She flipped on the light in the art studio and went right to the paintings her mom had been sending Penelope over the years. There were seven in all—seven pieces of artwork that appeared to have no connection to one another—until now. Mattie found the one she was looking for. When she and Lilith lived in Austin, Mattie painted a jack-o'-lantern that perfectly matched the face Lucy carved tonight.

"You okay?" Jonathan asked from the doorway. Mattie responded by showing him the painting. His brow creased. "Is that Lucy's pumpkin?"

"Painted when I was twelve." Mattie positioned the seven paintings so they could see each one. "My mom kept these seven paintings out of all the ones I've created. I had no idea she was sending them to Penelope. Do you see what's happening here?"

Jonathan stood beside her. She pointed to each piece in turn. "I planted coneflowers beside lavender in the backyard, task one. This walking stick looks like the one Mona Degaré had at the festival, task four. That looks a lot like Lenora at Butterfingers, task three. We planted sage at the Green Planet Initiative, task five, and you see those blue stones? My mom's favorite stone, lapis lazuli. The basil looks exactly like what we used at the pizza class, task two. Lucy's pumpkin is task seven, the Halloween party."

Jonathan pointed at the final canvas that depicted the campfire couple beneath a starry sky. "Is that us?"

"Task six," Mattie whispered. She placed her cool hand on her forehead. Her pulse fluttered at her neck. "I feel light-headed. You *can't* make this up."

"You were right about your mom," Jonathan said, slipping his arm around her waist. "The Russells are all a little bit magic, aren't they? Magic is all around you."

Mattie turned toward him and placed her hands on his chest. "You're not freaked out by all of this?"

"Of course I am," he said lightly. "But I've always known you were different." He tucked a piece of her hair behind her ear, and she caught his gaze. "Ever since the night we met." Jonathan's cell phone started playing "I Put a Spell on You," startling them both. He stared at his phone and then looked at her with disbelieving eyes. "You've been doing the phone thing?"

Mattie stepped backward. Wasn't it enough that he just found out about the eerie premonition paintings? Now she had to explain how music sometimes changed around her? "What phone thing?"

He silenced the phone and tugged her toward him. Mattie fell against his chest, forcing out the tightness in her throat with a laugh. "Music, painting, putting spells on me. What else are you hiding, Mattie Russell?"

He didn't sound disturbed by Mattie's talents. The knot in her stomach loosened. "I can't tell you all my secrets right away."

"Take your time," he said and kissed her. "I've got all the time in the world to ease them out of you."

"Hey, you two!" Lucy yelled from downstairs. "We're still here! Remember us, your best friends?"

"We should go back down," Mattie said reluctantly. She propped the paintings against the wall, placing Lucy's pumpkin picture in the front. "I can't believe my mom has been orchestrating this for years."

"It's borderline unbelievable." Jonathan slipped his hand into hers. "Have you decided when you're going to talk to Mr. Moreno?"

Mattie had been rehearsing what she might say to Raoul for days, but she kept putting it off. Thinking about confronting an almost stranger and professing that she might be his child made her want to throw up. Every day she told herself the same thing she said to Jonathan. "Tomorrow." But she meant it this time.

"Do you want me to go with you?"

Mattie shook her head. The inevitable stomach clenching followed. "I think I need to do this on my own. Less of an audience. Lucy's going to be here with the flower arrangements, so it's a good time to sneak off to the nursery on a fake errand."

He lifted her hand, with their entwined fingers, and kissed the top. "I'll be around if you need me."

But for how long? She stopped herself from blurting the question before she ruined a perfectly good moment with an incredibly handsome man. It didn't matter how long he'd be here, her mom would say. What mattered was *right now*, and right now she wasn't confronting her maybe dad or saying goodbye to anyone. Right now Mattie was full of hope and happiness and teetering on the edge of falling in love.

In the parking lot of Green Clover, Mattie gripped the steering wheel and closed her eyes, inhaling slow, intentional breaths. The car's heater warmed her initially, but now the heat combined with her nerves caused nausea to shudder through her. So she blasted the air-conditioning and shivered in the seat. After one more deep breath she grabbed her bag, opened the door, and lurched out of the car. *Am I doing the right thing?*

As though knowing Mattie would arrive today with life-altering news, Raoul walked around the side of a greenhouse and stopped when he saw her in the parking lot. They held eye contact for a few moments before Mattie marched toward him. *I can do this.* Her black boots crunched against the mulched pathway.

Raoul put down the potted orange mum he'd been holding and shoved his hands into the pockets of his brown cargo pants. A tentative smile lifted his cheeks. "Hey, Mattie, I wondered when you might show up."

Stunned, Mattie stopped a few feet from him. "You did?"

Raoul nodded. He removed his ball cap and rubbed his hand

through his mop of dark curls. His knuckles whitened in the grip he had on the cap. Then his hands relaxed. "You want to know about Lilith and me."

Mattie opened her bag and took out the photos and letter. "Mom didn't have a lot of things, but she kept these."

Raoul returned the cap to his head and reached for the offered mementos. His expression turned nostalgic, almost dreamy. He read the letter and then stared at it. It wasn't a long letter, so what was he thinking? Had she made a mistake?

Mattie cleared her throat, breaking the spell cast over Raoul. "You wrote that?"

"Lilith was easy to love," he said. "Not so easy to hold on to. Still, I was surprised when she left Ivy Ridge without telling anyone where she was going, including me. After I moved my family back to Ivy Ridge, I found out Lilith had a daughter who was a few years older than my two kids. I did the math. I assumed she left town because she was pregnant."

Everything around Mattie paused like the whole world was holding its breath. Her body felt like she was clicking her way up the first roller-coaster incline. A few more *click, click, clicks* and down she went, heart pounding and eyes wide. "You knew?"

"Knew what?" Raoul asked.

His intelligent brown eyes knew exactly what she meant, but Mattie had to say it. "That I might be your daughter."

Raoul gripped the back of his neck and released a quiet laugh that sounded strangled and nervous. "I suspected it, but I never would have said anything. What would be the point? Lilith must have had her reasons for not wanting me to know."

"She didn't give you a choice," Mattie said. Anger pricked her insides. "She didn't give *any* of us a choice about it. She told me I was dropped on the doorstep in a pumpkin. Why? You seem like a great guy. Why wouldn't she want me to know about you?"

Raoul sighed. "Did you have a bad life, Mattie? An unhappy childhood?"

Mattie hesitated. She wouldn't have described her life with Lilith as miserable. On the contrary, her memories were filled with excitement and travel and curiosity. "No."

"Lilith was complex, and I don't know why she kept this from you for so long, but she had a way of seeing how things *needed* to be, not always what you wanted them to be. Did you know I gave her that necklace you're wearing? I'm surprised she kept it all these years."

Mattie stared at the blue stone in her necklace. "She loved lapis lazuli because of *you*?" Mattie closed her hands around the stone and hung her head. "My whole life has been surrounded by things that were because of you. Because she knew one day I'd need to find you, and she wanted us to make a connection. You eat my favorite kind of pizza," Mattie blubbered, embarrassed by the tears and the way her voice pinched.

"You eat beet pesto with kale and goat cheese?" he asked. "Hey, you look like you need a hug. Okay if I do?" Mattie wiped at her runny nose and nodded. Raoul folded her in his arms. The embrace was solid, grounding, and Mattie's first experience with what it felt like to be hugged by a father, to feel safe and protected by him. When he pulled away from her, he said, "Give me a day or so to talk to my family? I know you and Lucy are close, which is odd and yet not odd, but I'd like to tell them myself."

Mattie hadn't thought far enough ahead. How would Lucy respond to news of a half sister? Would she be furious, welcoming, shocked, supportive? What about his wife? Mattie didn't want to ruin their family.

"Don't look so alarmed," Raoul said in his deep, calming voice. "It was a long time ago, and something I would have shared years ago had I known for certain. But we all have our reasons for letting things go."

"We should probably do a paternity test, right? To make sure?" Mattie swayed on her feet. What if, by some horribly small chance, Raoul wasn't her dad?

Raoul put his hand on her shoulder. "You look like Lucy just before she goes into panic mode about a floral arrangement gone awry. Yes, we can do the test, but no, I don't think we need it. I think your mom was certain about this, or else she would have led you to someone else."

Mattie sniffed loudly. Raoul's words resonated. Lilith's "clues" wouldn't have brought her to Raoul if he wasn't her dad. Mattie awkwardly thanked Raoul, gave him her number, and promised she wouldn't say a word until she heard from him. Then she climbed back into the car, a jumble of relief and anxiety bubbling in her stomach. There was nothing more to do except go home, keep planning the party, and try not to focus so hard on the biggest question in her mind. *What happens next?*

Chapter 33

JONATHAN

THE NIGHT OF THE HALLOWEEN BASH THE RUSSELL backyard was a hive of people and animated in a way Jonathan had never seen. Not that he knew the family all that well—not until recently—but as long as he'd known the Russells, they'd been a quiet family. Never throwing parties, never playing their music too loud. Whereas Jonathan's family, full of rowdy boys and parents known for hosting boisterous get-togethers, was the opposite of serene.

This lively evening was unlike the Carlisle parties though. The Russell home, and especially the Russell women, dazzled and sparkled like the string lights shining from the trees. The illuminated windows of the house set against its dark brick exterior, along with the setting sun turning the sky the color of mulberries, created a scene fit for Halloween movies. The feel-good movies Lucy and Mattie discussed while pumpkin carving, not the ones he and Luca suggested. This party was more *Practical Magic* and nothing like *A Nightmare on Elm Street*.

The hired DJ set up in one corner of the yard and shuffled through a mix of '50s, classic rock, Halloween favorites, and contemporary music. The catered food from Toasties and Butterfingers fit the party theme. There were grilled cheese sandwiches shaped like ghosts and tombstones. More elaborate sandwiches resembled Frankenstein's monster, and there were also spider sliders with pretzel legs. A long, slender hoagie was arranged to resemble a winding meat-trio snake with olives for eyes.

Lenora's creations, nestled together on orange-and-black platters, offered a variety of options, like ghost meringues, mummy sandwich cookies, and graveyard pudding cups. Cauldron cupcakes were decorated with bubbly green icing and witches' legs poking out. The eyeball chocolate truffles were Jonathan's favorite, and so far, he'd eaten one every time he walked by the table.

But the most enticing part of the whole evening was Mattie. Wearing a black-and-indigo dress, an early birthday gift from her aunt, Mattie twirled around the guests like a midnight fairy come to life after sleeping a thousand years. He'd never seen her so vivacious. The closed-off woman he'd met on the sidewalk in August had transformed. Did he have anything to do with it? She'd exposed desires inside Jonathan, dreams he didn't know were lying dormant like seeds waiting to break open with new life.

Jonathan weaved his way over to Mattie, who was chatting with his mom. He hooked his arm around hers and excused the interruption. "They're playing our song. Dance with me." His mom's pleased smile told him Virginia wasn't bothered by him pulling Mattie away from the conversation.

Mattie draped her arms over his shoulders and swayed to the beat. She smirked at him. "'Never Gonna Give You Up' is our song?"

"An excuse to get you close."

She reached up and turned his baseball cap around backward. "You don't need an excuse. Have I mentioned how much I like you in uniform?"

He leaned down to kiss her. "How impressed are you that my college baseball uniform still fits?" He pressed his lips to hers before she could respond. The song abruptly stopped and switched to "Every Little Thing She Does Is Magic." Jonathan pulled back. "Did you do that?" He glanced toward the DJ, whose brows were knit together in confusion.

"Do what?" Mattie asked in a voice that revealed she knew exactly what. "Maybe *you* did it." She poked her finger into his chest.

"Mattie!" Lucy squealed from across the yard. She leaped— literally *leaped*—over a group of pumpkins huddled together on the patio and rushed toward them wearing a Ms. Marvel costume. A small bouquet of pink roses wrapped in gold-and-black ribbons was pressed against her chest. She skidded to a halt in front of them. "Mattie," she wheezed.

Mattie stiffened in Jonathan's arms. "Everything okay?"

Lucy thrust the flowers at Mattie. "These are for you. They symbolize joy and happiness, and my dad said they'd be a good choice."

Mattie wrapped her hands around the bouquet, and Jonathan rubbed circles on her back, trying to loosen the tight muscles. Was she trembling?

"He told me, Mattie," Lucy said. "I mean, wow, what the heck, can you believe it? You and I . . ." Lucy's eyes sparkled with tears. "We're sisters?"

"Are you angry?" Mattie whispered. She traced her finger along the scalloped edge of a rose petal.

"Angry?" Lucy said. "Why would I be angry? I've *always* wanted a sister, but I got Luca. He's cool most of the time, and having a twin connection is rad, but he's not like a sister. No, I'm not angry.

Mom was taken aback, but she's probably the most understanding person on the planet, and she knows it happened light-years ago, and my dad had no idea about it. And neither did you! Were you shocked out of your socks?" Lucy flung her arms around Mattie and nearly crushed the roses between them. Then she whispered, "Does anyone else know?"

"I do," Jonathan said.

"No one else yet," Mattie said. "I promised I wouldn't say anything until your dad talked to you."

"Cat's outa the bag now. They'll be here shortly. I couldn't wait to get over here and talk to you first." Lucy scanned the party scene and latched onto Mattie's arm. "Are those Lenora's chocolate mousse cups made into tiny graveyard scenes?"

Jonathan's dad caught his eye from across the yard and waved him over. He leaned down and kissed the side of Mattie's head. "I'll be right back."

Over the past few weeks his dad's health had steadily improved until the limp and sag associated with his left side were barely perceptible. To his credit, Thomas had been following Virginia's diet plan as much as possible, and physical therapy strengthened his body and boosted his spirits.

Jonathan knew his mom coerced his dad into dressing up, but they were a dapper pair. Looking like they'd walked straight off the set of *Downton Abbey*, Thomas wore a black dinner jacket paired with a white tuxedo shirt, white bow tie, and black slacks. Virginia's slinky, beaded evening gown, paired with black satin elbow-length gloves, made chic look effortless.

In one hand, Virginia balanced a plate of mummy cookies with a half-eaten Frankenstein sandwich. In her other hand, she held a glass of bloodred Halloween punch. She noticed Jonathan's questioning gaze, and her cheeks colored. "It's a party, and we're allowed to enjoy ourselves sometimes. Your dad has celebratory news."

Thomas grabbed one of the mummy cookies and broke it in half. He passed one half to Jonathan. "The doctor gave me the green light today to return to work full-time."

Jonathan reflected his dad's smile. "That's great news! How do you feel about it?"

"I've been ready," Thomas said, casting a sideways glance at Virginia. "I know you have been too, son. I can't tell you how much I appreciate—"

"How much we *both* appreciate," Virginia interjected, raising her glass of punch like a toast.

"All of us," Thomas agreed. "You coming home and taking over these past few months, it was a blessing. But now you can go back to Chicago."

"Just the Two of Us" reverberated out of the speakers near him. Jonathan blinked down at the broken cookie in his hand, and one mummy eye stared back at him. The meaning of his dad's words soaked into his skin and spread through his chest, causing a sudden ache.

"I know you're ready to go," Virginia said, touching Jonathan's arm. "Life in Ivy Ridge is no comparison to your big city, but we've loved having you around. Now, go enjoy the party, and we can look at plane tickets tomorrow, my and your father's treat. Maybe I can talk you into booking a flight home for Christmas."

"One thing at a time, Virginia," Thomas said, and she laughed as she tugged him toward a group of revelers gathered near the drink table.

Jonathan stared at the empty spot where his parents had been standing. A swirl of fireflies darted by, and as he turned to follow their flight, his gaze found Mattie. Lucy had her deep in conversation, and then they both started laughing.

What *was* his regular life now? He'd been in Ivy Ridge for months, balancing two jobs—not always equally—living with his parents again, and falling in love with the next-door neighbor. His thoughts sent an electrical shock up his spine. Was he in love with Mattie? Even if he was, would that stop him from returning to Chicago? His life *was* there. At least a resemblance of a life, which consisted mostly of work. Could he change all of that for what his dad had called a "summer crush"?

Summer crush didn't accurately describe how he felt about Mattie. But after she received her inheritance, she would be freer than she'd ever been. They hadn't talked about what was next for her now that her final task was complete. What if her freedom didn't include him joining her? Did he want to join her?

"Hey," Mattie said, tapping him on the forehead. "What are you thinking so hard about? You look like you're calculating complex math equations in your mind."

Jonathan pulled her against him and crushed her into a hug. Her muffled laugh fluttered his baseball jersey. He didn't want Mattie sailing off toward the horizon, not without him on the same boat. A shocking idea blossomed in his mind.

"Why are you hugging me like you're about to go off on a dangerous mission?" Mattie joked, and Jonathan released her.

Happiness surrounded her like a halo of light. For a moment when she turned her face toward the trees and the string lights reflected in her eyes like starlight, she looked illuminated. He needed to talk to his dad, to see if his idea was even a possibility.

Lucy bounded over, perfect timing as always. "Last call for

guessing how many candy corns are in the jar. Winner gets that basket of goodies with donations from businesses all over town, including a 50-percent-off coupon to Green Clover." She grabbed Mattie's hand. "I'm guessing 375."

"Nah, there's way more than that," Mattie said, walking off with Lucy. She stopped and motioned to Jonathan. "Hey, you going to guess? There's a gift card to Toasties in the loot."

"Stuck on You" by Lionel Ritchie started playing, and Jonathan reached for Mattie's outstretched hand. When he left Chicago, he'd set an internal timer that counted down the days until he could return. Staying in Ivy Ridge had *never* been an option. His plan was to stay for a few weeks, help his family, and leave. Reconnecting with Mattie hadn't been part of the plan, but she'd been the highlight of his return home.

"I need to talk to my dad for second," Jonathan said. "Can you guess for me?"

"Nope," Lucy said with a laugh. "That's cheating. Or I could make an incredibly awful guess and sign your name to it."

Mattie squeezed his hand. "You okay?"

He nodded. "Be right back. Don't let Lucy sabotage my guess."

Jonathan found his dad in a group of family friends and asked if they could speak privately. Once they were away from everyone, Jonathan asked, "Have you ever thought about taking on a partner?"

Thomas frowned. "Why? Are you thinking my health isn't going to hold out?"

Jonathan shook his head and pointed to himself. "Me. I was wondering if you'd consider taking *me* on as a partner."

Thomas glanced over at Virginia, who was watching them, no doubt trying to read lips. His dad's expression shifted to confusion. "You want to open a branch in Chicago? I'm not sure we really *need* that. The branches we have are able to handle our national clients just fine. What do you think a branch in Chicago would offer that we don't have now?"

"No, Dad," Jonathan said, shaking his head. "What if I stayed here or moved back home and we became partners? I'm talking about leaving Chicago and starting over here."

"You're serious?" Thomas said. His smile was slow and sincere. "I never thought that would be an option, but yes. Yes, of course." He pulled Jonathan into a hug and squeezed. "But you can't move in with me and your mom. You need a place of your own."

Jonathan barked a laugh. "That's a definite. And, hey, don't tell Mom until after the party, okay? I want to talk to Mattie about it before everyone knows."

Thomas winked. "I hope she's as pleased with the news as I am."

Jonathan slapped his dad gently on the arm. *Me too.*

Chapter 34

MATTIE

At half past ten, the DJ had packed up and gone, no food remained on the tables, and the last partygoer drifted out of the yard, humming a Rolling Stones song. Penelope turned off the outdoor lights, and Stephen stood in the kitchen looking content but tired.

"Now that your last task is finished, I'll get to work finalizing the release of the inheritance," Stephen said to Mattie. He opened the flap of his jacket and pulled out a sealed envelope. "In the event you finished them, I was instructed to give you this."

Mattie took the standard white envelope and brushed her fingers over her name written across the front. Her fingers tingled, and her voice came out as a whisper. "This is Mom's handwriting."

Stephen nodded. "I've never opened it. She gave it to me sealed, but I'm assuming it's an explanation for you."

This flimsy piece of paper was like a treasured gift, and she grinned at Penelope. "It could just as easily be a scavenger hunt or a grocery list."

"Or her favorite Fleetwood Mac songs," Penelope added. "I left a box of things on your bed. They're from Raoul, which we can discuss later."

Mattie hustled up the stairs and Jonathan rushed after her. "You're faster than an outfielder chasing a fly ball," he joked, barely keeping up with her.

A battered Converse shoe box sat on her quilt, and Mattie reached for it but hesitated, her hands hovering over the lid.

"It's not a jack-in-the-box," Jonathan said.

Mattie looked at him. How could she explain the hope and uncertainty swirling inside her?

"Open it," he encouraged.

Mattie flipped off the lid, revealing a stack of letters, photos, and random keepsakes. The bed frame squeaked when she sat on the mattress and pulled the box into her lap. She opened the letter on top and scanned the words. "It's a love letter from Mom to Raoul." She shuffled through the other papers in the box. "All of these are." Mattie blew a strand of hair out of her face. "I don't know what's more surprising. That my mom wrote love letters or that Raoul kept them for the past twenty-some years."

Jonathan glanced at the open closet. "Is that my name on the wall?" He crossed the room.

Mattie chuckled. "From ten years ago."

He traced his finger across the names—his and Mattie's—and the heart in between. The writing was rounded and bubble-shaped like that of a teenager. "You were crushing *hard* on me," he teased. Then he grinned at her. "I was gone for you the night I ended up in your yard."

Mattie smiled and flipped through the photos. Jonathan sat beside her on the bed, and she instinctively leaned against him. She dropped the photos and papers back into the shoe box and replaced the lid. Mattie placed the sealed envelope from her mom on top of the box and brushed her fingers across the written words.

"You don't want to read it now?" he asked.

Mattie exhaled. "I do, but I don't. Part of me wants to rip it open right now, but the bigger part of me wants to wait until I can sit and savor the words. And there's a handsome man on my bed, so my ability to focus on other things is limited." She trailed a finger down his chest and leaned forward to kiss him.

He buried his hands in her hair. She leaned back on the bed, and he moved with her. Mattie touched his face and whispered, "I could kiss you forever."

Jonathan sat up abruptly, pulling Mattie with him. "I have to tell you something."

Mattie laughed playfully. "As long as you're not going to tell me you're married or you're dying or you're becoming a monk, I think I can handle whatever it is."

"I'm going to move back to Ivy Ridge," he said. "Dad's going to make me a partner in the business. I know we can make a go of this."

Mattie's eyebrows knit together. His words weren't connecting in her mind. "Make a go of what? You and your dad's business?"

Jonathan chuckled and entwined their hands. "Of us. You and me together. We're good together, Mattie. No, we're *great*. We could settle here in Ivy Ridge. Together."

Panic flared in Mattie's body. "Why would you give up your job in Chicago to move here? I thought you couldn't wait to get back to the city." She pulled her hands out of his.

Hurt rippled across Jonathan's expression, and his smile dropped. "That was before you, before us. I thought . . . I hoped you felt the same."

Mattie stood abruptly. What was happening? When had they gone from having a good time to something serious enough to cause Jonathan to change his life plans? Jonathan wanted to stay in Ivy Ridge. No, *settle down* in Ivy Ridge with her. And then what? Get married? Have a family? A normal life? What did Mattie know about a normal life? Absolutely nothing. All she knew was packing up and moving on repeat. She'd never even had a steady friendship. How would she maintain a relationship? Lilith was the furthest thing from a solid example of how to conduct partnerships.

Mattie pressed one hand to her chest and nearly sobbed. She knew that look in his eyes, even though she'd never seen it turned her way before. Jonathan Carlisle was *in love* with her. Deeply and seriously. Electric terror zipped through her. "But I'm leaving."

Shock dropped his mouth agape. "Where are you going?"

She looked away from him as she said, "San Francisco. I'm buying an art gallery. The owners want to close right away, and now that I have the money . . ."

"California? That's across the country, almost as far away from here as possible. Why haven't you said anything about it?"

Because she hadn't been 100 percent certain. Was she now? "I just heard back from them a few days ago, and I hadn't decided what I was going to do, but for the first time in my life, I've realized this is something I want for me. To open a gallery and sell my art."

Jonathan rubbed his hand across his chest. "I think I'm having a heart attack." He flexed his left hand. "This is . . . unexpected. Sounds like you've found what makes you happy. I should probably get going." He didn't move. Instead, he hooked his finger around hers.

For a brief second, Mattie wanted to take back everything she'd said. She wanted to go back to when they were kissing and life felt okay. "Thanks for all your help with the party tonight. I'll walk you out." Her words were more stilted than her body as she moved toward the bedroom door.

"Won't you miss this?" Jonathan asked, trailing after her down the stairs. "Life in Ivy Ridge with your family? You've just found your dad. Lucy and Luca. And me."

Mattie's resolve wavered. Could she really risk breaking Jonathan's heart when it turned out she was a disaster at relationships? Breaking her own heart was the better option. "We knew this was temporary," she said softly. "I'm used to packing up and moving on. Attachments are dangerous. We have the internet and cell phones. We can stay connected if we want to."

Mattie opened the front door, and Jonathan stepped out into the chilly night. The wind blew around clusters of leaves. They crunched and tumbled down the sidewalk. Thunder rumbled in the distance. He reached for her hand. For a second she let him lace his fingers with hers, and she let the feeling of love fill her one last time, but then she dropped his hand, said good night, and closed the door without another word.

Mattie's fingers lingered on the cold brass doorknob. She could almost feel Jonathan still standing on the other side of the door, staring in disbelief. She had tossed him out, but the alternative was worse. No way was she going to blubber all over him. She couldn't reveal what was actually going on inside—something that felt like a hurricane trapped in her body.

Laughter drifted out of the kitchen and into the foyer. It was the sort of intimate, hushed happiness shared by couples. Mattie felt like an intruder on Penelope and Stephen's privacy.

She moved for the staircase, and Penelope stepped out of the kitchen into the hallway. The carpet runner quieted the sound of her bare feet. "Did Jonathan leave?" The soft glow coming from the dimmed kitchen lighting reflected on Penelope's face. She stood casually, her body relaxed and calm. Years of heartache had encased Penelope in a rigid shell, but once she told Stephen the truth, cracks formed, followed by large pieces crumbling away. Now the gentle, loving Penelope underneath was emerging like a butterfly from a chrysalis. It was stunning to watch.

Mattie composed her face into a believable smile. She'd learned this practice from the first few times Lilith had come home and said, *"Time to hit the road, baby."* Those moments when Mattie felt like she was being snatched away from a bedroom she'd just gotten used to, from a school she liked, from the familiar that had only just become familiar. Lilith tried hard to make life a fun adventure, but scattered among her sparkly childhood memories were ones that left scars like the branches of a thornbush.

Mattie nodded. "I'm heading up to bed. Thanks again for a great party."

Penelope walked farther up the hallway. Mattie shifted beneath her aunt's stare. Could Penelope see into her heart? "Good night, sweet girl. We'll talk in the morning."

Mattie closed her bedroom door and changed out of her party dress and into a pair of Halloween pajamas. She hung her birthday dress in the closet and frowned at the names on the wall that the house refused to erase. "You can get rid of those now. He's *gone*. And I'll be gone soon enough."

In response, the letters darkened to crimson, arching around a pink heart that looked like it was beating. Mattie slammed the closet doors and the louvered doors bounced open, refusing to hide her teenage artwork. She dropped onto her bed and reached for the unopened envelope. Her silenced cell phone lit up, notifying her of a text from Jonathan.

Can we talk before you leave?

What more could they say? He wanted to leave his life in Chicago *for her*. Mattie squeezed her eyes shut. What if their relationship was a disaster? He'd resent her, and she'd resent not going to San Francisco when she had the chance.

Mattie didn't respond to Jonathan. Instead she slid her finger gently beneath the back flap on the envelope and created a slit across the top. The letter was written on plain notebook paper, the kind Mattie had used in grade school, wide ruled with three holes down one side. A bolt of lightning flashed outside and a window-rattling boom of thunder followed. She slid her legs beneath the quilt. Rain pelted the panes in an urgent, almost angry rhythm.

Dear Mattie,

I should have told you, but I don't regret not telling you everything. Not about your father, Raoul Moreno, not about our family, not about a million little pieces I was collecting and moving through the years, always with the hourglass running out of sand.

The best years of my life were spent with you. I kept you close because I couldn't bear to be too far from you, couldn't bear to share you too long with anyone else. Not even with Penelope, and believe me, she was fierce about you. Fiercely loyal and devoted. She would have raised you on her own in a heartbeat, but I never would have allowed it. Maybe I should have left you in Ivy Ridge with her. She would have offered you stability and security, things that were shaped differently in our lives. You were always safe with me, but were you happy?

You were my bright shining star, Mattie. You were the one

thing in my life I never regretted. How could I have given that up? How could I have sacrificed years without you when I knew my time was short? Penelope will call me selfish, but I was your mother, and I had the right to do what I wanted with my child. Maybe our lifestyle wasn't the best thing for you, but it was ours, and we had fun, didn't we?

I knew you were different. I knew you'd one day want to wake up to the same slant of light across your face every morning. I knew you'd cherish a garden of your own, a house that played your favorite songs, and a family who truly knew you and loved you. I also knew your heart would look for love, the kind of passion that turns your whole body to starlight. You wouldn't run from it the way I did. You would know love is worth the risk. You would hold it close and let it whisper promises to you, and you'd stick around to watch it unfold, petal by petal, like a soft pink rose.

I don't regret not telling you everything, Mattie. I wanted you to find yourself on your own. Find what brings you joy, what makes you laugh, what gives you wings. All your life, you followed me and my wild dreams. Now you can follow your heart, and I have a feeling that it belongs exactly where you are right now. In Ivy Ridge. But if I'm wrong, then I know you are brave enough to follow wherever your joy takes you.

I love you with all my heart, for all my days, and for infinity.

Mom

The notebook paper trembled in Mattie's fingers. Wind assaulted the house, wailing around the eaves and whooshing through the trees. Lightning flashed, much closer now, and the cannon blast of thunder caused Mattie to flinch. She reread the letter, slower this time, and when she was done, she pressed the folded paper against her chest and wailed, allowing the raging thunderstorm outside to drown out the sound of her cries. A few seconds later, the electricity went out, and the house was thrust into darkness. And Mattie wept.

Chapter 35

MATTIE

THE NEXT MORNING MATTIE GOT OUT OF BED LIKE SOME-one with an intense hangover. She made slow, deliberate move-ments, feeling like her head was stuck in a vise grip. She'd taken the act of sobbing to the next level, and even her bones ached from all the sorrow she'd wrung out of her body. She tugged open one of the bedroom curtains, revealing a clear, bright blue sky with not a cloud in sight. But the backyard was a disaster. String lights dangled from the tree limbs like limp tentacles. The folding tables they'd used for the party had overturned. Pumpkins lay scattered across the backyard like they were playing a game of hide-and-seek among the flowers.

Mattie gasped at the sight of the garden. Petals and leaves, yanked from their stalks, littered the grass. Some plants were bent in half, smashed down toward the saturated earth. Others leaned listlessly against one another like weary survivors. The greenhouse appeared unscathed except for hundreds of wet leaves plastered to the glass. The back door opened and closed, and Penelope stepped out into view on the patio with a mug in her hand. She drank slowly and surveyed the damage.

Mattie tugged open the other curtain. White squares of paper were stuck to the wet windowpanes. Were those the numbered plastic cards she'd staked in the garden? Still damp from rain, they'd been trapped against the glass by last night's wind. Mattie opened the window and carefully collected the cards, twelve in all. She tossed them onto her bed just as her cell phone dinged an email alert. The sellers confirmed a call for early afternoon.

Mattie dressed quickly and hurried outside. Penelope's peppermint tea filled the air around her with a sense of calm. "This is awful."

Penelope brushed a hand through the air. "It looks worse than it is." She caught Mattie's gaze. "Seems the garden isn't the only one who had a rough night."

The wet grass chilled Mattie's bare feet. All the stakes she'd put in the garden alongside her new plantings had uprooted, the labels ripped away by the winds. She glanced up at her bedroom window.

"I noticed that too," Penelope said. "With the way the winds were blowing last night, it was good of the house to collect the labels. All of this can be cleaned up and repaired." She lifted the mug to her lips. "Want to make breakfast and talk about it?"

Mattie pulled her fingers through her tangled hair. "How do you feel about cake for breakfast?"

"Time we finally make the Heart Mender?"

A couple of hours later Penelope swirled the last bit of dark chocolate pudding buttercream onto a three-tiered rich chocolate cake sandwiched together with a salted dark chocolate filling. Sophia and Robert sat in the breakfast nook, drinking tea and reading the newspaper. The kitchen smelled like chocolate and espresso, and Mattie's salivary glands were in overdrive. All through helping Penelope prepare the cake, filling, and frosting, Mattie told them about the clues that led to Raoul and about Jonathan's decision to move to Ivy Ridge. Then she eased her way into discussing the move to San Francisco.

"I don't want you to go," Penelope admitted. "But more than

that I want you to do what's best for you. I could probably talk Stephen into taking a trip out for your grand opening."

"Count on us being there too," Sophia said.

Mattie hugged Penelope tight, thankful for the support of her family. Telling them had eased the knots inside her. So why did she still feel unsettled? Was it nerves? She'd never been anxious about moving before. Penelope made a *ta-da* motion over the cake, and Mattie admired the finished dessert on the cobalt-blue stand. "I had my doubts. Could a cake *really* heal hearts? But seeing this masterpiece, I'm nearly convinced it will make everything better."

Penelope reached for the cake knife, and Mattie's phone lit up again. "Are you going to ignore him forever?"

Mattie slumped over her empty coffee cup. "I'm undecided." The phone went dark again. "You'd think after no responses, he'd give up."

Sophia walked over to compliment the cake. She tapped a manicured nail on the counter beside Mattie's phone. "He's not ready to give up yet, and I'm not sure you are either." Mattie responded with a huff. "Let's eat cake and see how we feel afterward."

Penelope slid the oversize cake knife gently through the layers. She plopped a fat slice onto a plate, handed it to Mattie, and then cut pieces for everyone else. The doorbell rang, and Penelope looked as surprised as Mattie.

Mattie slid off the barstool. "You don't think it's . . . him?"

Robert chuckled from the nook. "There are worse people it could be."

What would she say to Jonathan when she opened the door and found him on the porch? Mattie flung open the door and took a deep breath. Lucy bounced on the balls of her feet with her hands shoved into the front pocket of a green hoodie. She didn't wait for Mattie to say hello and instead bounded inside.

Pushing back the hood and allowing her wavy hair to fall free, she said, "What took you so long? It's freezing out there today. Why does it smell like a bakery in here?"

Mattie closed the door, questioning the twinge of disappointment she felt. "Good morning to you too. We made cake for breakfast. Want some?"

At the kitchen island, Lucy drank a cup of chai and ate a hearty slice of the decadent Heart Mender cake with Mattie. The chocolate cake seemed to capture the last remnants of grief inside Mattie and encase them in comfort and healing. She no longer felt frustrated for caring so much about Jonathan, for letting him into her heart. Lilith admitted to running from love when the roots wanted to push deeper, but she'd never run from taking the first step toward a chance at love. Mattie had taken a chance, and what she learned from opening up was worth it. Gone was the fear of abandonment she felt when Lilith died. Mattie still had a family, and looking at Lucy, she understood that her family had expanded.

While they ate, Lucy caught them up on the aftermath of the storm. There were downed power lines being repaired and fallen tree limbs and branches now grouped in piles along the streets. Many homes would need to replace missing shingles and roof tiles, but most of the town had power restored. Green Clover suffered minor damage, mostly overturned pots and mulch bags ripped open with their contents strewn. A young Japanese maple tree had landed upside down in the koi pond display, but the fish survived, and the maple would too.

Mattie's phone lit up on the countertop, and Lucy leaned over to see Jonathan's name. "You could at least let him tell you good-bye. You *are* going to make the deal with the sellers, aren't you?" Lucy read the indecision on Mattie's face. "Do you hate him?"

"Of course not." It wasn't hate that kept Mattie from responding. Fear created scenarios in her mind about how her heart would react if she read his texts, if she and Jonathan started responding like they were somehow going to keep up a long-distance relationship. She'd never had long-distance friendships, so how could a romance work? Based on the way her heart pounded a desperate tempo in her chest at the thought of him, she wasn't ready to let him go, but she had to.

"I owe it to myself to give San Francisco a try."

"Of course you do! But what does that have to do with Jonathan?" Lucy asked.

Mattie forked in her last bite of cake. "Only that I'm not interested in dating someone—or whatever we're doing—who lives across the country from me."

Lucy hummed in her throat. "I get that. Long-distance relationships have their challenges, and it's okay you don't want that. But Jonathan is a good guy, so you could at least tell him to have a good life."

Lucy was right. Jonathan had been good to her. He'd been there for her when she needed a friend. Her leaving didn't negate all the fun they had together. Her mind replayed Jonathan kissing her in the art studio, in the greenhouse, in the attic, on Blackberry Bluff.

Lucy interrupted Mattie's thoughts. "How long until you leave?"

Mattie shrugged. "I'll know more after I talk to the sellers, but I'll at least stay through Halloween. I want to spend my birthday here like I used to."

Penelope reached over and squeezed Mattie's hand. "We'd love that."

"Dad wants all of us to get together," Lucy said. "I was thinking we could all celebrate your birthday together at the Halloween festival."

Mattie looked at Penelope. "Remember how we used to go to the festival every year and then watch the fireworks together on Halloween?"

Penelope smiled. "Let's pick that tradition back up and add a new one that the Russells and the Morenos celebrate Halloween together."

"Here's to new family traditions," Mattie said, lifting her half-empty mug.

"And many more," Lucy sang horribly off-key, which triggered a burst of happiness and laughter.

Chapter 36

JONATHAN

THE PREVIOUS NIGHT'S STORM HAD KEPT HIM AWAKE FOR hours, but so had his thoughts. Mattie's closed-off expression as she shut the door on him replayed in his mind. Why wasn't she returning his texts? From the day they met on the sidewalk he knew her stay in Ivy Ridge was temporary, so why was she ignoring him now that the inevitable had happened? How could she change so quickly from adoring him to loathing him? Just because she was leaving didn't mean they had to end things.

He needed to book a flight to Chicago, return long enough to get all his affairs settled, and then move his life to Ivy Ridge. Was that still what he wanted to do, even if Mattie was gone? *Yes.*

He opened his suitcase on the bed and started pulling his clothes out of the dresser and the closet. Sunlight pooled on the floor. His phone vibrated on the end table, and he leaped for it, thinking it might be Mattie. A client from Chicago was calling, and Jonathan sat on his bed, sagged against the headboard, and answered. Hours later he was still working, answering emails, and updating his schedule. He'd informed everyone who needed to know that he would be back in Chicago tomorrow night to start the process of closing down his business there. Virginia brought in an armful of clean laundry, which she placed on the pile of clothes that hadn't yet made it into his suitcase.

"I see you're already back to the old Jonathan," his mom said, though not unkindly.

He looked up from his laptop. The sunlight in the room had shifted to the more intense midday brightness. How long had he been working? "The *old* Jonathan?"

"The one who buries himself in work," she said. "I kinda like the new one. The one who takes breaks and spends time with friends. The one I saw with Mattie."

Jonathan's whole body went rigid. But the gentle expression on his mom's face pulled a sigh from deep inside, and he closed his laptop. "Me too, Mom." He slid the computer from his lap and stood, stretching his long arms over his head and brushing his fingertips over the bottom of the ceiling fan blades.

"Maybe you can keep him around," she said with an uncharacteristic wink.

He dropped his arms. "She's ignoring me." The mirror reflected his petulant scowl.

Virginia smiled as though she knew the secrets hidden in women's hearts. "For now maybe, but not forever. I think she likes the new Mattie too."

Before he could ask his mom to explain, she breezed out of his bedroom. His phone illuminated with a text from Mattie.

I'm sorry for last night. I need some time.

Nothing more, but enough to cause a seed of hope to bury itself inside him with the belief that it might take root and grow.

Chapter 37

MATTIE

THE WEEK OF HALLOWEEN HAD BEEN JAM-PACKED WITH activities and spending as much time with everyone as possible before she packed her one suitcase and left for San Francisco. The final paperwork for buying the gallery would be signed in person, and the meeting was set up for next week. Mattie hadn't seen Jonathan again, but he texted twice. Once to let her know he was flying to Chicago for a few weeks and once on her birthday.

Standing in the departure terminal inside Hartsfield-Jackson Atlanta International Airport, Mattie hugged Penelope, Robert, Sophia, and Lucy in turn.

Penelope pushed Mattie's long hair over her shoulder. "Now let us know as soon as you land. And you checked to make sure the car will pick you up, right? The Airbnb is confirmed?"

"Penelope, honey, she's done this before," Sophia teased.

Robert slid his arm around Penelope's shoulder. "Never hurts to make sure our girl is safe, though, does it?" Penelope leaned into him with misty eyes.

"I'll text you as soon as the wheels hit the tarmac. I double-checked both the car service and the rental," Mattie said. "Before you ask, it's in a *very* nice section of town, near the gallery too."

Lucy grinned. "No slumming it for you now that you're basically a millionaire."

Mattie snorted a laugh. "You're coming to visit next month,

right? We'll window-shop the Christmas displays, ride the cable car and drink cocoa, and ice-skate in Union Square."

"Already packing my suitcase."

Mattie glanced around at the crowded space and the lengthening lines for security. "I'd better get going." She looked at her family and *felt* the love radiating off them. *I'm doing the right thing, aren't I? I have to do this for me, to choose something for myself.* "But I'll be home before you know it. Christmas is coming soon." After one more round of hugs, Mattie hurried away toward the security gates, turning once to wave. Seeing their smiles and lifted hands, Mattie almost ran back to them, but their support heightened her courage. She could do this. She could choose her own path. Squaring her shoulders, she filed into line with a mass of travelers.

⚮

The first few days in San Francisco after leaving Ivy Ridge felt like switching from taking a Sunday stroll to zooming on roller skates. San Francisco didn't have the same intensity level as Chicago or NYC, but Mattie had a long list of to-dos she needed to accomplish so she could settle in as quickly as possible. While waiting for the lawyer's meeting to review final paperwork, she searched for places to live. So far, there were a few viable options, but nothing felt cozy enough to call home. Could she request an enchanted house or apartment that felt like the Russell house? She'd also been interviewing possible candidates to help her manage the business side of owning a gallery. Finding someone knowledgeable about art, San Francisco city life, and running a gallery severely limited her choices and kept her busy on the hunt.

Busy was good though. Busy was the friend she could count on to keep her distracted from the uneasy feeling of loneliness that crept in. Busy also shifted her focus from how much she missed her family *and* Jonathan. She rarely heard from him, except for short texts a couple of times a week. She was embarrassed for anyone to know how much a few spare words from him improved her whole day. Even his random texts, like *Toasties debuted a November special: grilled cheese with cranberry sauce and turkey. Looks like a hot mess. Bet it tastes even better,* had her smiling hours later.

After she'd given it some thought, his decision to move back to Ivy Ridge didn't surprise her. Ivy Ridge grew on you with its birdsong mornings and vibrant sunsets. His family was there too. Her newfound longing for her own family shocked her. Now that she'd found her dad and gained instant siblings, Mattie wanted to know more about them. Lucy constantly shared news about Green Clover and her floral arrangements. She signed up for another baking class that, according to Lucy, wouldn't be as fun without Mattie. She promised to take one for the team and eat Mattie's share of brownies. Penelope and Sophia texted regularly to check in and send pictures from around the house and town. Mattie's home screen was currently an image of the green hummingbird spotted in the garden.

Swaths of oranges, from marmalade to rust, rippled across clouds the color of sangria in the San Francisco sky. She thought of the night she and Jonathan roasted s'mores on Blackberry Bluff and how they'd ended the night making out in his truck like high schoolers. Mattie's email dinged with an incoming message, then a text from Penelope vibrated her phone. The email was a reminder about tomorrow morning's meeting with the lawyer.

Penelope wrote, *Check flight options for Christmas. We can't wait to see you.* She included a selfie of her and Stephen, and neither one of them was looking at the camera lens. Mattie laughed and saved the image to her camera roll.

When she was home for the holidays, would Jonathan want to see her? And then what? The idea of seeing him kickstarted her heart racing. A reminder alarm sounded on her phone—time to tour a few more condos and apartments. Perfect distraction. She pocketed her cell phone and headed out into the temperate evening. San Francisco's weather was undeniably milder and more consistently pleasant than Ivy Ridge's. She was unlikely to swelter in one-hundred-degree temperatures here. No chance of melting into the sidewalk. A fact she could add to the plus-side column of her running mental list comparing San Francisco to Ivy Ridge. Should it bother her that Ivy Ridge was still winning, with more items on the plus side?

※

The following morning Mattie sat at the kitchen counter in her short-term rental drinking coffee and scrolling through her camera roll. Images from Ivy Ridge tugged a wistful smile onto her face. On a sigh she gazed toward the sliding glass doors that led to a sun-filled balcony. Striking out on her own had seemed like the best decision. So why was a shard of discomfort spreading through her? She wished her mom were there to ask. Was this how Lilith felt while settling into a new place? Or was this the feeling Lilith got when she was ready to leave?

Lilith's final letter to her was tucked into her suitcase. Maybe rereading it would soothe her. Mattie pulled her suitcase out of the closet. She unzipped it on the bed and flipped it open. A huddle of small square papers cluttered one corner. She'd forgotten about the plant label cards. How had they ended up in her suitcase? She tossed them on the bed, and they fanned out like a card game she didn't know how to play. Lilith had meticulously crafted all of the tasks to guide Mattie along, but even the final letter hadn't offered clarity regarding these specific numbers.

Mattie organized the twelve cards in a line. Ten of them had numbers, and two of them had one half of a heart. She slid the heart cards out of line and moved them together to form a whole heart. That's when she noticed the order of the remaining numbers. The first three numbers matched an area code for Georgia, and the next three digits were the exchange code for Ivy Ridge. Followed by four numbers that would finish off a telephone number.

Mattie tapped the number into her cell phone. The phone rang so many times she was about to hang up when an unexpected voice answered.

Chapter 38

PENELOPE

"WHO ELSE IS COMING OVER?" LUCY ASKED AS SHE grabbed two bunches of asparagus out of the refrigerator that was packed with salads, assorted fruits, and regular everyday food. "Based on the state of this fridge and the kitchen, it looks like we're feeding the whole block." She swiped her hand toward the island, which was covered in four different charcuterie boards—traditional meat, crackers, and cheese; crudités with dips; chocolates, candies, and popcorn; and one for building s'mores.

"It'll be the Morenos, the Carlisles, and us," Penelope said. "I've seen those boys eat, so we can have this conversation again after dinner."

Sophia took the asparagus from Lucy's hands and started preparing it for the grill. Penelope walked over to the kitchen window and glanced into the backyard. Raoul, his wife, Julia, and Stephen sat at the patio table chatting with Virginia and Thomas. Luca stood by the grill watching Jonathan place hamburger patties and chicken breasts on the hot grate. Jonathan handed Luca the tongs and walked toward the back porch.

Robert sat in the breakfast nook cast in the fire-orange glow of the setting sun. He swirled a cinnamon stick in a mug of mulled cider. Fifties crooners charmed the house from the Bluetooth radio Penelope had connected to her phone in the kitchen. She swayed her hips and hummed while she grabbed salad containers out of the refrigerator. Sophia placed asparagus spears into tinfoil packets and drizzled them with olive oil.

"Meat's on the grill," Jonathan said as he walked into the kitchen. He placed the dirty plate in the kitchen sink and washed his hands.

"Perfect timing," Sophia said. She arranged the asparagus packets on a tray and handed it to Jonathan.

Penelope stood at the island and removed the plastic lids from salad containers. A phone rang. No one responded right away, and the ringing continued.

"Whose phone is that?" Sophia asked, which was followed by a chorus of "Not mine." The music on the Bluetooth quieted, and the sound of the ringing phone echoed through the downstairs. "Is that the—"

Robert stood from the table. His mouth had gone slack.

"Is that the what?" Lucy asked.

"No," Penelope said, but she was already walking toward the sunporch. "It can't be."

Jonathan was the closest to the porch. He pointed at the blue rotary phone. "That thing actually works?"

Penelope whispered, "The dream phone is ringing."

Lucy laughed. "The what phone?"

Penelope and Sophia stood in similar positions with their hands over their mouths, staring at the long-silent phone now awakened and ringing.

Jonathan turned to look at Penelope. "Did you just call that the dream phone?"

"Answer it!" Robert said, taking the tray of asparagus from Jonathan's hands.

Jonathan snatched the receiver, causing the base to teeter on the edge of the table. "Hello?" he said, straightening the phone. No one responded. "Hello?" he said louder. His body tensed. "Mattie?" A collective gasp rose from the group, and Penelope leaped for the phone. Jonathan handed it over with an expression of shock.

Unexpected tears filled her eyes. "How are you calling the dream phone?"

"Penelope? I just called the dream phone? Why is Jonathan at the house?"

"What's wrong?" Penelope asked instead of answering. "What's happened?"

Mattie chuckled. "I need you to take a deep breath. Nothing's wrong. I'm as surprised as you. You're not going to believe this. You remember how the numbers we staked in the garden were blown against my window the night of the storm? They somehow ended up in my suitcase, and I just found them. The numbers are—"

"No way!" Penelope said in disbelief. She moved the handset away from her mouth. The gathered crowed watched expectantly. "The numbers Lilith told Mattie to stake with the plants—"

Sophia gripped Robert's arm. "They're the phone number for the dream phone?" Sophia's melodic laugh filled the space around them. With her hand over her heart, she said, "Beautiful, Lilith. That girl . . . she knew all along."

"What is going on?" Lucy asked, looking at Jonathan.

Jonathan shrugged. "All I know is that my dream girl is calling on the dream phone."

A green hummingbird fluttered outside the window, hovered in front of Penelope's sight for a few seconds, and then flew off. She turned to look at Jonathan and held out the receiver. "Maybe this call *is* for you. Lilith believed that when this phone rang, we would know that our dreams were coming true."

Jonathan took the offered phone. "Hey, Mattie . . . there's an audience here listening in, but I miss you and I hope you're doing okay in San Francisco. I'd love to see you at Christmas. Oh . . . Okay . . . I'll tell them . . . Sure, talk to you soon." Jonathan hung up the phone.

"Don't leave us hanging. What did she say?" Lucy asked.

The grin on his face reminded Penelope of the way Stephen sometimes looked at her—like a man totally in love.

"She's been looking for a sign," Jonathan said. "Now that she has it, she's coming home."

Penelope's heartbeat paused. "Is this—is this *home*?"

Sophia slipped her hand into Penelope's. "Of course it is."

EPILOGUE

DOWNTOWN IVY RIDGE COULD HAVE COMPETED FOR THE most festive town in Georgia, maybe even the country. Evergreen wreaths and bows adorned every light pole. Shop-window displays caused people to stop and marvel at the detailed and sometimes whimsical holiday scenes sparkling behind the glass. Music piped out from speakers, and thousands of string lights would light up as soon as the sun set.

Mattie stood inside one of the shops, looking through the front window at people strolling by on the sidewalk. This store's window display wasn't decorated, but this time next year, she knew it would be.

The front door swung open, and her real estate agent, Diana Dunson, rushed in. "Sorry to keep you waiting." Diana held out a key ring crowded with keys and a dangling charm advertising her real estate business. "Congratulations! It's all yours."

Mattie took the offered keys and grinned. Closing her fingers around the metal, she felt the keys warm in her hand. She turned a slow circle on the planked wood floors, taking in the high brick walls that would soon hold pieces of artwork. "It's perfect."

"A dream come true?" Diana asked.

"Something like that," Mattie said. "Thanks for dropping these off. I'll lock up now. My family and friends are next door at Butterfingers buying treats. We're going to celebrate."

Mattie locked the shop and pressed her hand to the cool wood of the front door. Diana's words resonated inside her. *A dream come true.* She stepped out onto the sidewalk and strolled the few short steps to the bakery, Butterfingers.

Jonathan leaned against a highboy table near the front. "Jingle Bells" played from the bakery's speakers, but the song suddenly switched to "Celebration." Jonathan laughed and stood to his full height when he saw her.

"Where is everyone?" she asked.

Jonathan reached for her hands and pulled her toward him. "They went on to The Pizza Box to make sure everything is set up for the celebration of you buying the gallery."

Mattie grinned up at him, then pressed her cheek against his chest. "It's not a gallery yet."

"I can't wait to see your art hanging on the walls," Jonathan said. "And, hey, I've been meaning to ask you something. It's kinda serious, but I want to give you something first."

Mattie put a bit of space between them, but Jonathan held on to her hands. Her heartbeat quickened.

"First the gift." He reached into a shopping bag and pulled out a Christmas ornament. A glittery green hummingbird hung from a golden loop. "I saw this on the way over and it made me think of you."

How could he have known? "Thank you. It's perfect."

Jonathan took the ornament from her and returned it to the bag. He twined their hands together. "Remember when you called on the dream phone?" Mattie nodded. "It's no coincidence that I was there to answer it, so does that mean I'm your dream guy?"

Mattie laughed. "You never give up, do you?"

"On you?" he said. "Never."

Jonathan leaned down and kissed her as the song shifted to "Shining Star." Mattie laughed against his lips. Opening a gallery, being close to her family, finding love, setting down roots . . . The list of her dreams stretched on and on, and Mattie couldn't wait to see where the next one would take her.

Acknowledgments

THERE ARE NEVER ENOUGH THANK-YOUS HANDED OUT— and how could there be?—given the multitude of people and the host of angels who work behind the scenes *and* front and center on helping create a complete book, from a (very) rough manuscript to sitting on a store's bookshelf. But I'll try to rain down as many thank-yous as I can, knowing there are always more to come.

Working on this book has been a wonderful, sometimes tear-filled experience as a writer. Without the support of wise, helpful, kind, and forthright people, this book might still be hiding out in a folder. Massive amounts of gratitude go to Natalie Banks, my soul sister, bestie, ride-or-not-die companion. Thanks for pinky swearing that you'll always drag me along when I can't take one more step and for being the most fabulous cheerleader anyone could ever dream of having. You make me think about sticking around and giving it another chance.

My pinch-hitting editor, aka associate publisher for Harper Muse Becky Monds, for taking on my manuscript when our beloved editor had her sweet baby a month early. Thank you for playing such a significant role in the shaping of this story and for challenging me to dig deeper, show more, tell less, and get to the heart of what Mattie *really* wants. This story wouldn't be the book it is today without your wisdom and guidance. Any writer would be lucky to have you on their team.

I am exceptionally blessed to work with the most fantastic and supportive publishing team, Harper Muse. Always professional, always helpful, and always sincerely excited about my victories.

Acknowledgments

Years ago, I thought it would be awesome to be published with HarperCollins, and I can verify this is true. Amanda Bostic, thank you for leading such a rock star group, and I couldn't be happier with where this adventure is taking us. Thank you sincerely to HarperCollins for continually breathing more life into my dreams.

Thank you to my editor Whitney Bak for your crazy-cool skills that give me pause long enough to think, *Wow!* Your attention to detail, consistency, timelines, and character development is such a gift. Just think, I could have ended up with a genius scientist who was barely twenty-three and a Kevin Bacon movie that someone watched when they were in middle school and a baby who was born in the wrong decade—a cool story, probably, but not *this* story. Thank you for your insight and for polishing this story like a treasured jewel.

Thank you, Jeanne Arnold, for always, always, always agreeing to read anything I write regardless of how rough, strange, or disjointed it is. You are absolutely the best early reader, and you're a sincere friend. I can't thank you enough for all of the nonwriting support you've given me through the years too.

Thank you, Hanelore Dumitrache, for reading the original short story of this book when it was still rough and unfinished. And thank you for a moment of blinding panic, followed by the loudest laughter in France. Remember when I was telling you about *The Magic All Around* at that café in Paris and you said, "I'm having déjà vu. I've read this story." And I adamantly said that was impossible because *this book* hadn't been released yet. Then I panicked because maybe someone else had already written this story and I had somehow copied it from a weird part of my brain, until—surprise!—we recalled that I sent you the rough draft nearly a year earlier. Crisis averted. Thank you for the subsequent laughter that lasted for days.

A massive heartfelt thank-you to my family, my earliest and often my loudest supporters. You could have *pfft*ed at my dreams, but not once has that happened. Anytime I had a creative idea and said, "I can do that!" you always agreed. Every time. Like you *knew* I could do anything I put my heart into, and you continually make me believe I *can*.

Saved the best for last! Thank you, dear reader. Thank you for being here with me, for loving stories and libraries and books and magic as much as I do—sometimes *more* than I do. Thank you for reading my stories, for asking for more stories, and for sharing in the wonderful excitement of watching our dreams come to life. You lift my heart and fill my days with extra smiles.

A Note from the Author

WHEN THE SPARK OF THIS STORY ARRIVED IN MY DREAMS, there was a girl and a boy meeting for the first time on Halloween. It was the girl's birthday, something magical was afoot, and they would never forget that night, and that was all I knew. Oh, and there was cake because cake makes life more enjoyable. So with this wisp of an idea and an even blurrier image in my mind, I drafted a short story. I called it *October*. I shared it with a few friends but did nothing more with it, so for months *October* lived in a computer folder full of one-day stories.

Then Harper Muse asked me to write a full-length novel, and the girl-meets-boy-on-Halloween short story returned to me. But how could I stretch it into a ninety-thousand-word novel? Could these two teenagers have grown up and never forgotten each other? Could they return to Ivy Ridge and meet again as adults? What would happen? Would sparks rekindle a brighter flame? Would there be more cake? With these questions, I was off and running—or typing—and creating a way for Mattie and Jonathan to find their way back into each other's lives.

As for the Russell house, I didn't intentionally set out to make the house its own character, but as the story unfolded, the house became just as much a part of the family as the people, and I grew attached to its quirky temperament and its loving care of the Russells. The house often understands the family's needs before they do. It keeps their secrets, shares in their joys, and embraces them (in its unique way) when they grieve. It also gives them a push when they need it. And don't we all need a push sometimes?

A Note from the Author

Finally, the hummingbird on the book's cover took my breath away the first time I saw the design. I've always loved hummingbirds—the enchanting flutter of their wings, the zippiness of their flight, the chittering calls they make as they zoom around my backyard. The hummingbird sightings in the book, directly connected to Lilith, brought me comfort, so when I saw the cover, it was the most perfectly magical way of piecing the heart of the story together. The cover is a reminder for me—maybe for you also—to keep our hearts open to receive the magic all around us every day.

Discussion Questions

1. In some ways, *The Magic All Around* is about the memories of places and people that we carry with us throughout our lives—sometimes physical mementos and other times things that are intangible. What are some things you've been carrying with you, either in your heart or in a box of memories? Why have you kept these particular items or memories?

2. The relationship between mothers and daughters is a big theme in this book. Some mothers we're born with, like Mattie's mom, Lilith. Others we receive as bonuses, like Penelope for Mattie. How do you relate to having multiple "moms" who have cared for you or for people close to you?

3. Friendship and love are also dominant themes in this book. Who is your Lucy? Who has pulled you out of your shell and opened your eyes to the beauty of friendship? Who is your Jonathan? Who has made you feel essential and important and seen?

4. Mattie has always loved painting, but she thought of it as more of a hobby until she started seeing the effect it had on others. What's something you're passionate about that others might view as a hobby? Can you see yourself turning this hobby into something more? Why or why not?

5. Mattie and Jonathan met when they were teenagers, and they never forgot that first meeting. It made quite an

impression on both of them. Do you know anyone you met when you were younger that you still think of even today? What was it about that person that resonated with you so deeply?

6. Lilith creates a scavenger hunt for Mattie that she is *not* thrilled about. What are your feelings about participating in a scavenger hunt? Do you find them boring or exciting? Would you change your mind about participating if the hunt led you to a hefty inheritance?

7. Some major themes of the book are being true to your feelings, figuring out who you are, and learning how to have faith in others. Mattie, Penelope, Stephen, and Jonathan all move through a season of learning about themselves and being honest about not only what they've done but also where they want to go. What parts of the story allow these transformations to happen for them? Have you ever experienced a season of self-realization? What or who helped you discover what was hidden in your heart?

8. There are a few love stories in this book. Which relationship was your favorite and why?

9. The Russell house has a personality of its own. What was your favorite aspect of the house? If given the opportunity, would you live in an enchanted house? Why or why not?

10. If you could go out for coffee or have lunch with one of the characters, who would you choose and why?

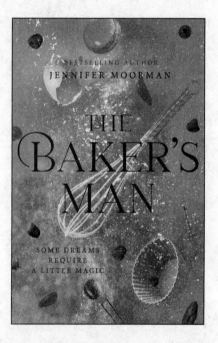

About the Author

Photo by Matt Andrews

BORN AND RAISED IN SOUTHERN GEORGIA, WHERE HONEY-suckle grows wild and the whippoorwills sing, Jennifer Moorman is the bestselling author of the magical realism Mystic Water series. Jennifer started writing in elementary school, crafting epic tales of adventure and love and magic. She wrote stories in Mead notebooks, on printer paper, on napkins, on the soles of her shoes. Her blog is full of dishes inspired by fiction, and she hosts baking classes showcasing these recipes. Jennifer considers herself a traveler, a baker, and a dreamer. She can always be won over with chocolate, unicorns, or rainbows. She believes in love—everlasting and forever.

Connect with Jennifer at jennifermoorman.com
Instagram: @jenniferrmoorman
Facebook: @jennifermoormanbooks
TikTok: @jennifermoormanbooks
BookBub: @JenniferMoorman